About the Authors

Anne Fraser always loved reading and never imagined that one day she would be writing for a living. She started life as a nurse and helpfully, for a writer of medical romances, is married to a hospital doctor! Anne and husband have lived and worked all over the world, including South Africa, Canada and Australia and many of their experiences as well as the settings found their way into her books. Anne lives in Glasgow with her husband and two children.

Jessica Matthews grew up on a farm in western Kansas where reading was her favourite pastime. Eventually, romances and adventure stories gave way to science textbooks and research papers as she became a medical technologist, but her love for microscopes and test tubes didn't diminish her passion for storytelling. Having her first book accepted for publication was a dream come true and now, she has written thirty books for Mills & Boon.

After completing a degree in journalism, then working in advertising and mothering her kids, **Robin Gianna** had what she calls her awakening. She decided she wanted to write the romance novels she'd loved since her teens, and now enjoys pushing her characters toward their own happily-ever-afters. When she's not writing, Robin's life is filled with a happily messy kitchen, a needy garden, a wonderful husband, three great kids, a drooling bulldog and one grouchy Siamese cat.

The Prince's

COLLECTION

Working For The Prince

ANNE FRASER

JESSICA MATTHEWS

ROBIN GIANNA

MILLS & BOON

First Published in Great Britain 2020
By Mills & Boon, an imprint of HarperCollins*Publishers*
1 London Bridge Street, London, SE1 9GF

WORKING FOR THE PRINCE © 2020 Harlequin Books S.A.

Prince Charming of Harley Street © 2010 Anne Fraser
The Royal Doctor's Bride © 2008 Jessica Matthews
Baby Surprise for the Doctor Prince © 2017 Robin Gianakopoulos

ISBN: 978-0-263-28120-0

0420

Printed and bound in Spain
by CPI, Barcelona

PRINCE CHARMING OF HARLEY STREET

ANNE FRASER

For Stewart –
Thanks for the idea and, as always, your help
and support.

CHAPTER ONE

ROSE whistled under her breath as she glanced around the reception area in the doctor's surgery. It was nothing like anything she had seen before. Instead of the usual hard plastic chairs, dog-eared magazines and dusty flower arrangements, there were deep leather armchairs, piles of glossy magazines and elaborate—she would even go as far to say ostentatious—flower arrangements. She sneezed as the pollen from the heavily scented lilies drifted up her nostrils. They were going to have to go. Otherwise she would spend her days behind the burled oak desk that was her station with a streaming nose.

Grabbing a tissue from the heavily disguised box on her table, she blew her nose loudly and pulled the list Mrs Smythe Jones, the receptionist—no, sorry, make that personal assistant—had left for her.

The writing was neat but cramped and Rose had to peer at the closely written words to decipher them.

It was Dr Cavendish's schedule for the week, and it didn't look very onerous. Apart from seeing patients three mornings a week, there were two afternoons blocked off for home visits. That was it. Nothing else, unless he had a hospital commitment that wasn't noted on the schedule. It seemed that Dr Cavendish must be winding down, possibly getting close to retirement. A vision of an elderly man with silver hair, an aristocratic nose and possibly a pince-nez popped into Rose's head.

Apart from the schedule Mrs Smythe Jones had also helpfully detailed Dr Cavendish's likes and dislikes. Apparently these included a cup of coffee from the cafetière—not instant—black, no sugar, served in a china cup and saucer which Rose would find in the cupboard above the sink in the kitchen in the back, and a biscuit, plain digestive, in the cupboard to the left of the one holding the cups. Patients were also to be offered tea— loose tea only, served in a teapot—on a tray, bottom-right cupboard, coffee, or bottled water, sparkling or still, from the fridge.

Looking at the schedule, it seemed that the first patient, an L. S. Hilton, wasn't due to arrive until 9.30. Plenty of time for Rose to have a good look around in advance. The cleaner, who had let Rose in a few minutes earlier, had dis-appeared, although she could hear the sound of a vacuum cleaner coming from somewhere further back.

There appeared to be two consulting rooms. Each of them bigger than most sitting rooms Rose had ever been in and almost identical to each other. There was the usual examina-tion couch and screen, a sink, a desk and two armchairs, as well as a two-seater sofa in the corner by the window. There were landscapes on the wall, traditional in one of the rooms but modern brightly painted ones in the other, slightly out of sync with the antique furnishings of the room.

Rose stepped across to study the pictures more closely. Whoever had painted them had a sure eye and a love of colour. Like the pictures in the other room, these were also landscapes, but that's where the similarity stopped. Unlike the sedate country images next door, these were painted in sure, bold brushstrokes and depicted wild, stormy scenes which spoke to Rose of passion and loss. Whoever had picked them for the wall was someone with unconventional taste.

A polite cough behind her made her whirl around. Standing by the door was a man in his late twenties dressed formally in a suit and tie with black shoes polished to within an inch of their lives. He had light brown hair that was worn slightly too long and fell across his forehead. His face was narrow, his nose straight, and startling green eyes were framed by dark brows. But it was his mouth that caught Rose's attention. It was wide and turned up at the corners as if this was a mouth that was used to laughing.

'I'm sorry,' she apologised. 'You must be here to see the doctor. I didn't hear you come in.' For the life of her she couldn't remember the name of the first patient, only that it reminded her of a famous hotel chain.

'And you are?' The words were softly spoken with just the merest hint of bemusement.

'I'm Rose Taylor, the temporary receptionist.' She stepped back towards the door but the man stayed where he was, blocking her path.

'Where's Tiggy?' he asked. 'I mean Mrs Smythe Jones.'

'Mrs Smythe Jones is on leave. Now, if you wouldn't mind taking a seat in the waiting room, I'll just get your notes out.'

'Take a seat? In the waiting room? My notes.' The smile widened. 'I see. I don't suppose there's any chance of a cup of coffee while I'm waiting?'

'Of course,' Rose replied smoothly. 'I'll just pop the kettle on.'

When she came back from the kitchen, carrying a tray

and trying not to feel too much like a waitress, he was sitting in her chair, leaning back with his arms behind his neck and his long legs propped on her desk.

'Excuse me, sir,' she said as politely as she could manage through gritted teeth. 'I think we agreed you'd take a seat in the waiting room.' He was beginning to annoy her. The way he was behaving as if he owned the place. However, on her first day she didn't want to cause a fuss. She needed this job. It paid well, extremely well paid, in fact, and the hours were flexible enough to give her time to help look after Dad. Perhaps this was the way all Harley Street patients behaved. How was she to know? Nevertheless, it was unacceptably rude of him to put her in this position. What if Dr Cavendish walked in to find she had allowed a patient to take over her desk? She couldn't imagine him being best pleased.

The man jumped to his feet and took the tray from her hands. 'Please let me,' he said, laying the tray down on the desk. He looked at the single cup and saucer and raised an enquiring eyebrow. 'What about you? Aren't you joining me?'

Rose forced a polite smile. 'No, thanks.' She slid behind her desk before he could reclaim her chair. 'Now, what did you say your name was?'

'Jonathan.' He stretched out a hand. 'Jonathan Cavendish.'

'You're related to Dr Cavendish?'

The smile grew wider. 'I *am* Dr Cavendish.'

Rose was aware her mouth had fallen open. She quickly closed it.

'But you're young,' she protested, feeling her cheeks grow warm. What an imbecilic thing to say.

He looked puzzled. 'Twenty-seven, since you ask. How old are you?' He leaned towards her and lazy eyes swept over her. 'No, don't tell me. Twenty-five?'

'Twenty-six, actually,' Rose conceded reluctantly. He was laughing at her, making her flustered. And she didn't do flustered. 'My name's Rose Taylor. The agency sent me over. To fill in until your usual receptionist returns.'

'Where did you say Mrs Smythe Jones was? I'm sure she didn't say anything about going on holiday.'

'I don't think it was a holiday.' Didn't this man know anything about the woman who worked for him? 'She had an emergency to do with her sister apparently. She called the agency on Friday, to ask for a temp.'

Jonathan frowned. 'I knew her sister hadn't been well. I was away this weekend, skiing. Couldn't get a signal on my phone—you know how it is.' He pulled his mobile out of his pocket. 'Still no message. I'll phone her later, after I've seen my patients.' He snapped the phone shut.

'Okay, so now we've that sorted, let's move on. Who's the first patient?'

Rose was still reeling from the discovery that this man was the doctor. Where was the elderly silver-haired man of her imagination? She was rapidly trying to process this new information. But it wasn't making any kind of sense.

As if he'd read her mind, Jonathan said, 'There is another Dr Cavendish, my uncle. But he retired last year. I took over the practice from him.'

Still confused, Rose studied the list in front of her. 'You have three patients this morning.' Only three! And each of them had been given half-hour slots. Half-hour slots! In the practice where she normally worked, the patients were lucky to get ten minutes with the overworked and harassed medical team. Either Dr Cavendish wasn't very good and no one wanted to come and see him, or he didn't like to work too hard. But it was none of her business how he ran his practice. 'And then you have a couple of home visits this afternoon. That's all Mrs Smythe Jones has marked down for you, unless there's another list somewhere?' Come to think of it, perhaps that was the answer?

She glanced around the desk. No, apart from this ornate leather-bound appointment book there was nothing else with information on it. Her eyes came to rest on the computer. That was it. There must be a computerised patient list. She stopped herself from smacking her head at her stupidity. Of course there would be a full list on the computer! The patients Mrs Smythe Jones had marked down in her neat hand must be additions.

Rose smiled apologetically at Jonathan, who was waiting patiently for a response, and booted up the hard drive. There had to be a password here somewhere.

'Oh, I'm sorry,' she apologised as the computer hummed into life. 'That must be the add-on list. As soon as I can get into the clinic on the computer, I'll be able to tell you who else is down for your clinic.'

The half-smile was back. 'You won't find anything on there. Mrs Smythe Jones doesn't believe in computers, I'm afraid. She uses it for letters, but that's it. The list you have in front of you is it.' He stood and straightened his already immaculately tied tie. 'Three patients sounds about right.' He held out his hand for the book. 'When the first patient arrives, just press this buzzer here.' He leaned back over the desk and Rose caught the scent of expensive after-shave. He straightened and pointed to a set of oak filing cabinets. 'Notes are in there. Now, if you'll excuse me. Vicki, my nurse, should be in shortly—she'll keep you right.' Without waiting for a reply, he retreated into the con-sulting room and closed the door behind him.

* * *

The first patient wasn't due to arrive for another half an hour. The cleaner came in and picked up the tray from the desk.

'His Lordship in, then? I'm Gladys by the way,' she said.

It was getting more confusing by the minute. His Lordship? Who the hell was she referring to? Did she mean Jonathan? In which case, it wasn't a very respectable way to speak about her boss.

Gladys chuckled. 'You haven't a clue what I'm talking about, dearie. Do you? His Lordship? Jonathan? The Honourable Jonathan Cavendish?'

Oh, my word. She was working for aristocracy.

Speechless, Rose could only indicate the closed door of the consulting room with a tip of her head.

'That's me, then, luvvie,' Gladys was shrugging into her coat. 'I'll get myself away home. Nurse will be in in a minute. I'll see you tomorrow. Ta-ra.'

Rose sat at the desk, completely stupefied. When a harassed staff member from the agency had rung her late on Friday afternoon, she'd been only too glad to get a job for the next few weeks. She hadn't stopped to ask about the practice, and even if she had wanted to, the voice on the other end of the line had made it clear she was in a rush.

'It's a minimum of four weeks, more likely five. Harley Street. Please say you can do it. They're new clients and we really want to keep them on our books. It involves the usual medical secretary work, plus manning the reception with possibly a bit of chaperoning thrown in. It'll be a piece of cake for someone with your experience.'

It had sounded right up Rose's street. Ever since Dad had had a stroke she'd known she would have to put her job in Edinburgh on hold and go and help her mother. Her parents hadn't wanted her to come home to London, but to Rose there had been no choice. Happily the practice she worked for as a practice nurse had been sympathetic and agreed to give her five weeks' leave, more if she needed it. The next few weeks would give her time to assess the situation at home and decide whether she should return to London permanently.

Harley Street was a couple of tube journeys away from her parents' house and meant an hour's commute at either end of the day, but it was a job and Rose had snatched the opportunity with both hands. Now she was wondering if she'd done the right thing. Then again, she hadn't much choice. There weren't that many temping jobs and she needed the money. Whatever reservations she might have about her new boss, the job was perfect.

She sighed and helped herself to another chocolate in the bowl on the desk. She let the rich flavours roll around her mouth. Delicious.

The door opened and an older woman with neatly coiffed hair and a small dog tucked under her arm swept into the room. Rose glanced at her sheet. Could this be L. S. Hilton?

'Such a naughty boy,' Mrs Hilton clucked. 'Snapping at that poor man's ankles. If you do that again, Mummy will get really angry with you.' Before Rose could react, she thrust the dog into Rose's arms. He was wearing a little coat that covered his legs and a scarlet ribbon in the hair on his head. 'Could you find him some chocolates? He always gets grumpy when his blood sugar gets low.' Then she peered at Rose over her spectacles. 'Oh, I don't think we've met, dear. Where is Tiggy?' She glanced around the room as if she might find her hiding somewhere.

'She's had to go away for a bit,' Rose said. The dog looked up at her with a distinctly unimpressed air. Rose was worried that he'd take a snap at her and she looked him firmly in the eye. She was used to dogs. Her parents had always had one when she had been growing up. You had to show them who was boss straight away. The dog whimpered and relaxed in her arms. She looked over to the desk for the chocolates. Her cheeks burned as she realised that she'd scoffed the lot. She should have known better than to leave the bowl in a place where her fingers could wander of their own accord. To her huge relief, Mrs Hilton didn't seem to notice the now empty bowl.

'Mr Chips likes you,' Mrs Hilton said approvingly. 'He doesn't usually take to strangers. And certainly not when he's grumpy.'

'If you could just take a seat, Mrs Hilton, I'll let the doctor know you're here. Then I'll see what I can find for Mr Chips. Can I get you something? A cup of tea, coffee?'

Mrs Hilton sat down on one of the chairs and picked up a magazine. 'No, thank you. Too much caffeine isn't good for my arthritis and…' she eyed Rose severely '…don't you know it's terribly bad for the skin? Like chocolates.' Her eyes flickered to the empty bowl and Rose felt her cheeks grow warmer. 'Although it seems you have good skin. Good girl. Most girls don't think about their skin until they reach my age and by then it's far too late to do anything about it. At least—' her eyes twinkled '—without the expertise of a good surgeon.'

Rose couldn't work out whether she was annoyed or flattered by Mrs Hilton's personal comments. But the gleam in older woman's eye made her go with the latter. She meant no harm.

Rose buzzed through to Jonathan to let him know Mrs Hilton had arrived.

'It's Lady Hilton,' he corrected mildly. 'I'll come out.'

The door opened almost before Rose had time to replace

the handset. Jonathan paused in the door way and his mouth twitched as he noticed Rose trying to juggle Mr Chips with one arm while she searched for Mrs Hilton's notes with the other.

'Sophia,' he said, striding towards the older woman. 'How lovely to see you.'

Lady Hilton raised her face to his and Jonathan kissed her on both cheeks.

'You know I would have come to the house to see you? It would have saved you a journey into town,' he said.

'I had to come in anyway. I needed to do some shopping. And I wanted to talk to you about Giles—away from the house. He doesn't know I've been feeling poorly. And…' she looked at Jonathan sternly '…he's not to know.'

'Sophia, everything that you tell me is always in complete confidence,' Jonathan said firmly. He placed an arm under her elbow and without appearing to add any pressure, eased her to her feet. Despite the look of resolve on the older woman's face, Rose could tell the movement caused her some discomfort. Probably arthritis. Or something like it.

'Do you mind awfully keeping Mr Chips while I'm in with the doctor? He gets so restless if I don't pay him my full attention,' Lady Hilton asked Rose.

It wasn't really a question. Dog-sitting hadn't been in the job description. But, hey, it wasn't as if she was overrun with work, and he seemed to have gone to sleep in her arms.

Rose smiled. 'Don't worry. He'll be fine with me. If he wakes up and starts looking for you, I'll bring him in.'

While Rose waited for the next patient to arrive, she looked around for something to do. She liked to keep busy. Not that she could do much with a dog asleep in her arms. Spotting her discarded cardigan hanging on the back of the chair, she used one hand to form it into a little bed on the floor under her desk. She placed the sleeping dog on top. He looked at her with one eye, then gave a contented sigh and settled back down to sleep. Okay, what next? Perhaps she should ask Jonathan whether he would mind if she brought in some textbooks and did some revision in between patients? She couldn't see why he'd object. Unless she had more to occupy her, she'd go mad with boredom.

Her glance fell on the pile of magazines Lady Hilton had picked up in the short time she'd been in the waiting room. They were a mix of high-fashion glossies and society-gossip magazines, the type Rose never ever looked through—or at least never bought. She had to admit taking a sneaky look once or twice when she was at the hairdressers, but that wasn't the same as buying them. Other people's lives didn't really interest her, not unless they were doing something remarkable, like climbing Everest or walking unaccompanied to the South Pole. Now, those were people with intriguing lives, not folk who were famous, well, because they were married to a footballer or had a rich father.

Casually she flicked through the first magazine she picked up, curious despite herself. She came to a few pages near the middle, which had photographs of celebrities out on the town. Suddenly she stopped. Staring out at her, his arm around the waist of a woman with long wavy red hair, a figure to die for and a dress that would have cost Rose a year's salary, was Jonathan. He was dressed in a dinner jacket and a white shirt and appeared relaxed and at ease. Rose peered closer. Although he was smiling, there was something in his eyes that suggested he wasn't best pleased to be photographed. The caption underneath read 'The Honourable Jonathan Cavendish and his girlfriend, actress

Jessamine Goldsmith, at the premiere of her film *One Night In Heaven*.'

Rose was having a hard time getting her head around it. He was an honourable, the son of a lord, his girlfriend was a movie star. And he was her boss. A GP. She felt her lips curl in disapproval. That wasn't the kind of doctor she approved of. People should go into medicine to help others, not to finance some gad-about lifestyle. However, it was nothing to do with her. She was here to do a job and as long as her new boss didn't actually go around killing his patients with his incompetence, who was she to judge?

The door swished open and she dropped the magazine as if it were a hot potato.

A woman with short curly hair and a look of panic rushed into the room. She ran past Rose without saying anything, heading straight for the staff bathroom. Once again, Rose was bemused. It was beginning to feel as if she had walked in to a madhouse. Who on earth was that? She hadn't rung the doorbell so she must have a key. And she knew exactly where the staff bathroom was. Could this be the missing Nurse Vicki?

A few minutes later, the woman reappeared. Although she still looked pale, some colour had returned to her cheeks.

'I'm so sorry,' she said collapsing into a chair. 'You must be the temp covering for Tiggy. She phoned me on Saturday to let me know she was going to be away and there would be a temp filling in.' She took a shuddering breath. 'You must think me incredibly rude, rushing in like that without so much as a good morning.'

Rose crossed to the woman's side. 'Are you all right?'

'Not really.' She grimaced before holding out a hand to Rose. 'I'm Victoria, my friends call me Vicki. I've just been terribly sick. Thank God I made it here in time. It would have been too embarrassing throwing up in public.'

'Should you be at work?' Rose said. 'Couldn't you have taken the day off?'

'I would have. If I hadn't known Tiggy was off. Or if I'd known I was going to feel this bad. I felt okay until I got off the tube, then I just started to feel worse and worse.'

'Dr Cavendish is in with a patient. Should I call him?' Vicki did look awful. There was no way she should stay at work. Rose watched in alarm as the colour drained from the nurse's cheeks again.

'Oh, no, sorry.' Vicki clamped a hand across her mouth and bolted for the bathroom.

While she waited for Vicki to re-emerge, Rose switched the kettle on again and finding some peppermint tea set about making a pot. She hoped the drink would help settle Vicki's stomach. There was no way she could be allowed to return home until she stopped feeling ill.

'You must wonder what kind of place you've walked into.' Vicki's voice came from behind her. 'The nurse more ill than the patients. And I see Lady Hilton has brought Mr Chips in again. I do hope he won't relieve himself in the plant pot again. Oh, is that tea? Could I have some?'

'I think you should try a couple of sips. Why don't you sit down? You look as if you could collapse at any minute.'

Vicki sat on one of the chairs at the kitchen table. 'Jonathan is not going to be happy about this,' she confided. 'The last time I was off the full eight months. He had to find someone to replace me, and she didn't turn out to be great.'

Realisation was beginning to dawn on Rose.

'You're pregnant?'

Vicki nodded. 'Oh, I'd better not do that again,' she moaned. 'Any movement just makes it worse.'

'And you had hyperemesis with the last pregnancy.'

'Hey, you're pretty switched on. Have you had it? Is that how you know?' She was too polite to say so, but Rose guessed she was wondering how a medical secretary would know about the condition an unfortunate few women suffered in pregnancy.

'I'm a trained nurse. Poor you. How badly did you have it last time?'

'Bad enough to put me in hospital, I'm afraid. And to keep me off work for most of my pregnancy.' She took a tentative sip of her tea. 'I'm dreading having to tell Jonathan.'

'He doesn't know you're pregnant?'

'I wasn't going to tell him just yet. I'm only eight weeks. And I hoped that I would be better this time around.'

'I'm sure he'll understand.'

'He's a real softy. Of course he'll understand. I just hate letting him down. The patients like to see me. They're used to me. Most of the older ones hate change. My obstetrician tells me it might get better by around twelve weeks, but I'm not holding my breath.'

The sound of a door opening alerted Rose to the fact that Jonathan's consultation with Lady Hilton had ended.

'I'll be back in a moment,' she reassured Vicki. 'Just you stay there until I get back.'

She scooped up Mr Chips from his nest in her cardigan and carried him over to Lady Hilton. The movement roused the dog from his nap and he reached up, attempting to lick Rose's face. She just managed to avert the doggy kiss by passing Mr Chips over to his owner.

'Has my baby been a good boy, then?' Lady Hilton cuddled her dog as if it had been days rather than minutes since they'd been together. But as she buried her face in her pet's fur, Rose noticed tears in the corner of her eyes.

'I'll come to the house to see you and Giles later this week,' Jonathan said. 'In the meantime, we'll try this new prescription. See if that makes a difference.' He patted her arm. 'The next few weeks are going to be rough,' he said. 'Call me any time. I mean it.'

He looked around. 'Rose, have you seen Vicki? She's usually in by now.'

'In the kitchen, having a cup of tea. I'm afraid she's not feeling very well.'

A look of concern swept across Jonathan's face. 'I'll go and check up on her. I'll see you soon, Sophia. Take care.' He kissed the woman on the cheek again and Rose showed her out.

Rose retreated behind her desk, giving Vicki the chance to tell Jonathan her news. She ran through the condition in her mind. Although hyperemesis was hugely debilitating, it was rarely life threatening. However, being constantly sick would prevent Vicki from working and might well require another stay in hospital.

Jonathan appeared with his arm around Vicki's shoulder. 'I'm going to take Vicki home,' he said. 'Do you think you could hold the fort until I come back? I'll be about an hour.'

'Your next patient is due in about ten minutes,' Rose reminded him. 'Lord Bletchley?'

'I can manage, Jonathan,' Vicki said weakly. 'I'll take a taxi. You stay and see your patient. You know what Lord Wretchley—I mean, Lord Bletchley's like. He'll go through the roof if he's kept waiting.'

'He'll just have to,' Jonathan replied, looking determined. 'I don't want you to go in a taxi. Not when you might throw up again. You know what some of these drivers are like. They might well kick you out.'

'Couldn't I take your car and drive Vicki home?' Rose

offered. 'My insurance allows me to drive any car. That way you could see Lord Bletchley on time. It does mean there wouldn't be anyone to cover reception, but seeing as it's only the one patient we're expecting, that shouldn't be too much of a problem. You can man the desk, whereas I'm not too sure he'd like to be seen by me.'

Jonathan smiled and Rose's heart gave a little blip. No man should have a smile like that, she thought. It just wasn't fair on women.

'Despite what anyone may have told you, I'm perfectly capable of answering the door.' He dug in his pocket. 'If you're sure you don't mind? My car's parked outside. Vicki knows which one it is.' He tossed a set of keys to Rose. 'It has satellite navigation so you should be able to find your way to Vicki's house and back okay.'

Ignoring Vicki's protests that really she could manage by herself, Rose retrieved a sick bowl from the treatment room and ushered her out the door.

'Okay, which one is his?'

Vicki pointed at a low-slung sports car. Rose felt the colour drain from her face. Although she knew relatively little about cars, she knew enough to know that the car must have cost at least as much as her parents' house. For a second, she was tempted to go back inside and tell Jonathan she had changed her mind. But one look at Vicki told her that she needed to be at home and in bed as soon as possible. If she put a scratch on the car, Little Lord Fauntleroy would just have to live with it.

Thankfully, Vicki knew how to work the sat nav and soon Rose was threading her way through the London traffic.

'You don't have to hold the steering-wheel as if it's a wild animal about to attack you,' Vicki said with a smile.

She was right. A child on a three-wheeler would move

faster. Rose forced herself to relax her grip. Now if only she could unclench her teeth, perhaps she could talk as well as drive.

But it seemed as if Vicki was no more capable of chatting than she was. The nurse leaned back against her seat and closed her eyes. Rose followed the instructions of the disembodied voice from the computer and by some miracle managed to find her way to Vicki's house without any disasters. Now all she had to do was make it back in one piece.

'Is there anyone at home to look after you?' she asked Vicki as they drew up in front of a small Victorian terrace.

'My husband,' Vicki replied. 'He's a police officer. He's on night duty so he'll be sleeping like the dead, but I'm sure he won't mind me waking him if I need anything. Our daughter is in nursery school.'

'I'll just see you safely in,' Rose said, and before Vicki could protest, she was out of the car and around the other side, helping her out.

Vicki smiled at her. 'Are you always this capable?' she said.

Rose smiled back. 'I can't help it. I was always the Guide who finished her badges long before anyone else did. The one who got the campfire going even when it was raining. It's social occasions that get to me. Doing is better than talking, if you know what I mean? Although I'm getting better at that. Needs must. In my other life I'm a nurse.'

Vicki frowned. 'Why are you covering for Tiggy as the receptionist? Oops, I mean personal assistant. That's how Tiggy prefers to be referred to. She's a sweetheart, but she thinks it's important everyone knows their place. Titles are important to her. And not just work ones either.'

'The job I was offered was as receptionist. I used to work as a medical secretary before I did my nurse training.

I was happy to do either since I just wanted something short term.'

Vicki pulled a bunch of keys from her bag and opened her front door. 'I can manage from here,' she said. 'I'm sorry that you've had all this dumped on you on your first day. I hope we haven't scared you off. Johnny will need help. Would you be a sweetheart and phone the nursing agency and find out about a replacement for me?'

'Don't worry, I'll sort it out. You get to bed and I'll see you whenever you come back to work.'

Vicki grimaced. 'God knows when that'll be. Jonathan made me promise not to come back until I've stopped being sick. If it follows the same pattern as last time, it could be months.'

'I'll speak to him about finding someone to cover for you as soon as I get back to the office.' Rose made her voice stern. 'Now, inside and off you go to bed.'

By the time Rose, with an enormous sigh of relief, returned to the surgery, it seemed as if Lord Bletchley had been and gone. Jonathan was back at her desk with his feet up, flicking through the magazine Rose had skimmed through earlier. He was scowling.

'Bloody paparazzi,' he muttered. 'Can never get their facts right.' He flung the magazine aside and got to his feet. 'How is Vicki?'

'She was going to go straight to bed. Her husband's on night duty, so he'll keep an eye on her.'

Jonathan pulled his hand through his thick dark hair. 'I can't see her being back for at least a month. If then. Would you mind getting onto the nursing agencies? You'll find the number of the one we use regularly in the diary. Ask if there's anyone who could cover on a day-to-day basis for the next four weeks at a minimum.'

An idea was beginning to form in Rose's head, but she liked to think things through before she spoke. Jonathan looked at his watch. 'I'll be in my room if you need me. I've a couple of phone calls to make.'

Could she? Should she? Rose rolled the idea around in her head. It would be the perfect solution. She was a trained nurse and there really wasn't that much to keep her busy at the desk. Mrs Smythe Jones had told her that she hoped to be back in a week or two. Rose could combine both roles for a short time. She'd much prefer to be kept busy. And if they needed someone to man the desk while she was in with a patient, she thought she had a solution to that too.

The ringing of the door interrupted her musings. She pressed the door release and watched bemused as a teenage boy with a resentful expression was almost dragged inside by an irate-looking woman.

'Come on, Richard,' the woman was saying. 'We might as well see the doctor now we're here.'

The boy looked at Rose through long hair that almost covered his face and Rose bit down the stab of sympathy that swept over her. He had the worst case of acne she had seen outside a textbook. His face was covered with angry raised bumps and he looked utterly miserable. Underneath the bad skin, Rose could see that he could be a good-looking boy, if it weren't for the surly expression and terrible acne. It brought back memories of her own teenage years, when she had felt as self-conscious with her height as this boy clearly did with his skin.

She smiled at the boy, knowing how embarrassed he would be feeling.

'You must be Richard Pearson,' she said. 'If you want to take a seat with your mother, I'll let the doctor know you're here.'

All Rose got in reply was a grunt. Nevertheless he sat down, dipping his head so his hair covered his face.

His mother looked at him with a mixture of frustration and love. 'I apologise for my son's rudeness,' she said. 'He didn't want to come.' She turned her back to her son, leaned across the desk and continued, her voice lowered to a whisper, 'I'm at my wits' end. He's refusing to go to school now. He just sits in his room, playing on his computer. I've tried other doctors. Dr Cavendish is my last hope. I heard from a friend that he helped her daughter.' She glanced behind her again. Richard was engrossed with his mobile; either playing a game or texting.

'I'm sure Dr Cavendish will do everything he can. I'll just let him know you're here.' Rose certainly hoped he could help. Nothing so far had given her any confidence in his medical ability. Oh, he was certainly charming. The way he had been with Lady Hilton had made that evident, but no amount of charm was going to help this poor unhappy boy. At the very least surely he would refer him to a dermatologist?

She buzzed through. 'I have Richard Pearson to see you,' she said.

'I'll be right out.' He really did have a lovely voice. Deep with just a hint of a Scottish accent.

As before, he was out of his room almost before she had a chance to put the phone down. He went over to the boy and held out his hand. 'I'm Dr Cavendish. But you can call me Jonathan, if you like. Why don't you come into my room and we can have a chat?'

Richard reluctantly got to his feet, and scowled at his mother.

Something in his expression must have caught Jonathan's attention. 'Why don't you stay here, Mrs

Pearson?' he said, his voice as smooth as silk. 'And have a cup of tea while I talk to your son on his own for a bit. Then if you have any questions, I'll be happy to answer them.'

'I'd like to come in with my son,' Mrs Pearson said stubbornly.

Richard looked at his feet and shuffled them uncomfortably.

'Richard? What would you like? I see from your notes that you're seventeen so I'm happy to see you on your own. However, if you'd prefer your mother to come in with you, that's perfectly all right too.'

'On my own,' Richard mumbled with an apologetic look at his mother. 'I'll be okay, Mum. As the doctor says, I'm almost eighteen.'

Mrs Pearson seemed unconvinced. Rose touched her gently on the elbow.

'Why don't I get us both a cup of tea?'

Mrs Pearson watched Jonathan lead her son away, but then let Rose guide her over to one of the armchairs and sit her down.

'I don't really want any tea,' she said. 'I just want to get my son helped. This time last year he was popular and outgoing, and he seemed so happy. But ever since the problem with his skin, he's become so withdrawn and miserable. I keep telling him that it'll get better in time, but he says he doesn't care. It's now that matters.' She drew a shaky breath. 'I'm so scared he'll do something silly.'

Rose sat down next to the distraught mother. 'There are medicines that can help. It's often just a case of finding the right one. As soon as he knows we can improve his skin, he'll be happier. It's too cruel that he's been hit with this just at a time when his hormones are already all over the place.'

'I hope you're right.' The woman sniffed and then

looked at Rose, puzzled. 'I guess you pick up all sorts of information working in a doctor's practice.'

'I guess you do.' Rose smiled. There was no point in telling her that she had spent the last four years studying nursing, and dermatology had been one of the last modules before she'd qualified. And as for understanding teenage angst, it hadn't been that long since she'd been through it herself. She remembered only too well how awful it felt to be the odd one out. Somehow at that age you could never accept that others had the same feelings of inadequacy and that they were just better at hiding it. Not that she could imagine Dr Jonathan Cavendish going through anything like it. She doubted that he'd had a moment's uncertainty about his looks in his life.

She chatted with Richard's mother until almost half an hour had passed. Eventually, Richard emerged with Jonathan. To her relief the teenager seemed much happier. He almost managed a smile for his mother.

'So take the tablets for a week and come back and see me. If things haven't improved substantially, we'll think of what to do next. One way or another, we'll get on top of this.'

Richard's mother looked uncomfortable for a moment. Rose guessed instantly that she might be worrying about the cost of the consultation and medication.

'Oh, and by the way, the follow-up consultations are included in the price of this appointment. I've also given Richard a letter to take to his GP, who'll be happy to give him the prescription on the NHS. I hope that's okay.'

There was no disguising Mrs Pearson's relief. Rose warmed to Jonathan. He had done that so gracefully she doubted Mrs Pearson or her son suspected for a moment that he was lying about the cost of the consultations. It was all there in the brochure she had read that morning.

Thankfully, Mrs Smythe Jones had said on her detailed list that she'd catch up with the billing on her return. So many of their patients had different arrangements for payment that it would be far too complicated for a temp to work out who was to be billed what and when.

As soon as mother and son had left, Rose turned to Jonathan.

'What did you prescribe?'

He looked at her baffled. 'Amoxicillin. Why do you want to know?'

Rose felt her cheeks grow warm. She hadn't decided whether to tell him she was a nurse, but now it seemed as if she had no choice.

'I'm a trained nurse,' she admitted finally. 'A practice nurse, and I not too long ago completed a course on dermatology, so I kind of wondered what you thought you could do for him. I know topical retinoids can help when antibiotics don't.'

His frown deepened. 'A nurse? Why are you working as a…?' He stopped in mid-sentence.

Rose had to smile at his obvious discomfort. 'I'm on leave from my job for a few weeks for personal reasons. I was a medical secretary until five years ago, so I'm also qualified to do this job. When I was working as a medical secretary, I realised as I typed up the notes for the doctors that what I was reading really fascinated me and I wanted to know more.'

Oops. What was she doing? There was something in the way he was looking at her with those steady curious green eyes that was making her babble. And she was usually so reticent when it came to talking about herself.

He did look genuinely interested, although Rose had the strong suspicion that was just part of his practised charm. In which case, why on earth was she telling him? But she could hardly stop now. 'Anyway, my boss encouraged me to study for my A levels in my spare time and then apply to university, and they accepted me.' Try as she would, she couldn't quite prevent the note of pride creeping into her voice. She was the first person in her family who had gone to university and her parents had almost burst with pride.

'So why are you here?' He sounded puzzled. 'Why didn't you take a nursing job? God knows, this city is desperate for trained nurses.' His eyes were casually moving up and down her body, as if he were a cat and she the cream. She should have been annoyed, but she knew it couldn't be because he found her attractive. Not this man. Suddenly she regretted wearing her old interview suit and primly buttoned-up blouse. Nevertheless, there was something deliciously unexpected about the way it made her feel. For a second she almost forgot the question.

'Rose?' he prompted.

Now see what she had started. This was where she should tell him about her home situation and despite his interested gaze she wasn't sure he would really want to know.

'Go on,' he encouraged. 'I'd really like to know,' he said as if reading her mind. He leaned against the filing cabinets and folded his arms, his eyes never straying from her face.

'Let's just say family circumstances and leave it at that?' She kept her voice light, but returned his stare directly. It really was none of his business. He was her boss but that didn't give him the right to give her the third degree. Okay, so it wasn't exactly the third degree, but it was more than she wanted to tell him.

He was still studying her intently and she could see the

same thought processes going through his head as had gone through hers earlier. She was a nurse. He needed a nurse, and quickly.

'Did you have any luck with the agency? About a replacement for Vicki?' he asked.

'I haven't called yet,' she admitted. 'I was thinking…' She took a deep breath. What if he hated her suggestion? For all she knew, practices like this wanted their nurses to have the right kind of accent. The right kind of image. Although there was nothing wrong with the way she spoke, her voice didn't have the plummy ring to it that Vicki's voice did.

'That since you're a nurse, you could fill in for her? Exactly what I was thinking. But what about the office? I'm not sure you could do both jobs.'

Rose hid a smile. She could easily manage both jobs if it were a simple case of workload, but he was right. There did need to be someone at the desk if she was in with a patient.

'I know just the person for the office,' she said. 'She's young, but keen. She's at a bit of a loose end while she's looking for a permanent job. I know she'll be glad to work any hours needed, but she also won't mind if you need to let her go at any time.'

'Cool. Can I leave you to sort it out? Tiggy always manages that side of things. I'm afraid I'm useless at anything except the medical side.' He glanced at his watch. 'Lunchtime! Where do you fancy eating?'

Rose gaped at him. There was no way she wanted to go to lunch with him. Not today, possibly never. She was having way too odd a reaction to him, and she wanted some time to examine what was happening. It had always worked in the past. Thinking about something logically made it easier to deal with. Besides, she had brought her own snack. She really couldn't afford to eat out.

'I brought a packed lunch,' she said primly. 'I'm quite happy to have it at my desk.'

His lips twitched, but he didn't try to persuade her. He was probably relieved she had said no. No doubt it was his impeccable manners that had prompted his offer in the first place and no doubt he would have been mortified had she said yes. Somehow she guessed that the hired help going out with the boss wasn't the way things were done in this part of London.

Jonathan ran down the stairs of his London consulting rooms and into the frosty spring air. He couldn't help smiling when he thought of the temp. She was a lot better looking than Mrs Smythe Jones, that was for sure. Although he had a soft spot for the elderly receptionist, who had been there since he'd been in short trousers, he was looking forward to the next few weeks. Rose Taylor intrigued him. The baggy cardigan she was wearing couldn't quite disguise a figure that would make most of his female acquaintances weep into their champagne. Luckily he was a connoisseur of women though; anyone else would have failed to see that she was a stunner under that shapeless cardigan and old-fashioned glasses. And he'd liked the way she had dealt with his patients. Solicitous but not overbearing. He couldn't help but notice the way they responded to her. Even Lady Hilton, who usually was as narky as the dog she insisted carrying every-where, had been like putty in her hands. She was the most intriguing woman he had met since—well, for a long time. The unusual mix of prickly personality, which reminded him of a teacher he'd had at school, and hidden sex appeal.

How could a woman be sexy and sexless at the same time? He whistled as he made his way to the restaurant. It was going to be interesting having Rose Taylor around.

CHAPTER TWO

ROSE waited until the door had closed behind Jonathan before she let out her breath. She collapsed in the chair. He was gorgeous—and that smile! Did he have any idea what it did to women? Of course he did. Rose's experience of men was limited but even she recognised a man who was used to being admired. She had never met anyone like him. After all, how could she have? Those weren't the circles she moved in. But good looking though he was, she was not sure whether she approved of him. She much preferred men who had a sense of purpose, men who had some ambition, and taking over the family practice in order to have an easy life was as far off ambition as she could imagine. Not that she'd had many boyfriends. Three at the last count and none of them could be called exciting. But at least they were reliable. Reliable and safe. Somehow she knew safe wasn't a word that could be applied to Jonathan Cavendish.

And it was just as well she preferred sensible men, she thought ruefully. The chances of Jonathan Cavendish being interested in her were less than zero. All she had to do was look at that flame-haired bombshell in the picture with him. She was so perfect—there was no way she would be found absent-mindedly munching her way through a bowl of chocolates.

She glanced around the surgery. Enough of that sort of thinking. What now? He had left her his Dictaphone with his notes about the patients he had seen, so she could type them up and have them ready for him to sign on his return. And as for the rest of the afternoon? There were three home visits marked down in the book. What was she supposed to do while he was away? She swallowed a sigh. It was going to be a long day.

As she'd expected, it only took her thirty minutes to type up the letters on the computer. The note paper was as grand as the rest of the consulting rooms.

Just as she was preparing to eat her lunch, there was a frantic knocking on the door. She opened it to find a woman about her age with a young child of about two in her arms.

'Please,' she gasped. 'Is there a doctor around? My daughter's having difficulty breathing. I don't know what happened—one minute she was okay then she started wheezing. My mobile's battery's flat or else I would have called an ambulance. Then I looked up and saw the doctor's name on the door. Please help me.'

Rose could see that the young mother wasn't far off hysteria. The little girl was having difficulty breathing but at least her lips were pink and the muscles in her neck weren't standing out with each breath. The little girl was clutching a teddy bear as if her life depended on it.

She gripped the woman's shoulder. 'I know it's difficult,' she said, 'but you have to calm down. Your little girl will get more distressed if she sees you panicking. Now what's her name?'

'Sally,' the woman replied after taking a couple of deep breaths. 'I'm Margaret.'

'Could she have choked on anything? Inhaled something? A button? A peanut? Anything?'

'Not as far as I know.'

'Sally, I'm just going to look inside your mouth. Okay?' Rose said calmly. The little girl looked at her with frightened eyes. Rose gently checked inside her mouth. There was nothing obvious blocking the little girl's throat. If there had been, her breathing would have been much noisier. It was still an emergency, but not one that was immediately life threatening.

'Okay, Margaret, come with me,' Rose said, taking the little girl from her mother's arms and walking briskly to the treatment room.

'I was just having a coffee in the café round the corner and she was fine then.' Margaret had calmed down a little, although anxiety and fear were still evident in her eyes.

'Has this happened before?' Rose asked. 'Any history of asthma or allergies?' There were two obvious possibilities as far as Rose could tell. Either Sally was having an asthma attack, in which case she needed a nebuliser, or she was having a severe allergic reaction, in which case she needed adrenaline. But which one was it?

'Could you open your mouth as wide as you can, Sally? I'm just going to shine a torch down your throat. It won't hurt at all, I promise.'

The little girl did as she was told. Rose shone the torch. As far as she could see, there was no swelling of the throat.

'Is it possible she's eaten a peanut? Or some other food she's not had before?'

The mother shook her head. 'She was in her high chair. All she had was the juice I gave her.'

In the background Rose heard the slamming of the door

and then a voice calling her name. A wave of relief washed over her. It was Jonathan. At least now she'd have help.

'In the treatment room,' she called out. 'Could you come, please?'

He appeared at the door of the room and took the situation in at a glance. He crouched next to the chair where Rose had plonked Sally back on her mother's lap.

He touched the little girl lightly on the cheek. 'Hello, there,' he said softly. 'What's all this, then? You're having difficulty breathing?'

While he was talking to the girl, Rose had located a nebuliser and some liquid salbutamol. As he started to listen to the little girl's chest she held the vial up to him and he nodded approvingly towards her.

'Margaret, do you know how much Sally weighs?' Rose asked. 'It'll help us work out how much medicine to give her.'

'I'm not sure, maybe about twelve kilograms. I haven't weighed her recently. There's been no need.'

Now that Margaret knew her daughter was getting the help she needed, some of the terror had left her voice.

'It's okay. We can make an estimate.'

Rose reached for a pulse oximeter. 'I'm just going to put this on your toe,' she said to Sally. 'It won't hurt either. It's just a little toy I have to help me. Okay?' Rose turned to Margaret. 'It'll monitor Sally's blood oxygen levels. Tell us how much oxygen she's taking in.'

The child was still having problems with her breathing, but now that her mother had calmed down, some of the panic had subsided and her breathing was becoming easier. Nevertheless, she still needed treatment.

'I think your daughter is having an asthma attack,' Jonathan said, taking the nebuliser from Rose. 'I'm just going to put this over your mouth, Sally, and I want you to take slow, deep breaths.'

The little girl shook her head from side to side, the panic beginning to return.

Frantically Rose looked around then she had an idea. She lifted the teddy from the little girl's arms and placed a second nebuliser over the toy bear's mouth. Rose crouched by Sally's side and, placing her hands on either side of the little face, forced her to look into her eyes.

'Watch me, Sally. We're going to play a game. Every time I take a breath, like this, Teddy's going to take a breath. You copy us, okay?

It seemed to work. Her eyes fixed on Rose and the teddy bear, Sally copied every breath Rose took. Jonathan watched carefully not saying anything. Slowly, Sally's breathing returned to normal and after a while Jonathan removed the mask from the little girl's face.

'Your breathing should be all right now, Sally.' He turned to her mother.

'This is the first time it's happened? Never before?'

Margaret shook her head.

'It probably didn't seem that way to you but I think that some of the problem was that Sally was getting quite panicky when she felt her breathing was tight. We could tell from looking at her breathing that she was still managing to take plenty of air into her lungs—her oxygen reading was ninety-eight per cent, which is pretty good, even when she was at her most distressed. Even so, it was a very scary experience for you both,' Jonathan explained.

Sally's mother looked weak with relief. The little girl hid her head in her mother's neck and closed her eyes. Rose knew that sleep would be the best thing for the child now.

'We had been to the park to feed the ducks with a friend.

Sally was sleepy so she went for a nap in my friend's arms. When she woke up she needed to go to the bathroom, so I took the chance to have a coffee. She had been coughing in the park a little, but I didn't think anything of it. It was only when we were in the coffee shop that she seemed to have difficulty getting her breath. I thought she'd be better in the fresh air but she kept on getting worse. Then I saw the name on the door. I hoped there would be someone who could help.'

She looked at Jonathan and Rose, her eyes glistening. 'Thank you, both. I don't know what I would have done if you hadn't helped me.'

'I think it's Rose who deserves most of the thanks,' Jonathan said, straightening. He looked at her as if she puzzled him—as if she were a crossword and he was missing several clues.

'You should see your own doctor as soon as you can. I suspect Sally is going to need regular medication for a while,' he told Margaret.

Rose was turning over what Sally's mother had said.

'Do you have pets, Margaret?'

'No, we don't. Sally's dad is allergic to animal fur.'

'What about this friend? The one you met in the park?'

'Linda? Oh, yes. She has about five cats. She loves them and is always rescuing another one.'

Rose caught Jonathan's eye and knew he was thinking the same thing she was.

'I think we might have found the culprit. It's possible your daughter is allergic to cat fur. Perhaps there were cat hairs clinging to your friend and when Sally fell asleep in her arms she inhaled some of the allergens. Anyway, it's only a possibility, but one worth thinking about and mentioning to your GP when you see him,' he said.

Margaret refused a cup of tea, but accepted Rose's offer to call her a taxi. Ten minutes later she was climbing into the cab, her sleeping child in her arms, still thanking Jonathan and Rose effusively.

When they had left, Rose turned to Jonathan. 'I hope you're all right with me bringing them in. I realise it wasn't anything to do with your practice and if I had messed up, you could have been held liable.'

Jonathan looked at her his expression serious. 'And if I told you that it was unforgivable, that you have never to help a passer-by again, what would you say?'

'I would say that you need to find another temp,' Rose replied hotly, before she noticed that corners of his mouth had lifted in a smile. 'You're kidding, right?' she said, embarrassed she had jumped to the wrong conclusion so quickly.

'Of course I'm kidding,' he said. 'I wouldn't dream of employing someone who would think of rules before they acted. That wouldn't be right and...' his smile grew wider and Rose felt the strangest feeling in the pit of her stomach "...so boring.'

He levered himself away from the wall against which he'd been leaning. 'I think you've had enough excitement for the day. Why don't you do the letters from this morning and then get away home?'

'Letters are done, just waiting for your signature,' Rose replied. What on earth did he think she'd being doing while he'd been out to lunch? She glanced at her watch. 'It's only two o'clock. I can't possibly leave this early.'

He looked thoughtful.

'How would you like to come on a home visit with me, then? From what I saw back there, the way you dealt with Margaret and Sally, you'd be perfect to step in for Vicki. What do you say? It'll mean more money, of course.'

The nervous flutter in the pit of her stomach spread upwards. The look in his eyes was a heady mixture—sexy, naughty, mischievous. Rose had never felt so flustered in her life, but she was damned if she was going to let him see the effect he was having on her. She held out her hand. 'You have a deal. And if you're happy for me to find someone for the office, I can do that too. I'll write down a name and number so you can check my references.'

He raised his eyebrows at her before shaking her hand. 'Somehow I get the feeling they're going to be first class.'

Rose tried to ignore the warmth that was spreading through her body.

'Is it usual for you to take the office staff on a home visit?' she asked.

'Not really. But the visit I have down for the afternoon isn't the easiest.'

For the first time since she'd met him, he looked uncomfortable. 'It's to Jessamine Goldsmith's house.' She was the actress, the one who had been with him in the photograph in the magazine. His girlfriend.

'And let's just say that it would make me feel much more comfortable having you there.'

'Isn't she your girlfriend?' What on earth was Jonathan thinking? It was completely against the rules for a doctor to date a patient.

He narrowed his eyes at her. 'What makes you say that?'

Involuntarily, Rose's eyes slid to the magazine.

Jonathan's eyes followed hers. He looked none too pleased when he realised what she'd seen.

'Let's clear one thing up,' he said. 'Never ever believe what you see in these magazines. Jessamine Goldsmith is *not* my girlfriend and never has been. She's a patient who just happens to move in the same social circles as I do.'

'In which case…' Rose raised an eyebrow while hiding a smile '…what are we waiting for?'

As he manoeuvred the car through the thick London traffic, he flicked a switch and the rich sounds of Debussy filled the car. It was a composer Rose loved. She sat back in her seat, aware of the scent of expensive aftershave mingling with the smell of leather. It was so much better being in this car without having to drive. All she had to do now was relax.

'How come we're going to see Miss Goldsmith at home? Is she really unwell?'

Jonathan flicked her a smile.

'Jessamine's almost certainly fine, believe me. She simply prefers to have me see her at her house. A lot of the patients do. They find it less stressful.' Again there was the smile. 'Naturally, if they need to come to the consulting rooms for tests, then they do. Or if they're shopping nearby. Some, however, prefer me to come to them. It's much more discreet. Take Jessamine, for example, the press follow her everywhere, as they do many of my patients. Any visit to the doctor is viewed with curiosity and speculation. As you can imagine, most people prefer not to have that kind of conjecture in the public domain.'

'But aren't they equally curious about a visit from the doctor?'

At this point they had left the traffic behind and were driving through one of the more exclusive parts of London. Jonathan pulled up outside a house that could have been a hotel it was so large. The Victorian façade was the grandest she had ever seen. Two tall pillars framed a massive front door.

Jonathan turned off the ignition. 'Except that they can never be sure whether I'm visiting as a doctor or as a friend. Most of my patients belong to the same social circle as I do. You can't imagine how many off-the-record consultations I do at a party or at Ascot.'

All this was more and more confusing. Rose frowned.

'That can't be good. Surely there needs to be some distinction between the doctor and the patient?'

He jumped out of the car. 'Nope. It works just fine, believe me.'

The door was opened, before they had a chance to knock, by a man dressed in a formal suit.

'Good afternoon, sir,' he said. 'And miss. Miss Goldsmith is waiting for you in the drawing room. She said I was to show you straight in.'

Rose wanted to giggle. It was like being caught in a time warp. But if Jonathan found it amusing, he gave no indication of it. Instead, he stepped back to allow Rose to go through the door in front of him.

She stepped into a hall, so enormous her parents' whole house could have easily fitted into it—possibly twice. The floor was marble, paintings hung on the wall, and sculptures and large vases holding extravagant flower arrangements were placed around the space. To one side was a fireplace and a small sofa.

'I know my way, thank you, Robert,' Jonathan said, and taking Rose by the elbow steered her across the hall and up a flight of stairs that wouldn't have looked out of place in the foyer of the grandest cruise ship. Everywhere Rose looked there were ornate statues and gilt ornaments. Although someone had lavished a fortune on the interior, it wasn't to her taste. Rose much preferred a minimalist, uncluttered look.

Inside another equally impressive room, almost hidden in the depths of a sofa, was a woman with fine features and a mass of red hair. As soon as she saw Jonathan, she jumped to her feet and came towards him, arms outstretched.

'I've been waiting all day for you to come.' She pouted, holding up her face to be kissed.

'I do have other patients, Jess,' Jonathan said, bending and kissing her on the cheek. 'I've brought someone with me. This is Rose Taylor, my...er...nurse for the next few weeks.'

Rose stood trying not to shuffle her feet like some sort of servant from the Middle Ages. She smiled and held out her hand. 'I'm pleased to meet you, Ms Goldsmith.'

Jessamine studied her for a second, her glance no doubt taking in the cheap suit Rose wore. Whatever she saw seemed to reassure her and she smiled, the famous smile Rose knew from the times she had seen her in the movies. It lit up her face, turning her from a petulant teenager into a woman of remarkable beauty.

Jessamine ignored Rose's outstretched hand and dropped two air kisses on either side of Rose's cheeks.

'Would you like something to drink? Champagne perhaps? Tea?'

'Tea would be lovely,' Jonathan said firmly. 'Now, Jessamine, what can I do for you?'

'It's my stomach,' she said. 'It hurts like crazy.'

'Why don't you lie down while I take a look?' Jonathan suggested.

'Perhaps Rose wouldn't mind going downstairs to organise the tea while you're examining me?' There was no mistaking the glint in Jessamine's eye.

'Sorry, Jess, I need Rose here.' He sent Rose a look that implied that if she even thought about leaving him alone, she would have him to answer to. 'In case I need to take blood. Now, don't be difficult, let's have a look. Have you been eating properly? You know we spoke about this before. Your tummy hurts because you're hungry. You have to have more than five hundred calories a day.'

'That's all very well for you to say.' Jessamine pouted again. 'You know how the camera adds pounds and I have an audition tomorrow.'

Jessamine lay down on the sofa and lifted her T shirt, revealing her stomach. It was, as Rose had suspected, as flat as a pancake. But Jonathan was right, she was too thin. Rose could almost count each individual rib poking through the skin. When Jonathan made Jessamine sit up, so he could listen to her breathing from her back, it was the same, each vertebrae sticking out like a railway track.

'Your chest is fine and so is your heart. Rose, could you take Jessamine's blood pressure, please?'

It took Rose about two seconds to wrap the cuff around the too-thin arms. The blood pressure was slightly on the low side, but nothing particularly concerning. Despite her thinness, Jessamine was, on the surface, in good physical condition. While Rose was taking her blood pressure, Jessamine was talking to Jonathan. She was speaking too fast, her eyes bright and feverish.

'I hope you haven't forgotten about the Wakeleys' yacht party next weekend, Johnny? All the crowd is going. I know you and Felicity aren't together any more, but you mustn't stay at home and mope. You must come too, Rose,' she added as an afterthought.

Rose knew it was only politeness that had made Jessamine invite her.

'I'm sure Rose would love to come,' Jonathan said before Rose could decline. 'In fact, I'll bring her myself.'

The response was obviously not what Jessamine had been hoping for. She narrowed her cat's eyes at Rose, and then with another dismissive glance seemed to remember that Rose offered no competition.

Rose opened her mouth to protest. She might be working for Jonathan, but that didn't give him the right to accept invitations on her behalf. Besides, she had her own plans. She would be going down to the pub, her old local, to meet up with friends she hadn't seen for months. Nevertheless, she felt slightly wistful. When was the last time she'd been to a party? And when would she ever have a chance to go to one like the one Jessamine was talking about? Never was the answer. But there was no point in even thinking about it: she'd be completely out of her depth. She caught Jonathan's eye. He was looking at her, willing her not to contradict him, so she wouldn't. She could always send her apologies with him on the night.

Eventually, after Jonathan had taken some blood and given Jessamine a lecture about eating properly and had received a promise in return that everyone in the room knew was empty, he made their excuses.

'We'll see you a week on Sunday, Jess,' he said. 'And I'll come back and see you before then. I don't think there's anything to worry about at the moment, but I'm going to keep an eye on you. But you have to eat more regularly. If you don't, you will continue to suffer from indigestion. But that's not the only thing. You're harming your body by starving yourself.' He frowned down at her. 'Is it really worth putting your health at risk, Jess?'

'Please don't tell me off, Johnny. I promise I'll be good. I just have to audition for this next film and then I'll put a few pounds back on, I promise.'

She held up two fingers in a salute Rose knew well. 'Brownies' honour.' She slid a pointed glance at Rose. Her look was mocking and challenging at the same time.

She had taken a dislike to Rose, that much was obvious, and Rose had no idea why.

Outside, Jonathan held open the door of his car. 'Can I drop you off at home?' he asked.

Rose shook her head. 'I think there's a tube station not far from here. I need to pick up a few things on my way home so, thanks, but no thanks.'

'Then I'll drop you off at the station. Hop in. We can have a chat about Jessamine on the way.'

Rose did as he suggested. 'You seemed pretty sure it was indigestion,' she said.

'I am. Given her lifestyle, it's the likely diagnosis. But I'm not ruling out other possibilities just yet either. I want to check her blood count—do a full blood screen, just to be on the safe side.'

Although it probably was just indigestion, Rose had been worried that Jonathan didn't seem to be taking the symptoms seriously enough. There was something about the casual way the consultations were held, the familiarity with the patients, that disturbed her. Jonathan's manner was so easygoing, her earlier doubts were resurfacing. Did he really know what he was doing? However nothing in the thorough way he examined the patients or his detailed notes suggested otherwise. Perhaps it was simply that this world was so different from anything she had ever encountered.

'You think it could be more than indigestion?' she asked.

'Let's just say I'm not going to take any chances.'

Rose was relieved by his reply. Apart from the ethical considerations of working with a less than thorough doctor, it had become important to her that Jonathan had a modicum of respect for the profession in which he was practising.

Suddenly he grinned at her and her heart gave a disconcerting lurch.

'How was your first day, then?'

'Not really what I'm used to,' Rose admitted. 'But interesting.'

She wasn't lying. But the most intriguing thing about the whole day was this man sitting beside her. She studied him surreptitiously from under her eyelashes. She had never met anyone like him before. How could she have? Her upbringing had been as different from his as it was possible to be. Her father and mother had worked hard just to keep their heads above water. Treats had been few and far between, but if material possessions had been in short supply, Rose had always felt treasured and loved.

She had always been studious, but she had never really been ambitious. After leaving school, without sitting A levels, she had done a secretarial course and had taken a job as a medical secretary with an out-of-town practice. It was there that she had realised that she wanted to do more with her life. The patients and their illnesses had fascinated her and she'd found herself becoming immersed in their lives. Soon the patients had been stopping by her desk on a regular basis to tell her the latest on their families, sharing their hopes and fears with her. One of the doctors had noticed how easily the patients spoke to her and how quickly she picked up the medical terminology and had suggested medicine or nursing as a possible career. She had taken her A levels at evening class and followed up her excellent results with four years studying for her nursing degree at Edinburgh University. The circle of friends she had formed there had shared her interests—walks, music, theatre and opera. University had introduced her to things she had never been exposed to before and she had lapped it up. After graduating, she had easily found a job she loved in Edinburgh, within walking distance of her flat.

It had been a warm, comfortable, if unexciting life. One she had cherished. Why, then, was she beginning to wonder if something had been missing?

CHAPTER THREE

'I'M HOME,' Rose called out, heaving a sigh of relief as she dropped her bags of shopping at the front door. The tube had been packed as usual, bodies pressed up against each other as the train had rattled and swayed. She had stopped off at the supermarket for something for tonight's dinner and had then had to complete the second half of her journey home. The walk from the station only took ten minutes but, laden as she was, combined with heels that, although sensible by most women's standards, were still an inch higher than Rose was used to, had felt every painful step of the walk home.

Her mother came out to greet her.

'How was it, love?' She reached for one of the shopping bags. 'Why don't you go in and see your dad while I put this away? Then you can tell us all about it over a nice cup of tea.'

'How is he, Mum? What sort of day has he had?'

'Not too bad. He ate his breakfast and his lunch, then we did the exercises the physio showed us. He's a bit tired now. I'll help him to bed once we've had supper.'

Rose found her father in his usual chair by the window. Her heart squeezed as she took in his useless arm and downturned mouth. The stroke had left one side of his body pretty much paralysed, as well as impairing his speech. Her father had been a vigorous man who had enjoyed going to football matches and playing cricket and golf, and now he was reduced to sitting by the window, watching the world go by. Rose knew how much he loathed needing help. If he would barely accept it from his wife, he hated taking it from his daughter. There had been a small improvement since he'd been discharged from hospital and Rose prayed with the proper treatment he'd continue to make progress.

'Hey, Daddy. How's it going? Seen any suspicious characters out there today?' She dropped a kiss on the top of his head and he gave her his lopsided smile.

'Hello, sweetheart,' he said. Although the words were indistinct, Rose knew that was what he was trying to say.

She sat down beside him and took his hand in hers. 'You have no idea what sort of day I've had, Dad.' She told him about the chocolates, Mr Chips, the visit to Jessamine's house, embellishing her stories to amuse him. Not that they needed much embellishment. She rubbed her stocking feet as she spoke, knowing she'd need a plaster or two before she could wear the shoes again.

'What's he like, then, this doctor you're working for?' Her mother appeared in the doorway, tea towel in hand. She had only very reluctantly agreed to Rose coming home to help look after her father. They had been so proud of her, the first in their family ever to get a university degree, and had wanted her to carry on building her career. In their minds, Rose knew they had her as Hospital Matron within a year or two. Rose had tried to tell them hospital matrons didn't exist any more, but they chose not to believe her.

Of course Rose had had to come home. She'd had to see her father for herself and she'd known the first weeks following her father's discharge would be tough, so she'd applied for, and been granted, five weeks' special leave. After that? She shrugged inwardly. She'd have to see. Her mother wasn't getting any younger.

'Dr Cavendish?' Rose paused. How could she describe him? 'Well, he's young. Not much older than I am. About six foot and kind of lean. Apparently he's the son of a lord.'

'Well, I never. The son of a lord! What's he doing working as a doctor, then?'

'Apparently the practice belonged to his uncle who was doctor for the Queen's household. The uncle's retired now and Jonathan has taken over.'

'Is he poor, then? That he has to work for a living?' Rose's mother crossed over and plumped the cushions behind her husband's back. 'I know not all of the aristocracy is well off.'

'I don't think so, Mum. He drives a Lotus, although I suppose that could belong to the business. I don't really know much more about him. I can't say I've ever heard of his family.'

She closed her eyes and immediately an image of smiling green eyes and a mischievous grin flickered in front of her. How could she even begin to explain someone like Jonathan Cavendish to her parents when she could hardly explain her reaction to him to herself?

'Let's just say that I think the next few weeks are going to be interesting. Instead of acting as receptionist and medical secretary, it seems as if I'm to be nurse and chaperone.' Rose filled her parents in about Vicki before continuing, 'He has patients all over the country, and in Europe, and he's asked me if I can travel with him.' She looked at her mother. 'It does mean I won't be around to help as much as I'd like.' She paused. 'Maybe I should tell him I can't do it. Come to think of it, I must be crazy.'

Her father reached out and patted her on the arm. 'Do it,' he said. 'I want you to. It would make me feel better knowing that I'm not holding you back.'

Rose hugged her father, feeling his too-thin frame under her arms. Where had the strong muscular father of her teens disappeared to? He had always been there for her, now she wanted to be there for him and her mother. But he hated being dependent. And she had to make sure she didn't make him feel worse.

'By the way, Miss Fairweather phoned.' Rose's mother mentioned the name of the neurosurgeon Rose had seen after her father's stroke. 'She wants you to call her at the hospital. She wouldn't say any more. There's nothing wrong, is there, love?'

Rose felt a shiver of alarm but pushed it away. Her father's GP had recommended she see the specialist after discovering her father's stroke had been caused by an aneurysm. He'd told Rose that the condition often ran in families and to be on the safe side she should have herself checked out. Miss Fairweather had agreed and advised Rose to have an MRI. That had been on Friday and she had refused to let herself think about it over the weekend. She had been positive that there was nothing to worry about. After all, it wasn't as if she had any symptoms. No head-aches, tingling sensations. Nothing. She dismissed the uneasy feeling that was creeping up her spine. No doubt the consultant just wanted to let her know that her results were all normal.

'I'm sure she just wants to let me know everything's okay, Mum. Don't worry. I'll give her a ring now.'

But when Miss Fairweather asked Rose to make an appointment to see her as soon as possible, Rose knew it wasn't okay. Had her results been fine, the neurosurgeon would have said so over the phone. Rose replaced the receiver, having made an appointment at the end of the week. She returned to the sitting room and her mother looked at her, alarm written all over her face.

'Not bad news, love?' she asked, the colour draining from her face.

There was no point in worrying her parents until she knew what Miss Fairweather had to say.

'No, Mum. Everything's fine,' Rose lied.

The following days at Jonathan's practice settled into a pattern. Patients would come to see Jonathan in the morning, then in the afternoon he would go out on visits, leaving Rose to type up notes if she wasn't needed. Some of the patients Rose recognised from the newspapers or TV, some she didn't recognise, but felt she should. Jonathan treated them all with the same easy grace and familiarity. Some afternoons she'd accompany him on his house visits, each home almost more spectacular than the last. Whenever Rose found herself thinking about her upcoming appointment with Miss Fairweather, she would push the thought away. There was no point in worrying until she knew what the neurosurgeon had to tell her.

But at home, in the privacy of her bedroom, she spent her evenings searching the net for information about aneurysms. None of it gave her much cause for optimism.

When Jonathan turned up for work in the morning, he'd sometimes look tired, as if he'd spent most of the night clubbing, although he never appeared hungover. And sure enough, there were photographs of him in the tabloid press, outside clubs and restaurants, with one glamorous woman after another on his arm. If it gave Rose a strangely uncomfortable feeling to see him with different women, she would dismiss the thought with a shake of her head. It was none of her business what he chose to do in his own time.

Once there was a photograph of him playing polo and she discovered that at least two of his free afternoons were given over to the sport. In the picture, he was swiping at an object with a long stick. Dressed in a white shirt and light-coloured trousers, his hair flopping over his eyes as he concentrated on his task, he looked like someone out of a regency romance. No wonder women seemed to find him irresistible.

She had managed to get in touch with Jenny, who had been delighted at the offer of some short-term work.

'I'm going mad having nothing to do,' Jenny had confided in Rose. 'I've sent out hundreds of applications but no luck yet. A bit of actual work experience can do me no harm. Especially if Dr Cavendish likes what I do and is prepared to put a word in for me.'

Rose had met Jenny the day she had gone to sign on with the agency. She was nineteen, having just finished her secretarial course, and full of boundless enthusiasm.

'Could you just tone down the hair?' Rose asked, remembering the spiky haircut. 'And perhaps remove the piercings, especially the ones from your nose and lip? Somehow I don't think it would be appropriate for the practice.' Even if quite a few of the patients had tattoos and piercings themselves.

'No problem,' Jenny said. 'I promise you you won't recognise me when you see me next.'

And true to her word, Jenny had turned up with hair neatly slicked into a bob, piercings removed and wearing a skirt that, while short, was just on the right side of decent.

She had regarded the consulting rooms with undisguised glee.

'This is a bit of all right,' she said. 'Now, where is this Honourable Dr Cavendish? And what do I call him? My Lord? Sir?'

Rose laughed. 'I think Dr Cavendish is just fine. Come on, I'll take you in to meet him.'

Happily, Jonathan seemed to take to Jenny. And the young girl, being smart and quick on the uptake, was soon ensconced behind the desk.

'He's a bit of all right,' Jenny confided. 'If he wasn't so old I could go for him myself.'

Rose laughed. 'He's hardly old. Twenty-seven.'

Jenny sent her a look that suggested that anyone over twenty-five was middle-aged in her opinion. Then she scrutinised Rose. 'But he's the right age for you.'

Rose smiled uncomfortably. 'I don't think I'm his type. Or he mine, for that matter,' she added quickly.

Jenny was still studying her critically. 'You know if you lost the glasses, maybe got some contacts, got a more modern hairstyle and some decent clothes, you'd be quite pretty.'

Rose couldn't make up her mind whether she was insulted or flattered. Get some new clothes and haircut indeed. Jenny watched too many films. Whatever, she knew Jenny didn't mean to be offensive.

'I appreciate your…' she searched for the right word '…opinion. But I'm happy the way I am. I like my clothes—they're comfortable. And I don't fancy poking my fingers into my eyes every morning and evening. Besides…' she glanced behind her just in case Jonathan was within earshot '…I'm not looking for a boyfriend. And if I were, Dr Cavendish wouldn't be him.'

'But…' Jenny started to protest.

'No buts.' Rose cut her off. 'Whatever thoughts are in that head of yours, get rid of them. I'm here to do a job. That's it.'

But after Jenny had returned to her work, she thought about what she had said. It was true she wasn't looking for a boyfriend, and even if she were, Jonathan wasn't for her, or she for him. Although he made her pulse race uncomfortably, she doubted whether he took anything in life seriously. And even if he were her type or she his, she had far more important things on her mind than the dishy Jonathan Cavendish.

One morning, towards the end of the week, a well-known footballer came to the surgery, accompanied by his wife. Rose vaguely remembered reading about their wedding in a magazine she had picked up on the train. The footballer was even better looking in real life, his wife petite next to his six-foot frame. Whereas he was dressed simply in a pair of jeans and T-shirt, his wife was dolled up to the nines.

While Jenny organised drinks for them Jonathan called Rose into his consulting room.

'Mark and Colette came to see me a couple of weeks ago as they are thinking of starting a family,' he said. 'The last time they were here I arranged for them to have some tests. I have the results back. And I'm afraid it's not going to be the best news they ever heard. IVF is the only way forward for them unless they adopt. I'm going to arrange for them to have further investigations at the London Fertility Clinic, but in the meantime I think it would be helpful if you could sit in while I chat to them. If they agree.'

Rose nodded. She often sat in with the doctors in her surgery when they were giving unwelcome news. That way she could be there if the patients telephoned later, looking for clarification. A large number of patients were unable to take in everything they were told when they first heard that there was a problem.

The couple were happy to have Rose present. From

their smiling faces, Rose knew they weren't expecting
bad news. At least until something in Jonathan's face
alerted Colette

'What is it, Jonathan? Something's wrong. I can tell
from the way you're looking at me.' Colette's voice shook
and Mark took her hand firmly in hers.

Jonathan pulled his seat around to the side of the
table where Colette was sitting. His green eyes were full
of sympathy.

'The initial bloods I took from Colette the last time she
came to see me suggest that her ovaries are working
normally. That's good. Although I think you should have
the test repeated at the London Fertility Clinic. They will
probably also suggest an ovarian scan, just to confirm the
results of the blood test.'

'So there isn't a problem, then. We should just keep
trying. We don't need to be referred.'

'There doesn't seem to be a problem with Colette.'
Jonathan kept his voice steady. 'Although that's not a
helpful way of looking at it. As if it's a problem belonging
to one of the partners. Whenever couples are having difficulty conceiving, we like to think of it as a couple thing.'

'Come on, Jonathan. Stop beating around the bush.
We come to you because we know we'll get straight
answers.' Mark said.

'The difficulty is on your side, I'm afraid,' Jonathan
said sympathetically. 'The semen sample you gave last
week had very few motile sperm. The clinic will want to
repeat the test again, but it would seem that you are
unlikely to conceive without ICSI. That's an IVF procedure
where Colette goes through IVF treatment to stimulate her
production of eggs then her eggs are injected with one of
your sperm. It's very successful. If…' He stressed the last

word while looking Mark directly in the eye. 'If they can find sperm that's healthy enough to do the procedure.'

Mark looked as if he'd been poleaxed. 'Are you kidding? But I'm healthy. You won't find anyone fitter this side of London.'

'I'm sorry, Mark. As I say, you'll need to have more tests, but I'm pretty sure. That's why it's a good thing you came to see me sooner rather than later. The quality of your sperm is only likely to deteriorate the longer we wait.'

The shock on the couple's faces tore at Rose's heart. She could see Colette making a determined effort to pull herself together.

'I don't mind, darling,' Colette said. 'I don't care about having IVF as long as we can have a baby. Jonathan's not saying we can't have children and that's all that matters.'

But Mark was still looking dumbfounded. Suddenly he got to his feet and lurched out of the room. Jonathan looked at Rose, and reading the unspoken question in his eyes she nodded. 'I'll stay with Colette.'

Jonathan followed Mark, leaving the two women alone.

'Jonathan can't be right,' Colette said after a moment. 'It's not possible. Mark won't accept it. We always assumed that if there was a problem it was me.'

Rose pulled a chair closer to where Colette sat and took her small hand. Her heart went out to the woman sitting next to her. In the last few days she too had had to face the real possibility that she might never have children. If she did have an aneurysm there would never be any children. Not even with IVF. A pregnancy would be too dangerous. Rose would never be able to carry a child. As her throat tightened, she pushed the thought away. She needed to focus on her patient.

'He'll come to terms with it in time, I'm sure. It's been

a shock. And it sounds, from what Jonathan's being saying, that a child is not out of the question. It might just take a little help, that's all.'

'We didn't seriously think there was a problem, you know. We just came to see Jonathan because we wanted to make sure we were doing everything right for the baby from the moment it was conceived. You know, folic acid, vitamins. All that stuff. But when he heard we'd been trying for almost a year already, he suggested doing the tests—just to be on the safe side.'

'The procedure Jonathan's talking about isn't too awful, you know. And if you have a healthy baby at the end of it, what does it matter if you've needed a little help on the way?'

Colette still looked doubtful. 'We always assumed we were going to have a family. At least three. Maybe four.' She smiled wanly. 'I think he wanted to start his own five-a-side football team.' Her voice cracked. 'The thing is, I don't know if he'll agree to IVF at all. I think he might take it as a slight to his masculinity—you know how some men are. What will we do then?'

'You'll need to give him time, Colette. Once he understands exactly what's involved, I'm sure he'll come round.'

'You don't know that!' Colette protested hotly. 'You don't have any idea how we're feeling. To think one day that you have everything happiness, wealth, fame, only to have your dreams stripped away the next.'

A wall of pain slammed into Rose.

Colette had no idea that she understood only too well.

Eventually Jonathan and Mark returned. 'We just walked around Regent's Park for a bit,' Jonathan told Colette. 'Mark's had time to think it over, and he's agreed that the best thing to do is have you both seen at the fertility clinic.

You just tell me when it suits you and I'll fix up an appointment. Then I'll see you back here and we can take it from there. Okay?'

The couple just nodded. Rose knew it would take them a little time to get their heads around what Jonathan told them and her heart went out to them. As Colette had said, what did wealth and fame matter if you couldn't have what your heart truly desired?

Jonathan was unusually sombre after the couple had left.

'They'll be okay, won't they?' Rose asked.

He pulled a hand through his thick, dark hair. 'I hope so. They've had a shock. They're a lovely couple. Despite Mark's fame, and despite his reputation for being a little wild on and off the field, he's down-to-earth, kind. So is she. If ever a couple would make great parents, it would be them. And as I told them, ICSI has a very high success rate. Even higher than getting pregnant naturally. As long as the embryologists can find any motile sperm.'

Jonathan gave his head a little shake as if to banish whatever thoughts were troubling him. He picked up tickets Mark had left on the desk when he'd first arrived.

'You fancy going to a football match?' he asked. 'Mark left some tickets for the Arsenal game next Saturday. I would go, but I already have tickets for the one-day International at Lords. I like football, but next to cricket...' He grinned. 'No competition, I'm afraid.'

'No, thanks,' she said regretfully, thinking of her father. 'Although you have no idea how much I'd like to accept. My Dad and I used to go all the time before I left home. He hates missing all the matches. He's been an Arsenal fan all his life.'

'Then give the tickets to him,' Jonathan said, thrusting them in her direction. 'They're for a box. He'll get a grand view.'

Rose wished she could accept on behalf of her father. It would be just the tonic he needed to lift his spirits. But getting him up and down flights of steps was more than she and her mother could manage.

'I wish he could go,' she said softly.

'So take him,' Jonathan persisted.

Rose turned away so Jonathan wouldn't see the tears that sprang to her eyes. 'He had a stroke about two weeks ago. He lost the use of his left side. He doesn't go out much any more. He hates the indignity of being seen out in public, and even if he didn't, until I get a new car that can take his wheelchair, he's pretty much trapped at home.'

Jonathan took a long look at her. Then he grinned and his eyes glittered. Rose's stomach flipped. 'You probably don't know this, but my family motto is *Where there's a will there's a way*. Actually, it's not, it's something far grander, but it means the same thing.'

Before Rose could ask him what he meant, his next patient arrived and Jonathan led him into his room.

'I'm so sorry,' Miss Fairweather told Rose. 'I really wish I was giving you better news.'

The room swayed as a wave of nausea hit Rose. She had known that there was a good chance the news would be bad, but she hadn't allowed herself to believe it. Now her worst fears were being realised. She did have an aneurysm.

Gathering her courage, she sat up straight in the hard backed chair and looked the young consultant in the eye.

'Okay, so what are my options?'

'You have two choices. You do nothing, and decide to live with the aneurysm.'

'Which would mean what exactly? Please, Doctor, don't mince your words. I need to know exactly what I'm facing.'

Miss Fairweather leaned forward. 'It is possible that you could live the rest of your life without the aneurysm bursting, but if it does, and there is no way of predicting how likely that would be, you could have a stroke and depending on the severity, you could be left with a number of physical problems—loss of speech, the use of your legs, or…'

'Or I could drop down dead,' Rose finished for her. 'Suddenly and without warning. Mmm, doesn't sound like much of a choice to me. What are my other options?'

'You can have an operation to remove it. Unfortunately there are a number of risks associated with the procedure too.'

'Such as?' Rose gripped her hands together to stop them shaking. Her mind flicked to her parents. They'd be devastated. She was their only child and knowing her father he would blame himself for passing on the genetic condition to his much-loved daughter. The same thing that had caused his stroke. How long had he been living with the time bomb inside his head? How long had she? She pushed the thoughts of her parents away. There would be time enough later to think about them. Once she had all the facts. Once she knew what she was going to do.

'Death, stroke. The complications of surgery aren't too different from the results should your aneurysm burst, I'm afraid. The problem is where your aneurysm is. The location makes the surgery riskier than usual.'

'Not a great choice, then.' Rose smiled wryly at the consultant. She *had* asked for her to be straight with her.

'On the other hand, if we manage to remove it through surgery, there is a good chance you could live to a ripe old age, have children, do everything you hoped for before this.'

'And if I don't? What then?' Rose knew the answer, but she wanted to hear it from Miss Fairweather. Maybe she had misunderstood what she had read about the condition on the internet.

'I'm sorry. You wouldn't be able to risk having children. It would put too great a strain on the blood vessels inside your brain. Otherwise, the risks are as I outlined earlier. But you don't have to decide straight away. You should go away and discuss it with your parents and boyfriend. Have a think. Make sure you understand the risks of both options. However, I wouldn't leave it too long. If you do decide to have the operation, the sooner you have it the better.'

Ten minutes later, Rose was outside the hospital. Although summer was supposed to be on its way, the wind still had a wintry feel to it. Wrapping her coat tightly around her, Rose stumbled to a bench and finally let the tears that had been clogging her throat for the last half an hour fall. She could die. Maybe tomorrow, maybe in ten years, maybe twenty. Miss Fairweather admitted that there was no way of telling. How could she live the rest of her life not knowing if every minute was going to be her last? On the other hand, if she had the operation Miss Fairweather had suggested, she could still die. Or be left paralysed, in a wheelchair—or worse. That prospect didn't have much going for it either. In fact, the thought was even worse than death. At least that would come quickly. The thought of a slow death, having to be looked after by her elderly parents, was infinitely worse. Being dependent on anyone didn't bear thinking about.

She blew her nose loudly. Behind her she could hear the sound of a baby crying. She had never imagined that she might not be able to have children one day. Never hold a child in her arms. Maybe never again go for a walk in the rain, watch an evening sky change colour as night approached. Never learn how to ski, or speak Spanish. All the things she had told herself she had plenty of time for. Perhaps it was just as well that she had never met anyone she cared enough about to marry. What should she tell her parents? Nothing. Not yet. They had enough on their plates right now with Dad's stroke without having to worry about her.

So there would be no more tears. No self-pity. She would do as Miss Fairweather had suggested. She would think long and hard about what to do. In the meantime she'd treat every minute of her life as if it were her last. No more hiding away. No more not doing something because it was too expensive, or scary, or any of the hundred reasons she had given herself in the past. From now on, she would say yes to every experience life had to offer. From now on, she would make the most of every second she had left.

During the long nights that followed her appointment with Miss Fairweather, Rose tossed and turned, trying to decide what to do. In the end, she decided she couldn't have the operation. What if it went wrong? And she ended up like her father, or worse? How would her mother cope with two invalids? Besides, if her father hadn't had a stroke, she would never have known about the ticking time bomb inside her head. She would have carried on living her life the way she was doing now.

In the small dark lonely hours of the night, she had tried to draw up a list of things she wanted to do before…well, before it was too late, but had given up on the list when she'd come to number fifty and scored it through. Instead, she promised herself she would try and live each day as best she could, taking any opportunities that came her way. She still couldn't get her head around the fact she could die any time. She felt so healthy and life had never seemed so painfully precious and filled with promise.

CHAPTER FOUR

JONATHAN habitually asked her if she wanted to go to lunch with him, but she always refused. The first sunny lunchtime, she asked him if it would be okay if she took a little longer than her usual half-hour.

'I'd like to take my lunch to the park,' she said. 'It's such a beautiful day and I could really do with some exercise. Jenny will be fine on her own for an hour.'

'Good idea,' he said. 'I'll come with you. There's a deli on the way, I could pick up something to eat from there. It will make a change from the stodge they serve up in my club. God, it reminds me of school dinners.'

Rose was taken aback, but she could hardly refuse. 'You can share mine, if you like. My mother always insists on making my lunch and she puts enough in to feed an army. I think she worries I don't eat enough.' Rose laughed. 'I eat like a horse, I just don't seem to put on any weight.'

Jonathan's eyes slid over her and she felt her cheeks flush under his gaze. She pulled her cardigan around her. What on earth had possessed her to say that? And as far as offering to share her lunch, she had the distinct impression Jonathan wasn't used to having egg and cress sandwiches or whatever her mother had packed for her. Didn't people like him have caviar or some other such stuff for snacks?

'Come on, then, if you're sure you've enough. We'll pick up a couple of coffees on the way.'

As they walked Rose felt inexplicably tongue-tied. It was different when they were working. Somehow, without patients to discuss, it was different.

After picking up their coffees they found a bench looking over a small lake. The good weather had brought out mothers and children, or was it their nannies? There were also a number of people strolling or jogging. Rose handed Jonathan a sandwich and lifted her face to the sun.

'Have you lived in London long?' he asked between mouthfuls.

'I was brought up here. My parents have lived in the same house all my life. I went away to university. Edinburgh, actually. I have an aunt who lives there so I was able to stay with her. It helped keep the cost down. What about you?'

'I boarded at Gordonstoun. I was almost six when my father sent me there. I studied medicine at Cambridge.'

Rose had heard of Gordonstoun. She knew it was a famous and very expensive school in the north of Scotland where many of the rich sent their children. She had also heard that the regime was very tough.

'Isn't that where Prince Charles went?'

'Yes. But long before my time.'

'How awful to be sent away to school when you were so young. Weren't you terribly homesick?'

Jonathan turned to her, looking surprised. He really did have the most amazing eyes, Rose thought. Dark green, and ringed with an even darker shade. He had the kind of eyes that made her feel he could see right into her soul.

'You know, I never really thought about it. It was just something that happened. I suppose the first few years were hard. I missed my home. But all the other boys were in the same situation. And there were the holidays—at least, some of the holidays. My father was away a lot, so I stayed with schoolfriends most of the time.' His eyes darkened and he looked away into the distance as if he found the memory unpleasant.

'I don't think I could ever send my child away. Especially at that age,' Rose said thoughtfully. 'But I guess your parents must have had their reasons. Would you send your child?'

Jonathan's eyes narrowed. If it were possible, he looked even bleaker. Rose could have kicked herself. She had no right to question the way he had been brought up.

'My child? You know, I can't say I've ever thought about it. Children have never really figured in my plans for the future. Somehow I don't ever see myself having them. They require commitment. And I'm not that kind of guy.' He grinned. 'Life is too full of possibilities to settle on one.'

Rose eyed him speculatively. Maybe when he met the right woman he would feel differently. Then again, maybe not. Somehow she couldn't see Jonathan giving up the lifestyle he enjoyed for the restrictions a domestic life would inevitably bring.

'I don't think my mother would have sent me if it had been up to her. She died when I was five, and my father sent me away soon after the funeral,' he continued after a moment.

Rose was shocked. How could a father send away a child who had just lost his mother? And not just down the road, but several hundred miles. An image of Jonathan as a little boy wearing long shorts and a peaked cap, standing alone outside the school while his father drove away, flashed through her mind and her heart twisted with sympathy for the little boy he'd been. What kind of man was his father if he could do that to his son? Rose thought if she ever met him, she would dislike him intensely. No wonder Jonathan seemed to have little faith in the joy children could bring. It was ironic: Jonathan didn't want children, although he almost certainly could have them; and she wanted them, desperately, yet couldn't have them. If she had been able to have children, she would never send them away. She would have kept them close to her, making the most of every precious moment with them. A wave of sadness washed over her. She forced her thoughts away. Thinking like that was pointless.

'I'm so sorry, Jonathan. I can't imagine what it was like for you. To lose your mother when you were so young and then be sent to boarding school.'

'Don't we all do things because we have to? I know duty is considered an old-fashioned concept, but you must believe in it too. You came back here to look after your father. You must have had a life in Edinburgh.'

Rose forced a smile. 'Of course. But as you say, sometimes we have to do what is right rather than what we want. My parents needed me.' She shrugged. 'So I came. My life in Edinburgh can wait.' *If* she had a life to live.

'No boyfriend?'

'No one serious.' She wanted to change the subject. It was far better for her to keep her mind off her future—and the possibility she might not have one.

'Why did you decide on medicine?' she asked him, genuinely interested. From what she had gathered, Jonathan's family was rich enough for there to be no need for him to work at all.

Jonathan smiled ruefully. 'As I told you, my uncle was

a doctor. He was apothecary to the Queen. He used to talk to me all the time about cases he had came across when he was still working in a hospital. I loved listening to him and I can hardly remember a time when I didn't want to be a doctor. I needed to do *something* with my life. My father hoped I'd take over the family business, but it wasn't for me.'

'But Harley Street.' Try as she would, Rose couldn't quite keep the disapproval from her voice.

'My uncle built up the practice. People liked coming to see the man who looks after the Queen's health. You can't get a better recommendation than that. I was going to set up a practice somewhere else, but then he became ill and wasn't able to carry on. Back to duty, I guess.' He took a gulp of his coffee. 'I couldn't let him down.'

'You don't miss real medicine, then?'

He looked at her, amusement making his eyes glint.

'You know, even the rich and famous get ill. In the end, birth and wealth don't prevent you from experiencing health problems. Like Mark, for example.'

Yes, she should know how arbitrary illness could be. Despite the warmth of the sun, she shivered.

He looked at his watch. 'Speaking of which, I have to visit Lord Hilton this afternoon. You remember his wife coming in to see me on your first day? She has arthritis and he has terminal cancer. He really should be in hospital, but he refuses point blank. Says he has no intention of dying anywhere except the home he's lived in all his life.' Jonathan studied Rose thoughtfully. 'How would you feel about coming too? If I remember correctly, she took a shine to you.'

'Poor Lady Hilton. I had no idea. Yes, of course I'll come. If you need me.'

What Rose didn't know and what Jonathan neglected to

tell her was that Lord and Lady Hilton lived a hundred
miles from London and that they were sending their private
helicopter to bring Jonathan to their country home. The
helipad was a ten-minute drive from the surgery.

Rose had never been in a helicopter before, let alone one
that had leather seats as wide as armchairs in the back.

'You didn't tell me we were flying to our visit,' she accused
Jonathan when he pulled up at the helipad on the Thames.

His eyebrows quirked in the way she was beginning to
know well. 'You didn't ask. About fifty per cent of my patients
live outside London. In fact, they sometimes fly me out to see
them when they're on holiday. Wherever that might be.'

'They don't see someone locally? Surely that would
be better?'

Jonathan gave her a half-smile. 'I see you have a lot to
learn, Rose Taylor. Most of my patients are so rich that is
doesn't occur to them not to fly their doctor out. In the same
way that they'd fly out their hairdresser or stylist. They like
to see the same physician.' He shrugged. 'And I don't mind
going. I've known some of my patients most of my life.'

It was a different world. One where Rose didn't know
the rules. But it was a job. As long as she got paid and as
long as Jonathan's patients didn't suffer, who was she to
judge? And, she had to admit, it was exciting to be part of
it, even for a short time. She sucked in a breath as she remembered the promise she had made to herself. *Live every
day to the full*. At least working with Jonathan was bringing
new experiences and every minute was exciting. How
much of the excitement was down to new experiences and
how much was due to being in the company of the man
sitting next to her, she didn't want to think about.

Jonathan gave her a radio set to wear, partly to drown
out the noise of the engine and partly so they could hear

each other speak. Below her the river Thames cut its way through London. She could see Buckingham Palace and the Tower of London as well as the pods of the London Eye revolving slowly.

'Have you been in it yet?' Jonathan asked, pointing to London's newest tourist attraction. 'Sorry, silly question. Of course you have.'

'As a matter of fact, no. I haven't had the time. I'd love to some time.' One more thing to add to her steadily growing list. 'Have you?'

'Once or twice.' He grinned. 'One of my friends is having a party there in a few weeks' time. You should come.' It was another invitation, but Rose knew that Jonathan was just issuing them out of politeness. If she accepted, he'd probably be dismayed.

Soon they were leaving London behind and passing over the countryside. A short time later they flew over a house bigger than most hotels Rose had stayed in and were touching down in what was the back garden, but which anywhere else would have been a park.

'Oh, my word,' Rose said as she stepped out of the helicopter. 'The last time I saw a house like this it was in a film. How many people live here?'

'Just Lord and Lady Hilton. His sons live in London. They come up when they can.'

A man dressed in the traditional garb of a butler walked towards them. Rose smiled. It was just like being on a movie set.

'Good afternoon, sir, miss,' the butler said. 'Lord and Lady Hilton are expecting you.' He turned to Rose. 'What name should I say?'

'This is Miss Taylor, Goodall. She's a nurse at the practice. Lady Hilton and Miss Taylor have already met.'

'Lord Hilton is in his bedroom. Lady Hilton said she'd like a word before you go in to see him, if that's all right?' Goodall said.

Jonathan chatted to the butler as they walked the few hundred yards to the front door. From the snippets of conversation Rose caught, it seemed they knew each other well. Following behind, Rose took in the formal garden with its neatly trimmed hedges and flower beds. Dotted throughout were nude sculptures, some modern, some more classic. It must have taken an army of gardeners, Rose reckoned, to keep it looking so perfect.

Inside, the hall was twice as large as the one in the town house belonging to Jessamine. There was a grand central staircase in the middle of a polished marble floor. Someone had lit a fire in the huge fireplace that dominated one side of the hall and with the large bowls of brightly coloured flowers it had a cheerful air. Despite the grandeur, Rose knew immediately she was in someone's much-loved home.

Goodall showed them into a room which, while as grand as the hall, had been decorated in thoughtful, homely fashion. Large squashy couches with brightly coloured cushions and a rug that had seen better days added a splash of colour to the otherwise muted room. Light was flooding in from the floor-to-ceiling windows overlooking the front garden, but a fire burned brightly in this room too. After the coolness outside, it was almost suffocating.

Mr Chips jumped down from an armchair and pattered across to them, his tail wagging. Rose bent to pat him, and in return received ecstatic doggy kisses on her hand. In an armchair next to the window was Sophia Hilton. Her silver hair was perfectly coiffed but despite the heat in the room her face was pale. Rose was sure there were more lines around her eyes and mouth than there had been when they'd first met. She was dressed in thick stockings and a tweed skirt and the hand she held out to Jonathan had the slightest tremble. Rose knew immediately that this was a woman who was under enormous strain, but desperately trying not to show it.

Jonathan bent down and kissed the older woman on each cheek.

'Sophia, how are you? And Lord Hilton?'

'Jonathan, dear boy. How good of you to come and see us. And Miss Taylor, an unexpected pleasure to see you again too. Jonathan told me you're filling in for Vicki until she's well enough to return.' Her mouth trembled slightly. 'Giles isn't good, I'm afraid.'

Jonathan pulled up a chair next to Lady Hilton and Rose sat on the sofa opposite. 'Tell me what's been happening,' he said gently.

'He's fading. He hardly eats at all now. He says he has no appetite. He gets up for an hour or two but that's all he can manage.' She dropped her voice to a whisper. 'We're losing him, I'm afraid.'

'You're both still sure you don't want to try another bout of chemotherapy? I could have him in hospital by this afternoon.'

Lady Hilton shook her head regretfully. 'He won't hear of it, I'm afraid, and I have told him I'll respect his wishes. That's why I don't want you to try and persuade him. He's too weak to put up a fight, so he made me promise to speak to you before you saw him.'

'The chemotherapy might help.'

'Will it prolong his life?'

Jonathan looked her directly in the eye. 'I'm not going to lie to you. It might give him a little more time, ease his symptoms, but, no, the outcome will be the same.'

'And the chemotherapy will make him feel even worse in the short term, won't it?'

'He didn't react to it very well before. So, yes, I'm guessing he'll feel even more rotten than he does right now.'

'Then nothing's changed since we last had this conversation. Except it's getting closer.'

'Have you thought any more about bringing in nurses to help? I thought Rose here might be able to convince you. She worked in general practice before she joined us in London.'

Rose leaned forward. 'If it's okay with you, I'd like to see your husband and have a chat with him before I advise you. But Dr Cavendish is right, there are lots of options that would allow you to keep him at home but help you keep him comfortable at the same time.'

'Of course.' Lady Hilton stood. 'I'll take you both upstairs.'

Rose and Jonathan found their patient sitting in a chair by the window with a rug over his knee. A book lay by his side, and a still full cup of tea sat ignored on the table next to him. His eyes were closed and his face had the grey gauntness that Rose had seen too often before. She knew immediately that Lord Hilton didn't have much longer.

His wife touched him gently on the shoulder.

'Darling, it's Jonathan and his nurse come to see how you are.'

Eyes flickered open and as they focused on his wife, a look of such love that Rose had rarely seen filled the pale blue eyes. Her heart contracted.

'Jonathan, my dear boy. How are you? And your family?' The voice was weak but clear.

'Father is always asking after you.' As he spoke, Jonathan placed his fingers on the old man's wrist.

'Any word of getting married yet? Isn't it time?'

Jonathan laughed. 'No. Can't find a woman who is crazy enough to have me.'

'What about this girl here?' For a moment Rose squirmed. He couldn't be alluding to her as a possible wife? The poor man must be confused.

'This girl, as you put it, is my nurse. Victoria's pregnant. Unfortunately she's being very sick again so has to take time off. Rose is filling in for the time being.'

Rose stepped closer so that she could be seen. 'Dr Cavendish thought I might be able to help make you more comfortable—or at least suggest some things that could help.'

Rose watched carefully as Jonathan finished his examination. While he was doing that she was assessing how Lord Hilton moved and how much pain he seemed to be in.

'Why don't we have a little chat while Jonathan talks to your husband?' Rose said to Lady Hilton. 'You can tell me what help you have at the moment.'

Once they were back in the sitting room, Rose broached the subject of nursing care.

'I don't want strangers looking after him,' Lady Hilton protested.

'What about a night nurse at least?' Rose suggested gently. 'Someone to sit with him through the night so you can get a good sleep?'

'There's Goodall,' Lady Hilton said firmly. 'He'll attend to Giles if he needs anything at night. He also helps him shave and wash. He's been with him for thirty years and knows his ways.'

Rose had to admit that having someone to help who Lord Hilton knew well would be far less stressful than bringing in new faces at this stage.

'I know Dr Cavendish—Jonathan—is likely to suggest a morphine pump. That way the pain can be controlled.

Will you consider it? You'll need to have a nurse call at least every second day to check on it, but that shouldn't be too intrusive.'

Lady Hilton blinked furiously. 'Why did Victoria have to be unwell now of all times? Oh, don't mind me, I'm just being selfish. Of course, it's important that she looks after herself now that she's pregnant. But Giles knows her. He would have been happy to have Goodall fetch her from town every day.'

'I'm sure there will be equally good nurses locally that would be happy to come to the house.'

'That would mean interviewing people. It would be terribly time-consuming. I don't want anything to interfere with the time we have left. I know there's not much time.' Her eyes locked onto Rose's and she could see the spark of hope there. But just as quickly it was replaced with resignation. 'You don't have to pretend otherwise, my dear. I know it and Giles knows it.' She paused for a moment. 'Couldn't you come? He's met you and he seems to have taken to you. And Jonathan wouldn't have brought you here if he didn't think highly of you. We could arrange for you to be collected and brought back every day. Please say you'll agree.'

Although Rose felt for the older woman's distress, she knew what she was suggesting would be impossible. Just as she was trying to find the words to let her down, Jonathan walked back into the room.

'He's sleeping now. Goodall and I helped him back into bed. I think he should have something more regular for the pain, however. I can come and see him whenever you want, but analgesia as and when he wants it would be better.'

'Miss Taylor was just suggesting the very same thing. But she tells me a nurse will have to come in regularly to check the pump. I asked her whether she could come. What do you think, Johnny? Could she?'

Jonathan looked at Rose. 'I'm afraid I need her in London,' he said.

The old lady looked so woebegone that Rose couldn't help herself. With Jenny manning the desk, she could come and help the Hiltons. It would keep her busy. She had too much time to brood as it was.

'What about if I came after my shift? Would that work?'

Jonathan frowned. 'Would you excuse us for just a moment?' he said, and taking Rose by the elbow steered her out of earshot.

'I know you want to help, but don't you have your own situation to think about? It'll be too much.' For a second Rose thought that somehow he had found out about her condition, even though she knew it was impossible. 'Coming here and putting in a full day's work before going home to help out with your father. I've your health to think about too. The last thing I need or want, is to have to find another nurse.'

'It's not as if I'm run off my feet at the surgery.' Rose glanced across at Lady Hilton who was studiously looking out the window. 'I just wanted to help. Anyway, there's at least three free afternoons a week where you don't have any patients. I know you keep them free for emergencies or un-scheduled home visits, but so far they've been quiet and I've just been twiddling my thumbs. I could come here then.'

Jonathan's eyes followed hers. Despite the determined look and the upright posture, Lady Hilton needed help and they both knew it.

'I'll agree to it on one condition,' Jonathan said. 'You come here only on those free afternoons and on the other two we shuffle my schedule around so that there aren't patients booked in for when you're here. Jenny and I can cover the odd drop in or emergency between us. If that suits you, we have a deal.' He didn't need to say what they were both thinking. It was unlikely that the arrangement would be required beyond a few weeks at the most.

He smiled sadly at Rose and her heart skipped a beat. 'Thank you for offering. I've known Lord and Lady Hilton all my life. Anything that will make these last few weeks and days easier for them would mean a great deal to them...and to me.'

Jonathan told Lady Hilton what they had agreed, emphasising that they still needed to get Jonathan's schedule sorted out but that he didn't think it would be a problem. The relief in her eyes brought a lump to Rose's throat.

Jonathan turned down Lady Hilton's invitation to dinner. 'Next time, I promise. But it's getting late, and I really have to get Rose home. I'll phone you tomorrow morning and let you know what we've managed to sort out between us.'

The journey back in the helicopter was a more subdued affair. Rose found herself wondering about Jonathan. On the one hand, he seemed to like nothing better than to be partying along with his social set; on the other, as a doctor, he seemed to genuinely care about his patients. She had been guilty of making assumptions about him that appeared to be no more than figments of her imagination. In that regard she was no better than the press. She slid a glance in his direction. Why couldn't she have met someone like him before? Before her world had been turned upside down? And why did she have the sinking sensation that what she was feeling was a good deal more than she should for her boss?

CHAPTER FIVE

ON SATURDAY morning, she was sitting reading to her father when there was a knock at the door. Rose glanced out of the window, surprised to see a large four-by-four parked outside. Baffled, she answered the door to find Jonathan standing there with a broad smile on his face. He was dressed in faded jeans and a short-sleeved shirt. It was the first time she had seen him in anything apart from his suit and if anything he looked even more handsome. Certainly more approachable.

For once the sun was shining and although it was cool, there was a hint of summer in the air.

Open-mouthed, Rose stood back and let Jonathan in.

'Who is it, love?' Her mother came to stand behind her.

'It's Dr Cavendish, Mum.'

'Please call me Jonathan,' he said, holding out his hand and smiling charmingly at her mother.

'Why are you here?' Rose asked, suddenly conscious of the small house with its comfortable but worn furnishings. Then, aware of how rude she sounded, she apologised. 'I'm sorry, I'm just a little surprised to see you. I didn't think you even knew where I lived.'

Jonathan's smile grew wider. 'Your address was on your

file.' Then he frowned. 'I should have phoned, but I thought we had an arrangement?' In the cramped dimensions of the hall she could smell his aftershave.

'Arrangement?' Rose echoed.

'The tickets to the match. Remember? I promised I'd find a way to get your father there. If he'd still like to go, that is.'

Rose was bewildered. 'You've come to take my father? Don't you have a cricket match to go to?'

'There will be other matches,' he said dismissively, but Rose knew enough about cricket to know that despite his words he was giving up one of the most looked-forward-to events of the year. 'I'm planning to go to a party afterwards. Perhaps you'll come too?'

Rose shook her head, still confused. He had given up his day to do something for her father, a man he'd never met, and he wanted her to go to a party. Her heart skipped a beat. 'I couldn't. I've nothing remotely suitable to wear. Besides, I'm needed here.' It wasn't the whole truth. Her father was improving daily and required only minimal help now. But her at one of Jonathan's parties? Not on your life. What on earth would she have to say to his friends or them to her? The idea was ridiculous. Nevertheless, she had to admit to a small stab of regret. It had been ages since she'd been out. Besides, she had to admit that she was intensely curious about what sort of party it would be. Like everything else these days, it would be another new experience to add to her growing list.

Suddenly aware that they were still standing in the small hall, Rose remembered her manners.

'You'd better come in.'

She ushered him into the small sitting room. Her parents looked up, curious.

'Dad. This is Dr Cavendish. He's come to ask if you'd like to go to the football match this afternoon.'

Jonathan crossed the room and shook her father's hand warmly. 'I'm pleased to meet you, Mr Taylor. Your daughter tells me you're an Arsenal fan. Well, it so happens that I have tickets to the match today and I wondered if you'd like to come?'

'That's kind of you, son,' Rose's father said. His words were still slurred and Rose doubted that Jonathan would be able to understand what he was saying. 'But my leg's a problem. I don't think I could get up the stairs.' Although he was continuing to improve, pretty much managing to get himself washed and dressed, he had to lean heavily on a stick to walk. Rose doubted he'd be able to manage more than a few metres without a wheelchair.

'I have a plan for that,' Jonathan said. It seemed as if Rose had been wrong and that he could make out the words her father was trying to say. 'If I told you that I thought Rose and I can manage to get you there and to your seat without too much trouble, what would you say?'

Rose saw her father's eyes light up and her heart ached for him. She remembered how he had taken her to football matches when she'd been young, hoisting her onto his shoulders so that she could see better. They had never missed a home match until she'd left for university in Scotland.

'I don't know, lad. Maybe you should take my Rose and go on your own. You'd enjoy it better.'

'I'm not going to the match, Dad. Unless you go too. And I don't think Dr Cavendish plans on staying. He has something else on.'

'Did I say that?' Jonathan asked innocently. 'Can't imagine why. There's nothing I'd rather be doing, but I don't care to go on my own. So you and Rose would be doing me a favour by coming with me.'

'Go on, love,' Rose's mother prompted. 'You haven't

been out of the house since…' She paused and Rose guessed she still found it difficult to admit even to herself. 'The stroke. A bit of fresh air will do you the world of good. And I could be doing with getting your father from under my feet for a few hours.'

Rose knew her mother didn't mean a word of it. Her parents still loved each other deeply. Her mother wanted to bring some joy back to her husband's life. Rose also knew her father wouldn't go without her.

'In that case, I say yes, I'd love to go.'

With Jonathan helping, it was difficult but manageable to get her father along with his wheelchair into the roomy back seat of the car Jonathan had brought instead of his sports car. When they arrived at the football stadium, Jonathan flashed something at the security guard and drove up to the front gate. With him on one side of her father and her on the other, they used the lift to reach the box where they were to be seated.

'Always wanted to see the footie from one of these fancy boxes,' Tommy said when they had seated him with a rug over his lap. 'Never could afford it.'

'We can go inside the lounge and have lunch first, if you like?' Jonathan suggested.

Tommy shook his head. 'You two go. I'm just as happy to stay here now I'm settled.'

'And I'd rather stay with you, Dad.' Rose turned to Jonathan. 'But please don't let us keep you from your lunch. We'll be fine here until the match starts.'

'Then I'll go and fetch us something to have here. I don't want to eat on my own. Any preferences?'

Several minutes later, Jonathan returned with a tray full of various goodies to eat. Rose noticed that he'd included several items that would be easy for her father to eat with his one good hand. Once more she was surprised and touched by his thoughtfulness. Her father was a proud man and wouldn't have touched anything that meant Rose had to help him in public.

As they waited for the match to begin, Jonathan and her father chatted about previous matches. It was the first time she had seen her father looked so animated since his stroke and she sent silent thanks to Jonathan. Doing this had surely been outside expected behaviour for an employer. She guessed it was to repay her for seeing to Lord Hilton. Whatever the reason, Rose knew she was in danger of falling for her boss. Her heart gave a sickening thud. Two more things she'd have to add to her list. Watching a football match from a box and falling in love for the first time.

Despite her father's team losing in the final seconds of the match, it was a good day and Rose was disappointed when it came to an end.

Jonathan drove them home, dissecting the game in excruciating detail with her father while Rose sat back in her seat, allowing their chat to wash over her. She was falling for a man with whom she had nothing in common. Why now? When, even if he could ever feel the same about her, she had no future to offer him? Perhaps it was because she didn't know what the future held that she believed herself in love? If what she was feeling *was* love. It was certainly lust. Infatuation. Every time he smiled her stomach somersaulted. Whenever he was in the room her heart would start pounding and she would feel short of breath. If he touched her, even the slightest pressure of his hands as he passed her a mug of coffee or a set of notes, her knees would go all rubbery. But it was more than that, she knew, and her heart dropped to her boots. Regardless of his reputation as a womaniser, he was kind and gentle. Would anyone else have given up what he had just to take the ailing father of an employee to a football match? Rose doubted it.

Her mother was waiting for them when they arrived home. She too seemed better for having an afternoon off, although Rose knew that the sight of her father looking as he once had was worth more to her mother than any number of afternoons with her feet up.

Jonathan helped her father settle back into his chair. Rose could hardly look him in the eye in case he read her mind. It would be too mortifying for words if he guessed how she felt.

'I've asked Rose if she'd like to come to a party with me tonight,' Jonathan said suddenly. 'But she's turned me down.' He turned the full voltage of his charm on her mother, who was already putty in his hands.

'Rose?' Her mother turned to her. 'You didn't say no, did you?'

'I can't go, Mum. I'm needed here,' Rose said.

'Don't be silly. We can manage. Besides, you could do with some fun. You've been looking awfully peaky lately.' Rose could see the worry in her mother's searching look.

'And I don't like my staff to look peaky,' Jonathan added. 'I promise you, if you get there and you aren't enjoying yourself, I'll bring you straight home. Or we can miss the party. Do something else.'

Rose capitulated. The truth was, right now she could think of nothing she wanted more than to have more time with Jonathan. Who knew how many opportunities she had left? If she only had a short time left, this was how she wanted to spend it.

'Okay, you're on,' she said. 'On one condition. Tonight

you come with me and meet some of my friends.' She held her breath as she waited for his reply. Whatever he wanted from her, she had to know if it included wanting to spend time with her on her own territory. If he wasn't simply using her as an excuse to avoid whatever demons he had in his life, she needed to know that too.

'You're on.' Jonathan grinned. 'Lead me to it.'

Jonathan sat in the pub feeling, he had to admit, slightly awkward. Rose had been engulfed by a load of her friends and he hadn't seen her for at least ten minutes. Someone, he couldn't remember who, had stuck a pint of beer in his hand and instructed him to drink up. Why was he here? And more importantly, why was he so driven to find out more about Rose Taylor? There were any amount of women he could be dating, ninety nine per cent of them less prickly than her and none of whom would be insisting that he get up and sing. He groaned internally. Apparently getting up on stage was part of the evening entertainment. And Rose had made no attempt to hide her glee when she had told him that he'd be expected to stand up and do his bit. Still, he was damned if he was going to admit defeat. He just prayed that none of the paparazzi had followed him here. Thankfully, it was extremely unlikely. It would never cross their minds that he'd be found in a pub on the outskirts of London.

The pub was packed for a special Scottish themed night, with people coming from all over London for it. The place was filled with laughter and the chinking of glasses.

Rose squeezed her way into the seat behind him. Instead of the usual tied-back hair she had loosened it until it fell about her shoulders in a sleek glossy wave. Her eyes sparkled and a small smile played on her lips. He had never seen her so animated.

Suddenly there was a call for silence and after a few minutes everyone quietened down. A man Rose had introduced earlier as Jack, an old friend, had climbed onto the make-shift stage and was speaking into a microphone.

"Most of you know Rose,' he said.

There was loud applause as everyone cheered and stamped their feet. Rose blanched slightly and muttered something under her breath. 'What some of you don't know is that Rose composes her own songs and plays the guitar as if she's making love to it.'

There were more wild cheers. Jonathan slid a glance at Rose. She played the guitar. This was the first he had heard of it. And wrote her own songs.

'I know she'll be happy to play us a tune—if we give her a loud cheer.'

There was more applause and stamping of feet. If anything, the uproar was even louder than before. Rose was shaking her head, her hair falling across her crimson-stained face. Then she got to her feet and amid more cheering made her way to the stage.

She took the microphone from Jack's hand. 'Sorry, everyone,' she said into the mike. 'I didn't bring my guitar with me tonight. So I'm afraid I can't play for you.' There was a sigh of disappointment then Jack turned round, holding a guitar which someone had passed to him.

'Sorry, darling,' he said. 'But we just so happen to have one here for you to play. Go on, you can't let everyone down.'

Reluctantly, Rose took the guitar from him. Someone pulled a chair across for her and she sat down, trying a few tentative chords. All the noise dropped away until there was complete silence.

'Okay, I'll play one song for you.' She held up a finger to emphasise her words. 'I'm going to play "*Fear A Bhata*".

It's a Gaelic song my mother used to sing to me when I was a little girl. She sang it to me whenever she was missing Scotland, which was often. I'm playing it tonight for everyone who is far from home.'

In the silence Rose strummed a few chords then her husky voice wrapped itself around the packed room. Jonathan didn't need to be able to understand the words to know it was full of longing and loss. The sound of her voice did something to his heartstrings that he'd never experienced before. He was transported to a world where people longed for something they couldn't have. The Rose up there on the stage was a revelation to him. In the place of the shy, mousy Rose he had come to admire and respect was a beautiful woman who sang as if she knew all about heartache and loss. A woman with depths to her he had never guessed existed. A woman he found exciting yet restful. In that moment he knew that he was falling for Rose and the thought scared him witless.

When the final notes of Rose's song had faded away, there was complete silence followed by a burst of applause. There were cries of 'More' but Rose just shook her head and passed the guitar back before stepping off the make-shift stage.

Jonathan was finding it difficult to concentrate. For once he didn't know what to do. She slid back into the seat next to him, her cheeks flushed and her eyes bright.

'You didn't tell me you could sing like that!' Jonathan said.

Rose smiled briefly. 'It's not as if it's ever come up. It's just something I do for fun. When I'm in on my own and it's raining outside. Sometimes, when something touches me, I make up my own songs. I guess it's my way of relaxing.' She glanced at him and he could see the teasing look in her eyes. 'I've never sung in public before. I didn't think I could.' If he had found her interesting before, now he knew he wanted to know everything about this woman who was so unlike anyone he had ever met.

Then there was a sudden movement as chairs and tables were lifted and piled up at the sides. A group of three had taken to the stage. One was carrying an accordion, the other two fiddles.

Rose flashed him a grin. 'Can you dance?' she asked. 'It looks like you're getting away with singing tonight.'

Jonathan breathed a sigh of relief. 'Depends what kind of dancing you're talking about. I do a fairly mean waltz and not a bad foxtrot, but I'm getting the distinct impression that it's not the kind of dancing you're talking about, is it?'

'Nope.' Rose's grin grew wider. 'They do two types of dancing here. One is Scottish country dancing, the other line dancing. You must have learned Scottish country dance at your school in Scotland, surely?' Jonathan felt a wave of relief. They had been taught the formal Scottish dances with their intricate steps. He could do that all right. But, still, there was that suspicious little smile hovering on Rose's lips. It unnerved him.

He stood up and as the band struck up a tune and invited everyone to take their places for an eight-some reel, he held out his hand to Rose. 'Shall we?' he asked.

But if he'd thought he was going to be dancing a dance that he had learned, he soon found out he was badly mistaken. Oh, the steps were the same, but the pace was quite different. It all happened at breakneck speed and in response to the fervour of the dancers, the band increased their tempo. Soon he was part of a dervish dance where everyone's feet were moving at the speed of light. As he whirled Rose around, her hair fanned out behind her. Then he was dancing with another partner who was forcing him to move ever faster. Not before time, the dance ended and Jonathan was able to get his breath back. But the respite was brief. Immediately the music struck up again. The Canadian barn dance was followed by the Boston two-step and the Highland Scottische. All carried out at break-neck speed. He just gave in to it and soon he found he was enjoying the exhilarating pace and being swept up by the rest of the dancers. For the last dance, the tempo slowed and the band asked everyone to take their partners for a St Bernard's waltz.

He pulled Rose into his arms, breathing in the scent of her as she placed her head on his shoulder. At first she was stiff in his arms, but as the music continued he felt her relax against him. It was strange how they seemed to fit together.

'So what do you think so far?' She raised her face and looked into his face with her amazing china-blue eyes. 'Not your cup of tea, I'm guessing?'

'Then it's clear you don't know me at all, Rose Taylor. How about we go to that party Jessamine mentioned for our next date?'

His words took even him by surprise. Just what was he getting into here? He felt her pull away, but he wrapped her back in his arms.

'Our next date?' she said, her face flushing. 'But this isn't a date, is it? Just two friends out together.'

'Is that what you really think?' he said. 'Come on, Rose, pretending doesn't suit you. You and I both know that there's more to it than that. I want to get to know the real Rose Taylor and I suspect you're not immune to me either.'

She raised her face to look him directly in the eye. 'We both know that we can't have a relationship,' she said flatly.

'Why not?' he asked.

She looked back at him. 'You know why not,' she said steadily.

'I'm not sure I do.'

'I don't think mixing work and personal life is a good idea.'

'Why? Aren't we doing that now? I'm having a good time. Aren't you?'

'Yes but...' She trailed off, seemingly at a loss for words.

She was thinking she wasn't from his world and he wasn't from hers, Jonathan mused. Admittedly, they had different upbringings, different friends, different lives, but what the hell did it matter? Not to him. It did to her, though. Her expressive face couldn't hide her obvious disapproval of him and the frivolous lifestyle she believed he led. She seemed so sure they had nothing in common. But he had never felt this at ease in a woman's company. And he knew he had never wanted a woman the way he wanted her right now.

'Can't we just go out and have fun? As friends?' he asked, knowing damn well that he had no intention of just staying friends with her. 'Let's just see where this takes us? No promises on either side. Just two people who enjoy each other's company getting to know each other better.'

'I'm not very good at casual relationships, Jonathan,' she said. 'I know it's not very modern, but there you go, that's the way I am. I can do nothing about my background, but I won't change who I am just to suit you.'

'I'm not asking you to. I won't push you to sleep with me if that's what's worrying you.' He was unable to stop himself smiling at the thought of Rose naked in his arms. 'I promise I'll be a perfect gentleman. I'm guessing you could use a friend right now.'

'I do have friends,' Rose protested, waving her hand in the general direction of the room.

'But we can never have too many, can we? Come on,

what do you say? Have a little fun. If you don't need friends, you do need something to take your mind off work.' He dropped his voice. 'And what's happening at home.'

If only he knew that what was happening at home wasn't the whole of it. And hadn't she told herself she would make the most of whatever time she had left? Take tonight, for example. Although Jack had tried to get her to sing in public before, she had always refused; the thought had scared her senseless. But then she had remembered her promise to herself and had forced herself to take the guitar. By closing her eyes she had been able to let herself pretend she was back in her room, alone, and once she had started singing she had lost herself in it. She had poured her heart-ache, the loss of her future into the music. And it had felt good. The applause had taken her by surprise; she had almost forgotten there were other people in the room.

When she'd opened her eyes, it had been to meet Jonathan's green eyes looking at her with what? Admiration? Surprise? Something was changing inside her, and she wasn't convinced it was just down to her illness. Somehow being with Jonathan made her feel as if she could do anything. The thought took her breath away. This wasn't supposed to happen. This wasn't part of her plan. But if she couldn't offer him a future, well, neither was he suggesting one. She held out her hand. He looked at her in surprise before enveloping it in his. His hand was cool in hers, his long fingers those of a surgeon. A thrill ran up her spine. More than anything else in the world, she wanted to know what it would feel like to be held in his arms. To have his mouth pressing down on hers. To lose herself in him—even if it was only for a short time.

'Okay.' She found herself smiling. 'I give in. I'll go with you to the party tomorrow.' She wagged a playful finger at him. 'But only because I've never been to a party on a yacht before.'

Jonathan grinned. 'If that's what it takes, I've plenty more types of parties to tempt you with.'

CHAPTER SIX

IT WAS bucketing down, Rose saw as she peered out from her bedroom window the next morning. So much for the start of summer. Her stomach was a mass of butterflies as she thought about the day to come. If she hadn't been so determined to follow through on the promise she had made to herself she would have been tempted to find an excuse not to go. Once again, she wondered if she was admitting the whole truth to herself. It wasn't just her vow to grab life with both hands while she could, it was that the life, just tantalisingly out of her reach, now held Jonathan. Who knew how long he'd be in her life? And she wanted to spend every minute she could with him. She was making memories that would have to last her a lifetime, however long that might be.

Pushing away the morbid thoughts, she considered her meagre wardrobe critically. The trouble was she didn't have the vaguest idea what one was supposed to wear to a party on a yacht. In the end she settled on her standby little black dress she always wore when she needed something more formal than her usual skirts and jeans. The best thing about it was that it was cut in a way that made her bony frame look sophisticatedly curvaceous instead of the sharp angles she was used to seeing.

By the time she had showered and dressed, the rain had stopped and the sun was shining. Maybe the day wouldn't be a complete washout after all.

Jonathan arrived to collect her, looking as sexy as hell in his faded jeans and short-sleeved shirt. He whistled in appreciation when he saw her and Rose was uncomfortably aware of the blush warming her cheeks. With a bit of luck he wouldn't notice.

The first surprise was that the yacht wasn't on the Thames. Jonathan had laughed when he'd noticed her bewilderment.

'I don't think many people keep their boats on the Thames. No, this one is moored off the coast of the Isle of Wight. They're sending the helicopter for us.'

Is that how everyone travelled in his circle? Rose thought a little grumpily. What was wrong with a car, although, come to think of it, getting to the Isle of Wight by road was, of course, impossible. Her head was beginning to ache. It had been a crazy idea to come. She was sure to be completely out of her depth.

Jonathan slid a glance in her direction. His face took on an uncharacteristically sombre expression.

'You're not having second thoughts, are you?' he asked.

It was on the tip of Rose's tongue to say, yes, she was and would he mind just dropping her off at the nearest station? But she bit the words back. She promised herself that she was going to try and be more adventurous and she was damned if she was going to bail out just because she was terrified she wouldn't fit in. After all, what was the worst that could happen? If everyone ignored her, she could…what? Swim back to London?

'I'll look after you, I promise,' Jonathan said. 'They're really a good bunch of people. Some a bit wilder than others, but nothing too outrageous.'

Giving in to the inevitable, Rose made herself relax. At least, with Jonathan promising to stay close by, she wouldn't be left on her own.

The yacht was unlike anything Rose had ever seen before. For a start it was enormous, almost the length of a football pitch, and all gleaming white lines and stainless steel.

There were a number of people already there. Half of the guests were in bikinis or swimming costumes, the other half were dressed informally in shorts or jeans. Rose felt overdressed and uncomfortable. But there was no way, no way at all, she'd wear a swimming costume to a party, especially this early in the year.

Someone handed them a drink as soon as they stepped on board. Taking a sip, Rose grimaced and, looking around in case anyone was watching her, tipped her drink over the side of the boat. It was far too early to be drinking champagne.

Seconds later, to her dismay, Jonathan was swept up in a crowd and carried away. So much for his promise to watch out for her. To be fair, he wasn't to know just how cripplingly shy and out of her depth she felt right now. Rose leaned against the side of the boat, wondering how long she would have to stay before making her excuses. She knew she should introduce herself to one of the chatting groups, but she just couldn't make her hands let go of the rail.

'Hello.' A soft deep voice broke into her reverie. 'And who are you?'

Rose whirled around to find a blond-haired man with slightly unfocused eyes looking at her. Clearly he had been at the champagne.

'I'm Rose Taylor. Jonathan's nurse,' she said politely, proffering a hand.

'Pleased to meet you, Rose Taylor, Jonathan's nurse. I'm Henry. It's my sister's party.'

Rose craned her neck wondering which one of the guests was Henry's sister. It could have been any of the elegant women clustered on the deck. She could just make out the top of Jonathan's head in the centre of a group of attentive females. As if sensing her eyes on him, he turned and caught her eye and raised a questioning eyebrow. She shook her head slightly. Now someone was talking to her, she was no longer sticking out like a sore thumb.

Henry reached over and lifted Rose's glasses from her face. Her unease mounted as everything around her blurred. She reached for her glasses but Henry grinned and hid them behind his back. 'Hey, you're not bad looking when a person can see your face.' He swayed towards her, breathing the smell of stale alcohol on her face. 'Trust Jonathan to keep you as his little secret.'

Embarrassed and repulsed, Rose stepped back. But Henry stepped closer until she was almost pinned against the side of the boat. Over Henry's shoulder, she looked for Jonathan but all she could see were blurry shapes.

'Please give me my glasses back,' she said as steadily as she could. The last thing she wanted was to cause a scene in front of all these strangers.

Henry waved them in front of her. 'A little kiss in exchange?' he slurred.

Rose snatched the glasses from his hand. At least now she could see properly. Over Henry's shoulder, she caught Jonathan staring at them, frowning. Something in her face must have told him that she was extremely uncomfortable. Within moments he was by her side.

'Hey, Henry. Can I have my guest back?' Jonathan said

smoothly. 'I think I should show her around.' He took Rose by the elbow and steered her away.

'Henry is best avoided, I'm afraid. He eats girls like you for breakfast.'

Suddenly furious Rose shook his arm off.

'And what makes you think I can't handle him? Just because I don't mix with the rich and famous every day of my life, it doesn't mean I don't know how to handle snakes like him. If he hadn't taken my glasses and I couldn't see, I wouldn't have needed you to…rescue me.' She almost spat the last words, her mortification at being the centre of attention causing her to direct her fury at Jonathan. She should never have come, no matter what promises she had made herself. Being mortified wasn't on her list of must dos!

Jonathan laughed. Immediately the anger drained from her.

'I should have known better. Of course you could handle Henry. One look from those diamond eyes is enough to cut anyone down to size.'

The world stood still. Jonathan reached over and gently lifted the glasses from her face. 'You do have amazing eyes, you know.'

Rose felt the strength go from her legs. He shouldn't be looking at her like that. It wasn't fair. He was making her feel as if she was just as beautiful as the rest of the women, and that was rubbish. Next to them, she was like a gawky schoolgirl. She snatched her glasses back from his hands. Thankfully everything swam back into focus. Why, oh, why did he have to smile like that?

Desperate for him not to see her blushing, she turned on her heel, almost falling over in the process. Once again, he reached out and grabbed her, steadying her against him. She could feel the heat of his body, smell his aftershave and it was doing all sorts of confusing things to her head. She looked up to find amused eyes looking into hers. Did he know the effect he was having on her? Of course he did. Someone like him would be used to it. She pushed against his chest and drew herself up to her full height. 'You were going to show me around?' she said stiffly, wishing desperately that she could think of something more amusing, more light-hearted to say.

The grin still very much in evidence, Jonathan indicated a flight of steps leading down into the boat with a nod of his head.

'Let's start inside.'

At the bottom of the steps was a sitting area filled with people, laughing and chatting. Jonathan steered her through the group, stopping only to say a brief hello and promising to come back later for a proper chat. But before they could get to the other side of the room, a girl with hair like a silver waterfall ran up to Jonathan and threw her arms around him.

'Darling, I've being looking for you everywhere.' Rose was conscious of curious eyes on her. But she was damned if she was going to let anyone else see how uncomfortable she was. She left Jonathan and wandered off by herself.

Off the main sitting area there were a number of bedrooms which, although small, were kitted out with the latest electronic equipment. Flat-screen TVs and state-of-the-art speakers. Each bedroom had a small but fully equipped bathroom.

She threaded her way back through the main sitting area. Jonathan had disappeared, so she went back up the stairs. The deck wrapped around the boat, and there was a jacuzzi at one end, what was it called? The prow? Several guests were in the jacuzzi, lapping up the sun. A couple of waiters and waitresses circled around, carrying trays of drinks and canapés. Rose helped herself to an orange juice and a tiny tart of something unrecognisable but delicious. Thankfully Henry was nowhere to be seen.

'Here you are,' Jonathan said, appearing at her elbow with the blonde. 'I've been looking all over for you. May I introduce Summer? Summer, this is Rose.'

Well, of course she'd be called Summer with hair like that. The blonde smiled at her, but there was a speculative look in her eyes that made Rose wonder.

'My goodness,' she said. 'Where did you buy your dress? Was it from some vintage market?'

Ouch. Was everyone at this damn party determined to make her feel small? In the past she might have mumbled something and walked away, but that had been before... Before she'd known there were more important things in life to worry about than rude, obnoxious people who had nothing better to do than make themselves feel superior at her expense.

'Yes, it was. How clever of you to know that,' Rose responded. 'I love wearing clothes that other people have loved wearing in the past. It makes me feel as if I know them a little.'

She took in Summer's outfit. The blonde was wearing tights that looked as if they'd been fashioned from the skin of a tiger and a gold lamé dress that just covered her bottom. Although she did look gorgeous, it wasn't the kind of outfit Rose could ever see herself wearing in a hundred years. It was far too trendy and far too short for a start. No, whatever they thought of her clothes, she preferred the simple black dress she was wearing. And if it was a few years out of date, she didn't give a hoot. In fact, she had just about as much as she could take of being given the once over and found wanting. She should have stuck with her original gut instinct and stayed well away. What would she and this crowd ever have in common?

But just as she was searching for the words to make her excuses, a dark-haired girl with an impish expression sidled up to Jonathan and tucked her arm in his.

'I've been admiring your dress ever since you arrived,' she said. 'I'm sure it's exactly like the one I saw last week on the catwalk in Milan. And I have to say, it looks better on you than it did on the model. Don't you think so, Summer?' The new arrival flashed Summer a look from green eyes.

'Rose, could I introduce Lady Ashley, my cousin? Ashley, this is Rose.'

Ashley held out a slim hand and grasped Rose's in a firm grip. 'I'm so very pleased to meet you. Johnny's being telling me all about you. Are you enjoying yourself?' She turned to Summer and said sweetly, 'Summer, I don't suppose you would mind very much grabbing one of the waiters? I'm famished.'

Summer glared at her before stalking off. Ashley winked at Rose. 'She's harmless really. She just has the hots for my dear cousin here. She can't resist having a go at the opposition.'

Opposition? Her? Was she out of her mind?

Out of the corner of her eye, Rose caught a glimpse of Jonathan elbowing his cousin in the ribs.

'And my dear cousin likes to exaggerate,' he drawled. 'I'm sure Summer has no interest in me whatsoever.'

Ashley raised one perfectly groomed eyebrow. 'Don't be naïve, sweetie. You know her type as well as I do. Just because her daddy earns millions, she thinks she should be marrying into aristocracy. And I'm afraid it's you she has her sights on.'

'I'm sure Rose isn't interested in whatever fantasies are filling your brain, Ash.' Although his voice was cool it was evident in the way he looked at his cousin that he held her in very real affection. 'Besides, I've made it perfectly clear that I'm not in the market for a wife. Not now. Maybe never.'

'Hey.' Ashley laid a hand on his arm. 'You mustn't talk like that. Just because Uncle Charles can't stay married for five minutes, it doesn't mean some people don't make a go of it.'

'I think that's enough on that subject for now.' Jonathan's tone was light, but there was a note of warning in his voice. 'So, Rose, have you seen enough? What do you say we get out of here?'

There was nothing that Rose wanted more. But she didn't want to drag Jonathan away from the party. Especially when they'd only been there for an hour.

Suddenly there was a cry of alarm from the other side of the boat. 'David! Help me, someone! Oh, God, I can't see him.'

Jonathan spun away, making for the other side of the boat where a crowd was forming. Rose followed close behind. Everyone was looking down at the water, muttering and pointing.

'David jumped in. I can't see him.' The girl's voice was frantic. 'I told him he'd had too much to drink to even think of going in the water, but he wouldn't listen. God, where is he?'

Jonathan was pulling off his shoes and top.

'Where did he go in?'

The distraught girl pointed. 'He dived in over the side. I think he hit his head. Please, Johnny, help him.'

Jonathan balanced himself on the side of the railings before diving into the water. Everyone waited in silence as he surfaced and looked around wildly. Then he dived again and again, each time coming up and shaking his head. Finally, just as some of the other men were preparing to join him in the water, he rose to the surface again. This time he was holding a body in his arms. Rose held her breath as willing hands hauled them back onto the deck. The man Jonathan had pulled from the sea didn't seem to be breathing. There were cries of distress and alarm. The girl who had called out dropped to her knees and cradled the head of the man in her lap.

'David,' she cried. 'Please wake up. You have to wake up.'

Rose pushed her gently aside. 'Let me have a look,' she said quietly. By this time a sopping-wet Jonathan had joined her on deck. She bent her head and breathed into the unconscious man's mouth. One twice, fifteen times. She watched to see if his chest would move, but it didn't. She looked up to find Jonathan's eyes on hers. She knew he was thinking the same thing she was. They would have to get the water out of his lungs before they could get him breathing again.

Together, they worked to pump the water from his lungs until, to their relief, David coughed, bringing up a large amount of water.

'Has someone called for an ambulance?' Jonathan asked.

'I have,' Ashley replied.

'Okay, I need a hand to get him into the little boat,' Jonathan said. 'Tell the ambulance to meet us at the jetty.'

David had regained consciousness, but looked confused and bewildered. His head was bleeding copiously. Jonathan examined the wound with gentle fingers. 'It's pretty superficial,' he said. 'Does anyone have anything we could use to stop the bleeding?'

Rose ripped a piece of fabric from her dress and used the material to staunch the wound. Oh, well, as Summer had pointed out, it *had* seen better days.

'What happened?' David moaned.

'You idiot,' his girlfriend cried out, before bending over and hugging him. 'You could have killed yourself. If it hadn't been for Jonathan and his friend, you'd be dead. Don't you ever do that to me again.'

Rose touched her on the shoulder. 'David's going to be fine, but we still need to get him to hospital. Inhaling sea water isn't the best thing for a person's lungs. Is there a medical kit on board? I'd like to put a proper bandage on his head.'

A medical kit appeared in Jonathan's hand. He quickly found a bandage and wrapped it around the piece of cloth from Rose's dress. It was crude, but it would do until the ambulance arrived.

Rose led David's distraught girlfriend to the side, while Jonathan and some of the other men lifted the small boat onto the deck and laid him inside. Then Jonathan looked at her, so she moved forward and stepped into the boat.

'As soon as we get this lowered, I'll join you,' Jonathan said.

Rose nodded and hiking her skirt up settled herself in the boat beside the injured man. In the distance she could hear the wailing of an ambulance.

As soon as the dingy was back in the water, Jonathan let himself down the ladder and joined her. He started the outboard motor and headed the boat back towards land. Rose kept a close eye on David's vital signs, but it seemed as if he was going to be okay. Jonathan was still drenched to the skin but showed no sign of discomfort.

When they reached the shore, the ambulance crew took over. They asked a couple of questions and Jonathan brought them up to date. Soon the ambulance was speeding away with David on board.

'Well, that's one way of ending a party,' Jonathan said

grimly, watching the ambulance disappear. 'I guess he's going to have a sore head in the morning. I don't suppose you want to go back?'

'Not on your life,' Rose said vehemently. Then she could have bitten her tongue. She softened her voice. 'Look, it was kind of you to ask me to the party, but all this…' she waved her hand in the general direction of the yacht '…is not really my cup of tea. I'm sure your friends are great but, well, to be honest with you, I think I'd rather be out for a walk and then curl up with a good book. I know it all sounds very boring, but it's what I like.' She smiled. 'An added bonus is that I don't spend too much of my time rescuing my friends after they've jumped into the water under the influence and bashed their heads.'

'Okay, then. Look, no one is expecting you back home for another few hours so why don't we spend the rest of the day together and you can give me another chance? We can do whatever you want to do.'

'Slum it, you mean?'

Jonathan looked offended. 'I wouldn't consider it slumming. For some crazy reason, Rose Taylor, every-thing you do interests me. I'd also like to show you my other side.' He grinned and Rose's heart flipped. She couldn't believe he was really interested in her. She so wasn't his type and that was okay, it wasn't as if there could ever be anything between them, even if she didn't have this awful thing in her head. And even if he was the most exciting, gorgeous man she had ever met. Anyway, when he realised she truly wasn't kidding about her life, she wouldn't see him for dust. The thought sent her heart crashing to her boots. However awful the day had been so far, she wasn't ready for it to come to an end.

'When do you have to be back?' he asked.

'I'm not expected back until later tonight. One of Mum's friends is coming around for a visit later, and she's offered to help Mum get Dad into bed.'

'I could do with a change of clothes. How would you like to see my country house?' Jonathan grinned at her.

Rose pulled a face. 'Of course you have two houses. Why didn't I think of that?'

'Er, two houses here, plus the family home. I'm afraid there are another couple abroad.' He held up his hands. 'Nothing to do with me. My father collects houses like other people collect hats.'

'What? And just passes them on to you?'

Jonathan looked offended again. 'He gave me the town house. I admit that. Simply to avoid inheritance tax. But the one I'm planning to take you to is all mine. I think you'll find it interesting. Come on, what do you say? In fact, I'd really like your opinion. Ashley tells me I should decorate, but that's not really my forte and I haven't a clue what to do.'

'Why don't you pay an interior designer to do it? Their taste is bound to be much more like yours.' But she couldn't help feeling curious. What kind of house did Jonathan like to call home?

'Okay, then,' she capitulated. 'Why not? But I'm warning you, I'll tell you truly what I think—no messing around. I have to be honest, your town house is not my cup of tea.' She had seen it once when she had brought over some urgent letters for Jonathan to sign. The opulent interior hadn't seemed to fit with the Jonathan she was getting to know.

Jonathan's grin grew wider. 'To tell you the truth, it's not mine either. That's what happened when I let an interior designer loose—that was my cousin's idea—not mine by the way. It's like living in a boutique. Or a hotel. I'm not going to risk that again.'

So a medical secretary, a nurse, now an interior designer. If she wasn't careful, she'd be taking on the role of house-keeper too.

Once they had flown back to London the drive took just under an hour. Jonathan drove fast, but he was a careful driver and Rose settled back and watched the countryside flash past. She still wasn't sure what she was doing or, more to the point, what Jonathan wanted from her.

Eventually he turned into a long sweeping driveway. Instead of following the driveway, Jonathan pulled up outside a small house close to the gates. It was a typical gatehouse of the type Rose had seen at the gates of every stately home she had ever visited—as a fee-paying visitor, that was.

'Here we are,' Jonathan said as he switched off the ignition. 'We can go up to the main house and say hello to Mary later. She's the cook.' His eyes softened. 'Actually, she's a damn sight more than a cook. She's lived in the house since before my mother died. She's been like a second mother to me.'

He opened the door to the gatehouse and stood aside for Rose to enter. There was a small hallway, not much bigger than the one in her parents' house. To the left was a sitting room. It was furnished simply with deep leather sofas and a couple of side tables. There was an open fireplace and in front of it a worn but beautiful rug. All along the side were bookshelves, and directly opposite where they were standing a window seat overlooked the garden. On the walls were more paintings like the ones in Jonathan's con-sulting rooms. The house was unexpected and a delight. Rose instantly fell in love with the room.

'There's another sitting room through here and a dining room and a kitchen. Upstairs there are three bedrooms.'

Whatever Rose had expected, it wasn't this. Somehow

she'd imagined something full of boys' toys, not this cosy little house. It seemed she was constantly getting Jonathan wrong.

'It's perfect,' she said. 'I can't see why you want to redecorate.'

Jonathan looked baffled. 'That's what I keep telling people. But Ashley seems to think it needs to be brought up to date.'

'I wouldn't change a thing,' Rose said adamantly. 'But, of course, it's not my house.'

Jonathan smiled at her and her heart did the strange little somersault it always did whenever he looked at her that way.

'In that case, I'm going to leave it the way it is. I like it. I can put my feet up on the table and I can turn around without worrying I'm going to knock over some ornament or another.' He paused for a moment. 'It feels more like home than any place I've ever lived.'

While Jonathan disappeared to get changed, Rose walked across to the bookshelf. There were the usual classics as well as a number of thrillers. There was also a pile of medical journals on the floor. On the side table was a photograph of a woman and a man. They had their arms wrapped around each other as they picnicked on the lawn. Rose recognised the gatehouse in the background. She picked up the photograph for a better look. The woman was rather plain looking, except for her eyes which were an arresting shade of green. The man could have been a younger Jonathan.

'Your parents?' she asked Jonathan when he returned.

He took the photograph from her and Rose caught her breath at the look of sadness that washed over his face.

'Yes,' he said heavily. 'It was taken on their seventh wedding anniversary. Mother died shortly after that.' He placed the frame back on the table. It was the only photograph in the room. 'It didn't take long for Dad to remarry. Six months, I think it was. He recently divorced his third wife. I guess he's a man who can't stand his own company.'

The bitterness in his voice shook Rose.

'Don't you get on with him?'

Jonathan laughed harshly and turned away from her to look out of the window.

'No. I guess you could say we don't get on. He didn't want me to go in for medicine. He thought as the only son I should take over the family business. I don't think he's ever forgiven me for not doing what he wanted. And I can't forgive him for forgetting about my mother so soon. He could at least have waited a decent period before marrying again.'

'Maybe he wanted to provide some stability for you? Perhaps he thought he was doing the right thing?' She walked across the room and touched him on the shoulder. 'Perhaps he's never been able to forget her and that's why he keeps marrying?'

Jonathan turned to face her. He ran a finger down her jaw. 'Ah, Rose. Trying to find the best in people all the time. When will you learn that there's not many people like you?'

'Hey, don't make me out to be some kind of saint. It makes me sound so boring.'

'One thing you're not is boring, Rose Taylor.' She held her breath as he tipped her face so he could see into her eyes. She was sure he was going to kiss her and her heart was pounding so hard she could almost hear the rush of blood in her ears. She closed her eyes, anticipating the feel of his lips on hers.

His mouth brushed hers in the lightest of kisses. She opened her eyes to find him looking down at her intently.

'Come on, let's take a walk up to the main house. We

can see if there's any dinner going. If not, we'll go back to the village to find a pub. How does that sound?'

What just happened there? Rose thought, bewildered. Had she misread all his signals? It was perfectly possible. Once again she was reminded that she didn't know how men like Jonathan operated. All she did know was that she felt a thudding disappointment.

Jonathan read the confusion in Rose's eyes. She wasn't to know it had taken all his willpower to pull back from her. For the first time ever with a woman he wanted to take it slowly. She was becoming too important for him to rush things. He wanted to woo her gently—take his time, make everything perfect. She was too important to him to treat her as if she were simply another woman he took to his bed. He was beginning to suspect that he had found the missing part to him and the thought filled him with dismay. In his soul, he knew Rose wasn't someone who would love lightly. He owed it to her, and to himself, to be sure he wouldn't hurt her before he let things go any further. He bit back a groan. He had never thought about a future with any woman before, but it seemed finally he might have met the woman who could change his life. He was in deep trouble.

It was a substantial walk up to the house. As they turned a bend in the driveway the house came into view and Rose gasped. It was a beautiful large Georgian house, the facade grand but graceful. There were too many windows to count but Rose guessed that there had to be at least ten, possibly more, bedrooms.

'It's beautiful,' she whispered. 'Quite stunning.'

'I suppose it is,' Jonathan said thoughtfully. 'But to me it's just the house I was brought up in.'

They walked up a number of steps towards an ornate front door and stepped into the hall.

'Anyone at home?' Jonathan called out. 'It's Jonathan.'

His call was greeted with silence. 'Mrs Hammond, the housekeeper, is probably in her office. Let's have a look in the kitchen. Mary, our cook, is always in there. She's probably grabbing a snooze. Dad wanted to retire her years ago, but she won't have it. Says she'll go mad without anything to do. You'll like her. She still bakes every afternoon.' He sniffed the air appreciatively. 'In fact, I'm sure I can smell scones.'

He led her across the hall and down some stairs and along another passage with several doors leading off. 'In my grandparents' day this was the servants' quarters. At that time there were at least twenty people working in the house. Now it's just Mrs Hammond and Mary who live in. A couple of women come from the village every day to help with the cleaning. Most of the rooms are shut up. Dad only keeps the rooms he's using open, unless he has visitors. Then we draft in some more help.'

They followed the smell of baking to the end of the passage and turned left into the largest kitchen Rose had ever seen. There was an enormous old-fashioned range to one side and a huge scrubbed pine table in the centre. On top of the table was a pile of recently baked scones as well as a carrot cake. On the other side was a bowl of chopped vegetables. In the corner of the room was an armchair with a figure that, as he'd anticipated, was sleeping, snoring gently.

Jonathan tiptoed towards the sleeping figure and gently touched her on the arm. The old woman mumbled in her sleep before coming to. Faded grey eyes looked up in confusion, before the woman's face broke into a wide smile.

'Master Jonathan! How many times have I told you not

to sneak up on me like that? You'll frighten me to death one of these days. I keep telling you, this old heart can't take surprises.'

'And I keep telling you that there's nothing wrong with your old heart,' Jonathan teased.

'Who is this?' Mary struggled to get up. Jonathan placed a helping hand under her elbow until the older woman had heaved herself to her feet.

'This is Rose. A friend.'

The faded grey eyes grew sharp. 'A friend, huh? You've never brought a friend down here before. Does she know what she's letting herself in for? And what does Lord Cavendish have to say?'

'Who I'm friends with has nothing to do with my father, Mary.'

Rose stretched her hand out. 'I'm pleased to meet you, Mary. I don't think Lord Cavendish and I are very likely to meet. Jonathan and I aren't that kind of friends.' All the same, she couldn't help feel offended. Cheek.

'Hey, don't mind me, love.' She ruffled Jonathan's hair as if he were about ten years old. 'Jonathan here could do with a good woman. Someone with a bit of heart instead of the type he usually runs around with.' She sniffed disapprovingly.

'Shall I put the kettle on?' Rose offered, not knowing what else to say.

'No, away you go and wait in the drawing room. I'll bring up a tray shortly.'

'I'd rather stay down here, if we won't get in your way,' Rose said. 'It's such a cosy room.'

Mary sent another sharp look Rose's way. Then she seemed to make up her mind. Her mouth turned up in the faintest of smiles.

'I think you might have found a good 'un, Master

Jonathan. None of those other women would think of stepping down here to say hello to an old woman. It would be beneath them.' Her eyes grew moist. 'Not like your mother, love. No airs and graces about her. She was never happier than when she was down here, sitting in that chair, chatting away to me, her dress and her hands covered in paint. She'd even roll up her sleeves and tackle a bit of baking when the mood took her. She just laughed when your dad told her it wasn't appropriate.' There was another loud sniff. 'This place has never been the same since she passed away. Bless her soul.' Now Rose knew who had painted the wonderful landscapes that hung on his walls at the surgery and his home. Jonathan's mother had been a wonderfully talented artist.

She sat back down in her chair while Rose put the kettle on the stove and found the tea things.

'You said hello to your father yet, son?' Mary asked Jonathan, while she watched what Rose was doing from the corner of her eye.

'Dad is here?' Jonathan said, sounding surprised. 'I thought he was in America on business.'

'He came back last night. Brought some woman with him. She's staying the weekend, so he tells me. She's already making all sorts of demands as if she owns the place. Get the rooms all opened up! Send to the village for more staff! She won't believe me when I tell her that we can manage perfectly well. She's already wrapped Mrs Hammond around her little finger by saying she needs more help. Well, that's your father for you. There's nothing like an old fool.'

A bell jangled furiously. Mary glanced to her left where a row of old-fashioned bells hung in a row. 'That's her. Probably looking for her afternoon tea in the sitting room.'

Mary began to heave herself out of her chair. 'I suppose I'd better get a tray sorted for them.'

'You just stay where you are, Mary. They can wait a moment or two.' Jonathan squatted on his heels next to the old woman. 'Maybe they're right. More help would make life a lot easier for you. I thought you had people in from the village during the day? Where are they?'

'Oh, they're away home. They only do the cleaning. Said that's all they're paid for. And they're right. Mrs Hammond wants to get another cook, someone who's lighter on their feet. Someone who's younger and can manage to take trays up and down all day.' Mary folded her arms and her face took on a mutinous look. 'I'm not going anywhere. I've been here all my life and the only way anyone's going to get me out of here is in a wooden box.'

Although Rose's heart went out to the older woman, she had to hide a smile. She was getting the distinct impression that no one was able to make Mary do anything she didn't want to. This Mrs Hammond, whoever she was, sounded like a sergeant-major. And as for Lord Cavendish's friend, she sounded as if she'd be better off at the Ritz.

'Tell you what, why don't you and Jonathan have your tea and a chat? If you tell me how to fix the tray, I'll take it upstairs for you. I'll introduce myself while I'm at it. And while I'm away, you can tell Jonathan about those chest pains you've been having.'

'How did you know? I mean, what chest pains? There's nothing wrong with me.'

'Yes, there is,' Rose said gently. 'I saw the way you were rubbing your chest when you got up a few moments ago. And you seem a little short of breath. It's probably nothing, but worth getting checked out.' She pretended to look fierce. 'Especially if, as you say, you plan to stick around for a few years yet.'

'Now, Mary. Why didn't you tell me?' Jonathan said, frowning. 'You know I would have come to see you long before now if I'd thought you needed me.'

'Take no notice of Rose. She doesn't know what she's talking about.' But something in their expressions must have told her that further protests would be a waste of time. 'Oh, well, then, if you have to have a look, go on. But don't you go saying anything to anyone, mind.'

While Jonathan returned to the cottage to fetch his stethoscope, Rose laid the tray under Mary's guidance. 'Just point me in the right direction. I'll be back as soon as I've handed this over.'

'It's the third door on the right at the stop of the stairs.' She paused and her mouth lifted in a smile. 'And if you could tell Lady Muck or whatever her name is that there has never been dandelion tea in my kitchen as long as I've been cook and there's no way it will ever be served here as long as I've breath in my body, I'd appreciate it.'

Rose carried the tray up the sweeping staircase until she got to the top. She smiled to herself. Now waitress was being added to her list of jobs.

She found the room she was looking for. The door was open, so she coughed and entered. A man got to his feet and instantly she recognised Jonathan's father from his photograph. He shared the same arrogant nose and wide mouth as well as thick brown hair with his son.

'Hello?' Lord Cavendish raised an eyebrow. 'You must be new. I don't think I've met you before.' His voice was welcoming, but more than that, to her chagrin, Rose was aware of his eyes sweeping across her body in the most disconcerting way.

'Just leave the tray over there.' The woman who had been looking out the window turned and waved at Rose with a dismissive hand. She was considerably younger than Lord Cavendish, closer to Rose's age, possibly a year or two older.

'I'm not new,' Rose said, placing the tray on a coffee table in front of the sofa. 'I'm here with Jonathan. He's having a look at Mary downstairs. She's not feeling too great, so I offered to bring the tray up for her.'

Lord Cavendish's eyes clouded with concern and something else—could it be surprise?

'Jonathan is here? To see Mary? Why didn't she say she was feeling unwell? I'll go and see her myself.' He hurried out of the room, leaving Rose alone with his guest.

'I'm Rose Taylor,' Rose introduced herself. Cool grey eyes swept over her and this time Rose could tell Lord Cavendish's guest was taking in her clothes, her haircut, assessing the cost and then wondering what on earth she was doing with the son of a lord.

'I work with Jonathan. I'm his nurse.' Now, why had she said that? It was none of this woman's business.

The grey eyes narrowed and she nodded to herself as if something had been cleared up.

'How do you do, Miss Taylor?' The voice was as cool as the eyes and Rose noticed she didn't bother to introduce herself. 'Did cook manage to rustle up some dandelion tea? She certainly had enough time.'

Hadn't this woman taken in a thing Rose had said? For the first time in her life she found herself detesting someone on sight.

'I'm afraid Mary isn't feeling well,' she said stiffly. 'Now, if you'll excuse me, I'll leave you to your tea.'

She found Jonathan and his father deep in conversation. Rose could sense the strained atmosphere between father and son.

'Mary needs to rest, Father. For at least a week, possibly longer.'

'And I've tried to tell her that on more than one occasion, but she won't listen to me.'

'When did you tell her? You've hardly been here over the last six months,' Jonathan said sharply. The two men noticed Rose and stopped their conversation abruptly.

'Father, can I introduce Rose Taylor? Rose, this is my father, Lord Cavendish.' Rose suppressed the inane desire to curtsy.

'I apologise for my lack of manners upstairs,' he said. 'I was anxious to check on Mary myself and to see my son. Who…' he shot a look in Jonathan's direction '…hasn't seen fit to visit for quite some time.'

'Now is not the time or place, Father,' Jonathan said warningly. It was the first time Rose had seen him look so grim. Something was clearly badly wrong between father and son.

'You are quite right, Jonathan. Now, if you'll both excuse me, I'd better find Mrs Hammond and see what can be done to find someone to fill in for Mary while she's resting.'

As soon as he had left, Rose turned to Jonathan. His normal open and cheerful expression was tight. 'How is she?'

'I think she has mild ischaemic heart disease. I want to arrange to have her admitted to hospital for proper tests, but she's not keen. But I've threatened to call an ambulance if she doesn't agree. Father's right. I should have called in here more often, especially when he's away.'

'Look, why don't you make some calls, and I'll go and check on Mary? Add my voice to yours if you think it would make a difference.'

'I'm sorry to have got you mixed up in this.' He grinned

ruefully. 'So much for me trying to give you a relaxing day out away from work.'

He looked so regretful Rose's heart went out to him.

'I don't mind being mixed up in this, as you put it. Isn't that what friends are for? To help each other?'

Jonathan looked perplexed. 'Is it?' he said thoughtfully. 'I wouldn't know. I can't say I've ever had to rely on my friends before. They're always there when I need to let off steam and that's all I ever expected from them.' He smiled down at her. 'You're a good person, Rose Taylor. You know that, don't you?'

Ah, well, Rose thought dismally. It was good that Jonathan knew she was his friend—even if he didn't want her as his lover.

She found Mary right at the top of the house, several flights up. The older woman was sitting at the window, looking out at the garden. She folded her arms across her chest and glared at Rose.

'If you have come up here to try and persuade me to go into hospital, you're wasting your time. And you can tell Master Jonathan that from me.' She pursed her lips.

'You will probably only have to go in for a night, two at the most. Just while they do some tests. Then you can come back here, although I'm going to suggest that you move to a room that doesn't require quite as many stairs.'

'There's nowt wrong with this room. I've been in here since the day I started work thirty years ago and I see no reason to move now.' She blinked furiously, but she couldn't quite disguise the moisture in her eyes.

'What is it, Mary? What's truly worrying you? Come on, you can tell me.'

'If I leave here, I'll never come back. That woman down there with Lord Cavendish will persuade him to employ someone younger. I know she will. She's only been here a couple of days and already I can see that's she's imagining herself as the next Lady Cavendish.'

So that was what was worrying the old woman. Somehow Rose knew that Jonathan would never let that happen.

'This place is as much my home as anyone's. I don't have anywhere else to go. The only way I want to leave here is in a box.'

'How long have you been hiding your symptoms, Mary?'

'A month, maybe two. I thought it was indigestion at first. Then the pain started to get worse whenever I had to climb the stairs, so I knew it must be my heart.'

'Why didn't you call Jonathan? You must have known he'd be concerned enough to come and see you straight away.'

'Oh, he's got enough on his plate without me bothering him with my little problems. Anyway…' she leaned across and dropped her voice to a conspiratorial whisper. 'I can't make myself believe he's actually a doctor. Not the boy I've watched grow up. It doesn't seem right somehow.'

Rose pulled up a seat and sat down.

'You seem very fond of him,' she said.

'The poor mite was only little when his mother died. I'm probably the nearest, most constant person he had in his life as a child. Whenever he was home from school, he'd spend more time at the kitchen table with me than upstairs. When he wasn't running around outside, that was.'

'What about Lord Cavendish?'

'He was distraught when Jonathan's mother died. But his way of dealing with it was to throw himself into work. He couldn't see that Jonathan needed him more than ever. Then six months after Jonathan's mother died, Lord Cavendish returned from an overseas trip married to the second Lady Cavendish. That didn't last too long. He divorced the third wife a year or so ago, and now it looks as if he's preparing to marry again.'

'His fourth marriage?' Rose couldn't keep the shock from her voice. 'Surely that's a little excessive?'

'Ah, well. He always did have an eye for the women.' She moved her gaze back to the window and her eyes glistened. 'I don't think he's ever got over the first Lady Cavendish. Now, she was a real lady. Not in the sense of being from aristocracy, you understand, her own background was quite humble, but in terms of knowing how to treat people.' She pointed a gnarled finger to the floor. 'That woman will never compete in a hundred years.'

There was a tap at the door and Jonathan walked into the room. With a guilty start, Rose realised she had been gossiping.

'How's my favourite girl, then?' Jonathan said. 'Has Rose managed to talk you into going to the hospital?'

Before Mary had a chance to protest, Rose interrupted smoothly. 'I think Mary will agree to go to the hospital. She's just a wee bit worried that your father will replace her while she's away.'

It looked as if a thundercloud had descended on Jonathan's face. 'Whatever gave you that idea? I agree you could do with more help, but no one is thinking of replacing you. This house would fall down without you to look after it—and us. You've been here as long as I can remember. It's your home, Mary. Don't ever forget that.'

Mary looked relieved but then her mouth puckered. 'But it's not just to do with you, Master Jonathan, is it? At least, not for some time. Right now your father makes the decisions, and if he marries again, it'll be the new Lady Cavendish's wishes that take precedence.'

'My father might have his faults, Mary, Lord knows, but

he'll never agree to replacing you.' His eyes narrowed. 'I had no idea he was planning to marry again.'

'Now, don't you go saying anything,' Mary protested. 'It's not official yet. At least, he's not said as much. It's just I heard his guest speaking on the phone. She was telling them not to make plans for the summer because she was planning a big party.'

Jonathan's lips thinned. 'You leave my father to me, Mary. Come on, I'm going to drive you to the hospital. They're expecting us. If you want to get a few things together, I'll let my father know what's happening.' He turned to Rose. 'I can't apologise enough, but there's only room in my car for Mary and I. If I ask my father to take you to the railway station, would you manage to find your own way home from there?'

'Of course. Really, it's no problem.' She smiled. 'It's far more important that Mary gets investigated, and the sooner the better.' She got to her feet. 'We'll leave you alone to pack your things, Mary. Take your time. There's no rush.'

Jonathan still looked livid when they left Mary. 'I need to go and find my father. It shouldn't take too long. Would you like to wait downstairs?'

'I think I'll take a stroll in the garden while I'm waiting. And if it's inconvenient for your father to take me to the station, perhaps you can call me a taxi?'

'He'll take you,' Jonathan responded grimly. 'One thing you can say about my father is that his manners are impeccable.'

The grounds of the hall were as lavish as the inside. Rose kept close to the house in case she was needed. To her right, a small rose-coloured archway invited her to explore. She dipped her head and entered a small hidden garden. She gasped with pleasure. Someone had taken the time to make this little spot less formal than the rest of the gardens. It was a mass of flowers and the smell of rosemary, lavender and mint drifted up her nostrils. Seeing a bench with views out to the open hills off to one side, Rose took a seat and closed her eyes.

Something was badly wrong between Jonathan and his father. She wondered if he'd have taken her to the house, or even to the gatehouse, if he'd known his father was at home. Somehow she felt sure he wouldn't have. How could someone not get on with their father? Especially when he was the only family member Jonathan had left. Rose couldn't remember ever having cross words with her parents.

She was beginning to realise that Jonathan was a much more complex man than she had ever imagined and she knew that every moment she spent with him she was falling deeper and deeper in love. The realisation was not a welcome one.

Voices drifted from the open window behind her. She recognised Jonathan's and his father's. Both men sounded heated.

'How can you think of marrying yet again?' Jonathan's voice was raised.

'What I choose to do with my life is none of your goddamn business. And speaking of marriage, when are you going to stop seducing every woman on the planet and get into a real relationship? You can't carry on the way you do for the rest of your life. At some point you're going to accept you have responsibilities.'

'That's rich, coming from you.'

Rose got to her feet. The last thing she wanted was to overhear the argument between father and son. She started to edge away from the window.

'What about that prissy little thing you brought with you? She looks like she has a sensible head. Why, for God's sake, can't you find someone like her to settle down with?'

Rose froze in mid-stride. This was so embarrassing. How dare Lord Cavendish refer to her as prissy? Even if she supposed there was an element of truth in the description. But she had to admit she was dying to know how Jonathan would respond.

'Rose? As the future Lady Cavendish?' Jonathan laughed harshly. 'Now you mention it, she'd be a lot more suitable than the last two *you* chose to marry. At least she has brains and a kind heart under that prissy exterior, as you call it. I can tell you she's worth a hundred of the women you married after Mother.'

Lord Cavendish dropped his voice and Rose could hear the sadness and regret in it. 'Why are we always arguing, son? You know I need your help. I'm not getting any younger and running my businesses as well as this estate is getting too much.'

'Are you all right? You've not being feeling ill, have you? When did you last have a check-up?' This time it was Jonathan's voice that was full of concern. Despite their earlier angry words, Rose could tell the two men cared about one another.

'I'm fine. I promise. I'd feel a lot better if I knew that you were settling down. You can't keep on living the way you do. God, man, your name is in the paper every other day. Always with a different woman. You need to get married—have children. I need to know before I die that there is going to be someone to carry on the family line.'

'You're a fine person to talk.' The anger was back in Jonathan's voice. 'Is that why you married Mother? Just

to provide an heir for the future? My God, didn't you love
her at all?'

'Love her? Of course I loved her. She was the best thing
that ever happened to me.'

'Which is why you married again within six months of
her death.'

Rose couldn't bear to hear any more. She tiptoed away
until she could no longer hear the voices and waited by the
front door of the house. She was tingling as she recalled
the words Jonathan had used to describe her. Kind and
clever. Well, she hoped she was. But she would have liked
to hear herself described as beautiful and sexy as well, even
if it was untrue. This way she felt like Jonathan's sister and
that wasn't how she wanted him to see her at all. She
wanted someone to find her exciting and interesting. She
wanted *Jonathan* to find her exciting and interesting. If she
didn't have a future, she wanted a here and now. And why
not? Where had playing safe got her? She felt her blood
heat her veins. Prissy. She'd give them prissy. She could
be as exciting and interesting as the next woman and with
a bit of help—possibly a lot of help—she could do sexy as
well. It was as if she'd been sleeping up until the moment
she'd realised her life could be snatched away at any time.
Now she wanted to wake up and experience life before it
was too late. And who better to show her that life than
Jonathan Cavendish? After all, it wasn't as if she could
break his heart.

CHAPTER SEVEN

'I CAN'T wait for it! Do you think there'll be loads of celebrities there?' Jenny was practically bouncing out of her
chair with excitement. Jonathan had informed everyone
that he was taking a table at the annual fundraising ball and
they were all invited. It had been on the tip of Rose's
tongue to refuse, but instead she had found herself
agreeing. What harm could it do? And it was one more
thing to add to her list. Besides, it was another opportunity
to be with Jonathan outside work and although she knew
she was storing up heartache for the future, she couldn't
bring herself to deny herself a moment of him.

'I get the feeling there will be one or two.' Rose had to
smile at Jenny's enthusiasm.

'We'll have to go shopping for something to wear,'
Jenny said. 'And you'll have to go to the hairdresser.' She
pulled out her mobile. 'You must go to mine. He's fantastic. He'll know exactly what to do with your hair.'

'What's wrong with my hair?' Rose protested. She eyed
her colleague doubtfully, recalling the spiky hairdo she
usually sported outside her job. If Jenny thought she was
going to go punk, she had another think coming.

Jenny looked at Rose thoughtfully. 'I would die for hair

like yours. It's just a little old-fashioned, you know. It could do with an update. In fact, and I don't mean to be rude or anything, the whole of you could do with an update.' She wrinkled her nose. 'That cardigan you're so fond of wearing, for example. That has to go.'

'Hey, there's nothing wrong with it. It's warm and comfortable,' Rose protested.

'And makes it seem as if you're wearing a sack. Come on, Rose. You don't want to look like someone's maiden aunt. Not when all those glamorous people are going to be there.' She held up her hand, cutting Rose's protests off. 'You will not let the side down. I simply won't allow it.'

Dowdy? Someone's maiden aunt? Now she had two more derogatory adjectives to add to the steadily growing list. Up until recently nobody had ever complained about the way she looked. Or complimented her either, she had to admit. But she hadn't minded. Hadn't she always told herself that external appearances weren't important? But this was the new Rose, she reminded herself. The one who was determined to break out of her shell. Hadn't she promised herself to try different things? And if that included a new image, so be it.

By Saturday afternoon, Rose had been done to within an inch of her life. Jenny's hairdresser had cut her hair into a sharp modern style while keeping it long. He had parted it to one side and now it fell over one side of her face. If she had to keep blowing out little puffs of hair so she could see what she was doing—as Jenny had said, what did it matter if she looked chic and alluring? But the hair over her eyes wasn't the only thing obscuring her vision. Jenny had insisted that no way was she allowed to wear her glasses. She had marched her to the optician and Rose was now trying contact lenses. She finally managed to get them in and blinked furiously as water streamed from her eyes. She'd give them until she had to apply her make-up and if they hadn't settled it was on with the glasses. The last thing she needed was to turn up looking like she had spent the day crying.

She and Jenny had been shopping for a dress and eventually, after what had seemed like hours of tramping around London, had settled on a silky, two-tone red number that shimmered as Rose walked.

'Wow! I had no idea you had a figure like that underneath those dreadful clothes you insist on wearing,' Jenny had said. 'I could diet for a year and still not have a body like that. Why on earth do you cover it up?'

'I'm too thin,' Rose had said. 'I hate the way my bones stick out all over the place. They used to call me pin legs when I was in school. Someone even accused me of being anorexic.' The memory brought painful feelings flooding back. At school she had been teased for being too thin and she had never lost that gawky, unattractive feeling. Now all the worries and anxieties about the way she looked seemed so petty and pointless. And Jenny was right. The dress did amazing things to her figure. The way it hung, the way it moved when she moved. For the first time in her life, Rose felt glamorous.

'And don't even think you're going to get out of buying new underwear,' Jenny had said. 'Are these mum pants or what?'

'There is nothing wrong with my underwear,' Rose protested. 'Okay, they might be serviceable rather than sexy, but who is going to see?'

'Seeing, as you put it, isn't really the point. At least not all of it. If you don't feel sexy under your clothes, how are you going to look sexy?'

Rose had to laugh. She let Jenny steer her to the lingerie department and allowed her to bully her into buying several lacy bras with matching panties. Rose dreaded to think what her credit-card bill was going to be like. But she had to admit she had plenty money in the bank and it was fun. It was the first time she could remember that she had spent so much money on herself. After all, she reminded herself with a stab, who knew if she would ever have the opportunity to dress up like this again? And right now saving her pennies for a rainy day seemed like an exercise in futility. One thing her illness had done was to free her from the small pointless worries of everyday life.

As she finished putting the finishing touches to her make-up, almost the way the girl at the cosmetics counter had shown her, she had to admit that now she was as far away from prissy as it was possible to be. She giggled. All she needed was a cigarette holder in one hand and a glass of champagne in the other, and she'd look like Mata Hari, even though she didn't smoke. And while the contacts had settled, she was sure the famous seductress hadn't blinked quite so often.

She sashayed down the stairs, revelling in the feel of the soft fabric of her dress against her skin.

Her father glanced up when she entered the sitting room and attempted a wolf whistle.

'Can this really be my little girl?' he said, his eyes glistening. 'So grown up and so beautiful?'

Over the last couple of weeks his condition had continued to improve. He was getting about fairly easily with one stick and his speech was less slurred. He was able to manage more of the activities of daily living by himself, even if it still took him twice as long as it used to. Being more independent had cheered him up enormously and

Rose knew that soon her parents would be able to cope without her. It lifted some of the burden from her shoulders when she thought about what the future could bring—for them as well as her.

'Yes, Dad. I know it's hard to believe.' She whirled around. 'I find it hard to believe too.'

'I've never seen you so lit up,' her mother said quietly. 'Is it just the night out or is there another reason why you're glowing inside and out?' Rose had made sure her mother didn't see her torment and worry. Around her mother, she forced herself to think only about things that made her happy. Like Jonathan.

He had insisted on sending a car for her. She had tried to protest, saying she'd be quite happy to take the tube, but he had been adamant.

'You and the rest of the gang are my guests. There is no way I'm going to let you arrive on foot.' He had smiled down at her and her heart banged against her ribs. 'Just give in gracefully, kid. For once.'

But she hadn't expected to find him at her door. He looked jaw-droppingly handsome in his dinner suit and bow-tie. When he saw her, he looked taken aback. He bowed briefly from the waist. Then he whistled. 'You look absolutely stunning,' he said. 'Have you had your hair cut? It suits you.' Rose felt a wave of pleasure wash over her. Perhaps he was just being polite, but the look in his eyes told her he meant ever word.

'You don't look so bad yourself,' she quipped.

'I'll just wish your parents good evening,' Jonathan said, stepping inside the small hallway. He was so close she could smell the faint scent of his shampoo and the familiar spice of his aftershave. He touched her briefly on her shoulder and a shiver ran down her spine. 'There are going to be a few women there tonight with their noses severely out of joint. You do know that, don't you?' His breath was like a caress on her skin.

After a few brief words with her parents, he ushered Rose out to the waiting car.

Inside the stretch limousine was an over-excited Jenny, as well as Vicki and her husband. It was another new experience for Rose. There were seats along one side as well as a small bar. Jonathan reached into the bar and brought out a chilled bottle of champagne, which he popped with a flourish. When everyone had their glasses filled he toasted them. 'I hope you all have a great time tonight and remember it's all for a good cause.'

'I'm so glad you could manage,' Rose said to Vicki after she had introduced her husband, Russell. 'How are you feeling?'

'Much better. I don't know how long I'll last, but I couldn't miss it. It's my favourite night of the year. The one and only night I really get to let my hair down.'

Vicki, who had declined the champagne in favour of fresh orange juice, waved her glass at Jonathan. 'Are you going to be auctioned as usual tonight?'

'Not if I can help it,' Jonathan replied. 'I made a deal with the organisers this year. They've agreed I don't have to take part as long as I match the highest bid for one of the other guests.'

'Auctioned?' Jenny said, sounding puzzled. 'What do you mean?'

'Every year at this do they ask some of the eligible bachelors to agree to auction a date. They have to parade up and down a catwalk while women bid for a date with them. It can get quite heated. At least, it did last year,' Vicki replied, grinning.

'What happened?'

Jonathan was frowning at Vicki, shaking his head from side to side. But she wasn't to be deterred.

'It almost caused a riot. The organiser made Jonathan remove his jacket and shirt. He was allowed to leave his bow-tie on. Not that that gave him much to hide behind.' Vicki chuckled. Jonathan was looking mortified.

Rose almost spluttered into her champagne. The image of a semi-naked Jonathan strolling down a catwalk was almost too much.

'Who won?' Jenny asked.

'That was the best part. It was one of the elderly matrons. You should have seen her excitement when she learned her bid was the highest.'

Everyone, even Jonathan, laughed. 'She actually bought the date for her daughter. I don't know who was more embarrassed, her or me. Still, we had a pleasant enough meal. But I will never do that again. No way. Uhuh.'

By this time they were pulling up outside the hotel where the dinner-dance was to be held. Although the hotel was famous, Rose had never been inside before.

As they climbed out of the car, they were swarmed by photographers.

'Look this way, Jonathan,' they called out. She pulled back inside the car. She hadn't expected this. There was no way she wanted to be photographed, even if it wasn't her they were after.

But she had reckoned without Jonathan. As the rest of the group made their way into the hotel, he jumped back into the car and pulled the door closed.

'What's wrong?' he asked.

'I don't want to go out there,' Rose whispered. 'I hate having my photograph taken.'

'I don't much like it either,' Jonathan replied, 'but the best way to cope with it is to pose for a couple of photographs and then walk away.'

'I can't.' Rose shook her head.

'Yes, you can,' Jonathan said firmly. 'They are going to want a picture of the amazingly beautiful woman who has arrived with me.' He looked regretful. 'I'm an idiot. If I had thought for one minute that you'd hate the attention, I would have arrived separately. But it's too late now. The more you hide away, the more curious they're going to be. There's nothing else for it. We have to brave the lions in their den.' He grinned. 'Just follow my lead and it'll be over in a few minutes. Okay?'

Rose nodded and, head held high, stepped out of the car. Once again, there was an explosion of blinding flashes.

'Who is your lady friend, Jonathan? Is it serious? Are you settling down?'

Rose's heart sank as she realised that her climbing back into the car had only made matters worse. Now they thought she was someone.

'Hey, guys, give us a break.' Jonathan kept his tone even. 'Ms Taylor is just one of several guests I have with me this evening.'

'Does this mean your relationship with Jessamine Goldsmith is over?' another reporter asked.

'Ms Goldsmith and I are good friends and have never been anything more.'

'So there's no truth that she dumped you because you refused to name the day?'

'None at all. Now, if you'll excuse us,' Jonathan replied smoothly, 'I have guests waiting inside.'

'Could you tell us a bit about yourself, Ms Taylor?' Another reporter thrust his microphone into Rose's face and she almost stumbled. As quick as a flash, Jonathan reached out to steady her with one hand while with the other took hold of the microphone and pushed it away. 'Just carry on walking,' he said into her ear. 'I'll keep them busy.'

'It's okay,' Rose replied, lifting her head again. 'I can deal with this.' She took a deep breath and turned to the journalists with the biggest smile she could manage. 'I'm afraid there isn't much to tell. I work with Dr Cavendish. I'm his practice nurse. As he's told you, I'm one of a party of his staff. Now, I know that you are all interested in what this evening is in aid of. Perhaps you'd like me to bring you up to speed with the work of the charity?'

From the corner of her eye she saw the look of surprise on Jonathan's face, followed by a look of approval. She had made a point of looking the charity up on the Internet during a quiet spell at the clinic. She carried on, inching her way towards the hotel door as she briefly outlined the work of the charity, making sure that she kept smiling. Fortunately it seemed to work. As soon as another car pulled up at the kerb, the reporters turned away to catch the new arrival.

Inside, Jonathan was immediately surrounded by people. Rose left him to greet his friends and acquaint-ances, and spying Jenny and Victoria from the corner of her eye went over to their table. Jenny's eyes were alive with excitement.

'I've already spotted at least ten famous people,' she told Rose. 'Everywhere I look there is someone whose face I recognise. Isn't this brilliant? I can hardly believe I'm here.' She pointed across the room. 'I saw her film last week. Isn't she beautiful? Even more than she is in her films? And as for that dress, isn't it to die for?'

It was overwhelming. Rose felt drab and shy in the

presence of so many well-known people, all of whom looked relaxed and confident. In the crowd she noticed Lady Hilton. Although she had a smile painted on her face, Rose could tell instantly, even from a distance, that she was worried. When she thought no one was looking her smile disappeared, to be replaced with lines of worry around her mouth and eyes. Forgetting her shyness, Rose made her way through the throng until she was by her side.

'Lady Hilton,' she murmured in her ear. 'Are you okay?'

'My dear girl, I didn't know you were coming. It's lovely to see you.' She raised her face for Rose to kiss. Although the older woman's voice was bright, she didn't fool Rose.

'How is Lord Hilton?' she asked quietly.

'Much the same as when you last saw him, my dear.'

As promised, Rose had been making regular trips to their estate to check up on Lord Hilton.

'He insisted I come tonight, even though I told him I'd rather stay with him. But he wouldn't hear of it. He said that the Hiltons had never missed this fundraiser in twenty years and we weren't going to start now.' Sophia smiled wanly. 'You know how much we both owe you, don't you, dear? Without your help we would never have been able to keep him at home. Jonathan's a lucky man. Goodall is with Giles tonight. I'll stay until the auction then I'll go home.' She glanced around the room. 'Where is Jonathan? I'd like to speak to him.' Her voice regained some of its familiar strength.

It was kind of Sophia to think Jonathan was lucky to have her as a nurse. But Rose knew that the small help she had been able to give the couple had made a difference to the dark days they were facing. It had helped her too. There was a bitter-sweet poignancy in helping the couple through their last days together.

'Why don't you join us at our table?' Rose suggested. Then felt immediately embarrassed. Lady Hilton was bound to have friends to sit with. But, to her surprise, Sophia looked relieved.

'Thank you, my dear. I'd like that. It would save me having to answer questions about my Giles. Everyone means to be kind, but it gets a little difficult.'

'Come on, then.' Rose smiled. 'Let's get you seated and you can rest your feet. Vicki and her husband are at our table too. I'm sure she'd like to see you.'

Lady Hilton seemed glad to see Vicki. Jenny, on the other hand, was struck dumb for the first time Rose could remember. Rose suppressed a smile when Jenny attempted a small curtsy when she was introduced to Lady Hilton, and then, realising what she had done, blushed to the roots of her hair.

'Apparently the auction is going to start before dinner and continue all the way through,' Vicki told everyone at the table. 'There's a list of what's being auctioned under the menu.'

Rose picked up the bound, heavy pages of the auction items. There were cars and weeks on private islands, trips on personal Lear jets, diamonds, paintings and—she smiled—the date with one of London's eligible bachelors. That must be the event Jonathan had told them about. She wished there was something she could afford to bid on, but there was nothing she could afford. She would have to sit back and watch the fun.

'Are you bidding on anything, my dear? I think I'll make an offer on one of the paintings. I usually do and then slip it back into the auction the following year. We have far too many paintings as it is.'

'I'm afraid there is nothing here I can afford,' Rose admitted.

'Lady Hilton, Sophia, what an unexpected pleasure.' Jonathan's voice came from behind her. 'And to have you sit with us is a double honour.'

'I haven't taken your seat, have I?' Lady Hilton. 'If I have, I can easily return to my own table. I'm sure Rose would rather sit next to you than an old lady like me.' Her eyes slid to Rose and the sadness was replaced with a twinkle. 'Doesn't she look beautiful?'

'Yes, she does,' Jonathan replied quietly. 'Easily the most beautiful woman in the room.'

Rose felt a blush steal up her cheeks. But she knew better than to take his words seriously. No doubt it was the way he spoke to all women.

'Unfortunately, I won't be needing my seat for the next hour. Despite my best efforts, Lady Somerville has roped me into the bachelor date auction. She won't take no for an answer.'

Rose stifled a giggle. It was the first time she had seen him look ill at ease.

'Isn't that the thing you were telling us about in the car? The one you said you would never do again?' Jenny leant over, dragging her eyes away from the seemingly endless parade of actresses, models and pop stars.

Jonathan sighed heavily. 'I tried to tell her that I'd match the highest amount bid for any of the men in the auction, but she wouldn't hear of it. She says she needs me to make the numbers up, and I was the highest earner last year.'

'If I had the money, I'd bid for you,' Jenny said stoutly.

'Just remember it's all for a good cause,' Lady Hilton reminded Jonathan.

A woman was waving frantically from the other side of the room, trying to get his attention.

'Looks like I'm up. Wish me luck, everyone.' Then, with a last rueful grimace, Jonathan left them.

'You should bid for him,' Lady Hilton told Rose. 'He could do with a good woman. Someone to settle him down. I know his father worries about him.'

Rose was mortified. Jonathan and her? It was inconceivable. Lady Hilton should know that.

'I hardly think Jonathan and I are suited,' she said, keeping her voice mild.

'Why ever not? Don't you find him good looking and charming? He'll inherit a title when his father dies. Half the women in this room would jump at the chance to be the future Lady Cavendish.' She peered after Jonathan. 'What's wrong with him?'

'There's nothing wrong with him.' Rose wished the floor would open up and swallow her. 'It's just that I'm hardly suited to being the lady of the manor, am I?' And if that wasn't bad enough, she had no future to offer any man. But she wasn't going to talk about that.

'Rubbish, girl. If you think just because you're a commoner, and he belongs to aristocracy, think again. His mother, the current Lord Cavendish's first wife, was a commoner too. Things are changing. And for the better, I would say.' She looked thoughtful for a moment. 'I don't think his father ever got over the death of his first wife. She was the love of his life.'

'What happened to her?'

'She died when Jonathan was five. Pneumonia, would you believe? The poor mite was devastated. His father sent him away to boarding school just when Jonathan needed him most. I don't think Jonathan has ever forgiven him and I suspect he blames him for not noticing how unwell Clara was. How can a child understand that Cavendish sending him away was nothing to do with him? That his father just couldn't cope? The sight of him every day was just too much of a painful reminder. It was the way things were done. I'm not saying it was right. Then his father married again. Within six months. I think it was because he was lonely, but Jonathan never forgave him for that either.'

It explained the tension and anger between Jonathan and his father.

'Why didn't Lord Cavendish explain? Tell his son how he felt?'

Lady Hilton looked surprised. 'Men don't speak of these things, my dear. At least, not then. Oh, I know these days it's the done thing to talk about your feelings, endlessly. But that isn't the way Jonathan and his father were brought up.'

Rose felt a pang for the child Jonathan had been. How terrible to lose your mother and then to be sent away into a strange environment from the only home you had known. What would that do to a grieving child? At least she had always been surrounded by the love of her parents and had always known that they would do anything for her happiness.

There was no more time to talk as everyone was instructed to take their seats by a tall woman with short, platinum-blonde hair.

'That's Mrs Tenant, Rose.' Lady Hilton whispered. 'She used to be a model in the sixties. Her father was enormously wealthy. Perhaps even wealthier than Lord Cavendish. She married for love and she's been blissfully happy. She helps Lady Somerville run the auction. I have to say, between them, they've helped raise hundreds of thousands of pounds over the years.'

Mrs Tenant—Julia—welcomed everyone in a rich Yorkshire accent that was as far away from the plush London tones all around her as it was possible to be.

'We are going to start with the eligible bachelors' auction,' she said after she had spoken briefly about the charity. 'I know this is a favourite event for most of you. Now, we have five men, all single and all looking forward to their dates with the lucky women who win the auction. Don't be mean, anyone. Dig deep into those pockets.'

Everyone settled down, looking towards the runway that had been erected near the front of the room. A hush descended as Julia introduced the first 'bachelor'—a British tennis player who had been taking the country by storm over the last year. He swaggered onto the stage in a pair of tennis shorts and nothing else, looking, Rose thought, extremely self-conscious with a nervous grin on his face. There were a number of wolf whistles as he walked to the edge of the stage and flexed his forearm in a way that had become familiar to millions of tennis fans around the world.

'Who'll start the bidding? Come on, now, ladies, don't be shy. Who'll give me a hundred pounds?'

A sea of arms shot up. 'A hundred and fifty,' came a call from the back. Rose swivelled around in her seat to find a young woman waving her arms in the air, a bundle of notes in each hand.

'Two hundred,' came another voice. Soon the bidding was up to four hundred and after Julia had promised that the player was throwing in a couple of prime seats for Wimbledon in June, the bidding rose to five hundred pounds before the triumphant girl who had started the bidding won her date.

Three others followed in quick succession. Rose felt sorry for the aristocrat with an unfortunate smile who only managed to raise two hundred pounds and she suspected his mother was behind that.

Jonathan was last to take the stage. He had, or someone had made him, remove his shirt. He strolled up the runway in his dinner trousers, bow-tie and jacket, his exposed chest smooth and muscular. If he felt self-conscious no one would have known from his confident grin. Rose felt a shiver run down her spine. He really was the sexiest man she had ever known.

The bidding started at three hundred pounds and quickly rose to five hundred.

'Come on, ladies. You can do better than that. Jonathan is one of London's most eligible bachelors. As far as I'm aware, there is no one in his life at the moment.'

The bidding rose by another hundred pounds. And even further. Suddenly, Lady Hilton's hand shot up. 'One thousand pounds,' she said firmly. Rose looked at the old lady in astonishment and was even more surprised when she received a saucy wink in response.

'One thousand pounds. Sold to Lady Hilton,' Julia said with a flourish. 'A new record.'

As she thanked everyone and the music faded away, Jenny and Vicki turned surprised faces towards Lady Hilton, who leaned closer to Rose and whispered in a conspiratorial voice, 'I bought him for you, dear.'

'Me?' Rose squeaked, thinking that Lady Hilton had lost her marbles. 'Whatever for?'

She leaned over and took Rose's hand in one of hers. 'Because I think you're right for each other, that's why. Even if he can't see it yet.'

Lady Hilton hadn't a clue how wrong she was. Rose was hardly the catch of the century. Even if she didn't have an uncertain future, unable to have children, bookish, what would anyone ever see in her? Let alone a man like Jonathan, who had dated some of the most beautiful and confident women in the world? Her heart stumbled. She'd enjoyed Jonathan's company over the last few weeks. More than enjoyed it, but soon it would be over. She'd be leaving, going back to her life in Edinburgh, whatever she decided to do about the operation. Her empty life, she thought miserably. She had been happy with it once, but that had been before Jonathan. Now she knew, however long she lived, her life would be lonely and grey without him.

Jonathan, who had replaced his shirt, slipped into the chair beside her. 'Thank God, that's over,' he said. 'I think I might just make my excuses for next year. But thank you, Sophia, for making the winning bid. Where would you like me to take you? Horseracing? To a polo match? I know you love both.'

Lady Hilton smiled wryly. 'As much as I'd like to go somewhere with you, Jonathan, I rather suspect that this will be my last outing for a while.' She turned her head to the side, but not before Rose saw a tear slip down her cheek. 'That's why I've passed my date on to Rose here. I know she's been working hard. Not least as she keeps popping in to see how we are, bless her. And I don't think polo or the racecourse is altogether what's needed. I need you to come up with something much more...' she hesitated. 'Appropriate for Rose.'

Rose was thoroughly embarrassed. Imagine Jonathan being tasked with taking her out as if she were a bag of shopping or a pet requiring to be walked. It was too much.

'There's no need at all to take me out,' she muttered into his ear. 'But perhaps we should pretend—as if it's ever going to happen—for Lady Hilton's sake?'

Jonathan grinned and Rose's heart pinged.

'I'm not one to back out of anything,' he said into her ear. She felt his warm breath on the nape of her neck and a delicious thrill ran down her spine. Goose-bumps prickled her arms, making her shiver. 'And I didn't have you down as a quitter either,' he continued. 'In the meantime…' he held out a hand '…shall we dance?'

Almost in a daze, Rose let him lead her to the dance floor. Thankfully she knew how to waltz. Memories of her father twirling her and her mother around their small sitting room to the music of Mozart and Strauss brought a lump to her throat. She had never dreamed she would be putting it into practice in such a setting.

Jonathan held her tightly. She could smell his aftershave and feel the hard muscles of his chest against her head. An image of his bare chest, tanned, defined muscles made her want to groan out loud. Who would have ever suspected he had a body like that? All that polo playing must help. She pushed the thought of heavily muscled thighs away before she became any more flustered.

She looked into his eyes. He looked back and her world tipped. Damn the man. Damn everything. Why did she have to go and fall for him? And why did she have to be facing an uncertain future? Why? Why? Why?

'You are the most beautiful woman in the room tonight and the most remarkable,' Jonathan whispered into her hair.

All at once, Rose had had enough. If Jonathan thought he could play games with her he had another think coming. No matter how she felt about him. *Particularly* because of how she felt about him.

She pulled away from him so she could see his face. 'What do you want from me, Jonathan?' she asked.

'What do you mean?' he asked as he whirled around the dance floor.

'I'm not the woman for you, believe me.'

He frowned. 'Don't you think I should be the judge of

that? Believe me, Rose Taylor. You're exactly the woman for me.' He paused by a door leading outside and pulled her into the fresh evening air. The scent of climbing roses drifted up her nostrils, intoxicating her.

Jonathan's finger stroked her hair away from her face. 'I don't think you have any idea just how lovely you are.' He smiled. 'But it's not just the way you look, you're a very special woman, Rose. Don't you know that? I can't believe that no one has won your heart yet.' He frowned and a shadow passed across his face. 'Or has someone? Of course. What an idiot I've been. There's bound to be someone back in Edinburgh, waiting for you. God, do you love him? Would you dump him? Come out with me instead?' His smile was warm and tender. 'I promise you, you won't regret it.'

Rose's head was swirling. There was nothing she wanted more right now than to tell him that there was no one else and, yes, she would go out with him. Every day for the rest of her life. However long that would be. But she couldn't. It wasn't fair to her or to him. All at once she knew he was falling in love with her and it made her heart soar, but she also knew she already cared too much to deny him the happy-ever-after ending he deserved.

'There's no future for us,' she said bleakly.

'So there is someone else.'

Rose hesitated. It would be easier to let him believe that. But she wasn't going to lie to him. Even if she couldn't tell him the truth.

'No, there isn't anyone.'

'In that case, I'm not going to take no for an answer. I owe you a date. And a date is what we're going to go on. Like it or not.' Although he smiled, Rose sensed the determination behind his words. And even though she knew she should avoid him, for his sake if not hers, she couldn't resist the temptation. Another memory. A few more moments with Jonathan to store away like a squirrel.

'Okay, then. If you insist, I'll go out with you. I guess it's not really a date anyway.' She tried to sound casual.

'Not really a date,' Jonathan muttered under his breath. 'If I insist? Well, I do insist. So that's sorted. This weekend. I'll let you know when and where later.'

Back at his flat, Jonathan prowled around restlessly. What was it about Rose that had got under his skin? Okay, so she was beautiful, but God knew he had dated beautiful women before. Even a supermodel. No, it wasn't that. It was her. That dogged air of determination mixed with an underlying vulnerability and genuineness that he had never come across before. She wasn't the least bit interested in his title or his wealth. She wasn't bowled over by him the way most women were. In fact, she gave the distinct impression she was unimpressed by him, almost disapproving.

That probably hit the nail on the head. She probably thought he didn't have a serious, committed bone in his body. And what was wrong with that? Wasn't it important to have fun in life? There would be plenty time for settling down in the future. A shiver of revulsion ran through him. The words 'settling down' and 'Jonathan Cavendish' didn't really go in the same sentence. Hell, he just had to look at his father and his serial marriages to know what a waste of time getting married was. He had a damn cheek to accuse him of a lack of commitment and responsibility. Look at the way he had treated his mother. She had hardly been cold before he had taken up with some one new. What kind of recommendation for married life was that?

But Rose was different. He suspected when she gave her

heart, it would be for keeps. And the man she gave it to would have to be deserving. She was a challenge. That was it. That was the true reason he was attracted to her. Never before had he been turned down by a woman and it wasn't going to happen now. He would take her on the kind of date that she would like. Something that would convince her that he saw her for who she was and not just another woman. It was obvious that parties on yachts weren't for her. What did she say she liked? Being outdoors. Long walks, sitting in with a book when it was raining outside. Playing her guitar. What else? Picnicking.

He had gone about trying to impress her the wrong way. When they went for their date, he would show her he was sensitive and thoughtful and that he didn't need wild parties or crowds of people. He sat down on a chair by the window and looked out at the lights of London below. An idea was beginning to form in his head. He thought he knew exactly where to take her. Somewhere she would get to know the real Jonathan Cavendish.

CHAPTER EIGHT

JONATHAN collected Rose, as promised, on Saturday morning. He came in and spent a few minutes making small talk with her parents, accepting a cup of coffee from Rose's mother and engaging her father in a dissection of the latest football results.

'Just let me know when you fancy going to another match. I can always get tickets.' He paused. 'I don't suppose you're a cricket fan, are you? I've a couple of tickets for Lords next weekend.'

Rose suppressed a groan. If anything, her father preferred cricket to football. If the two of them started talking cricket, goodness knew when it would stop. She was delighted in her father's improvement. Managing at the football match had given him a lift. Every day he was more like the man he had been before the stroke and for that alone she could have kissed Jonathan.

'Now, you two. That's enough talk about cricket. Shouldn't you and Rose be getting on your way?' Rose's mother stepped in.

Jonathan rose to his feet. 'You know my flat actually overlooks Lords. Why don't you come to lunch the next time there's a match on? We get a great view from the drawing-room window.'

Rose's father slid a glance at his daughter. She knew he would love to go, but didn't want to agree without knowing how his daughter felt about it.

'It's up to you, Dad,' she said. But she gave him a small shake of her head. She really didn't want to be any more beholden to Jonathan than they already were. Despite her best intentions, they were being drawn increasingly into Jonathan's life, and she had to remember that no good could come of it.

'One day perhaps, son,' Rose's father answered.

'Any time, at all. Just let Rose know.' Jonathan jumped to his feet. 'I'll have your daughter back before it gets too late.'

She was back in a time warp. Get her home before it gets too late indeed. Who did he think she was? Cinderella?

'Don't wait up, Mum, Dad. It's just possible I'll go the pub and catch up with the gang when we get back.' Put that in your pipe and smoke it, she thought, pleased that she had made the point. She would decide when she came home. Not him.

'Where are we going?' Rose asked as they sped up the motorway, heading north. She hadn't known what to wear. He could be taking her anywhere, another party, lunch with some of his friends, anywhere. Not knowing, she had decided on a simple summer dress, hoping that it would see her through most eventualities. Her glasses were back in place as, try as she would, she still didn't quite have the hang of the contact lenses. But at least with her glasses she could see, and with her hair tied back in its usual plait, she felt collected and in control.

'You'll have to wait and see,' Jonathan said obliquely. 'I had the damnedest time trying to decide where to take you, but I hope I've got it right.'

'As long as I'm appropriately dressed, I don't care.'

'You would be appropriately dressed even if you wore a sack,' Jonathan replied.

Huh. More of his empty compliments. If she wore a sack, she would look like a bag lady. Who was he trying to kid? On the other hand, Jonathan would look perfectly at home where ever they went. Even in the faded jeans and open-necked, short-sleeved shirt he was wearing. A lock of hair flopped across his forehead and he kept brushing it away as he drove.

After an hour he turned off the motorway and onto a road bordered by fields which, in turn, gave way to a smattering of houses. A sign welcomed them to Cambridge.

'I don't know if this was the right place to take you,' he said. 'But I thought we could hire a punt and stop along the bank for a picnic. I used to do that regularly when I was a student here and I know just the place where we can tie up the boat.'

He looks nervous, Rose thought, her heart melting. She liked this more vulnerable side to him.

'Just as well it's not bucketing with rain, then.' She smiled to let him know she was teasing. 'Isn't this pretty close to where you live?'

'Yes. Cavendish House is just over half an hour to the west. And don't worry, if it had rained, I would have come up with another plan.'

'And the picnic? Did you make it yourself?'

He shook his head, looking sheepish. 'I had it delivered from Harrods.' Then they both laughed. 'Sorry, I guess old habits die hard. But, honestly, Rose, I don't think you would have found anything I made edible.'

He parked the car close to the river, near the town centre. Rose was curious. She knew little about Cambridge other than that it was a famous university town and people punted on the river. 'Show me the college you went to,' she said. She really wanted to know more about him.

He looked perplexed. 'Are you sure you're interested? They all look pretty much the same really.'

'Not to me they don't. I'd love to see where Newton, Darwin and Wordsworth lived and worked. And all the others. Go on. Indulge me.'

He bowed from the waist. 'Your wish is my command. Come on, then. I went to Trinity. In fact, we can hire a punt from there. It's in the main street. Let's see if the porters remember me. They might even let me have a look at the room I was in.' He looked pleased, Rose thought. As if he wasn't used to anyone taking an interest.

He took her by the hand and led her down streets, past several modern buildings and ancient colleges. Rose kept swivelling her head to look at buildings, a round church, a medieval house, but Jonathan propelled her on.

'I want to show you the Bridge of Sighs first,' he said. He was like an excited schoolboy and Rose warmed to this new side of him. He was constantly challenging her pre-conceptions of him.

'It connects the older part of St John's College to the newer part.' He pulled her through heavy wooden gates, past the porter's lodge and into a courtyard. Rose stopped in her tracks. Elegant buildings with intricate stained-glass windows looked down from every side. Students scurried about chatting, books under their arms, oblivious to their surroundings.

'Wow,' she breathed. 'I think if I came here to study I'd never get any work done. I'd just want to sit and take in my surroundings.'

Jonathan looked at her strangely. 'I suppose it is magnificent,' he said. 'I guess I stopped seeing it after a while.'

His mouth turned up at the corners in the way that always made her knees go weak. 'I love seeing it all through your eyes. It's like I never really saw it before.'

Rose's heart squeezed. Why did he keep saying those things? Making her believe he could love her?

'Come on,' he said. 'It gets better.' He led her through another archway that led onto a covered bridge. The stone bridge was intricately carved. Someone must have spent years working on it. Her father would love to see it, as only one artisan could really appreciate the work of another.

'I can see why it's called the Bridge of Sighs,' Rose said. 'It's so beautiful, you just want to sigh with pleasure when you see it.'

'It's named after the Bridge of Sighs in Venice,' Jonathan told her. 'People think it's a copy but, apart from the romanticism of the two bridges, all they have in common is that they are both covered.'

'Hey, don't spoil it for me. Imagine being able to do that.' Rose half smiled. 'I love that so I'll have one built just like it where I live.' She turned to Jonathan. 'That's the kind of world you live in,' she said softly. 'Where money and position makes anything possible.'

'You don't approve?'

'I don't approve or disapprove. I just can't imagine ever being in that position.' And that was the truth. Her world and Jonathan's were miles apart. They could have come from different planets for all they had in common.

'We're not so different, really, you and I, Rose.' Jonathan lifted his hand and tipped her chin until she was looking directly in his eyes.

Strange feelings were fizzing around inside Rose, making her breathless. What was he doing? Was he *trying* to make her fall in love with him? Didn't he know he had already succeeded? She pulled away, putting distance between them. If she stayed near him, she knew she wouldn't be able to stop herself from winding her arms around his neck.

'So where's the college you went to? What did you say it was called?'

'Trinity. We can get to it this way.' He took her hand again and led her towards a building covered in what looked like ivy, but which was what Jonathan told her was Virginia creeper. He pointed upwards. 'My last room was up there. It had a view of the river. Come and see the chapel.'

The chapel was breathtaking with its high arched ceilings and stained-glass windows. Pews lined either side, with a candle at each seat. Rose could imagine evening service, especially in the winter with the snow lying thickly outside and the music of the choir in the soft candlelight. She could appreciate the history in every stone, every worn flagstone and see, in her mind's eye, the centuries of scholars who had walked down the aisle before her.

'Seen enough?' Jonathan said quietly. He had been standing behind her, watching her closely.

She nodded. The more she knew about Jonathan the more she knew how much she wished things could have been different. The Jonathan she was learning about was someone she could imagine a future with. If she had one. The knowledge that soon she would be leaving, probably never to see him again, was tearing her up inside.

'If you want to look around some more, I'll just get the picnic from the car. When you've seen enough, wait for me down by the river. I'll only be a few minutes.'

Rose wandered around, torn up inside. In this chapel she could let herself hope that somehow everything would work out fine and that some kind of miracle would happen, freeing her from the threat of death hanging over her, giving her back her future. But she couldn't let herself think like that. Even if this thing inside her head never changed, even if she lived a long time, she still couldn't ever risk having children.

Pain lanced through her. She would have loved babies. Two, maybe three. Why did life have to be so unfair? She shook her head, angrily brushing away the tears that stung her eyes. There was no point in feeling sorry for herself. She had to stay positive. Back in Edinburgh she had a job she loved, many friends and her music. It was entirely possible that she would have many years in front of her to enjoy life. That would have to be enough. She would *make* it enough. Even if it was to be a life without children—or Jonathan.

By the time she made her way down to the river bank, she had managed to get her emotions back under control and when Jonathan appeared with the picnic basket, she laughed. Grief, how many did he think he was catering for? She couldn't help but look past him, half expecting a stream of his friends to be following close behind. But, no, it seemed as if it really was just the two of them.

'What on earth have you got in there? A kitchen sink? The kitchen?'

'I don't know, but it's damned heavy. They kept on asking me what I wanted and I didn't have a clue, so I said yes to everything. They did say there was wine, plates, a tablecloth. For all I know, they've stuck a set of tables and chairs in there while they were at it.'

'As long as the weight doesn't sink us.'

'Nope, we should be fine.' He lugged the basket down to the bank of the river. After a few words with the person hiring out the punts Jonathan jumped into one and set the basket down. He then helped Rose into the boat. She was delighted to find that her seat was padded and comfortable. She sat back, trailing her hand in the water as Jonathan balanced on the other end of the punt, using the long pole to push away from the side of the river.

Rose closed her eyes, letting the sun warm her face and allowing the gentle splash of water as Jonathan pushed them along to soothe her. They passed under overhanging trees of willows, their long branches reaching into the river. Rose was pleasantly surprised. This was exactly the kind of day out she loved. Jonathan had got it exactly right. It seemed she was always having to reassess her opinion of him. And the more she found out about him, the deeper she fell in love. Her heart contracted with the pain of it. How was she going to find the strength to leave him when the time came? She pushed the thought away, not wanting to spoil another moment of whatever time she had left with him.

'Aren't you going to serenade me?' she asked, looking at him through slitted eyes. 'Isn't that a necessary part of the deal?'

'You obviously haven't heard me sing, or you wouldn't be suggesting it.' He grinned back. 'But you can sing well enough for both of us.'

She shook her head sleepily. 'I can't sing without my guitar. Don't know why. Maybe it's because it gives me something to hide behind.'

As soon as the words were out, she could have bitten her tongue.

Jonathan looked at her curiously. 'Why would you want to hide? Do you truly not know how beautiful you are?'

Rose snorted. 'Nice try, Jonathan, but save the compliments for someone who believes them.'

'Has anyone ever told you that you are the most exasperating woman? Or that when someone gives you a compliment, a sincere compliment, you should accept it with good grace?'

'In which case, thank you, kind sir. And has anyone ever told you that you have a fine punting action?'

Jonathan laughed and passed a hand across his forehead. 'It's much warmer than I thought it would be. Would you mind if I took my shirt off?'

Ever the gentleman. All the men of Rose's acquaintance would have removed their shirts whenever they felt like it. But as Jonathan shrugged out of his, she bit down on her lip. Maybe she should have insisted he keep it on. Now she was going to have to keep her eyes averted from his chest lest he read some of the thoughts that were going through her head. She smiled. A man like Jonathan probably had a very good idea of was going through her mind.

'Would you like to try?' he asked. 'It's really very easy.'

'Sure,' Rose said.

'Okay, come over to where I am.'

Rose picked her way to the stern of the boat, where Jonathan was standing. As she came alongside him, the boat wobbled. In a flash Jonathan wrapped his arm around her waist to steady her. A tingling sensation started in her waist and was soon fizzing around her body. Just for a second she let herself breath in heady scent of his after-shave mixed with the masculine smell of his sweat. Then he released her gently.

'Stand with your legs slightly apart for balance. Then you push the pole all the way down until it touches the bottom. Push hard then pull it all the way up. No, that's not enough.' His hands were on hers, guiding them, and she could feel the heat of his body as he stood behind her. It was making her flustered. 'You have to pull the pole through your hands until you're almost gripping the bottom. And if you want to steer, you push the pole, when it's in the water, to the left or the right. Got it?'

It was much more difficult than Jonathan had made it look. The pole was heavy, unwieldy and Rose was glad Jonathan stayed where he was to help her. Nevertheless, she was determined to do it on her own, and after a little while she got into a rhythm.

'I can manage by myself from here on,' she told Jonathan. 'You sit down.'

'Er, are you sure? It can be hard work.'

She turned to look into his face. 'I can do this. Now, scoot. Go and relax.'

Okay, so their progress wasn't quite as smooth as it had been. The punt had a disconcerting habit of weaving from one side of the river bank to another, almost as if the damn thing had a life of its own, but at least she hadn't crashed it, and they were heading in the right general direction.

'The bridge we're passing under now is called the mathematical bridge,' Jonathan said. Rose allowed herself a quick glance up and away from what she was doing. The bridge was an odd-looking wooden affair, as if a child had taken giant wooden Meccano and stuck it all together. It didn't look very mathematical.

'Why do they call it that?'

'I'm not absolutely sure. Rumour has it that it was originally put together without nuts and bolts and a mathematician at one of the colleges wanted to know how it was done. So he pulled it apart. Only he couldn't get it to go back together without nuts and bolts.'

Rose peered at the bridge again, trying to see better. But with her attention distracted, she suddenly realised that she had forgotten to lift the pole from the water and it was now behind her. Panicking lest she drop the pole into the river, she held on for dear life. But all that happened was that she was pulled out of the punt and into the water.

She shrieked as she was submerged in water the colour of pea soup. Disoriented, she bobbed to the surface, gasping.

Jonathan had retrieved an oar from the bottom of the punt and was making his way back to her.

'You should have told me you fancied a swim,' he said, reaching an arm out to her. 'I would have found a better place.'

Rose was mortified and scowled when she saw the broad grin on his face.

She grabbed his hand and found herself unceremoniously hauled back into the punt where she lay gasping like a fish that had just been landed.

'Are you okay?' Jonathan had lost the smile and was looking concerned. But Rose could have sworn there was a hint of laughter in his words.

'Apart from the fact I feel like a prize idiot and that I'm soaked, yes, I'm fine. You could even say I've never been better.' She glared at him, but then despite herself she had to laugh. It hadn't been Jonathan's fault and from his point of view it must have been funny.

Jonathan retrieved the pole from the water.

'Shall we go back?'

'I'd rather get dried out first. I don't fancy having to walk through Cambridge town centre like this.'

'The place I was going to stop is just a little further.'

A few metres on and Rose was being helped out of the punt onto dry land. Jonathan heaved the picnic basket on shore and opened it. He pulled out a white linen tablecloth.

'Take this,' he said 'Remove your wet things and wrap this around you.' He pointed to some trees. 'There's a little hollow over there. You can't be seen unless someone actually stands over you. Your things will dry out in the sun.'

It was getting worse and worse. But Rose knew the sensible thing was to do as he suggested. The alternative, waiting for her clothes to dry while she was actually in them, wasn't really an option. She would freeze.

In the relative privacy of the hollow, she slipped out of her sundress. Leaving on her bra and pants, she wrapped the sheet around her toga style. Making sure the ends were firmly tucked in, she laid her dress on the grass to dry. At least she had taken her shoes off when she had first stepped on to the punt, otherwise they'd be ruined.

By the time she returned, Jonathan had emptied the picnic basket. He raised an eye at her unconventional outfit before opening a Thermos flask and pouring a cup of steaming-hot coffee.

'Here, this will warm you up.' Then he laughed. 'You look like a Greek goddess in that get-up.'

Rose squirmed with embarrassment under his gaze. Greek goddess, her foot. More like a drowned rat, she would have thought.

He handed her his shirt. 'Put this round your shoulders. It will help keep you warm.'

Rose shrugged into the shirt, which smelled faintly of him. It came to just above her knees and realising it would cover the essentials she slithered out of the tablecloth. Now she felt almost normal again. She used the tablecloth to blot the worst of the river from her hair.

'So much for the tablecloth, I'm afraid.' She laid it next to her dress. The sun would dry it along with her clothes.

'You're still cold.' Jonathan reached out and took her feet in his hands. He began massaging them with the pads of his thumbs. Delicious ripples ran from her feet before pooling in her belly. She tried to pull her feet away, but Jonathan held them firmly. Giving up, she relaxed, propping herself on her elbows and closing her eyes, giving in to the interesting sensations his touch was provoking. The sun emerged from the clouds, warming her face. In the distance she could hear laughter as children played and the gentle sound of the breeze through the leaves of the tree. In all her dreams she would never have imagined this scenario. She and Jonathan, just the two of them, as if they were meant to be together, for ever. If she had known, she would have run and kept on running. Fate was cruel. To show her love now, to give her a glimpse of what might have been, was so unfair.

'That's better,' Jonathan said, releasing her feet. 'Now, what about something to eat?'

Rose wasn't sure whether she could eat anything. Her mouth was as dry as dust. She nodded, not trusting herself to speak. Jonathan unpacked the basket, laying out a bottle of wine, glasses, china plates and cutlery. Next came the food. There were tiny quiches, olives, crusty bread, cheese, cold meats. As Rose had suspected, there was enough to feed an army. Her mouth began to water. It had been a long time since breakfast.

Jonathan lifted an olive. 'You like?' he asked with a quirk of his lips. Rose nodded.

He held the olive to her lips. Her eyes looked into his and her breath stopped in her throat as her chest tightened. Involuntarily her lips parted and he popped the olive into her mouth. He watched as she chewed slowly, never taking his eyes off her. Rose's heart was beating like a pneumatic drill and she couldn't believe he didn't hear it. He trailed a finger across her lips, catching a slick of olive oil. Then slowly, ever so slowly, he leaned forward and placed his mouth gently on hers. Her head swam as she tasted him. The firm pressure of his mouth. His tongue flicking across hers. He groaned and pulled her into his arms where she rested between his long legs. His kisses grew more demanding. Rose gave in to the sensations coursing through her body, returning kiss for kiss. Letting her hands drift behind his head to pull him closer, revelling in the taste of him, the warmth of his skin, the solid strength of his muscles.

He trailed a hand across her neck, sending sparks of desire coursing through her. His hand slipped under the shirt she was wearing, searching, caressing her skin until she thought she would go mad with her need from him.

They lay down, stretching their bodies along each other, straining to meet along their whole length. She could feel the hardness of his desire for her against her hips and she shifted her body so that she fitted against him perfectly.

'I've never met anyone like you,' Jonathan said eventually. 'I can't believe I've lived almost thirty years without meeting you. I think I've been looking for you all my life.'

A cold breeze fluttered down Rose's spine. This wasn't supposed to happen. She wasn't supposed to fall in love with him, or him with her. It was meant to be harmless fun. No broken hearts on either side. A few more days, then she'd be out of his life for good. The sun vanished behind a cloud. She shivered.

'You're cold,' Jonathan said. He reached out a hand and pulled her to her feet. 'Why don't we take the rest of this back to my place? I can light a fire, and we can eat the rest of the picnic in bed.' His eyes were glowing. There was no mistaking his intent. His green eyes were dark, almost pleading.

Rose knew she should run, but she also knew she couldn't. If all she had was this one night, then she had to have it. She could no more deny herself than fly to the moon.

* * *

Jonathan watched as Rose packed the food back into the basket. When he had seen her emerge from behind the tree, her damp hair in disarray, he had thought he had never seen anyone more beautiful, or more desirable. Then when she had slipped into his shirt, her long legs appearing to go for miles where his shirt skimmed her bottom, her nipples evident through the sheer fabric, she had sent his libido into overdrive. He much preferred this Rose even to the elegant woman of the fundraising dinner. Damn. He much preferred this woman to any of the sleek, polished women he had been out with over the years. What he had felt for them had been lust, pure and simple. What he felt for Rose was different. Desire, yes. So much it hit him like a punch to his solar plexus. But so much more. Tenderness. Joy in her company. Delight in seeing his world through her eyes. He reeled from the mixture of fear and excitement as he realised the truth. He loved Rose Taylor. He had been waiting for her all his life, and from now on nothing would ever be the same.

They were silent in the drive to his house. Rose kept sneaking little glances at Jonathan. The air between them sizzled with anticipation. Every time he caught her looking at him he would smile and her heart would flutter as if a hundred butterflies were trapped within her chest.

Inside his house, Jonathan closed the door and, taking her by the hand, led her to the bedroom. Kicking the bedroom door closed, he reached for her and pulled her into his arms.

'I've never wanted a woman the way I want you, Rose,' he said hoarsely.

Rose raised her face to his, knowing that whatever the next few days, weeks and months brought, she was exactly where she wanted to be for the rest of her life.

She wound her arms around his neck then his mouth was on hers and she gave herself up to him.

Much later they cuddled up in front of the fire, and finished off their picnic.

Rose leaned against his chest. His arms were wrapped around her as they watched the flickering flames.

'It won't be long before I go back,' she said quietly.

She sensed him take a deep intake of breath. 'You don't have to go. Stay with me.'

She twisted her head until she could see his face. 'I'm not talking just about tonight. I mean go back to Edinburgh. I have a life there. A home. Friends. Whatever this is, you and I know it can't last.'

'What do you mean? It can last as long as we both want it to.'

Sadness washed over her. Jonathan couldn't know that each moment could be their last. He couldn't know and, what was more, she was determined he would never know. She knew she could never hurt him like that. This thing in her brain could burst at any time. If it didn't kill her, it could leave her helpless and she would never be a burden on anyone. It scared her more than death.

'We're different, you and I,' she said softly. 'You have your life and I have mine. That's okay.'

Jonathan threw back his head and laughed. 'You think because I'm the son of a lord, because I'll inherit a title one day, that that means we can't be together. My God, Rose. This is the twenty-first century. Even princes marry who they want.'

'But we're not talking marriage, are we? We hardly know each other.' She shook her head, forcing a laugh. 'Let's not make more of this than it is.' She turned away so she couldn't see his eyes, knowing she was hurting him.

'I know you well enough to know you are everything I ever wanted. But I don't expect you to feel the same. That's why we need time. Time for me to convince you that I'm not beyond redemption.' He smiled wryly. 'Somehow I know my partying days are behind me.' He hugged her tighter. 'Don't give up on me, Rose. Not yet.'

His hands were on her body again. She wished he wouldn't do that. How was she expected to think clearly when her head was full of him? Her body burning at his touch, her need for him so strong? But this right now was all she could offer him. All she had. She turned around and sat facing him, wrapping her legs around his hips.

'Enough talking,' she said, before pulling his face towards hers.

The next days were the most bitter-sweet of Rose's life. She burned every memory of Jonathan into her head. During the day, they would steal kisses, small touches and share glances. Then at night, after she'd been home to check up on her father, he would collect her from her parents' house and drive her back to his town house. As soon as the door closed behind them, they would be in each other's arms, tearing at each other's clothes, often not even making it to the bedroom.

On the rare occasions they didn't see other she would sit in her room, strumming her guitar, composing lyrics to new songs in her head. It was the happiest time of her life—and the saddest. Sometimes her head would ache and she would be terrified it was a sign the aneurysm was going to burst. She spent hours on the internet going over the options, but if she was hoping to find an easy solution she was disappointed. As the doctors had pointed out, there were only two. She could have surgery. Or not. Whatever she decided, the outcome could be the same. Paralysis, possibly death.

Not much of a choice, then. Do nothing and continue to live as she had been. Making the most of every day. But it was a life without a future. A day-to-day existence. A life where she wouldn't marry, have children or, worst of all, Jonathan. And the other option? Have the operation, knowing the consequences, but also knowing it offered at least a chance for a future. One where she was free to love and be loved. Have children. Grow old.

Until she had met Jonathan, doing nothing had made sense. Now she wanted more.

She paced her little room, her throat tightening as she remembered happier times. Her father strong and healthy, the house filled with love and laughter, the future still a merciful blank.

One thing she knew for certain. She couldn't tell Jonathan. He would insist on sticking by her whatever happened, and she couldn't allow that to happen. How soon would it be before his love changed to duty, regret, even loathing. Instinctively she knew he would never leave her.

Neither could she talk to him about it. He would want to help her make a decision. Then whatever she did, whatever the consequences, he would feel responsible. She loved him too much for that. No, only one person could decide what to do, and that was her.

Her aching heart told her the truth before her brain could accept it. She would have the operation. Place her fate in the hands of the gods. She would leave Jonathan behind, convince him somehow she didn't love him, then disappear from his life and have the operation. If it was a success, she would find him again and tell him the truth. And if it wasn't? At least she had set him free to live his life. She had a week left with him. And she would make the most of every minute.

* * *

'So I'll be back next week. On Monday, if that's okay with you?' Vicki propped a hip against the desk. 'I can't believe how much better I feel now that I've stopped being sick.' She dropped a hand to the curve of her belly and Rose felt a stab of longing that almost took her breath away. Now Vicki was coming back, she no longer had an excuse to put it off. Miss Fairweather had scheduled the operation for two weeks' time. Now that she had made the decision, she had told her parents. It had been one of the worst nights of her life. But she had found comfort at last as she had cried in her mother's arms.

Vicki glanced over at Jonathan's closed door. He was seeing a patient. 'He's going to miss you. I don't suppose you are free to cover my maternity leave?'

Rose smiled wryly. Vicki had no idea how much she hoped she would be able to be in a position to do that.

'I still have my job in Edinburgh. They're expecting me back. I don't think you can count on me covering you, although…' she reached out a hand '…I'll come back and see you when the baby is born.' Rose swallowed the lump in her throat. Please, God, let her be telling the truth.

'I'm going to miss you. Hard to imagine returning to the way it was here before you and Jenny.' Vicki indicated Jenny with a nod of her head. 'I think the patients actually prefer Jenny now they're used to her. She makes them laugh.'

'Just as well, then, because Jonathan's offered her a permanent job. Mrs Smythe Jones called into see Jonathan the other day. Apparently she's decided to emigrate to New Zealand to be with her sister.'

Vicki whistled under her breath. 'I didn't think she'd ever leave. This practice has been her life for nearly forty years. She was here when Jonathan's uncle started. She wouldn't retire last year even when Jonathan assured her that the pension the company would settle on her is almost as much as her salary. She said she'd be lonely at home. I guess if she's going to stay with her sister, lack of company won't be an issue.'

The two women turned to look across at Jenny who was patiently listening to the voice on the other end of the phone, offering periodic *oh, dear*s and *poor you*. They smiled at each other. 'I gather Jenny was out at lunch when Mrs Smythe Jones came for her chat. Somehow I can't imagine her letting Jonathan employ Jenny if she had seen the hairdo.'

Over the weeks Jenny's hair had reverted to the spiky look she loved. No one had said anything. Rose had only been glad that the piercings remained at home. Even if Jonathan and his patients accepted the hair, a nose ring was bound to be a step too far.

Rose would be leaving all this behind soon, maybe forever, and the thought was breaking her heart.

CHAPTER NINE

LATER on that day they received word that Lord Hilton had died in his sleep. Rose had become fond of the couple over the last few weeks and when Jonathan broke the news she was unsurprised at how sad she felt.

Jonathan pulled her into his arms and she rested her head there. It felt so good, so safe, and she wished she could stay there for ever. With him she could face anything, except what she feared most.

'How is Lady Hilton taking it?' Rose asked. 'Should I go to her?'

'She said to tell you that she is very grateful for everything you did for them. She has friends and family around right now, but she asks if you would come to the funeral. She says Giles wanted it.'

'Of course I'll go,' Rose said softly. She looked up at him. 'You'll be there?'

'I'm always going to be there, Rose Taylor,' Jonathan said firmly. 'Don't you know that by now?' The look of love in his eyes made her heart shatter. 'She's also asked if you could back to the house with the others after the funeral. She has something to tell you.'

Rose could hardly speak. Her throat was tight. He loved

her. She knew that without doubt, even if he hadn't said the words. Little did he know they could only have these last few days to do them for the rest of their lives. She had handed in her notice in Edinburgh, effective immediately, as the operation had been scheduled for the end of the next week. But she wouldn't tell Jonathan. For his sake, she would make him believe that she wasn't in love with him, that she wanted to go back to her life in Edinburgh. It would be hard to convince him, and the thought of hurting him was tearing her apart, but for his sake she had to make him believe her. If the operation was a success she would come back to him and tell him everything. If not? At least he would be free to live his life.

That evening Jonathan came down to her local again. They had been a couple of times and Jonathan was surprised how relaxing he found the pub and how welcoming Rose's friends were. Every time they had been there, Rose had taken her guitar and sung. Every day he fell deeper in love.

Tonight she took her guitar and perched on a chair on the stage. She caught his eye across the crowded room.

'I've a new song I'd like to sing tonight,' she said softly. 'It's something I composed recently. I hope you all like it. It's called, "All my tomorrows".'

Her voice was husky as she sang directly to him. The song was about love and loss, about making the most of every moment. The last line of the chorus was 'All my tomorrows are wrapped up in you today,' and as she sang the line her voice cracked a little. Something in the way she sang the song and in the way her eyes filled as the last notes died away scared him.

When she'd finished singing, she smiled a little shakily. The room erupted as everyone clapped and cheered, but

Jonathan sat stunned. If he hadn't known better, he would think she was saying goodbye.

Lord Hilton's funeral was held a couple of days later in the family church. Summer had arrived and the mourners gathered under a blazing sun. Rose tried not to think that soon a similar crowd might be gathered to say their last farewells to her. Instead, she resolutely pushed the thought away. She wasn't going to waste a moment of whatever time she had left thinking gloomy thoughts.

And Giles's funeral wasn't gloomy. It was a celebration of a remarkable man who, as it was pointed out, had stayed in love with his wife of fifty years right until the end.

Jonathan's father was there and after the burial he came up to Rose.

'It's good to see you again, my dear,' he said. 'Won't you ask Jonathan to bring you home for dinner so we can get to know each other better?'

Rose looked him directly in the eye. If anything happened to her, Jonathan would need his father. She didn't know if she could make things right between father and son, but she had to try.

'I don't know if I can persuade him,' she said softly. 'He seems to be very angry with you.' She took a deep breath and hurried on before she lost her nerve. 'He seems to think that you don't care about him. That perhaps you never did.'

Lord Cavendish looked aghast. Whether it was because Rose had the audacity to talk to him about what he almost certainly saw as a private matter, or whether it was because he didn't want to acknowledge the way his son felt, Rose couldn't be sure.

Suddenly his expression relaxed and he smiled grimly.

'I can see why my son is so besotted with you,' he said. 'But he can't think I don't care about him. My God, he is the most important thing in my life. Why would he think otherwise?'

'Maybe because you sent him away to boarding school after his mother died? I understand he's never lived at home since.'

Lord Cavendish pulled a hand through his still dark and thick hair that was so much like his son's. 'I sent him away because I thought it was for the best,' he said stiffly. 'I was away so much on business and without his mother...' He shrugged. 'There would be no one at home to look after him.'

Rose plunged on. Out of the corner of her eye, she could see Jonathan chatting to Lady Hilton.

'He was only a child,' she said. 'And you took him away from everything he knew and loved, just when he had suffered the most devastating loss. Didn't it occur to you that he'd need his father? At least for a while?'

Jonathan's father looked even more taken aback, if that was possible. He looked into the distance. 'I met Jonathan's mother when I was a young man at university. I loved her instantly. She was like a bright star in my otherwise lonely existence. A bit like I suspect you are to Jonathan. Like you, she didn't come from aristocracy and my parents didn't approve. It was different back then. Nobody cares these days. But it didn't matter what they thought. I couldn't imagine a future without her. I would have married her even if my family had thrown me on the street.' He smiled. 'Luckily it didn't come to that. We married and had a few short years together. She was a painter, you know. I understand from Lady Hilton that you compose songs? My Clara and you were very much alike. I was working all hours setting up my businesses while she painted. I guess it made her less lonely. Then Jonathan came along and I thought she would miss me less, so I spent even more time away from home.' His eyes were bleak. 'I missed her every second, but I thought we had years together.' His voice was hoarse as if tears weren't far away.

Unable to stop herself, Rose touched him gently on the arm, wanting to let him know she understood.

'Then when Jonathan was five, my darling Clara died. I thought I'd go mad with the pain of it. Every time I looked at Jonathan I saw his mother. I couldn't bear it. I had to throw myself into work. And I had to know they were being looked after. So, yes. I sent him away. I regret it now. I hardly know my son, and it's my fault.'

'But you married again. Several times, I gather.' Rose smiled to take the sting from her words.

'I wanted what I had with Clara, but it was no use. I never found it again.' He looked directly into her eyes.

'Have you ever been in love, Rose? I mean so in love that it feels that he's the missing part of your soul?'

Rose bit hard on her lip to stop the tears. She nodded.

'Then you'll know that no one else can ever measure up, no matter how they try. Your soul remains in two bits. A chunk of you is always missing, no matter how much you search.'

'But you still have part of her. In Jonathan,' Rose said, forcing the words past her frozen throat.

She followed his gaze until it rested on Jonathan. His eyes softened. 'I know I do. But I think I may have left it too late.'

'It's never too late.' Then, at the realisation of what she'd said, she added, 'At least, it's not for you two. Talk to him. I know it's difficult. But tell him what you told me, about Clara. I think you'll find he understands.'

Lord Cavendish gave her a long appraising look. He

grinned and Rose's heart skipped a beat. In that instant she could see the man Jonathan would become as he aged. What she would give to be around to see it. 'I think I'm going to like having you around, Rose Taylor,' Lord Cavendish said slowly. 'Now, if you'll excuse me, I think I should go and talk to my son.'

Rose watched as Lord Cavendish walked over to his son. He placed a hand on Jonathan's shoulder and after a few words the two men walked off together.

Later, back in the Hiltons' home, Sophia asked Rose to come into her study for a few moments. Rose was baffled. The day was taking its toll on her and she didn't know how much she could hold it all together. But if Sophia Hilton could keep a brave face even if she was breaking up inside, so could she.

Lady Hilton opened a desk drawer and pulled out an envelope. She handed it to Rose.

'Giles wanted you to have this, my dear. In the short time we've known you, we've come to look on you as a daughter.'

Intrigued, Rose opened the envelope. Inside was a cheque, the sum of which made her gasp.

'What on earth...? You can't possibly mean to give this to me. It's far too generous and completely unnecessary.'

Sophia smiled. 'It's for your wedding. Giles and I both see the way things are with you and Jonathan. We don't have daughters of our own, and it gives us both...' She drew a shaky breath. ' I mean, the thought of you using it to get married gave us so much pleasure.'

'But I'm not getting married. J-Jonathan and I haven't even s-spoken of it,' Rose stuttered.

'But you will, my dear.'

Rose thrust the envelope back at Sophia. 'I'm sorry. I

really can't take this. There isn't going to be a wedding, whatever you might think.' Her throat was clogging with tears and she could barely speak.

'Don't you believe he loves you? Is that what you think? Or do you think he won't marry you because you have some misguided idea about class? But, my dear, Jonathan's mother was the same and it didn't stop his father from marrying her. And back then people did make more of it.'

It was all too much. The funeral. The Hiltons' kindness. That a couple she barely knew had been thinking of her even while going through the most horrible and sad time. Knowing that her days with Jonathan were about to come to an end. She couldn't bear it.

'I'm sorry,' she managed. 'I really have to go.' And before she could disgrace herself by breaking down completely, she fled.

CHAPTER TEN

ON WHAT was to be their last night together, although of course Jonathan had no idea that it would be, Rose suggested they spend the night at his house near Cambridge. It was where they had first made love and the place she had been happiest in all her life.

If Jonathan suspected something, he gave no sign of it. In fact, he looked as if he was up to something. There was a hidden air of excitement about him that Rose had never seen before. Her heart was cracking with the unbearable realisation that this could be the last time she would ever be in his arms.

'We can pop into to see Mary first, if you don't mind. She's back at work after her time off and I want to check she's not doing too much.'

'Of course,' Rose agreed. The doctors at the hospital had diagnosed angina but with some changes to her diet and some additional gentle exercise they were hopeful she would live for many years yet.

They found Mary ensconced in her kitchen domain. The older lady had lost a little weight and was delighted to see them.

'Jonathan and Rose! Thank you for coming to see

me.' She sent Jonathan a mock severe look. 'Although how you smelled my baking all the way from London is anyone's guess.'

'Is Father here?' Jonathan asked Mary, after hugging her.

'He is. Thankfully without that woman. She seems to have been chucked. Thank God he saw sense before it was too late.' She dropped her voice. 'Why don't you go and see him? He's always talking about you, you know. Telling me how proud you make him and how very proud your mother would be.'

Jonathan smiled awkwardly.

'So he keeps telling me. This new father is taking a bit of getting used to,' he said. 'I wonder what brought about this change.' But the look he slid Rose told her he knew about their conversation, although until now, he hadn't mentioned it.

'Ah, my dear boy. It makes an old woman happy to know that you two have made up. He loves you, you know.'

Jonathan shuffled his feet uncomfortably. 'And I him, Mary. Now, any chance of us raiding your kitchen for some food? I'm going to steal Rose away for a private dinner in my cottage.'

His look sent bitter-sweet memories ricocheting around Rose's head. More than anything she didn't want to waste a single moment that they had left.

'Can't you stay for dinner? Your father would love to have the company.'

Jonathan looked at Rose for agreement and when she nodded her head he said, 'Okay. I suppose Rose and I will have plenty other times.'

Blast Lord Cavendish and blast her interference, Rose thought briefly. But wasn't this exactly what she'd engineered? Jonathan wasn't to know this was their last night.

Dinner seemed to go on for ever, although Lord Cavendish was surprisingly amusing company. It was good to see the two men, so alike, sharing jokes and later their memories of Clara. It seemed astonishing to Rose that Jonathan knew so little about his mother. Lord Cavendish included Rose in the conversation, making it obvious that his interest in her was genuine.

Finally, when it was almost ten o'clock, dinner was over and Jonathan made their excuses.

Once inside his house, he reached out for and brought his mouth down on hers as if he were drowning and she were a life raft. Although Rose wanted nothing more than to be naked beside him in his bed, there was another memory she needed to leave him with. A memory she hoped that when she was gone he would recall and know deep down that she had loved him and her leaving hadn't been her choice. She wanted to sing to him one last time, so that one day in the future he would understand why she had acted as she had.

She disentangled herself from his arms. 'I want you to sit there and not move,' she ordered.

Bemused, Jonathan wasn't having it. 'No way. Right now I want you too much to keep my hands off you.' And then he was kissing her again and Rose was lost. She gave herself up to him greedily, wanting to burn every part of him into her soul.

Later she lay in his arms and he looked at her through half-closed lids.

'I love you, Rose,' he said huskily. 'And I'll go to my grave loving you.'

Rose's heart sang. But she couldn't say the words he longed to hear. If she did, he would never stop looking for her.

She forced a laugh. 'Wow! That's a surprise. I had no

idea you felt that way.' She slipped out of bed and started to get dressed, avoiding his eyes. If he saw her eyes, she knew her anguish would be plain to see.

She sensed his puzzlement.

'Is that all you have to say?' He leapt out of bed and came to stand behind her, wrapping her in his arms. 'Don't you get it? I love you and I want to spend the rest of my life with you. I want you to do me the honour of becoming my wife, Rose.'

Rose wriggled out of his grasp. 'But I don't want to marry you. I'm sorry, Jonathan, whatever we had, whatever this was…' She indicated the unmade bed with a sweep of her hand. 'For me it was just an interlude. Some fun. I'm going back to Edinburgh. My life is there.'

'Going back? You can't. What about us? Even if you don't love me now, I know you feel something.' He pulled his hand through his hair. 'I can't be wrong. Everything tells me I'm not wrong.'

She forced herself to continue dressing.

'I'm sorry, Jonathan, I could never marry someone like you. All you're really interested in is having a good time. When I marry…' Her voice cracked and she breathed deeply, knowing how much she was hurting him. 'It will be to someone who knows that there is more to life than having fun. Someone I can respect.'

'My God, Rose, I know I'm not the kind of man you would have wished for yourself. But I love you. I can change. No more parties, I promise. I didn't tell you but I've taken a part-time job at the local hospital. I'm going to complete my surgical training. It's what I always wanted to do.'

'What about your uncle's practice?'

'I'll employ someone else to keep it on. You've made me realise that I need more in my life. What I had before I met you was meaningless. Empty.'

'You shouldn't change your whole life around because of me,' Rose said sadly, 'especially when after tonight I'm no longer going to be in it.'

She turned and looked him directly in the eye. She knew the tears would come later. But she had to hurt him now, even if it broke her heart.

'I've had a good time, Jonathan. You showed me a different side to life and I'll always be grateful to you. But it's over. I'm going back to Edinburgh and there's nothing you can do, or say, that'll make me change my mind. I don't love you and I never will.'

Jonathan's green eyes turned cool.

'You've been stringing me along all this time, haven't you?' he said bitterly. 'None of this meant anything to you, did it?' He pulled his jeans over his hips. 'Well, I can't say I haven't deserved to be taken for a ride. God knows, I've hurt others. Now it seems it's my turn.' He laughed sourly. 'And the irony of it all is that I've spent all my life not believing that it was possible to love one person for the whole of my life. Until you showed me that that was exactly how my father felt about my mother. I guess at least I have you to thank for that.'

Rose recoiled from the look in his eyes. She longed to put her arms around him and tell him the truth. But she couldn't. If she touched him, she'd be undone.

He slipped his shirt on and picked up his car keys. 'I think I should take you home now.'

CHAPTER ELEVEN

ROSE lay on the hospital bed, feeling groggy. The premeds were taking the edge off her anxiety, but couldn't quite take it away. She wondered if these few minutes would be the last she would know.

'You can still change your mind,' her mother whispered. Behind the forced smile, Rose could see her terror.

Rose smiled faintly. She reached for her mother's hand. 'I've made up my mind, Mum. I'm going through with it.' Her head had been shaved where they were planning to operate. Knowing that they would do that, she had gone to the hairdresser yesterday and insisted they crop her hair. She hardly recognised herself. And not just because of the haircut. Her face was gaunt, her eyes haunted. She wondered what Jonathan would think of her new hairstyle. She closed her eyes. She could see him clearly, his smile, his eyes. She could almost taste his skin. She pushed the image away. She couldn't think of Jonathan. Not now. If she did she might not have the strength to go through with it; she might just persuade herself that whatever days she had left were better spent with him. But she knew she could never risk breaking his heart.

'Please let me call him.' It was as if her mother could

read her mind. She had begged Rose to let Jonathan know, but Rose had held steadfast. Instead, she had written the words to the song she had written for him, and asked her mother to give it to him should anything happen to her. Her father was at home, refusing to say what might be his last goodbyes to his only child. His doctor had advised him against coming to the hospital earlier, worried that the added strain would set him back.

'I'll be there when you wake up,' he had said before she left for the hospital. He had held her and kissed her hair, murmuring words that she remembered from her childhood.

'We've been through this, Mum, and you promised.' Rose squeezed her mother's hand. 'And if something happens to me, if I survive the operation but am brain damaged, remember you swore you won't tell him. I'd rather he remembered me how I was.'

'But…' her mother smiled weakly, '…you're going to be fine. Everything is going to be just fine.'

All too soon, they came to take her to Theatre. Rose could hardly bear the pain in her mother's eyes as they kissed for what could be the last time. Then she was in Theatre and the anaesthetist was asking her to count backwards from a hundred. Now she allowed herself to think of Jonathan. To bring his dear face into her mind, and as she drifted off, she imagined his lips on hers.

Jonathan was restless. Since Rose had left him, nothing could distract him from the thoughts and memories of her. He couldn't bring himself to attend any of the parties or lunches to which he still got invited. All he wanted was Rose. The only thing that kept him sane were his patients and his work. If it hadn't been for them he would have gone stark, staring mad. Several times, more often than he cared to count, he had considered jumping on a plane to Edinburgh to go searching for her. Maybe he could still persuade her to come back to him. He just couldn't believe she didn't love him, even a little bit.

Picking up his car keys, he made up his mind. He would call in on her parents. See how her father was doing. Maybe he could get an address out of them. At the very least, he could be where she lived. If he couldn't be with her, being where she was until recently would be the next best thing.

Half an hour later, he rang the doorbell. A taxi pulled up behind his car. After a long pause Rose's father came to the door. He was still leaning on his stick, but Jonathan was pleased to see he seemed to hardly need it. The droop to the side of his mouth had also improved. All in all he appeared to be making a good recovery. But it was the look in his eyes that shocked Jonathan. Never before had he seen him look so sad, or so frightened, not even when he had first met him.

'What is it?' Jonathan asked. 'Is something wrong?' His heart was pounding like a runaway train. Had something happened to Rose? Please, God, no.

Tommy shook his head despairingly. 'I'm sorry, Jonathan, I can't talk to you at the moment. My taxi's waiting for me.'

'Where's Rose's mother? Why isn't she here? Something's wrong. Is it Rose?' He blocked Tommy's path. He had to know.

'Please, Jonathan, I don't have time for this. I need to get to the hospital.'

'The hospital?' His alarm was growing stronger. There was no way that Rose's mother would let Tommy go by himself. There was something wrong. He knew it. It took every ounce of his strength not to shake the fragile man in front of him. Tommy looked at him steadily. 'She made us promise not to tell you. I think she was wrong, but I promised her.'

'Just tell me where she is.'

'I can't. I need to get to the hospital, but if you were to follow the taxi there, I couldn't stop you, could I?'

Jonathan read the message in his eyes. It was all he was going to get and it would have to do. But as he followed the painfully slow taxi through the thick London traffic, his mind was whirling with images he couldn't bear. His Rose. Dead or dying. Here in London. Why had she told them not to tell him? He didn't care. All he wanted was to know that she was all right. If he knew that, he could live the rest of his life without her. As long as he knew she was in it somewhere.

His fear almost threatened to crush him as the taxi pulled up outside the London Hospital for Neurological Sciences. Little clicks were going on inside his head. The sadness in her eyes. Her refusal to talk about the future. That song she had composed. What had the last line been? *All my tomorrows are wrapped up in you today.* What hadn't she been telling him?

Fear clutching his throat, he abandoned his car on a double yellow line—he couldn't care less if he never saw it again—and caught up with Tommy. He placed his hand under his elbow.

'She's here, isn't she?' he said flatly.

Tommy simply nodded. Something squeezed Jonathan's chest when he saw tears glisten in Tommy's eyes.

'Is she alive? Please, you have to tell me that.'

'I don't know,' Tommy said slowly. 'She's in Theatre, having an operation for a brain aneurysm. It seems it's the same thing that caused my stroke. The doctors knew it was the hereditary kind, so they screened her for it.' His voice cracked.

'And they found something?' Jonathan could hardly breathe. It all made sense now. Terrible, heart-breaking sense.

'She's being operated on today. I'm here to sit with her mother and wait. We don't know if she'll survive the operation.'

'Survive?' he could hardly force the words past his clenched jaw. 'Of course she's going to survive.' But try as he may, he couldn't completely remove the fear from his voice. 'It's Rose we're talking about. And the woman I know is a fighter.'

When Rose opened her eyes she thought she was dreaming. Either that, or she had died and she was in heaven. But as soon as he spoke, she knew this was no dream and that she was very much alive.

'Hey, how're you feeling?' His eyes looked different somehow. Almost damp. As if he'd being crying. Which was ridiculous. Jonathan didn't cry.

'I'm alive?' The words were all she could manage. A vague memory of her parents' faces, their eyes bright with tears, swam into her head.

Jonathan slipped a hand under her shoulders and helped her take a sip of cold water. It tasted like nectar. She was alive and she could hardly believe it.

'The operation went well. Even better than the surgeon hoped. You are going to be fine. You have to take it easy for a while, but after that you can do whatever you want.'

She still couldn't quite believe what he was telling her. She wriggled her toes. That was good. Then she stretched her fingers. Movement there too. She could move, she could speak, she could see and she could understand.

Her eyes were growing heavy. 'You found me,' she whispered, before she let herself give in to sleep.

He was still there when she opened them again. He was watching her, as if he couldn't bear to tear his eyes away from her.

'Hello, love.' Her mother's voice came from the other side of the bed. Beside her was her father. They were smiling and holding hands. Her mother stood and kissed her on the cheek. 'Welcome back to us.' She stood back and let Tommy come closer. Rose watched a fat tear slide down his cheek. Rose had never seen her father cry before and her heart ached for him.

'My child,' he said simply. 'My baby girl. You are going to have a long and happy life. Thank God.'

'We're going to leave you two alone for a few minutes,' her mother said. 'Jonathan refuses to go home until he's sure you're okay.'

She swivelled her head to look at him. His face was grey and he was unshaven. How long had he been here? Had she imagined seeing him earlier when she'd first come round?

'Don't try to speak,' he said. 'You've been sedated since the operation and you need time to rest.'

'How long?' she whispered.

'Two days. Two of the longest, hardest, scariest days of my life. How much worse for you and your parents to have lived with this for all these weeks.'

He touched her cheek with his finger. 'You need to sleep now. But when you wake up, I'll still be here. I'm never going to leave your side again.' He smiled sadly. 'No matter what you say. You're stuck with me.'

CHAPTER TWELVE

THE day was bright with promise. The sun shining just for them as Rose walked down the flower-edged path towards Jonathan. Her parents were sitting in the front row. Apart from a slight droop to the side of his mouth and a residual limp, her father had made an almost complete recovery. These days he was forever telling whoever would listen that his stroke had been the best thing that ever happened to him. After all, if it hadn't happened, Rose would never have discovered she had inherited the condition. He never finished the sentence, and he didn't need to. If her condition hadn't been discovered, if the aneurysm hadn't been removed, it was possible she might not be here. Not walking down the aisle to the man who in a few minutes would become her husband.

Instead of the traditional wedding march, a band was playing the song she had written for Jonathan. 'All my tomorrows are wrapped up in you today.' Rose's heart soared. She and Jonathan had many, many tomorrows in store for them. She still wasn't sure how she felt about being the future Lady Cavendish, but what did anything matter when she had Jonathan by her side? And he had promised it wouldn't change a thing—except perhaps end his party days. And that, he said, was no loss at all. He had everything he'd ever dreamed of. With the possible exception of four or five children. And they both agreed it would be fun making their babies.

She finished her walk up the aisle and as Jonathan looked at her, she caught her breath. She knew without a shadow of doubt that he loved her more than she'd ever thought it possible to be loved.

Holding her hand, his voice ringing out, he repeated the words from the Bible.

'"Do not urge me to leave you or turn back from following you; for where you go, I will go, and where you lodge, I will lodge. Your people shall be my people, and your God my God."' He touched her lips with his.

'Remember that, my darling. No matter what, you must never ever shut me out again. Do you promise me?' His voice was urgent, the pain of the days when he had thought he would lose her still evident in his voice.

Rose grinned at him. 'Are you kidding? You and I are stuck with each other. For better for worse, for richer, for poorer. In sickness and in health. And I for one am going nowhere. Not ever.' Happiness bubbled up inside her, filling her with a joy she had never known was possible. 'I'm here for all your tomorrows. I promise.'

THE ROYAL
DOCTOR'S BRIDE

JESSICA MATTHEWS

To everyone who ever pretended to be a princess.
I hope you all found your prince…

CHAPTER ONE

"DR SUTTON, we have a problem."

In the process of jotting down a script and mentally calculating a drug dosage for her patient, Gina Sutton answered absent-mindedly, "I'll be right there."

"This can't wait too long," Nurse Lucy Fields urged.

A warning note in her tone pulled Gina's attention away from her task. She glanced at the normally unflappable woman and saw the distress written all over her face. While the unusual was the norm in Belmont Memorial's Emergency Department, something had upset their nursing supervisor.

"Noted," she said calmly, before turning back to her patient, forty-year-old Jim Pearce. "According to the X-rays, you've sprained, not broken, your wrist. You'll need to keep it immobilized for several weeks to give the muscles time to recover. Here's a prescription…" she tore off the sheet "…for an anti-inflammatory. Take as directed. And if your wrist isn't better in a few weeks, either come back or visit your family doctor. Any questions?"

Jim shook his head.

"Just remember, no more hammering or heavy lifting in the meantime," she cautioned. "Wearing a splint for support doesn't mean you can do everything you did before. If you don't give yourself time to heal, you'll have worse problems."

His face colored slightly, as if she'd read his mind and knew his intent. "OK. A few weeks is all, right?"

"At least three, maybe more."

"Doctor," Lucy urged from the door.

Telling her patient goodbye, Gina followed Lucy into the hallway. "What's the big problem that couldn't wait two more minutes?"

"It's Dr Nevins. He's gone *crazy*!"

"What's he done now?" Gina asked tiredly, already wondering what mistake she'd have to correct this time. Bill Nevins may be the Director of Emergency Services, but an intern could do a better job. On the few occasions when he assisted with a trauma, he was usually more hindrance than help. If he didn't have connections, she believed, he wouldn't have been hired in the first place.

"The man has completely lost his sanity," Lucy declared. "He's storming around his office and when I tried to go inside, he threw his glass paperweight at me!"

"He's always been high-strung," Gina soothed. "What upset him today?"

"I don't know, but he was fine until he got a phone call. You have to talk to him, Gina. You're the only one in the entire department he'll listen to."

For some reason, during the two years she'd been in Belmont's ER, she'd always been able to reason with the man, even when he was at his most unreasonable. When he'd wanted to fire a nurse for dropping a syringe during a code blue, she'd convinced him to give the poor girl a second chance. When he refused to spend the money to replace their defibrillator, she'd calmly reminded him of how costly a potential lawsuit would be, not to mention how his reputation would suffer.

Now, apparently, her negotiation skills would be needed once again to deal with his latest temper tantrum.

"All right," Gina said resignedly, as she handed over Jim

Pearson's chart and tucked her pen into the breast pocket of her lab coat. "Let's beard the lion in his den."

To her surprise, his door stood open and she cautiously walked in, noticing how the normally neat office now looked as if a tornado had whirled through. Papers and medical books covered the floor, boxes stood on top of Bill's desk, and file drawers were yanked off their tracks. Even the philodendron she'd brought to soften the stark white walls lay on its side, dirt spilling out of the pot across the top of the filing cabinet.

"What's up?" she asked calmly as she righted the plant.

Bill paused from riffling through the papers on his desk. "I've been fired, that's what."

It's about time, she thought. "Really?" she asked, trying to sound horrified but certain she failed miserably. "Whatever for?"

He waved aside her question. "The reasons don't matter. The point is, I've given my all to this place, and this is how they repay me."

Privately, Gina wondered how a man who worked three, maybe four hours a day could claim "he'd given his all", but it wasn't her place to argue. Her goal now was to bring calm to a potentially unstable situation.

"What happens now?" she asked, more concerned about the repercussions to their department rather than to Bill's professional life.

He waved furiously at the wall clock. "Who knows? I have thirty minutes to pack up and get out. *Thirty minutes*," he ranted. "After ten years of unfailing service, struggling to operate on the shoestring budget they gave me…well, it's unthinkable and insulting!" He grabbed his coffee-mug, then hefted it in his hand. In the next breath, he heaved it at the metal filing cabinet.

Gina didn't have time to dodge before the ceramic cup shattered into a hundred pieces. A sharp sting bit into her cheek and she instinctively touched her face. No real damage as far as she could tell. Although she was somewhat disconcerted because Bill had never injured anyone before during one of his tirades, the burden of restoring his reason clearly fell to her.

She ignored the lingering discomfort and began in her most placating tone, "Now, Bill—"

She didn't get past his name before a tall, dark-haired man burst into the office, wearing an expensively tailored dark gray suit and a grim expression.

"Throw one more thing and you'll be flying through the air, too," he snarled as he moved in front of her, effectively blocking her from her irate superior. In the next instant, he whipped out a snowy white handkerchief and pressed it into her hand. "You'd better take care of that, Gina."

Too curious about the scene unfolding, especially when two more men arrived who were more stocky and not quite as tall or as handsome, she didn't ask how this stranger knew her name. She simply nodded and did as she was told.

To her surprise, a large smear of blood—*her* blood—stained the expensive cotton square. Quickly, she pressed it to her cheek again, more curious about the drama than about her scratch, especially when her rescuer approached Bill behind his desk.

"You, Dr Nevins," the authoritative man accused in a deep, stern voice, "have forfeited your right to collect your things. Leave the premises immediately."

Bill straightened to his full five feet five inches and his beady little eyes narrowed. "Who are *you* to tell *me* what I can and cannot do?"

"I'm your replacement," the fellow stated calmly and firmly. "Goodbye, Dr Nevins."

He raised one hand and in the blink of an eye the two men moved round the desk from opposite directions to grab Bill's arms and lead him toward the door.

"But I didn't hurt her on purpose," Bill screeched. "Tell him, Gina."

Everyone's gaze landed on Gina. "Bill wouldn't hurt me," Gina responded. "Not intentionally."

Her handsome knight folded his arms and regarded her cooly. "A man with such an obvious lack of control can't be trusted."

"You can't do this," Bill shouted. "I have thirty minutes left."

Bill's replacement, with his regal bearing and handsomely aristocratic features, looked down his aquiline nose. "You now have none. Take him away."

"But my things," Bill wailed over his shoulder as the two henchmen literally lifted him off the ground.

"Dr Sutton will ship your personal possessions to you." And with that, the two apparent security guards carried him out, kicking and screaming.

Gina stared at the now empty doorway. "At the risk of sounding completely ridiculous, what just happened?"

"Changing of the guard," the man said as he stood in front of her. "Let me look at that." Without waiting for her permission, he tipped her chin upward, pulled away the handkerchief and peered at her face.

Strangely enough, an attack of self-consciousness swept over Gina. The most handsome man she'd seen in ages had burst into her department like an avenging angel and now was studying her face as if he'd never seen a scratch before.

"It's nothing," she said inanely, extremely conscious of two things—his six-foot-plus frame, which made her feel petite at five foot eight, and a delightfully masculine scent that made her appreciate being a female.

He pressed on her cheekbone and frowned. "You need a stitch."

"I don't think so."

He raised both eyebrows, eyebrows framing chocolate brown eyes that were deep, dark pools. "Are you questioning my medical judgement?"

"I believe so. Yes."

A huge grin spread across his face. The dazzling brilliance of his smile made him seem younger, more approachable, and less formidable.

"At least you're honest," he said.

"It's the best policy," she answered.

"Have a seat," he ordered. "I'll be right back."

She might have obeyed, but it wasn't in her nature to ignore the obvious. Because she weighed her problems more easily if she was busy, she carefully picked up the shattered remnants of Bill's mug while she contemplated the sharp turn that the morning had taken.

Bill was gone. While she took a few seconds to rejoice, she knew life in Belmont's ER might not turn out better than it had been under Bill's administration. Clearly, his successor—whoever he was—had a definite take-charge attitude. Once he'd plotted his course of action, he followed it, which was a good thing provided he based his decisions upon facts and logic. But if he didn't, they would be in trouble, because she doubted if she'd be as successful at negotiating with him as she had been with Bill.

No matter. She'd learned the art of persuasion at a young age and had developed it fully as she had taken care of her father near the end of his too-short life. She hadn't met a man yet who came close to Arthur John Sutton in stubbornness.

With any luck, however, the new ED Director would be more reasonable than Bill, although after watching him mercilessly throw Bill out of the department, she hoped he didn't normally manage his subordinates with the same dictatorial style.

"I see you're a person who doesn't follow orders," he said behind her a minute later.

"I follow them when they're rational," she replied pertly.

"Do I detect shades of a warning?"

"If the shoe fits." She dumped the last shard of china in the trash can. "I thought I'd get a head start on cleaning up the mess."

"I appreciate the offer, but someone can take care of it later."

She eyed the piles of papers and hesitated, but when he added, "Please," she couldn't disobey.

He cleared off a corner of the desk with one swipe of his hand, then placed a bottle of alcohol, several sterile gauze squares and a suture kit on the surface before he faced her. "Don't worry. Rational is my middle name. Are you ready?"

She eyed his supplies. "You don't stitch a scratch. It's hardly bleeding now anyway."

He whipped a small mirror out of his pocket. "See for yourself."

Her reflection revealed a large drop of blood that welled up in the cut which was dangerously close to her right eye. "No stitches," she insisted.

"If you're worried about my sewing ability…"

"Your abilities aren't in question. I simply don't think it's necessary."

He perched on the edge of the desk. "I'll call a plastic surgeon, then. We'll get his opinion."

"You will do no such thing," she stated firmly. "A butterfly bandage will do the job. You're overreacting. So the cut is a little deep. One stitch isn't worth the trouble."

"You'll have a scar," he warned.

She eyed the cut before she dabbed the blood away. "Probably, but it won't be so big that make-up won't cover it." She grinned as she handed the mirror back. "It will blend in with the normal wrinkles. No one will ever notice."

"Your significant other might."

"If he can't look past a hairline scar, then he won't be my significant other, will he?" she asked lightly. "Would it bother you if *your* significant other had a scar on her face?"

"Of course not." He appeared affronted.

She smiled. "Then I rest my case."

He hesitated for a heartbeat. "I can't talk you into this, can I?"

"Nope. Not a chance. As a patient, I have the right to refuse or accept treatment."

"OK. Butterfly bandage it is." He rose to shrug off his jacket, revealing a white shirt that covered deliciously wide shoulders.

"And I'll take care of it myself."

He poured alcohol on a gauze pad. "I'm sure you can, but you aren't. This is going to sting a bit."

She nearly howled as he pressed the saturated pad to her face and disinfected the wound, but she bit back her yelp. To take her mind off the burning sensation, she concentrated on him.

Whoever he was, he was too handsome, too well built, too *everything* for words. His short hair was the color of dark molasses and seemed just as thick. His features reflected an aristocratic heritage and his long eyelashes were every woman's dream.

As he probed and prodded, she noticed his long fingers and light touch. Idly, she wondered how he'd look in a scrub suit, and if they could find any lab coats that would fit.

"The man should be drawn and quartered," he muttered as he ripped open another package of gauze.

"Who, Bill?"

"Who else?"

"He's harmless. Incompetent but, overall, harmless."

"From where I'm standing, I'd disagree."

Perhaps he was right. The room was a mess, and he *had* thrown a paperweight at Lucy before he'd pitched his coffee-mug in a fit of pique.

"You shouldn't have gotten in the way," he chided.

"Someone had to talk to him, calm him down. I've done it before. Given a few more minutes, I would have again."

"The diplomat."

She hadn't ever described herself with that term before, but it fit. "At times."

He pulled the butterfly bandage tight to hold the cut edges of her skin together. "Don't get it wet," he informed her.

"Yes, I know. Thank you." She straightened in her chair. "Now, if you don't mind, I'd like a few answers."

He perched against the edge of the desk in front of her. "What do you want to know?"

"Your name, for starters."

His perfect smile was sheepish. "In all the excitement, I left out the formalities, didn't I?"

"Given the circumstances, it was understandable."

"I'm Dr Ruark Thomas, at your service."

She held out her hand. "Pleased to meet you, Dr Thomas. Welcome to Belmont Memorial."

"Thank you."

Gina became instantly aware of two things, the touch of his fingers against hers and his deep voice. Both caused her nerve endings to tingle pleasantly and create a surprisingly powerful attraction that tugged at her middle. She couldn't remember the last time she'd felt more than a glimmer of interest in someone she'd met, but this was certainly not the time for her hormones to kick in or her subconscious to get caught up in the moment. Yet, in spite of her mental scolding, she reluctantly withdrew her hand and forced herself to concentrate.

"You have a lot of ER experience?" she asked.

"Some. I moved here from California, thinking it would be nice to try life in the Great Midwest," he said smoothly. "I trained in Great Britain, specialized in emergency medicine in New York, and spent most of my time over the years with a number of relief agencies."

"Interesting. And now you've come to boring little Belmont Memorial."

He chuckled. "From indications so far, being here will be anything but boring."

The men who'd carried Bill away suddenly appeared in her mind's eye. "And the two men with you?"

"Security guards. You'll probably see Hugh and Joachim a lot in the days ahead. Then again, you may not. They work best behind the scenes, or so I've been told."

The two men certainly outclassed Belmont's regular department security guards. Oscar Burns, who, with an extra fifty pounds around his mid-section, only moved fast when someone brought homemade goodies to share and Hal Jarvis, who, at twenty-four, looked like he was thirteen, and hadn't filled out his gangly teenage frame yet.

In contrast, Hugh and Joachim were professionals through and through. Their muscles had muscles and a mere glance from those piercing eyes would coax co-operation from the most difficult of patients and visitors. They'd definitely be handy to have around on a Friday or Saturday night.

"Is Dr Lansing afraid Bill will make trouble?" Lansing was the Chief of Medicine and he was the sort who didn't act upon anything until the i's were dotted and t's were all properly crossed.

"It's a possibility."

"Bill is all bluster," she told him. "He won't make trouble if he suspects those two are hanging around. He'll be too embarrassed, especially if he might be hauled outside like a bag of dirty laundry again. Frankly, after what I saw, I'd hate to run into them in a dark alley."

The corners of his mouth twitched. "Stay on Hugh and Joachim's good side and you won't have any problems."

"You're already on a first-name basis?"

"It seemed appropriate."

The dull throb in her cheek demanded a couple of acetaminophen, but she wanted answers more than she wanted a painkiller. "I can't believe Bill's gone. Do you know what prompted his sudden exit?"

"I'm not privy to all the details, but your administration hasn't been happy with the way he's managed this department."

"They actually noticed?"

"Yes, they did."

"When did they decide to take matters into their own hands?"

"Apparently they began making discreet inquiries several months ago. I heard about the position and thought it would be a challenge, so I completed my other commitments and here I am." His face darkened. "However, if I'd known he was such a volatile man, I would have arranged my schedule differently."

She hardly knew what to say, but a warm, fuzzy feeling spread through her. No one, since her father had died, had been so concerned about her safety. What woman wouldn't feel flattered?

"You, on the other hand," he scolded, "shouldn't have gone into his office when he was so upset."

"We've been over this before. I had to go in. There was no one else."

"There is now," he stated firmly. "You won't do anything like that again."

"Are you planning to go ballistic at some point in time, too?" she asked lightly.

He smiled. "No, but one never knows what will happen. You're too valuable to put yourself in harm's way."

Why today's incident bothered Ruark so much she didn't know, other than he didn't want to find a replacement physician. Even so, working in Emergency carried a normal element of risk and danger, especially if one considered some of the situations they handled on Saturday nights. Mentioning a few of those incidents seemed counterproductive, so she changed the subject.

"You're truly taking over the department?" she asked.

"I intended to call a staff meeting as soon as Bill left, but we got sidetracked," he said wryly.

No doubt he referred to tending the scratch on her face. "We can call one now, unless you'd rather tidy your office first."

He glanced around. "From the looks of things, it will take a long time. I'll meet our group instead."

"Good idea. I'd bet they're all dying of curiosity."

A knock at the door interrupted. "Come in," he called out.

Lucy poked her head inside. "Is everything OK in here?"

"It's fine," Gina responded.

"Can I get either of you anything?" she asked. "Coffee, tea, or…?"

"Thank you, but not at the moment," Ruark answered politely.

Disappointment flitted across Lucy's features. "If you should change your mind…"

"We'll let you know," Gina assured her.

"OK." The nurse disappeared and Gina faced Ruark. "The natives are definitely dying of curiosity."

"I'll deal with them in a minute," he said. "But before I do, I'd like to discuss a more personal matter."

Knowing she had nothing to hide, she shrugged. "Sure."

He studied her intently. "You truly didn't know I was coming?"

"Didn't have a clue," she responded cheerfully.

"My name didn't sound familiar?"

She shook her head. "Should it?"

"Really?"

"Really. Have you been in the news?" She hoped not. If he was a household name and she didn't recognize it, she'd feel horribly awkward.

"Not lately."

She smiled. "Good, because otherwise I'd have to apologize. I rarely watch television," she admitted.

His gaze held hers. "What if I told you I'm originally from Marestonia."

Marestonia? A warning bell sounded in her head and her smile froze in place. *Stay calm*, she told herself. Lots of people lived in Marestonia.

She pretended ignorance. "Someplace in Eastern Europe, isn't it?"

"Next door to Avelogne."

Her heart pounded painfully in her chest. She hadn't heard the name of her father's country since she'd turned sixteen and he'd told her the entire tale of his life.

A life he'd given up rather than sacrifice his principles.

A life where he'd gained a wife and daughter and lost everything else.

"Your father and mine were friends years ago."

The past wasn't supposed to surface after all these years. Her father had left that life behind, never to embrace it again. Acknowledging it now seemed rather disloyal to her parents' memory.

"Was your father an aeronautical engineer, too?" She sounded stiffly polite as she pretended ignorance of her family background. "Did the two of them do business together?"

"Their friendship began long before your father moved to Seattle. *Countess*."

She drew herself up at the title she had a right to use but didn't. "Do *not* call me that."

"Deny your heritage all you want, but I have the proof."

"And what if you do? It means nothing. I don't have any official ties to Avelogne."

"Ah, but you admit you do have ties."

Feeling like a mouse caught in a trap, she bit her lip, reluctant to say anything else.

"You do," he insisted. "You have a grandmother, aunts, uncles and cousins."

"Whom I never met," she countered. "I'm thirty years old and

I've lived my entire life without them. I'm not interested in changing my family dynamics now."

With a blinding flash of insight, the pieces of the puzzle making up Ruark Thomas began to align themselves in a picture she didn't like. His aristocratic bearing, his take-charge attitude, his familiarity with the security guards all suggested he was more than a physician, more than the new chief of emergency services.

She studied him with the same intensity she used when searching for bacteria under a microscope. "Who *are* you, Dr Thomas?"

CHAPTER TWO

RUARK watched the woman in front of him. Her green eyes flashed with fire and she bristled with a combination of indignation and suspicion. Breaking the news to her wouldn't be easy; he'd known it for some time, which was why he'd planned and orchestrated the proper timing.

He clicked his heels together and bowed slightly. "Ruark Benjamin Mikael Thomas, Prince of Marestonia."

"Prince?" she asked on a near squeak. "I thought you were a physician."

"They aren't mutually exclusive. I happen to be both."

"What brings a physician slash prince of Marestonia to Belmont Memorial?"

"To work, like everyone else," he promptly answered.

"Since when do princes need to earn a living?"

"It's called serving the people," he said lightly. "As the third son, I was free to choose my own career, and I chose medicine. Just as your cousin, Leander, did."

Curiosity flashed in her eyes at the mention of a cousin who shared her interest and her profession, but a few seconds later indifference appeared, as if she simply refused to acknowledge any sort of connection between her and her father's family. "And you chose to work in the US?"

"When I'm not involved in relief work."

"How noble."

"Please, feel free to tell me what you *truly* think."

His gentle rebuke brought color to her face. "I apologize," she said stiffly. "As a physician, I was out of line to say something so unforgivable."

"Apology accepted." Gina was many things, but she didn't hesitate to speak her mind, he decided. From the reports he'd read about her, he hadn't expected her to do otherwise.

She crossed her arms. "OK, you're a prince who works for a living, but out of all the hospitals in this country, what made you choose Belmont?"

"Because you're here," he said simply.

She scoffed. "Oh, please. You can't be serious."

"It's true," he insisted. "I came as soon as a job was available."

She looked puzzled. "But why? We don't know each other."

"Your grandmother and my father sent me." He reached into the left inside pocket of his suit coat, retrieved a white envelope and held it out to her. "The Queen Mother asked if I would deliver this."

Recognition flashed in her eyes as her gaze traveled from one corner emblazoned with the royal crest of the House of Avelogne to the middle where her name appeared in large, beautifully precise script. "Why would the royal family send a letter to me?" she asked suspiciously.

"You'll have to read the explanation for yourself."

She eyed the envelope as if it were a pure culture of *Hantavirus*, but indecision flickered across her face. He hoped her curiosity would overrule the hard feelings she so plainly felt.

Reluctantly, she accepted the offering and hefted it in her hand before tapping the long edge against one palm. "If you wanted to be the Queen Mother's errand boy, you didn't have to accept a job at Belmont to do so."

Although amused by her bluntness, he hid a smile. "For the

record, your uncle is now King, which makes your grandmother the Queen Mother, but to answer your question, no, I didn't."

"Then why did a Prince of Marestonia, a *Doctor* Prince no less, move here just to deliver her mail?"

"You'll understand when you read what your grandmother has to say."

"If this is a 'hi, how are you' note, I'm not interested," she warned.

"Read it," he repeated. "I'll answer your questions *after* you read the letter."

"All right, I will."

Suspecting she'd leave under the guise of needing privacy and then, when she was alone, she would destroy her grand-mother's letter unopened, Ruark positioned himself in front of the room's only exit. "I'll give you all the time you need, without saying a word."

She clutched the envelope until it wrinkled. "I can't deal with this right now."

"Of course you can. You're not afraid, are you?" he asked, hoping she'd respond to the challenge in his voice.

She did. She squared her shoulders and met his gaze as she defiantly slid her finger under the glued flap and pulled out a piece of expensive stationery. "Happy now?" she asked crossly.

"Not until you read it."

"Then stop hovering," she snapped.

Once again, he hid his amusement and moved closer to the door. "Sorry," he said, unapologetically. It was clear she was as irritated with him as she was at her grandmother for breaking years of silence, but a journey began with a single step and Gina had taken hers.

Gina took a deep breath as she unfolded the single sheet. The words written in the same beautiful script as on the envelope jumped off the page.

Greetings, dearest Granddaughter,

We trust this letter finds you well. Although we have
never met, we still consider you an integral part of our family.

Gina inwardly scoffed, but read on.

You will never know how much I deeply regret the family
differences that have separated us all these years, but I hope
you will find it in your heart to put the past behind us and
look to the future.

Avelogne needs your help, my dearest Gina. Its alliances
with Marestonia are threatened and neither country can
afford to lose the goodwill we've enjoyed for centuries. We
realize your loyalties do not lie with us, but your parents
are at the heart of the matter and I hope you will find it in
your heart to honor them by being part of the solution.
Prince Ruark shall relay all the details and explanations
necessary.

We know our request will come as a great surprise, but
your decision will affect countless people. You are a
woman who chose a profession because you care about
others and we are confident you shall follow your nature
and choose the right course of action.

We shall look forward to hearing from you and soon
meeting each other face to face.

With best wishes,

Your Grandmother, Juliana

"What does she mean, my parents are at the heart of the
matter?" she asked.

"Today's problems are linked to the government's decision to
withhold approval for your parents' marriage."

Her father had mentioned something about that, but had glossed over the details. "Sounds to me like the government made its own dilemma, so they can fix it."

"My family was involved, too."

"Then *you* can do whatever it is you need to do, but count me out." She stepped closer and tried to reach around him for the doorknob.

He gripped her arm and didn't budge. "My aunt gave questionable information to the committee which led them to refuse your father's petition to marry your mother."

"You mean, someone *lied*, and they believed her?" No wonder her parents hadn't spoken of those days except in the most general terms. Her dad, especially, must have felt betrayed by his countrymen who'd trusted the testimony of an outsider instead of his own.

"Unfortunately, yes. Now, after all these years, the truth has come out and tensions are running high. The fate of our nations depends on us."

If not for one woman's pettiness, her entire life might have been different…she might have grown up as a member of a royal family, with doting aunts and uncles, cousins, grandparents marking every major event in her life, sharing in her triumphs and failures, and, most importantly, supporting her after her father's death.

But even if Ruark's aunt had been involved, the decision ultimately rested upon the members of Parliament. In her opinion, they were as much at fault as Ruark's relative, if not more so.

As she'd already pointed out, it was too late to change the past. Neither was it her responsibility. One thing, however, was certain. She didn't count gullibility among her faults.

"Oh, puhleeze," she scoffed. "Fates of two countries. You can't be serious."

"I am."

According to the grim set to his jaw, he was. "Why would I want to help the same government who carelessly changed my family's life?" she asked.

"Avelogne is your heritage," he said simply. "You also hold dual citizenship, which means you have a legal as well as a moral obligation to Avelogne." He paused. "Do you honestly believe your father wouldn't want you to help his homeland avert a crisis?"

Admittedly, her dad had stayed abreast of all the happenings across the Atlantic. Their home had been littered with newspapers and magazines from various cities. In later years, those had given way to Internet news and emails. Arthur Sutton may not have been in close physical proximity to the land of his birth, but his heart had never left.

"This is quite melodramatic, wouldn't you say?" she asked, struggling to shore up her wavering resolve. "Avelogne and Marestonia losing centuries-old goodwill over a thirty-year-old incident that most don't remember."

"The past hasn't been forgotten," he assured her. "The people of Avelogne lost a favored prince and demand restitution for your parents going into exile. If not, they plan to break off all ties with Marestonia."

She crossed her arms. "So?"

"Each country provides goods and services to the other, which makes them somewhat trade-dependent. This includes everything from agriculture to military technology. If ties are broken, thousands of jobs on both sides of the border will be lost and the economic impact will be huge. It will take years to recover. Meanwhile, people will lose their homes and businesses, farmers won't have an accessible market for their products, children will go hungry. The list goes on."

She'd treated patients who couldn't scrounge together enough money for bus fare, much less their medication. She'd lost track of the number of families she'd fed, either in the cafeteria or a nearby restaurant. As much as she wanted to help them all, she couldn't take responsibility for everyone who walked through Belmont's doors.

"I sympathize with your situation, but the last time I checked, my credentials were limited to medicine, not détente. You'll have to ask someone else."

"There *is* no one else to ask. You're my only option."

"I'm sorry, but my answer is still no." She tried to nudge him aside, but he didn't budge.

"You're a coward."

She stared at him, incredulous. "Because I choose not to immerse myself in the politics that sent my father away from the home he loved, I'm a coward?"

"You don't even know what we're asking," he accused. "The least you can do is listen to the unabridged story before you decide. Refusing to do that is either a show of cowardice or being self-centered. Take your pick."

For a terse moment, the silence became so complete, only the distant ringing of a telephone could be heard.

"I'm sorry Avelogne and Marestonia are suffering a diplomatic crisis," she said quietly. "But I'm just an average woman on the street, so to speak. I work in a hospital in a relatively bad part of town and deal with drug addicts and gang members on a daily basis. I don't know what you or my grandmother think I can accomplish. I can't undo the past and I don't run in lofty social or political circles of influence, so you're only wasting your time."

"I disagree. You are not an 'average' woman. If you reestablished ties with your family, you would enter influential circles," he pointed out. "You are, after all, a countess."

"What if I like my life the way it is? I don't *want* to be known as *Countess*. Anonymity suits me just fine."

"You can remain anonymous and still become reacquainted with your family. The point is, life is too short to bear grudges."

Thinking of her father, who'd died as much from heartache as heart disease, Gina's eyes burned with unexpected moisture.

"Aren't you the least bit interested in hearing their side of the story?" he coaxed, as if hoping curiosity would sway her.

"Will it change anything?" she demanded. "Rewrite the past? Restore my father to the family he loved? Take away my mother's sorrow and guilt for causing him to choose between her and his family? I think not."

"I agree those wrongs can't be undone, but we have to resolve this crisis."

"I don't have to do anything," she retorted, blinking away her unshed tears. "My father left Avelogne and his family long ago. I don't intend to get involved with either now."

He fell silent for a moment, then nodded slowly. "If you don't want to deal with the royal family, you don't have to."

"I don't?"

He shook his head. "The real solution lies between the two of us anyway."

She stared at him, puzzled. "You've lost me."

"While it would help matters if Avelogne could show the world a reunited royal house—namely that Arthur's daughter has been reinstated into the fold—it isn't required. Your relationship with me is the important thing."

"Because of your aunt?" she guessed.

"Yes. On behalf of my entire family, I'd like to apologize for her selfish actions."

She tapped one foot on the floor. "What exactly *was* her motive for ruining my parents' lives?"

He didn't comment, although he heaved a great sigh. "Margret fell in love with your father and believed that if your mother, Lizbet, disappeared from the scene, she would be able to earn Arthur's affections." He paused. "She was quite shocked when he relinquished his claim to the throne and moved to America. The situation didn't play out quite as she'd planned."

"I'll say," she said wryly. "Whatever her reasons, though, I don't hold you responsible. Neither the past nor your royal connections will interfere with our employer-employee status. As far as I'm concerned, we're simply two physicians who happen to work together in the same department, in the same hospital. So you can call whomever you need to and announce the good news. Then life for everyone can return to normal."

He smiled, as if she'd amused him with her simplistic solution. "It's a start, but, as I've already said, your people demand more than an apology. They want their prince back."

Do you hear that, Dad? A pain shot through her heart. If only he'd lived long enough to see this day. "Impossible," she said flatly.

He nodded. "Which is why the situation is complicated."

"I was afraid you would say that," she said dryly. "But, complicated or not, I can't help you."

He started to speak, but the door edged open and Lucy poked her head inside.

"We're getting a couple of traumas in about five minutes. Two stabbing victims."

Gina had never been so relieved to have patients coming into the ED before. She could deal with medical situations far better than she could sort out diplomatic problems of countries she'd only seen on the map and in occasional family photos.

"Thanks, Lucy," she said. "We'll be right there."

Lucy vanished, apparently without noticing the tension in the office. From the look on Ruark's face, he was clearly glad for the reprieve as well.

"We'll discuss this further tonight," he said. "When we won't be interrupted or distracted."

"There isn't anything to discuss," she protested.

"You need to hear everything," he insisted. "The least you can do is listen."

She wanted to refuse but, after seeing the fierce determination on his face, she knew he wouldn't give up.

She faced him squarely. "OK, but in the meantime you will not breathe a syllable of this conversation to *anyone*. No one knows my background and I prefer to keep it that way."

"You have my word," he agreed. Immediately, he opened the door. "After you, Dr Sutton."

Setting aside her host of questions to mentally gear up for her patients, Gina hurried toward the centrally located nurses' station. "Page Frank," she told Ruby, the desk clerk, referring to their surgical resident, Frank Horton.

With the phone tucked under one ear, Ruby mouthed, "I'm already on it." Then she spoke into the receiver. "I don't care where you have to find him, just do it. We need him in the ER, stat!"

Gina rushed into the opposite hallway to check if Trauma Room One was available, and found Ruark following her like a shadow. "What are you doing here? Bill didn't—"

"It's a new day. Bill isn't here any longer," he pointed out. "As I understand the job, I'm supposed to be available for traumas, and here I am."

Only if I need you, she wanted to protest. But then, with two patients coming in and not knowing the condition of either, she might need an extra pair of hands. The only question was, would he function like Bill and be more hindrance than help?

"Afraid I'll find your department doesn't run smoothly?" he asked.

"We run just fine," she defended tartly. "Feel free to observe for yourself." Already dismissing him, she asked no one in particular, "Where's Casey?"

Another nurse scurried past. "Dr Casey left for his dentist appointment ten minutes ago. Remember?"

How could she have forgotten? Of all the days for him to lose a temporary filling. But considering what had happened so far this morning, she would count herself fortunate if a natural disaster didn't occur.

"Dr Powers is supposed to cover, but he can't come until one-thirty." Toby Powers was a physician who was close to retirement and worked two shifts a week.

"Staff problems?" Ruark asked.

"Nothing we can't work around."

The ambulance bay doors near the nurses' station swooshed open and she rushed forward to greet the two paramedics and the gurney carrying her first patient.

"Twenty-five-year-old male with multiple wounds to the chest," one of the paramedics, Tim Abbott, reported. "Open pneumothorax. BP is one ten over sixty-five..."

Gina listened to his recitation as she donned her protective gear, including a face shield, while following the gurney into the trauma room. Not only was the man's blood pressure low and his heart rate increased, but his skin was cold and clammy and he appeared restless in spite of his cervical and thoracic spine immobilization. Tim had already inserted an endotracheal tube in the field, but her patient still struggled to breathe and showed jugular vein distension.

She raised the large bandage covering his bloody chest and saw eight puncture wounds, with the largest one near the heart showing frothy blood. Because air and blood were leaking into his thoracic cavity, his lungs couldn't inflate properly. Her work was cut out for her.

To her surprise, a similarly gowned and gloved Ruark appeared in the room. "I've got it under control," she said as she, Tim, Lucy, another nurse and now Ruark prepared to move her patient from the ambulance gurney to a hospital bed.

"Are you warning me away from your patient, Dr Sutton?" he asked coolly.

She mentally noted that she didn't need to take charge, but old habits were hard to break. While she'd have to defer to him for the time being, she'd maintain a watchful eye until she assured herself that the royal doctor truly knew what he was doing.

"Not at all," she answered. "One, two, three, lift!" On Gina's command, their patient made the transition with minimal jostling. Seconds later, she began barking her orders to the nurses who were busy affixing a pulse oximeter, monitoring the IV and taking over ventilation duties. "Get me a chest tube on the double, a CBC and type and cross-match for four units. Where's Horton?"

Becky answered. "He's not here yet."

"Page him again. If he doesn't answer in the next sixty seconds, page Dr Ahmadi too." Ahmadi was Frank Horton's supervisor.

Gina wiped blood away from the largest and most worrisome puncture and revealed heavily tattooed skin. A closer look at his torso showed her what she'd missed before—his entire body was tattooed with mythical creatures. The detailed dragon which was prominently featured on his left bicep was quite distinctive.

"I see we've gotten another one of Picasso's customers."

"Who?" Ruark asked.

"Pablo Picasso. Pablo's his real name and being a local tattoo artist, he calls his parlor Picasso's," she said as she began to palpate along the man's rib cage to determine the chest tube placement site. "He thought the famous name would give his place some class. We see a lot of his work in here."

"Doesn't say much for his choice of clientele," Ruark remarked.

"Pablo is interested in his art, not in people's lifestyle choices," she defended.

"How did you meet him? I wouldn't think a physician and a tattooist would have much in common."

"He came into the ER with pneumonia when I was an intern and we started to talk about all sorts of things. He invited me to his workplace—he dared me to visit, actually, and I did. His drawings are fantastic."

"Did you pick one for yourself?" Lucy asked.

"Sure did. Lidocaine."

Lucy slapped the required syringe into Gina's hand. "Oh, my gosh. You have a tattoo?"

Conscious of Ruark listening intently, Gina wished she hadn't said a word. Her tattoo was none of his business, even if she wasn't ashamed of it. "Yeah."

"You're kidding."

"Come on, Lucy, it isn't that big a deal," Gina defended.

"Hey, any time you veer off the straight and narrow path of respectability to walk on the wild side, it's interesting," Lucy announced. "So what did you choose, and where is it? Don't keep us in suspense."

"It's a frog," Gina snapped. "On my foot. Scalpel."

"I should have guessed. You collect them, don't you?" Lucy slapped the instrument into her hand.

"Yeah." From the sheer volume of inked skin, Gina suspected her patient took as much pride in his body art as Pablo did, so she made the smallest incision possible to accomplish what had to be done. As she punctured the pleura with a Kelly clamp, blood spurted from the hole.

Working frantically, she hardly noticed the appearance of another nurse, and two more paramedics as they wheeled in a second victim who, like the first, had an IV line established and wore an oxygen mask.

"We've got problems here, Doc," Andy Carter, one of the paramedics, announced.

"Tell me about it," she muttered.

"What's wrong?" Ruark abandoned Gina's patient for the new arrival.

"He's got a pneumothorax and I couldn't intubate him before we brought him in. I tried, but couldn't get through and I didn't want to waste more time trying in the field."

Gina inserted the tube into her John Doe's chest. Immediately blood filled the line and ran into the attached drainage bag. "Hang on, buddy," she told her patient. "We're taking good care of you."

"Give me an endotrachael tube," Ruark ordered as he moved to the head of his patient's gurney.

Andy glanced between her and Ruark. "Doc?"

"Where's Frank?" she asked no one in particular.

"I asked for an endotrach tube," Ruark ground out. "Must I get one myself?"

Everyone froze, including Gina. "What do you think you're doing?" she asked.

"Trying to save this man's life, if someone will give me a damn tube!" he roared as he stood over the second man, who was audibly rasping for breath.

Immediately, the nurses sprang into action.

Gina exchanged a brief glance with Lucy. Ruark would be furious that no one had instantly obeyed his orders. Apparently her days as staff liaison hadn't ended yet but, in all fairness, what could he expect? No one knew of the official leadership change—it all had happened so fast. If he'd called his staff meeting instead of springing international problems on her that were beyond her control, none of this would have happened, she thought uncharitably.

"By the way," Gina announced offhandedly as she tended her patient, "I'm afraid none of you have met our new emergency director, Dr Ruark Thomas. In case you haven't figured it out yet, he's replaced Bill."

Under the wary greetings offered by the subdued staff, Gina muttered to Lucy, "Keep an eye on him and signal me if you notice he's in over his head."

Lucy obeyed, quietly trading places with the other nurse.

While Gina finished securing the chest tube with sutures and dressed the wound she'd created, she listened to the quiet con-versation over the second gurney.

"We can't get through," Ruark declared. "His larynx is frac-tured and the upper airway is blocked."

"Then he needs a cricothyroidotomy," she interrupted from across the room. Having worked with her share of unseasoned physicians, she was accustomed to sharing her opinions during the trickier situations. "Can we get by with—?"

Ruark must have read her mind. "Ventilating him with only a needle and catheter is a temporary measure. The surgical method will make it easier for placement of a tracheostomy tube later, which he will definitely need."

"OK. I'll be there in a few seconds." But as she watched the blood pour out of her patient's chest into the drainage bag and heard only muffled heart sounds, she knew she couldn't leave his side.

She hated to ask, but she had no choice. "Can you do it on your own?"

"I'm two steps ahead of you," he answered. "Never fear. I've done this once or twice."

Once or twice? Gina mentally groaned. Yet, for a man with such limited experience, he didn't seem flustered or act out of his depth. And while she was relieved by his calm, matter-of-fact manner, she couldn't squelch the irrational notion that he might need the benefit of her expertise. After all, a patient's life was at stake.

"Find the cricoid cartilage, which is approximately two to three centimeters below the thyroid notch," she instructed. "Once the membrane is exposed, puncture it midline. Be careful of the vocal cords and don't puncture—"

"The back wall of the larynx and enter the esophagus. Yes, Gina, I know, but thanks for the reminder."

He didn't sound upset and wasn't yelling at the nurses for not providing the proper supplies at the exact moment he wanted them, which was a one-eighty-degree change from working alongside Bill. Her fears that he was simply a more polished version of their previous director slowly faded as she listened to his calm voice ask questions and give directions. No, it was obvious she didn't need to review his curriculum vitae—his actions spoke of his abilities far better than a list of positions held ever would. If he could handle his current patient's condition, he was a colleague she could trust.

Within seconds, Ruark's patient's audible symptoms of respiratory stridor disappeared, and with it all of her fears about his medical skills. Suddenly, a burden she hadn't realized she'd been carrying lifted.

"Airway's in," he said, sounding quite pleased. "His pneumothorax is next on the agenda."

The activity on the other side of the room faded into the background as the nurse at her side interrupted with a terse "BP is falling".

Gina immediately noticed her patient's visibly distended jugular veins and muffled heart sounds—Beck's triad—and knew the man's heart was failing. "His pericardium or coronary artery must have been nicked," she said aloud. "He needs his chest opened, but…"

"But what?" Ruark asked from across the room. Apparently he also had the ability to listen in on two conversations at once.

"But I'm not qualified to perform the procedure," she admitted. "He needs a surgeon. We belong upstairs, now!"

Dr Horton suddenly nudged her aside. "He won't make it as far as the elevator. Move over."

"Nice of you to join us, *Frank*," she replied caustically as she traded places with the tardy surgeon.

"Hey, I'm here now." He turned to Candy. "It'll ruin his tattoos, but get ready for a thoracotomy."

"At least he'll be alive to complain," Gina muttered.

"Only if we stop the bleeding before he goes into cardiac arrest. Scalpel."

While Frank began to work, Gina glanced at the paramedics hovering nearby. "Do we have names for these two yet?"

"I'll check." Andy slipped from the room.

Intent on assisting Frank and urging her patient to hang on, Gina didn't notice Ruark until he stood at the foot of the bed. "How's your fellow?" she asked.

"Better than yours," he answered. "He's on his way to an operating room as we speak. They're also holding a suite open for your patient."

"And here we have it," Frank announced with distinct arrogance at discovering the problem. "His coronary artery is nicked. I'm cross-clamping the aorta and then we're out of here."

A few minutes later, Frank and the John Doe were gone. Lucy and Candy immediately began the unenviable task of dealing with the mess and, oh, what a mess it was. Instruments littered every available surface, paper wrappers and used gloves covered the blood-slickened floor.

Gina tiredly stripped off her face shield and blood-stained gown before removing her gloves, conscious of Ruark doing the same. She started to slip out of the room with the other extraneous personnel, but the sound of his voice stopped her, and everyone else, in their tracks.

"Nobody move," he commanded.

CHAPTER THREE

EVERYONE froze. Most appeared resigned, as if they were already bracing themselves for a coming storm. Determined to protect her staff, Gina immediately began her defense. "Don't blame them for not instantly following your orders. You could have been a medical student for all they knew."

Anyone with two eyes and an ounce of common sense would never believe he was a mere med student—he was far too confident and authoritative, not to mention distinguished. From the wry expression on his face, he recognized the feeble excuse for what it was.

"I'm well aware we didn't get a chance to observe the formalities, Dr Sutton," he stated as he met her gaze. "So we'll put this incident behind us. However, I am the new emergency director and I can assure every one of you I am fully qualified to handle the position."

Gina's face warmed at his rebuke. Clearly, he'd known she had sent Lucy to monitor him. Her embarrassment grew as he shared his experiences in other emergency departments and during the course of his medical relief efforts. At first, she felt guilty for having thought he was only a figurehead—a royal prince who didn't do more than lend his name in support of a cause—but how was she to have known otherwise? She hadn't even known his name before he'd waltzed in and took over. No, if anything, *he* should feel remorse for sneaking into Belmont like a burglar.

"I don't plan to change your routine overnight," he continued, "but I will be looking at your operations closely and fine-tuning those processes that need it. No matter how well a department functions, there's always room for improvement. Rest assured, I will not tolerate slipshod performances. I expect one hundred and ten percent from each of you, and intend to put forth the same effort."

Gazes met and shoulders squared as everyone seemed willing to meet his demands. It was almost surprising to see the staff co-operate so wholeheartedly this soon, but he *had* proved himself with his first case. Clearly, they were eager to impress him as well.

"What's the possibility of budgeting for more staff?" someone asked.

"If the numbers justify it, I'll do what I can to get them," he promised.

Those who had still appeared suspicious now nodded as if satisfied with Ruark's response. Slowly, skepticism and stoicism faded as he shared his vision for the department as well as a few personal facts. By the end of his impromptu meeting, not only was everyone smiling and joking with him, but they'd also learned he liked all flavors of coffee as long as they were strong, loved fresh pastries and any dessert containing apples. No doubt there would be donuts and apple pie tomorrow.

"I'm certain you'll have more questions as time goes on, but if you have a problem, my door is always open," he added in conclusion. "Meanwhile, you can return to work."

Gina accompanied him from the room while the rest of the staff headed off to deal with their respective tasks. "You had them eating out of your hand," she remarked.

His wide grin only enhanced his handsome features. "People

usually produce in accordance with the level of expectation. If they know I expect a lot, they'll deliver. If not..." He shrugged.

Determined to clear the air, she squared her shoulders and met his gaze. "For the record, I'm not sorry I'd asked Lucy to report any problems you had to me. Having never seen you in action, I'd do it again in a heartbeat."

"Under similar circumstances, I would have done the same, as would any physician who cares about his patients. I trust I've satisfied your curiosity and relieved your doubts?"

"Yes."

"Then we'll put this behind us, too."

"Why didn't you tell them you were a prince?"

"They need to see I'm a physician first and a prince second," he said simply, "otherwise they won't look past the issues of royalty and we can't form the cohesive unit we need to be."

He was obviously speaking from experience. "You told me who you are."

"Given our backgrounds, I made an exception for you."

Lucky her, she thought glumly. "I thought you prided yourself on honesty."

"I do, but do *you* want reporters swarming all over the place, digging into your past? Believe me, it only takes one curious reporter for all of your secrets to become tomorrow's headlines. Are you ready for that, Countess?"

She gritted her teeth. "I told you before, I consider that title purely academic. I prefer to use the one I earned, and I'd appreciate it you did, too."

"I stand corrected. In any case, my personal background is irrelevant."

She scoffed. "Do you really believe that? The staff aren't blind. People will notice your bodyguards and ask questions."

"After what happened today with Bill Nevins, no one will give two extra guards a second thought. Besides, my men are professionals. They're experts at blending in. But if someone does ask questions, I'll tell them the truth. They'll find out soon enough, anyway."

His ready reply caught her off guard. "You have all the answers, don't you?" she asked waspishly, lumping in their earlier, more private discussion with this one.

"What sort of leader would I be if I didn't?" he countered. "You see, Gina, I don't like surprises."

After today, neither did she.

Ruark spent what remained of the morning observing the work flow of the department. Fortunately, no other traumas arrived, which left him free to talk individually with the staff regarding everything from scheduling to ordering supplies. He would have preferred Gina acting as his guide, but she often disappeared in other directions—"to take care of patients," she'd said.

It was only an excuse. The whiteboard indicating room assignments and diagnoses plainly showed nothing that the physician's assistant couldn't handle. However, he was willing to cut her some slack today. She clearly wanted space to digest the information he'd given her, although little did she know he'd barely scratched the surface. The rest would come this evening, when he outlined their families' proposed plan in complete detail.

When his father had first approached him and he'd read the dossier on Gina that had been compiled by the palace security team, he'd been resigned to fulfilling his obligations. After meeting her, talking to her, watching the way she handled a difficult situation, he'd become more…hopeful? about the long-term success of the scheme they had devised. Doing his duty to restore his family's honor wouldn't pose a hardship at all.

In fact, if he'd come to Belmont without any ulterior motive or agenda, if he'd only arrived as a physician who merely intended to use his medical skills until the next career move presented itself, Gina still would have captured his attention. Her elfin features, willowy frame, tawny-colored hair and special smile charmed him more than he'd imagined possible. After he'd touched her soft skin, seen the damage done by the shard of china and her blood staining his white handkerchief, he'd wanted Bill Nevins's head. For a man who prided himself on his control, his reaction amazed him.

He was almost tempted to pull rank and follow as she went about her business, to compare what he learned about her first-hand with what he'd gathered from her file, but he had to be patient. If she felt threatened and he couldn't win her over tonight, then the next few weeks wouldn't pass by pleasantly.

To his surprise and delight, he'd learned more interesting things about Gina and Belmont's emergency department from Gina's colleagues than he would have learned from her. More often than not, he heard what had fast become a familiar refrain.

"Dr Sutton takes care of that."

"Dr Sutton completes those reports."

"Dr Sutton always talks the supply department into giving us what we need."

"Dr Sutton is a stickler for continuing education," one nurse said proudly. "We're the only department in the hospital where all staff certifications are current."

At first, he'd wondered how it could be possible for one woman to accomplish so much in a given day, until he stood at the nurses' station and merely watched her go from one task to another. She might deny her heritage, but she still possessed the innate grace and regal bearing of her ancestors.

"If you're waiting until she has a free minute to talk to her, you'll be waiting a long time," Lucy warned.

He pulled his attention away from Gina and his thoughts at the sound of the nurse's voice. "Excuse me?"

"If you ever want to catch Dr Sutton, you have to do like the rest of us and just interrupt," Lucy commented. "She's in constant motion. The only time she sits down is when she's at her desk or at lunch, which she takes on a hit-and-miss basis. Sometimes just thinking about everything she does makes me tired. I don't know how she has the energy to run at full speed all day, but she does."

"I assume she stays past her shift," he said before he caught a glimpse of Gina slipping out of one exam room and into another.

"All the time," Lucy told him bluntly. "The woman doesn't have a life. She's here at 6:00 a.m. and stays until eight or nine at night, five days a week. I keep telling her she's going to burn out, but she only laughs. If you ask me, Bill Nevins took advantage of her good nature."

Ruark suspected as much.

"To be honest…" Lucy cast a sidelong glance at him "…we'd hoped that when Bill decided to retire, Gina, er, Dr Sutton would take over."

"Did you?" he replied mildly.

Lucy raised her chin. "She's done a lot for us. The staff are intensely loyal to her."

Ruark locked his gaze on hers, but she held her ground. "Is this a warning?"

"Not unless it needs to be."

He grinned at her tart tone. "Dr Sutton's place remains secure," he assured her. "Although I would appreciate it if, when Dr Sutton is relieved of some of her duties, the staff will understand it isn't because she hasn't done an excellent job. As head of Belmont's emergency department, I don't intend to follow in Bill Nevins's footsteps and shirk my own responsibilities."

"They'll understand," she promised, a smile returning to her face. "I'll see to it myself."

Certain he'd gained the head nurse's co-operation, which meant everyone else's would follow, he pointed to the schedule taped to the counter's backsplash. "Other than Gina, I rarely see the same doctor's name twice in a week."

"Because it doesn't take long for most doctors to get fed up with being overworked and underpaid, so they leave. When Gina assigns the shifts, she relies heavily on locums, friends, or previous on-staff physicians who just can't say no."

She sighed. "Then again, none of us seem to be able to say no to her. It's impossible to refuse someone who works harder and more hours than you do. She takes up a lot of the slack herself."

He thought about Frank Horton. "What about residents? Shouldn't a surgeon be available all the time?"

"Belmont only has a few residents," Lucy mentioned. "An OB-GYN who spends most of her time on the maternity floor and a neurology fellow who's usually in ICU or Rehab."

"And Frank?"

"Oh, don't let him hear you call him anything but a board-certified physician," she warned. "He's hired as a hospitalist and is assigned to our department, but he only drops by when we call him."

"He's allowed to do that?"

She shrugged. "Who's going to stop him? Gina's tried, but without having the authority she didn't get very far."

"Why didn't Nevins stand behind her?"

"As long as Frank responded in a 'timely' manner…" she emphasized the word with quotes in the air "…Bill wasn't going to force the issue." She glanced at him slyly. "If you're looking for quality improvement ideas, you should start with that one."

After dealing with cases she could have handled blindfolded, Gina had silently begged the fates to send a patient with something more complicated than shingles or an ingrown toenail. After suffering two major personal surprises today, with the arrival of both Prince Ruark and a letter from a grandmother she'd never met, she suspected the upcoming evening would have more surprises in store. Already her imagination was running rampant with possibilities of what a famous radio commentator liked to refer to as "the *rest* of the story". Rather than waste her time worrying or second-guessing what Ruark would tell her, she needed a case that required her full attention.

Fortunately for her, twenty-one-year-old Janice Myers arrived, complaining of abdominal pain.

Gina flipped through the latest lab and radiology reports. In spite of all the tests she'd run, she still couldn't pinpoint the woman's problem.

She wasn't going to give up, though.

"Your beta HCG is negative, so we can rule out an ectopic pregnancy," Gina informed Janice and her fiancé Kyle Burnham.

"I told you I wasn't pregnant," Janice said weakly as she lay on the gurney, clutching Kyle's hand in a white-knuckled grip.

"I know, but I had to check as a precaution," Gina told her kindly. "You'd be surprised how many women claim they aren't expecting and the test turns up positive."

"Then what's wrong with her, Doctor?" Kyle demanded. Tall, lanky, and wearing a mechanic's uniform, his worry was as obvious as the grease stains on his clothing. "She's been like this since last night."

"Abdominal pain, fever and your slightly elevated white blood count suggest appendicitis," Gina admitted, "although those symptoms could be due to a number of other things as well."

"Like what?"

She stuck to the more minor conditions on the list of possibilities. Suggesting Crohn's disease or cancer at this stage was premature. "Pelvic inflammatory disease," she said, thinking of how Janice only noted tenderness during her pelvic exam. "A hernia or diverticulitis, to name a few."

"What about food poisoning?" Janice asked.

"Food-borne illnesses usually manifest themselves rather abruptly. You mentioned your pain actually started two days ago and gradually grew stronger, which doesn't fit the picture."

"So what do we do now?" Kyle asked, his gaze focused on Janice. "Wait and see if the pain goes away on its own?"

Gina tucked the metal chart under one arm. "Absolutely not. I'm going to ask for a surgical consult."

"Surgery?"

Noting the horrified look the couple exchanged, Gina explained, "Your ultrasound didn't show anything unusual, so he may decide it would be best to take a peek inside you with a laparoscope. But we'll let him decide." She patted Janice's shoulder. "Try to relax. Dr Horton should be in shortly."

She strode toward the nurses' station and plunked the chart on the counter, conscious of Ruark and Lucy at the opposite end. "Call Horton for a stat consult," she told Ruby. "Possible appendicitis in room three."

"He won't be happy," Ruby warned, her kohl-lined eyes matching her short black-out-of-a-bottle hair. "He only left a little while ago."

"I don't care if he walked out the door and has to turn around and come back—it can't be helped. My patient needs a surgery consult. If he won't come, he should send someone else."

"I'll get right on it."

"Please do."

"When you're free, Dr Sutton," Ruark interrupted as Ruby picked up the phone, "I'd like a few minutes."

She couldn't refuse, although she wanted to. At times she'd been able to pretend the events of that morning had all been a bad dream. At others the throbbing in her cheek and the occasional whiff of his expensively masculine cologne as she stepped out of a patient's cubicle reminded her otherwise. Now, with hope borne of desperation, she glanced at the whiteboard room grid.

To her regret, other than Janice's name written in room three's square, someone had wiped the board clean. "OK," she said.

If he heard her reluctance, he didn't comment. Instead, he politely followed her into his office.

She immediately noted the room's appearance as she gingerly took the chair he offered. "You've been busy."

He propped one hip on the edge of his desk. "It wasn't as bad as it looked," he admitted. "Most of the papers didn't stray too far from their folders, so it was a matter of slipping them back inside. Until I figure out the filing system, I thought it best to enlist help and Ruby obliged. According to her, you might know where these belong." He handed her a thin stack.

She quickly scanned them. "Contracts are kept in the accounting department. We certainly don't deal with real estate down here." She turned another page. "Selling equipment? We didn't sell anything..." The list of items caught her attention.

"Why, that rotten...scoundrel," she muttered under her breath.

"From your reaction, I assume you weren't aware he was selling the department's medical equipment?"

"Not at all." She shook her head before one entry caught her eye and she pointed to it. "I recognize this ophthalmology scope. We had a patient with a scratched cornea and I couldn't find it. Bill said he'd sent it out for repairs and we had to scrounge an ancient model out of storage."

"No wonder he reacted so strongly when I wouldn't give him time to clear out his desk," he mused.

"He didn't have time to hide the evidence," she agreed, handing the papers back to Ruark. "Lucky for us he threw that coffee-cup."

His gaze moved to her scratch and a muscle tensed in his jaw. "I don't happen to agree. How're you feeling?"

She gingerly touched the adhesive strip. "I'm fine. Other than an occasional throb, I hardly know it happened."

Amusement flitted into his eyes, as if he knew she wasn't being completely truthful, and she quickly changed the subject.

"Did you find anything else of interest in Bill's files?"

He folded his arms across his chest, which only emphasized the broad shoulders she found so appealing. How odd for her to be attracted to him, of all people. He was a man who represented everything her father had given up, from his responsibilities to his extended family, so how could she possibly entertain any fantasies about him?

She should get out more, she decided. She should get involved in a cause more personal than treating patients day in and day out. As rewarding as she found her job, she clearly needed an activity that met *her* needs. With nothing more than a houseplant to call her own, her hormones were plainly running amuck.

Once again, she vacillated between wanting to hear the rest of his news immediately and wanting to postpone tonight's meeting indefinitely.

"I did." His deep voice yanked her attention back where it belonged—on her job. "Surprisingly enough, underneath the mess was an organized office. After meeting my predecessor, I would never have guessed."

"First impressions can be deceiving," she said lightly.

"I also find it hard to believe he was the driving force behind the department's relatively smooth operation. But he wasn't, was he?"

Because she didn't know where he intended to go with this conversation, Gina's smile faltered. "I couldn't say," she prevaricated.

"I've been talking to our personnel," he began. "From the things they've told me of your accomplishments, I'd almost begun to wonder if you could walk on water."

She chuckled. "Trust me, I can't."

"Your people are extremely loyal to you."

The direction he was going now became clear—he was concerned about a power struggle. "Bill wasn't the easiest man to get along with. If people had a problem that I could handle, I did. And if I couldn't, I took it to him." She reflected on the times he'd blustered and bellowed, fussed and fumed, until she'd persuaded him to consider other possibilities. She definitely wouldn't miss her former boss at all. "Fortunately, I usually convinced him the situation wasn't as bad as it first appeared, or I offered more sensible options."

"Ever the diplomat."

"I did what was necessary. Otherwise we wouldn't have had a soul willing to work here longer than a week." She met his gaze. "I assume things will be different now?"

"Without question," he assured her. "I expect people to come directly to me, not hide behind you."

His command was inevitable. Although she'd wished Bill had met his responsibilities rather than leaving them for her to assume, facing the new reality was harder than she'd imagined. Whatever would she do with herself if she didn't work eighty-hour weeks?

She hid her disappointment. "Of course."

"I'm curious, though. Why didn't you let Nevins sink or swim on his own?"

"Because I got tired of dealing with crises that shouldn't have occurred, whether it was broken equipment, staffing issues, or proper procedures. I'd tried going over his head and was told to follow the proper chain of command. So, in order to treat patients, I chose to work *with* him instead of against him. I learned what made him tick."

"Which was?"

"His ego. When he complained about a certain task, I volunteered to handle it on the grounds that his time was too important to spend on trivial matters." She motioned to the papers Ruark had shown her, and smiled ruefully. "Apparently I gave him too much time."

"Did you look through his files?"

"No!" She was aghast.

"Then you shouldn't feel guilty," he said. "In the meantime,

I'll alert Administration. They'll probably decide to initiate punitive action."

She nodded.

"You should also know this, Gina. I don't plan to shirk my duties."

"I'm glad to hear it."

Ruby knocked on the door. "Excuse me, Dr Sutton? Dr Horton is here and—"

Gina heard his raised voice and mentally geared herself for the inevitable confrontation. "He's not happy," she finished as she stood. "I'm coming." Without waiting for Ruark's dismissal, she joined a blustering Frank Horton at the nurses' station.

As soon as he saw her, he glared. "What is the meaning of this?" He slapped Janice Myers's chart with his knuckles.

Gina fell into her ultra-calm mode, the same tone she used to deal with recalcitrant patients as well as staff. "I asked for a surgical consult. I suspect she has appendicitis."

"I read her chart. From her symptoms, she could have any number of conditions. Check her for food poisoning." He slid the chart across the counter where Gina caught it.

"Have you examined her yet?"

He frowned. "No. The woman doesn't need surgery. Have you thought of PID?"

"Yes, I did, but she doesn't have a history of pelvic inflammatory disease. And if PID is her problem, a laparoscopy would be helpful in the diagnosis."

"Check for parasites."

Gina held on to her temper. "I know my job," she pointed out through gritted teeth. "The test isn't necessary because her problem isn't due to intestinal parasites. She hasn't had any exposure and even if she had, the symptoms don't match."

"Surgery is already running behind schedule," he pointed out. "If she isn't better by tomorrow—"

"And if her appendix ruptures tonight?" she asked. "Or what if I'm wrong and she has a perforated peptic ulcer, acute gangrenous cholecystitis or some other surgical condition? Are you willing to risk the consequences of waiting another day? Because if you are, I hope you've paid your malpractice insurance premiums."

Frank hesitated. "She doesn't have appendicitis," he insisted. "She doesn't have rebound tenderness and her white count is hardly elevated."

"Fine. Do a laparoscopy and prove me wrong. I'll be happy to let you say 'I told you so'. You can post it on the bulletin board in the cafeteria too, if you'd like."

"I'm not taking her to surgery."

"Suit yourself." She moved behind the counter and grabbed the phone.

"What are you doing?" he asked.

"I'm transferring her to St Bridgit's."

"You can't do that!" he blustered.

"Watch me."

"But the paperwork! You can't justify a transfer. There'll be hell to pay," he warned.

"Yes, but I won't be the one paying. As for the paperwork? It won't be any worse than the paperwork you'll have if this woman dies."

"Don't be so melodramatic." He sounded disgusted. "She's not going to die."

"You two." Ruark's voice interrupted. "Bring this into my office. Now." He delivered his order in a tone that didn't leave room for argument.

Once inside, with the door closed, he asked, "What's the problem?"

Frank shot a triumphant look at Gina before he began. Even as he straightened to his full height, Ruark still stood several inches over him. "Gina wants me to perform unnecessary surgery.

Because I won't, she intends to transfer the patient to another hospital."

"It's not unnecessary," she countered hotly.

Ruark raised his hands. "One at a time. Dr Horton?"

Fuming inside, Gina pressed her lips together and began counting to ten.

Apparently sensing the new ED chief would be an ally, Frank ran through Janice's symptoms and test results to back his diagnosis.

"I see your dilemma," Ruark said after Frank finished.

Gina gasped, and he continued as if she hadn't made a sound. "However, it's been my experience that possible appendicitis is nothing to ignore. If Dr Sutton believes the woman needs a laparoscopy, you should honor her request."

Frank's expression changed to disbelief. "But...but—" he blustered.

"Furthermore," Ruark added, "if you can't convince Surgery to hold a suite open, perhaps your boss can arrange for one. Dr Ahmadi is the chief of surgical services, isn't he?"

"Yes, but..." Frank's face turned red.

"On second thoughts," Ruark mused, "you don't appear as if you're in the right frame of mind to operate. I'll call upstairs and locate a more *co-operative* and open-minded surgeon. After I talk to Dr Ahmadi."

Frank frowned as he squared his shoulders. "I'm a professional," he said stiffly. "I'll handle it."

"I thought you would," Ruark said smoothly. "Remember this, Dr Horton. Question Dr Sutton's judgement with such hostility again, and it will be the last time you set foot in this department."

Ruark's quiet warning took a few seconds to sink in, but eventually Frank understood. His Adam's apple bobbed as he swallowed before nodding. An instant later, he grabbed the chart out of Gina's hand and stormed away.

Gina was speechless. She'd been prepared to defend herself on behalf of Ms Myers, and now that it was completely unnecessary, she felt cheated. She should have been thrilled by the outcome, and yet…she wasn't. Ruark had defused the situation so handily, she was left with anger simmering in her veins.

"I would never demand a patient undergo unnecessary surgery," she protested.

"I know."

"I checked the woman thoroughly. She doesn't present with the classic symptoms, but my gut says—"

"Gina, I trust your instincts. Frank Horton won't give you any more trouble."

He sounded far too pleased with himself, which only added to her ire. "Apparently not," she replied stiffly.

He frowned. "I thought you'd be pleased."

"I can fight my own battles, Dr Thomas," she ground out.

"I'm sure you can, but you weren't winning this one."

She advanced. "Do you realize what you've done?"

"Saved a patient?"

"How will my colleagues ever respect my opinion if you threaten them should we ever disagree?"

"What did you want me to do? Let him yell at you as if you were a green first-year medical student?"

"No, but—"

"I stand behind my staff, and you, Gina, are mine. I don't tolerate rudeness and the sooner everyone in this hospital realizes it, the better."

It took a few seconds for his words to sink in, and when they did, she felt foolish. "I apologize for overreacting."

"Accepted. We are a *team*," he stressed. "Problems that arise aren't yours or mine. They're *ours*. We are in this together. Remember that."

His intent gaze and the promise in his voice sent a shiver down her spine. *We are in this together. You, Gina, are mine.* She might not be an expert at reading between the lines, but she sensed undertones that he had a more proprietorial relationship in mind—a relationship that went beyond a professional employer-employee one.

In that instant, her life seemed to change before her eyes. Whether she wanted it or not, agreed to it or not, he was going to sweep her into something larger than her small world. For a woman who'd managed her life on her own, without anyone's help or interference, the idea scared her to death.

Desperate to escape until she could regain her equilibrium, she said, "I've got to go."

"Gina."

She stopped at the door. "Yes?"

"My driver will pick you up at seven."

"I'd rather drive myself."

"Not an option. Unless you'd rather we meet at your house?"

Did she want him in her home, filling it with his presence? She didn't think so. "What if I can't leave work on time?"

"Then I'll send the car here for you."

That option was worse because of the questions it would raise if anyone saw her or realized she'd left her vehicle in the parking lot. The ER staff was a sharp-eyed bunch.

Hating to give in, she had no choice. He'd won this round. "Fine," she said curtly. "I'll be ready at seven."

CHAPTER FOUR

"YOU have a lovely home," Gina remarked politely after Hugh had delivered her into Ruark's company later that evening.

"Thank you," he said. "May I take your jacket?"

She shrugged off the cardigan that complemented her yellow sleeveless knee-length sheath. It had taken her an hour to decide what to wear before she'd settled on this simple outfit, but after seeing Ruark, she wished she'd opted for something more elegant. He appeared informal with the sleeves of his white silk shirt rolled to his forearms and his collar and top button unfastened, but wearing his clothes in such casual abandon didn't hide the fabric's quality or the tailored fit.

"I'm surprised you found a place to live so quickly."

"Dr Lansing and his wife made the arrangements," he said. "I told them what I needed and they did the legwork."

The large foyer with its winding oak staircase and crystal chandelier definitely did not grace the houses in her moderately price neighborhood.

"It's huge. You must entertain a lot," she remarked.

"Hardly ever," he answered with a smile. "That's not to say I don't invite a few friends over, but nothing on a grand scale."

"No diplomatic events?"

"On occasion, but I don't host them at my private residence.

As for the size of the house, my staff live here as well." He grinned. "Tripping over each other isn't a good idea. We all need our privacy."

As a handsome prince, much less an eligible doctor, he probably needed more privacy than most, she thought irritably.

Before she could ask what staff requirements the modern working-man prince needed, he changed the subject. "Which would you prefer first, dinner or drinks?"

"Dinner, please," she said promptly. "Lunch was a long time ago."

He grinned. "A woman after my own heart. I hope you enjoy salmon."

"I do."

"Henri will be pleased. He's been fussing over the menu all afternoon." He seated her in the formal dining room where two places had been set at one end of a table capable of serving twelve. "I'll tell him to begin serving."

Gina studied the beautiful china before her. The crystal sparkled under the chandelier's lighting and she saw her reflection in the polished silver. Not quite the same as her chipped stoneware and stainless-steel utensils, she thought. At the same time, she realized exactly what her father had given up when he'd defied Parliament's decision—everything from having staff to see to his every need to the day-to-day tableware. Had he ever regretted his decision? She liked to think he hadn't.

Yet something he'd always told her popped into her mind. *People matter, Gina, not things.*

Ruark returned a minute later and sat at the head of the table. "Did you have a comfortable ride across town?"

She'd been expecting a limo and had been pleasantly surprised her escort had arrived in a more modest vehicle instead. "Yes, although I can tell you don't need to worry about your staff spilling any secrets. I could barely drag his name out of him."

Nervous about her upcoming evening, she'd tried to draw Hugh into a normal conversation about Marestonia and, of course, Ruark, but the security guard had limited his answers to one- or two-word replies.

He smiled. "Hugh's somewhat shy, but he makes up for it in other ways. His powers of observation are phenomenal. Nothing gets by his eagle eyes."

Great, she thought irritably. He'd probably seen her flexing her Italian charm bracelet and recognized it as the nervous mannerism it was. Realizing she was toying with it now, she let go of the metal with a decided snap and dug her fingers into the napkin on her lap.

A door leading from the kitchen swung open and a portly, middle-aged balding fellow appeared with two plates in hand.

"Gina, this is Henri. Henri, Dr Sutton."

"Pleased to meet you, *mademoiselle*." Henri set a plate of spinach salad before her. "The prince has spoken of you often."

She raised an eyebrow at Ruark before turning to smile at his chef. "Good things, I hope," she answered lightly.

"Oh, my, yes. All good things. Enjoy your meal." After placing Ruark's salad in front of him, he bowed, then disappeared.

"Henri's been with me for several years," Ruark offered. "He's quite temperamental when it comes to food."

"Oh?" She took a bite and nearly groaned with delight. The dressing had definitely not come out of a bottle.

"He's a stickler for timing. If anyone is five minutes late, he complains about dinner being ruined."

"You and your staff eat together?"

"Are you shocked?"

"A little," she admitted. "I didn't think a prince would associate with hired help. Protocol and all that."

"There are a few lines I don't cross, but dinner isn't one of them. You see, I hate to eat alone."

Gina did, too. Which was why she often stayed at the hospital and ate her evening meal at the cafeteria. Even if she sat by herself, hearing bits and pieces of conversations at other tables was better than having the television for company.

Maybe she should get a dog, although it wouldn't be fair for the poor creature to be alone all day.

"Perhaps you'll agree to join our group some time," he added.

"Perhaps," she answered, unwilling to commit herself although the idea intrigued her.

While Henri's grilled salmon, herb-roasted potatoes and glazed baby carrots gave her taste buds a real treat, Ruark entertained her with humorous stories from his previous jobs. Halfway through the meal, she became so focused on her companion and so caught up in their conversation, that she forgot the purpose behind her visit and began enjoying herself. Reality, however, set in after Ruark offered to serve coffee and dessert in his study. She hadn't made a purely social call.

"I'd like to thank you for coming tonight so we can discuss the problem before us," he said as he guided her into a room filled with a large oak desk, several Queen Anne chairs and a sofa covered in matching maroon and gold brocade, and built-in bookcases filled with tomes of all shapes and sizes.

She sank into a chair, noting he'd taken the one opposite. "I'm not convinced this is my problem."

"Poor choice of words. The *situation* before us."

"Why don't you cut to the bottom line and save us both some time?" she suggested.

"I'd rather start at the beginning. Just to be sure you understand what happened and why it affects current events."

"Suit yourself, but I'm not promising anything," she warned.

"Understood." He took a deep breath. "As you may know, in Avelogne, as in Marestonia, the government approves the marriages of the royal family as a formality. Unfortunately, when your father requested permission to marry your mother, Parliament denied his petition."

"Which was why he relinquished his claim to the throne and came to America," she finished. "Yes, I've heard the story of how a group of small-minded men in power didn't feel my mother had the right…" she drew imaginary quotation marks in the air "…'connections'. I never understood what the right connections would have been, other than she was a commoner instead of a royal."

"Our governments are more progressive in their beliefs than to get hung up on the royalty-versus-commoner issue," he pointed out somewhat defensively. "However, their decision was based on what appeared to be irrefutable evidence indicating that the royal family could be placed in a compromising position if Prince Arthur and Lizbet VanHorn married."

Her father had never mentioned any so-called evidence. "And this information was…?"

He hesitated, and Gina pressed on. "There can't be any secrets, Ruark. I have to know *everything*, good or bad."

Ruark cleared his throat. "Lizbet's father worked for a man who dealt in illegal activities, so there were suspicions of his involvement."

Illegal activities? Her dear, sweet grandpapa Jorge had been a criminal? He'd died when she'd been six—about five years before her mother's accident—but she couldn't believe the man who'd smelt of peppermints and tobacco and taken her to the park with a bag of day-old bread to feed the pigeons had been a part of the criminal element. Had her whole life, her family's seemingly normal life, all been a lie?

"Those activities were?" She raised an eyebrow.

"Drugs, prostitution, and anything else you can think of. Because of that association, your parents conducted their romance in secret. Your mother taught music at the primary level, lived a quiet, sedate life and was well liked, so Arthur believed his petition to marry her would be granted. After all, she couldn't be blamed or held accountable for her father's or his employer's actions.

"Unfortunately, as I've already told you, my aunt Margret had developed feelings for Arthur and was crushed when he didn't return her affections. Consequently, she, shall we say, *embellished* certain facts and arranged for the committee to receive information that called Lizbet's character into question."

"Embellished? Let's not sugar-coat this, Ruark. In other words, she *lied*."

He sighed. "Whatever term you wish to use, there was enough truth in the story to make the evidence appear irrefutable. That, coupled with a doubt here, a question there, and the members of the committee subsequently hesitated to give their approval."

"So that's why they denied his request." For the first time in her life she'd heard specific details, and her heart ached for her parents.

"Prince Arthur refused to let the government dictate his personal life so, against the Queen's wishes, he relinquished any future claims to the throne. His decision rocked the country but, being a second son, he was able to smooth over the issue with reminders that his chances of assuming the position of King were minimal at best. Because he publicly insisted how much he loved his future wife."

"He did," she insisted.

"No one is denying that. However, the people of Avelogne were incensed with Marestonia, accusing them of dishonesty and all manner of evil plots. In order to defuse the volatile situation, Arthur played on the people's romantic sympathies. He worked tirelessly for the two countries to maintain diplomatic ties, citing that this was a private matter and not a political one. Eventually, tempers softened as his appearances with your mother proved his sincerity, so everyone bowed to the inevitable and reluctantly accepted his decision. He married Lizbet and they moved to America, where you were born."

The story brought tears to Gina's eyes, but she blinked them away. "Didn't they try and prove Mother's innocence, not to mention my grandfather's?"

"The circumstantial evidence was too strong. And, I'm sorry to say, the royal family wanted the incident to die down as quickly as possible." He met her gaze. "I don't believe your grandmother expected Arthur to act as he did, but once he set the wheels in motion, she had to uphold the laws governing succession."

"And Margret? What happened to her?"

"She never married."

Gina swallowed the lump in her throat. "How did you learn the truth? If no one had been able to ferret out the facts at the time, how could anyone thirty years later?"

"Your uncle and my father quietly investigated from the beginning, but they kept running into dead ends. Witnesses disappeared, documents vanished, memories failed, until finally Arthur insisted they accept what they couldn't change. A few years ago Margret was diagnosed with a virulent form of brain cancer. In her diary, which we found shortly after her death, she admitted to her role in the scandal."

"Was she honest?"

"As honest as anyone would be when faced with their own mortality," Ruark replied. "We didn't have reason to doubt her account as she supplied all the information we needed. Names, dates, places."

"I see."

"It seemed pointless to act. Arthur and Lizbet had both died by then, too. Dredging up the old memories seemed counterproductive, although the few members of the committee who still sat in Parliament quietly resigned their positions."

"Bully for them."

"For the record," he continued, "your grandmother, the Queen Mother, regrets the events leading to your father's decision to leave Avelogne. She'd always hoped for a reconciliation, and his death upset her greatly. They would be grateful if you would agree to visit them some day soon."

"You can thank them for the invitation, but it isn't likely," she said politely. "It's too difficult to get away from the hospital."

Her excuse was flimsy, especially as the man who could arrange it in a heartbeat sat a few feet away, but he didn't argue.

"Regardless of the role Prince Arthur's family played in these events," he continued, "the bulk of the blame falls on the house of Marestonia."

Gina tried to tie the ends together, but couldn't. "Assigning blame isn't necessary," she mused aloud. "I appreciate finally knowing the truth, but it doesn't change what happened. Honestly? I don't see why this should be causing a problem now if the appropriate people knew the truth several years ago."

"Margret's diary recently fell into the wrong hands," he admitted, "and the information went public. The hostilities resurfaced because to the people of Avelogne this was one more in a long line of what they considered as poor decisions made by the ruling class."

"None of this makes sense," she protested. "If you're unhappy with your officials, you don't cause problems for other countries."

"You do if you feel the government has given those other countries, Marestonia in particular, favored status. You see, in trying to increase imports and exports, they granted special tax dispensations to Marestonian citizens who opened businesses or conducted trade in Avelogne. Now, with this news coming out, it's the proverbial last straw and they want their pound of flesh."

"Which is why they're pressuring Parliament to vote on

severing economic ties to Marestonia," she finished, finally understanding the dynamics.

"Yes. I've already explained the repercussions to both countries should that happen."

"Then offer an official apology. Take away the tax exemptions."

"Both Avelogne and Marestonia have prided themselves on their openness and honesty with each other. Many feel an apology isn't enough. As for the tax, I believe your Parliament plans to address the issue."

"Your family could build a new hospital or a school in my father's honor. That should make everyone happy."

"Excuse me, Your Highness." Hugh stepped into the room. "You must see this latest news report."

While Ruark opened the oak cabinet which hid the large-screen TV, Hugh immediately retrieved the remote and clicked on the set.

A picture flashed to a street where hundreds of people lined the sidewalks in front of a large building that Gina recognized as Avelogne's Parliament. Some carried signs, others chanted or waved angry fists at police who stood nearby in full riot gear.

A female reporter's voice explained the scene.

"As you can see," the nameless woman began, "people have come to the seat of government in response to a grass-roots effort to force Parliament into correcting what is perceived as a careless decision some thirty years ago involving Prince Arthur and his bride-to-be, Lizbet VanHorn. The mood is tense as most people here demand the authorities sever diplomatic ties with Marestonia. A number of people have already been arrested for inciting the crowd and it's obvious neither the government nor the royal family has a ready solution to this growing discontent.

"Businesses owned by Marestonians are being boycotted and many of them report they cannot keep their doors open or will be forced to lay off their employees if this continues. A number have reported increased amounts of vandalism ranging from broken windows to obscene graffiti."

The camera panned to one area where fisticuffs had broken out between several young men and police, then switched to show several others breaking car windows with rocks and tire irons. One view zoomed in on a child crying in his mother's arms after the family had been evicted from their apartment.

"As you can see," the announcer continued, "we have a volatile situation and if it escalates, Parliament has already threatened to set curfews and deploy national troops to maintain order."

Gina hardly noticed when Ruark clicked off the television. The screen had gone dark, but she was still taking in what she had seen and heard. "I thought you were exaggerating," she admitted, reeling from what she'd seen. "But you weren't, were you?"

He shook his head, then sat down. "No."

She faced him. "According to the reporter, no one in authority has a solution. What do you think I can do?"

"Diplomacy doesn't seem to be having an effect. The experts believe a more 'personal' solution between our families is required."

"We're already working with each other," she reminded him.

The corners of his mouth turned up slightly. "It's a start, but they're hoping to tie the two royal houses together."

"How would you tie two royal houses…?" Her voice died as she realized exactly the sort of "personal" relationship he wanted. "You can't possibly be thinking of…"

He finished her sentence. "Marriage."

Marriage.

The word echoed in her head.

Marriage.

To a man she'd only met earlier in the day.

After years of working in the ER, she'd always considered

herself unshockable, but that one word definitely shifted the ground underneath her. "We're supposed to get married?" she managed to croak.

He leaned forward and rested his elbows on his knees. "Yes."

Her heart pounded and an urge to escape swept over her. "This is a joke, right?"

"Not at all."

Her mind raced with possibilities. "You mean to tell me the diplomats of two countries can't dream up a better solution than to ask two strangers to marry?"

"We considered other options, but lawsuits, financial settlements, and economic sanctions are cold comfort to a person's pride. Those solutions would also cause undue hardship on both countries. I've seen too many hungry children in my relief work. I don't have a desire to see the same sad faces and malnourished bodies at home."

"Of course I don't want anyone to lose his job or go hungry," she snapped. "What kind of person do you think I am?"

"The sort who will do the right thing."

The enormity of the situation struck her and she rubbed the back of her neck. "This day can*not* be happening," she muttered. "It can't. First Bill, and now this. It's all a dream."

"I assure you it isn't," Ruark said.

She met his gaze. "The idea of using marriage as a diplomatic measure is so *medieval*!"

"Medieval or not, the practice isn't unheard of. Wars have been started over the very issue standing between Avelogne and Marestonia."

"Not in this day and age."

He raised an eyebrow. "Really? Tell that to all the countries who believe another has slighted them for whatever reason."

"Oh, great. You're going to hold me responsible for starting a war?"

"Matters won't go to that extreme, but strained relations won't do either country any good."

She shook her head. "No, but I can't believe a sane person actually proposed this as a solution or that two entire families gave it merit."

"I can assure you the Queen Mother of Avelogne is perfectly sane. As for the idea having merit, desperate times call for desperate measures."

Desperate times, desperate measures. She understood the concept.

"Look," she began, "I'm flattered you think I can help. I'm flattered that you, as a prince, would seriously consider marrying me sight unseen, but no one will believe we're sincere. Things are moving much too fast to be believable, unless you're thinking of a platonic marriage which we'll annul in a year or so." She raised an eyebrow.

"No annulment. No platonic marriage. This is for real."

So much for that idea. "Marriage is a big step to a couple who know each other, much less between two people who don't. The fact we're complete strangers may be a small, insignificant detail to you, but it isn't to me and I doubt if it is to everyone else. The people of both countries will see it as a ploy to manipulate them and they'll be right."

"Not if we convince everyone otherwise."

"I'm a physician, not an actress," she reminded him.

"Exactly." He sounded pleased. "No one will question a romantic relationship between two people who share the same career and work in the same facility."

The pieces fell into place—delivering the letter from her grandmother had only been a small part of the overall scheme. "You'd planned this all along, didn't you?"

His gaze locked on hers. "Of course. A marriage with the two of us on opposite sides of the country would draw suspicion."

"No one can pack up and move overnight. Job openings don't appear because you want them either."

"They don't," he agreed. "I began making inquiries several months ago."

Several months ago? "Don't tell me you had Bill Nevins fired so you could take his place." She didn't want to think of the sort of power Ruark might hold if he'd accomplished that feat.

"According to what I was told, Bill's management style had concerned Administration for some time. They'd been biding their time and quietly looking for a replacement so when I approached them about a position here, they were ready to act. It was the perfect opportunity for all of us. Except Nevins, of course."

Now she understood how a game piece token felt as the player moved it along according to the roll of the dice. Arranging the events that had brought the two of them to this point must have been as precisely orchestrated as a military campaign.

"Aren't you going out on a limb?" she asked, certain she'd found an ace up her sleeve. "What if I walk out that door and don't come back? You'll be stuck here, I'll be gone, and your grand scheme will fall apart."

"You won't leave."

She snorted at his confidence. "Don't be too sure."

"Oh, I'm sure, Gina." His dark gaze grew more intent and she sensed he would be a formidable opponent. "You see, you need this job because you're as proud as your father. As a matter of principle, he didn't use the funds the royal family provided when he left Avelogne and you haven't either, even though it would have made it completely unnecessary to borrow money to finance medical school. In fact, you and your father have already planned to leave the money to charity should anything happen to you. Half to an orphanage in Avelogne and the other half to—"

She was amazed by his unerring accuracy. "How do you know that?"

"You would be surprised what I know, but I can safely say you won't run away." He ticked off his points on his fingers. "One, you need a job, so you either must keep this one or find another. Two, you won't find another without a reference and guess who currently is responsible for writing one on your behalf?

"Three," he continued, "your contract states you must give ninety days' written notice. If you fail to honor those terms, we're back to reason number two. So, your argument about marrying a stranger is inconsequential because, one way or another, we'll be together for the next three months. We won't be strangers for long."

Darn the man, he was right!

"And if I refuse your gracious proposal?"

He raised one eyebrow. "I'm known to be quite persuasive."

She didn't doubt that a bit. Having met him less than twelve hours ago, she'd already seen evidence of his dogged determination to succeed at any cost. Plus, she was on *his* turf, without any form of transportation other than her own two feet, which meant he could hold her here for hours. Clearly, the odds of standing her ground weren't in her favor.

"Why are you accepting arrangements made without your consent?" she wanted to know. "It isn't as if you're the heir apparent. If you can choose your own career, you can surely choose your own wife."

As she spoke, she wondered what sort of woman he would have married if given the choice. Irrationally, the thought that she might not have attracted his attention under normal circumstances pricked her self-esteem.

"I can," he assured her. "For me, though, this is a matter of family honor and duty."

How could she argue with something so intangible, yet so powerful? "Just what every woman wants to hear," she said dryly. "A proposal offered out of duty."

He raised an eyebrow. "Would you rather I had pursued you for several weeks, professed enduring love and then rushed you to the altar? Eventually, you would have learned the truth and hated me for my dishonesty, which wouldn't have boded well for any marriage."

Once again, he was right, and she found his uncanny perception as irritating as his impersonal proposal. "What if I already *have* a fiancé?" she blustered.

CHAPTER FIVE

RUARK smiled, as if he knew she was grasping for an excuse. "You don't. You haven't dated anyone seriously for a number of months."

At least he hadn't pointed out her last date had been for the previous year's hospital Christmas party. Even so, he didn't need to sound so pleased with himself for pointing it out.

"I know more about you, Gina," he continued, "than you think I do."

What a scary thought. "There has to be an alternative," she said, desperately trying to think of one and failing miserably.

"If you think of one that our diplomats and scholars have overlooked, I'm willing to listen."

She had nothing, at least at the moment. "Look," she began, "for your plan to work, you're assuming we're compatible. What if we're not?"

"What if we are?" he countered. "We'll never know if we don't put in an effort."

She argued her case from another angle. "Why don't you issue a press release announcing that you proposed but I refused? You can claim you tried to do the right thing, but I didn't co-operate."

"Do you think my countrymen will be satisfied once they hear you've rejected their prince without cause, after knowing him less than twenty-four hours? They'll take it as a personal insult."

"Better to feel insulted than manipulated," she pointed out. "Knowing you proposed less than a day after meeting me isn't going to promote good public relations either. Neither is inventing a story to fool millions of people. Two wrongs don't make a right and being anything less than perfectly honest is a prescription for disaster."

"Stretching the truth goes against the grain with me, too," he admitted, "but we simply state the barest of facts and allow the press to draw their own conclusions. As luck would have it, we both attended the emergency medicine conference in Los Angeles six months ago. Registration records from both the conference and the hotel will prove it to anyone who questions us. People will logically believe we met and struck up a long-distance romance that led to me relocating to Belmont."

"You were at the conference?" Granted, there had been thousands in attendance, but how could she have missed him?

"All five days," he assured her.

This whole situation was spiraling more and more out of control. "Am I the only one who sees the inherent failure in this so-called *plan*?"

"We won't allow it to fail. It's the best solution, as far as I can see."

The man had to be blind, she thought, exasperated by his calm acceptance of the situation. "I don't know the first thing about being a princess. And in case you haven't noticed, things like this *just aren't done these days!*"

"Being a princess won't be any different than being a countess. You'll wake up every morning, go to work, and come home at night to your family."

Family. The term implied a husband, children, and everything associated with them—piano recitals, ball games, school events. She'd wished for relatives after her mother had died in a car accident and she'd had no one left except her father, but the demands of medical school and her career had pushed those dreams to the back of her mind. Realizing they could now be within reach, that they now fell in the realm of probability rather than possibility, was almost more than she dared to imagine. More importantly, the prospect of Ruark playing a prominent role in that scenario caused her toes to curl.

Yet, she'd learned a few lessons over the years. Few situations were as simple as they initially appeared.

"You've clearly forgotten how I was raised. My royal background was simply historical information, like having an ancestor who served in the First World War. It didn't factor into who I am today."

"Perhaps not entirely," he agreed. "We chose medicine as our profession and I doubt if either of us will give it up, so the major part of our lives won't change. Oh, we may have to appear at a diplomatic event every now and then but, I can assure you, those instances are rare. Probably a few times a year."

He was entirely too agreeable to a scenario that could end in a lifetime of disaster. She narrowed her gaze. "What's in this for you? Is someone giving you the keys to the national treasury, or what?"

His eyes reflected his gentle smile. "I had my doubts, too," he admitted, "but when I considered the repercussions if I refused to put the needs of my people before my own, my worries seemed insignificant in comparison."

While she hadn't expected him to swear undying love after a few hours and wouldn't have believed him if he had, she would like to think she was more than another obligation he had to fulfill. And yet it was silly to wish for that—they'd only met ten hours ago.

"I realize this idea is difficult to consider, much less accept," he said kindly. "But your father worked tirelessly to prevent what you saw from happening thirty years ago. Are you willing to let it happen today, when you have the power to prevent it?"

People matter, Gina, not things.

Knowing how much her father had loved Avelogne, she found herself actually giving Ruark's proposal serious thought…

"I don't want my father's efforts to have been in vain," she admitted, "but marriage should be based on more than politics, especially if it's supposed to endure through good times as well as bad."

"Ours will be," he assured her. "We have enough common interests to form a foundation for a satisfying life together."

Common interests. A satisfying life. It sounded as exciting as a bland diet. "When have you and your cronies planned this happy event, provided I agree, of course?"

"As soon as it can be arranged."

"As soon as…?" She didn't attempt to hide her shock. Marrying Ruark at some distant point in the future was a difficult enough concept to wrap her head around, but doing so as soon as possible? A shiver went down her spine, but she couldn't decide if fear or some twisted sense of anticipation caused her reaction.

"Why the rush? Why not, say, six months?" Surely in that length of time the crisis would resolve itself or she would find a another solution.

"Six months? Impossible. Time is of the essence. Discontent grows with every day we delay."

She'd seen the newscast, so she couldn't argue his point. "Yes, but rushing to the altar will only raise more questions." She eyed him closely. "I do hope you aren't going to hint a royal baby's involved."

He grinned. "That's an idea no one's considered. I'm sure we'll make beautiful babies."

A mental picture of a long, lean masculine form tangled in sheets, his whisker-rough face relaxed in sleep as he spooned his body against hers created a sudden and unsettling ache in her core. She rubbed her forehead with an unsteady hand to dispel the image, and it instantly changed. A boy with Ruark's dark hair and impish smile appeared, followed by a little girl who resembled Gina in her childhood photos. They were definitely beautiful children, but this wasn't the time to think about offspring.

She drew a cleansing breath as she blinked away the vision. "Whether we will or won't isn't the issue," she stated firmly. "The point is, don't you dare suggest I'm pregnant because I can guarantee your story will backfire."

He raised one eyebrow. "Will it?"

Something in his eyes suggested that he wouldn't mind making a baby a reality. As for her, the notion of sharing a bed, feeling his intimate touch on her bare skin, was enough to send another wave of heat coursing through her. Marrying a man out of duty—a man she'd just met—wasn't supposed to cause such an intense reaction, was it?

She struggled to rein in her thoughts. "We aren't going to muddy the waters any more than they already are," she ordered, hoping he hadn't noticed how breathless she sounded.

He paused. "Perhaps it's for the best," he mused, "but, as I said before, time is our enemy. Parliament will vote at the end of October to sever diplomatic ties, so the sooner we act, the better."

"Maybe everyone will be satisfied with an engagement announcement," she suggested hopefully.

He shook his head. "If we don't follow through with a wedding, the whole plan will seem contrived and we'll have worse problems. There's truly no sense in prolonging the inevitable."

Reluctantly, she saw his point. Better to rip off the adhesive bandage rather than tear it off in tiny, painful increments. "Tell me how this is going to work," she said tiredly, hoping he hadn't noticed how she'd slipped and used the present tense.

"I'll arrange for a civil ceremony as soon as possible. Once our union is official, my father will announce our marriage and we'll begin our life as a couple."

A civil ceremony. Not quite the wedding she'd imagined but,

then, she'd never dreamed about marrying a man she didn't love in a business arrangement.

"How do you explain why we're not having an official state wedding?"

"You want to be married in the US because it's been your home," he said simply. "With your father deceased, you preferred a private gathering with only your closest friends. No one will question your decision."

"Other than we're rushing into this."

"Rushing only adds to the romanticism," he assured her. "Especially if we hint at our impatience to be together after I moved to Belmont."

He'd thought of everything, which irritated her. "Am I allowed to choose my own dress, or have you organized that, too?"

He went on as if he hadn't noticed the sarcasm in her voice.

"After the ceremony, we act as any married couple. A few photos and a couple of carefully screened interviews should convince everyone in Marestonia and Avelogne to put the past behind them."

"And if we fight like cats and dogs?"

His now-familiar half-smile appeared. "We won't."

"How can you be so sure?"

"Gut feeling."

"And if you're wrong?"

"I'm not."

"But if you are?" she persisted.

He leaned forward. "We're both adults and know what's at stake. We have to make this work, Gina. We *can* make it work."

He sounded so certain, but was he trying to convince himself or her?

She couldn't deny her physical attraction to him, but she'd always imagined experiencing a grand passion. Considering how her father had sacrificed everything to marry the woman he'd loved, how could she do any less, no matter how handsome or charming the man was? And yet how could she ignore the repercussions if she didn't do something to calm the troubled waters?

"You may not find me as distasteful as you imagine."

He'd spoken lightly, but she sensed his hurt. He'd argued his case in such coolly logical terms that she'd forgotten her lack of co-operation was as much a rejection of him as it was for the plan he'd presented.

Her face warmed and she tried to minimize the damage. "I'm sorry, Ruark. My objections aren't directed toward you personally. I'd always imagined I'd have a marriage like my parents', not one borne out of convenience or duty. And certainly not one that was forced upon me to solve a national crisis."

He nodded, as if he understood. "It does take a bit of time to grow accustomed to the idea."

She met his gaze. "How long did it take *you* to become a willing participant in this…this plan?"

He shrugged. "You forget I was raised to place my country's needs before my own. If one looks at the big picture, there are far worse things I could do than marry a beautiful woman who shares my passion for medicine."

She wondered if he was simply spouting flattery to get on her good side, but there probably *were* worse things she could have been asked to do. However, at the moment she couldn't think of what could be worse than marrying a man she'd just met, regardless of how attractive he was.

"And if this grand scheme doesn't work?" she asked. "If people don't care about our marriage?"

"They will," he assured her. "Trust me." He paused. "Are you willing to marry me, Gina?"

Ruark's question hung in the air. Was she willing?

Hardly, she thought. Unfortunately, as Gina glanced at the now-darkened television screen, the newscast and Ruark's predictions haunted her. As much as she hated to be a pawn, she *was* her father's daughter, which meant she had to uphold her father's reputation. How well would the people of his homeland remember him if she, as his daughter, ignored their problems?

She may not have been raised under the same strict code of duty and honor that Ruark had been, but she, too, had learned similar lessons from her father. More importantly, she carried enough royal blood in her veins to know she couldn't besmirch Arthur Sutton's memory or do anything that would reflect poorly on her beloved papa. Holding out for a so-called "grand passion" that might never occur was too high a price to pay.

"I'll go along with the plan," she reluctantly agreed, "but I'm concerned about one thing." She met his gaze with steel in her own.

"Which is?"

"What if you meet someone else? Someone you fall in love with? What then?"

"I won't."

She eyed him with skepticism. "You don't know that."

"I'm thirty-five years old, Gina. I've dated my share of women and been involved in a number of relationships. Falling in love is an overrated concept, especially when one considers the problems Margret's so-called love for your father has created," he added dryly. "Far better for both parties to build a relationship on respect and mutual interests rather than on something as changeable as emotions."

Thinking of her parents' love for each other, the lengths they had gone to just to be together, she disagreed. "You have a rather cynical view."

He shrugged. "The best one can hope for is congenial companionship. I believe we can find it in the course of carrying out our duty."

He'd used that word again. Duty. Never had such a tiny word carried such a heavy burden, but she'd made a promise. As she studied her future husband, a variety of emotions swirled around her. Marriage to a handsome man who wore sex appeal like a well-fitting garment was both exciting and nerve-racking. For a woman who'd placed the prospect at some distant point in the future, knowing that the future was *now* was quite scary, too.

"Let's hope so," she agreed. "But this marriage…" She paused. "You truly want it to be real."

He nodded. "In every sense."

Once again, her hand trembled. "Yes, but—"

"We won't be convincing if it isn't," he said gently.

"I know, but making…" Knowing his views on the subject, she bit off the word "love" and corrected herself. "Having sex with a stranger, much less my boss, is going to be difficult."

"Not if you think of me as your husband first."

Husband. Her mouth suddenly went dry at the thought.

"But," he continued, nodding as if he understood her dilemma, "I understand your concerns so I'll give you time to adjust."

"How much?"

He met her gaze and the heat she saw in those depths reminded her of a lion she'd seen on television eyeing a tasty doe. "We'll play it by ear," he finally said.

While she would have preferred a specific date, knowing he would give her the luxury of getting to know each other first helped ease her mind about their quasi-business arrangement. "OK."

"Good. I'll set the wheels in motion." He rose then, as if he'd sensed her inner turmoil, stopped in front of her chair, pulled her into his embrace and tucked her head underneath his chin. "This will work out, you'll see."

"I'm not as sold on the idea as you are," she said wryly as she held herself stiffly against him.

"I have enough confidence for both of us," he said before he tipped her chin up to kiss her.

The pressure of his mouth was gentle, his hold on her loose

enough that she could break free if she wanted to, but that made all the difference. Instead of feeling trapped, she felt reassured, as if he'd transferred his faith to her through that small but intimate contact. Earlier in the day her instincts had told her she could trust him as a physician. Now her trust had somehow expanded to include the entire man.

As she inhaled his scent and found it utterly delightful, she relaxed against him, conscious of how this simple kiss had sealed their agreement in a way that mere words or a handshake could never have accomplished.

Slowly, almost reluctantly, he raised his head, and she pulled away as the special moment passed. Unsure of what to say or do next, she simply met his gaze and offered a small smile, which he returned.

"Your father would be proud of you," he said simply.

She'd like to think so, but she also knew how strongly he adhered to his principles. "Would he? I'm not so sure he'd approve of a pretend romance. After all, we're not being completely honest, are we?"

"We're being honest enough. As for a romance, few will concern themselves with how it begins. Only with how it ends."

Ruark strolled into Belmont's ER the next morning with a smile on his face and a spring in his step. Last night had gone better than he'd initially hoped. In fact, he suspected the newscast had done more to persuade her than anything he'd said. No matter how it had happened, Gina had finally agreed, and that was all that mattered.

It wasn't until he began the detailed tour of what would soon become her home that he realized the enormity of his situation.

He was getting married.

Acquiring Gina as his wife wasn't a mere theory or a step-by-step plan any longer. Promises had been exchanged and he felt more committed now than he had when he'd first agreed to perform his duty.

He would have a spouse and, eventually, children to call his own.

The additional responsibility bore down on him, but he wasn't afraid or nervous. As he'd kissed her, the most delightful hungry sensation had swept over him. Her feminine scent and the way she had felt in his arms had made it difficult to maintain his control. Pouncing on her while they had been sealing their bargain would have been completely inappropriate, but he would be patient. Their strong physical attraction seemed to confirm that they would enjoy the same companionship his parents did.

In spite of his parents' urging over the years, he hadn't met anyone he'd wanted to marry or whom he'd considered a potential bride until Gina. But with her, he'd felt an indefinable "click" between them, as if fate had already decreed they belonged together. That feeling was more important than the nebulous emotion of love that so many searched for and rarely found.

Her worries about him falling in love with someone after they were married were completely groundless. He'd been with plenty of women who'd professed to love him, then had left when their eyes had landed on someone else. Friendship, coupled with a significant dose of lust, was love enough for him and certainly didn't make one as vulnerable. He wasn't looking for, or expecting, more than that and he believed he'd made his feelings clear. He didn't want her to harbor any false expectations.

As for Gina's expectations, she'd been remarkably closemouthed during their tour of his home. He'd half expected her to balk and protest at sharing his bedroom, but she hadn't. Her face had paled, but she hadn't shown any other reaction. Instead, she'd tentatively asked if she could move her mother's oak quilt stand into a corner.

It had been the first—and only—request she'd made. By then he would have agreed to anything just to see a smile.

Something inside him cautioned him on the importance of smoothing her transition into her new life. If not, they'd never develop the sort of amicable relationship he wanted, much less the sort necessary for their plan to work.

Yet he had other reasons for wanting to minimize the stress of a quick wedding. She'd looked lost, as if everything she'd ever known or believed in had been ripped out from under her and her forlorn expression had tugged at his gut.

When she found her footing again, he wanted to figure prominently in the picture, to be the rock she leaned on, just as his friends' wives leaned on their husbands. It was the only way their relationship would work.

Of course, their mutual interest in medicine was a plus, and the physical attraction that arced between them practically guaranteed a successful marriage. He'd been resigned to performing his duty, but now he was actually looking forward to it.

In fact, he was quite glad the political analysts didn't believe a mere engagement would solve Marestonia and Avelogne's problems. Nothing but a wedding ring on her finger would prove the two families had worked through their differences, and he was more than happy to oblige.

While he might be eager to fulfill his royal obligations, Gina clearly was not. Working together would present ample opportunity to develop a relationship that would calm her fears, starting now….

He rounded the corner and saw her standing with several staff members at the nurses' station, wearing a freshly starched lab coat over a deep purple scrub suit. Her shoulder-length hair gleamed under the fluorescent lights and reminded him of the young lioness he'd seen at the grand opening of the Marestonia National Zoo. Just seeing her made him forget his briefcase full of papers to review and the rainy-day forecast.

"Good morning," he said casually as he approached, trying to tone down his enthusiasm at seeing her again.

Gina's face turned a becoming shade of pink. "Good morning," she mumbled warily.

Determined to set her at ease, he turned on his professional demeanor.

"Anything interesting?" he asked as he glanced at the board. Four rooms were occupied, which wasn't unusual for a morning. After translating the shorthand, the diagnoses included emphysema, an orthopedic consult, a diabetic, and the one thing that sent people running to the ED—chest pain.

"Um, yeah, the orthopedic consult."

"Unusual sports injury?"

"In a manner of speaking. A lady fell off her high heels. Poor thing."

"What happened?"

"She'd overslept this morning and was running out to her car when her heel caught in a sidewalk crack. She started to fall, and twisted her knee in the hope she'd save her panty hose."

"No kidding?"

"Hey, snagging one's last pair of panty hose is serious business. Anyway, she landed wrong and heard her knee pop."

"Torn ACL?" he asked, using the abbreviation for the anterior cruciate ligament.

"I'd say so, but I'm waiting for Tribble, the orthopedic surgeon, to drop by. If it is her ACL, she's looking at surgery and lots of physical therapy. In the meantime, she's icing her knee and swearing off high heels." She smiled ruefully. "The price we pay for fashion."

"You have to admit, high heels are rather sexy."

"Really? You think so?" She sounded interested in his opinion.

"Trust me, they are." He raised his briefcase as he dropped his teasing tone. "About our ceremony…"

"What about it?" she asked hurriedly, taking one step toward his office in an obvious attempt to hold their conversation in more private surroundings.

Sensing Lucy's and the ward clerk's interest, he didn't budge. "It's tomorrow night, eight o'clock. In the chapel upstairs."

Her eyes widened. "How…? When…did you arrange that?"

"'Where there's a will, there's a way'." He cheerfully quoted the cliché. "Actually, I've been busy this morning."

In truth, he'd hardly slept at all last night. After he'd taken Gina home, he'd dialed his father's private extension to break the news to his ecstatic parents. Not only did Gina's acceptance signal the beginning of the end to their current problems, but their youngest son, who'd fiercely vowed to remain single, was getting married after all.

No doubt the palace staff had been as busy as his own after their conversation had ended.

"What ceremony?" Lucy asked, curiosity oozing out of her.

Ruark slid one arm around Gina's waist and hugged her close. "We're getting married and everyone's invited."

CHAPTER SIX

WE'RE getting married....

Ruark's announcement couldn't have been more shocking or exciting to the ER staff than a ten-million-dollar lottery win. Staff members suddenly appeared from out of nowhere and fired question after question until her head spun.

"How did you two meet? We want details," someone cried out.

"How long have you planned this?"

"Are you going on a honeymoon?"

Gina had never run from problems before, but certainly wanted to now. Ruark had created this sideshow and he could deal with it, she thought unreasonably, yet she knew she belonged at his side. Leaving him to fend questions by himself would cause people to speculate and draw the wrong conclusions, which would cause the plan to fall apart.

So she allowed him to anchor her to his hip and tried to look like an excited soon-to-be bride. It was difficult at first, but being surrounded by his masculine scent, tucked under his arm and plastered against him helped her assume the role.

After her alarm had gone off that morning, she'd almost assured herself that yesterday, and more specifically last night, had been part of a strange quasi-nightmare, but as soon as Ruark had breezed in wearing a cheery smile and looking quite satisfied with the world, she knew she hadn't dreamed a single minute.

Dinner, their bizarre conversation, agreeing to his marriage proposal—they had all actually taken place. And when he'd suggested they'd marry as soon as it could be arranged, she'd been half-afraid Ruark would whip a minister out of the closet by the time Henri served coffee and chocolate éclairs. She'd honestly believed she'd had at least a week, but a day? Why, she couldn't think of a suitable item in her closet to wear!

Her wedding garment aside, she would have one final evening to herself. After that, she'd be with Ruark in one capacity or another twenty-four seven, which would be enough to send her into a panic, if she were the panicky sort.

Idly, she wondered if he realized she wasn't a social butterfly, didn't belong to any ladies' or civic groups, and didn't have any serious hobbies. She jogged for exercise, preferred quiet evenings at home or in the company of a few close friends, and had memorized the take-out phone numbers for nearly every restaurant within a two-mile radius of her apartment. If he was looking for a socialite, the proverbial Earth Mother, or Suzy Homemaker, he would be sorely disappointed.

Disappointing him concerned her, although why she should worry if she did or not, she didn't know. She was what she was, and he would have to deal with her flaws and idiosyncrasies just like everyone else.

Fortunately, by the time she'd come to those terms, Ruark was finishing his speech. "We'll expect you all there," he told the excited staff moments before he tugged her into his office.

"Next time, could you give me a few minutes to pull my thoughts together before you drop your bombshells?" she asked waspishly as soon as they were alone. "Or maybe you'd like me to run out and announce who you really are, *Your Royal Highness*."

"They'll find out tomorrow when we make our vows," he

said, sounding unconcerned by her threat to expose his secret. "By the way, I need your house keys."

She eyed him suspiciously. "What for? I'll pack my own things, thank you very much."

"Hugh and Joachim need access to your home in order to install a security system."

"A security system?" she echoed. "Why?"

"Because it needs one," he informed her. "Until we decide how we're going to combine households, we either have a state-of-the-art system in place or I hire more security. Considering your place is rather small, I can either station people outside or bring in an RV to use as their base of operation."

She shuddered, both from the thought of what the neighbors would think to the way he made it sound as if guarding her was a military exercise. The idea of anyone observing her every move, even for her own protection, was daunting and thoroughly foreign. She didn't like it. Better to have an electronic watchdog than a real one.

"My keys are in my locker. I'll get them."

She hurried out and, after dodging the gauntlet of well-wishers, returned a few minutes later. "Here," she said, dropping both the front and back door keys into his palm. "Anything else?"

"Not at the moment."

With that, she fled, hoping, *praying* for a patient she could tend to. Luckily, she walked past several cubicles with charts waiting in the bins outside the doors. Grabbing the first medical record like a lifeline, she focused her attention on her job, although she soon found herself fielding situations that went beyond her new responsibilities. Ruark had been adamant about handling the administrative issues himself, so she passed them off to him all day long.

"Dr Sutton, Dr Casey called in sick again. He needs someone to take his place."

"Tell Dr Thomas."

"Dr Sutton, Central Supply says we can't have three-cc syringes because they're back-ordered. What do we want, ones or tens?"

"Tens, but tell Dr Thomas."

"Dr Sutton, we have a patient who insists one of us misplaced his false teeth while he was here yesterday, but no one remembers a patient with dentures."

"Tell Dr Thomas."

Unfortunately, he bounced those same issues back at her. It wasn't his fault. He was still trying to find his footing, but it meant she dealt with the problems twice. She simply had to be patient until he learned the ins and outs of their department's management.

"Gina, where's the list of locum physicians?"

"File cabinet, top drawer."

"Gina, who's in charge of Central Supply?"

"Jessie Ames. Extension 4125."

Amazingly enough, he didn't ask her to look into the missing denture problem, so when she interrupted him for a patient consultation, she brought up the subject herself.

"Oh, that," he said when questioned. "He wasn't our patient. He'd gone to St Bridgit's, so I happily referred him over there."

St Bridgit's was a small hospital across town, about half the size of Belmont, but in spite of being Belmont's competitor, they shared a congenial working relationship.

"I'm glad it was them and not us," she commented, thinking of all the paperwork they'd been spared.

"Tell me about it," he said fervently, before he leaned back in his chair and steepled his fingers. "What's on your mind?"

Think of me as your husband first. Although he'd made that statement in regard to their hours spent privately, it was far too easy to think of him in that light every time she saw him. Perhaps once the shock wore off, she'd become better at compartmentalizing her life, but right now she was having difficulty separating Ruark, her future husband, from Ruark Thomas, her boss.

As his calm gaze met hers, she clutched the chart in her hand and forced herself to focus on her patient. "Roger Davis is sixty-three years old and has a history of type-two diabetes. He's been vomiting since yesterday morning and hasn't been able to keep anything down."

"Has he taken his insulin?"

"He claims he has." Gina ran through his symptoms. "He doesn't have fever, diarrhea, headache, achiness or chest pain. As expected, his electrolytes show he's slightly dehydrated so he's presently on IV fluids."

"Any history of GI problems?"

"None."

"Lab work?"

"Pending. His bedside glucose was 405, which is four times the normal. Critical, in fact."

"Food poisoning?"

"It's possible," she admitted. "Diabetics who are sick can have results in the two or three hundreds, but four hundred seems excessive for a simple case of food poisoning."

"Want me to take a look?" he asked.

"Would you mind?"

She escorted him to room two. Mr Davis sat on the edge of the bed, wearing a green Hawaiian-print shirt and pressed tan slacks. His dark brown hair was clearly courtesy of a toupee, but the IV in his hand, coupled with him retching into a plastic basin in his lap, spoiled the effect of a vacationing businessman.

"This is Dr Thomas," Gina announced. "And this is your lucky day. You get to see two of us for the price of one."

"I don't feel too lucky right now. In fact, I feel awful. Can't you do something to stop me heaving up my insides?"

"We're working on it," Ruark promised. "Are you able to keep anything down? Water? Tea?"

"Not for long."

"Are you having trouble urinating?"

"Haven't noticed, so I guess not."

He turned to Gina. "I want a urine sample."

"He already gave one. We're waiting for the lab report."

Ruark turned back to Roger. "Sit tight. We'll be right back."

He nodded right before another spate of retching struck. The two of them left him clutching his emesis basin.

"Any ideas?" she asked once they'd stepped into the hallway.

"I know it's easy for us to explain the unexplainable as a virus or food poisoning, but the other signs aren't there."

"I agree."

"He might have a urinary tract infection."

"I thought of that." She approached Ruby. "Check on Davis's urinalysis results, will you?"

Ruby handed her a page. "They came through a minute ago."

Gina scanned the document. "Bingo," she said before handing it to Ruark.

"The only problem is," he said slowly, "simple bladder infections don't cause vomiting, even in diabetics."

"What are you thinking?"

He shrugged. "Hard to say. His temperature, pulse and respirations are all normal, as is his blood pressure. How do you take temperatures here?"

"Ear probe."

"Can we get a rectal temp?"

"Sure, why not?" She waved at Lucy and made her request.

The nurse frowned as she listened, but she agreed to take the required temp. "I hope you aren't going to want these on everybody," she grumbled before she disappeared into Davis's cubicle. A few minutes later, she returned with a wide smile on her face. "It's 102."

"Then he *does* have a fever," Gina mused. "A urine infection, plus fever, plus vomiting adds up to—"

"Sepsis," Ruark finished.

Somehow, the bacteria invading Roger Davis's bladder had spread into his bloodstream and were attacking the man's natural defense systems. Left untreated, his blood vessels would collapse and his kidneys would fail.

Gina turned to Ruby. "Call the lab. I want stat blood cultures and then we're going to admit him." She faced Ruark and walked him back to his office. "A heavy dose of antibiotics is in order, wouldn't you say?"

He grinned. "Well done, Doctor."

She'd been set to congratulate herself on treating him as she would any other colleague, but before she could, he'd covered her hand with both of his. After Ruark's announcement, no one would comment or question if they were seen, but he was doing more than hold her hand. The small circles he traced in her palm nearly drove her crazy and caused her knees to grow weak. His touch sent a delicious shiver down her spine, but she found herself powerless to break contact.

And his eyes held such promise…such passion…and such frustration, as if he wanted to do much, much more….

Surprisingly enough, she wanted it, too. What was it about this man that he could so easily cause her to react like an infatuated teenager?

He'd said they'd take things slow and play having a physical relationship by ear. At this rate, they'd both be jiggling the bedsprings before the ink had dried on their marriage license.

"Same to you," she managed to say. "I wouldn't have considered taking a rectal temp."

He shrugged. "Sometimes you learn a few tricks. By the way, I forgot to tell you last night about Janice Myers."

His gentle caress befuddled her to the point where she had to forcibly think about who Janice Myers was. When she did, she was pleased her voice sounded normal, even though her pulse rate wasn't. "What did Horton find?"

A twinkle appeared in his eyes. "It was her appendix. Red, swollen, and ready to burst. If he'd delayed a few more hours, she'd be fighting peritonitis."

Gina's spirits soared. "I was right."

"And everyone knows it. From what I heard, Frank grumbled about doing the procedure from the time they wheeled her into the OR until he opened her up and it nearly jumped out at him. According to rumor, the nurses are hounding him to apologize, so be prepared."

She laughed, thrilled her instincts hadn't failed her. As much as she hated confrontation, arguing with the man had been worth every tense moment. "OK, but I won't hold my breath. Meanwhile, do you want to tell our patient his good news?"

"Go ahead. I have a ton of paperwork to finish before our date tonight."

"Our date?" she repeated.

"Sure. I thought we'd go to dinner."

"Sorry," she shook her head. "It's bad luck for the groom to see the bride before the wedding."

"I thought that applied to the day of the ceremony."

"Could be," she admitted, "but I have a hundred and one things to do before tomorrow."

"Then it's a good thing I've changed the schedule so we both have the next couple of days off. It won't be the longest of honeymoons, but we'll still have one."

Her face warmed as she'd hadn't given thought to anything other than the ceremony. In fact, she would have probably reported for her shift the next day as usual. So much for presenting the picture of wedded bliss. Suddenly, what they were about to do, and the ramifications if they—*she*—took a false step and committed a social error, overwhelmed her.

He shook his head and smiled. "Can't have the newlyweds working the day after, can we?"

She managed a smile. "Honestly? I hadn't thought about it."

"I have," he said firmly.

"Yes, but I didn't. And there's the problem." She tried to tug her hand free, but he didn't release it.

"I don't see one."

"Then you aren't looking. It's as plain as the nose on your face." She met his gaze, certain he would read the sorrow in her eyes. "This isn't going to work."

He frowned, before he pulled her into the nearest empty exam room. "Why do you say that?" he asked as soon as he'd closed the door and blocked it with his foot.

"Because I'm going to make a mistake and we won't convince anyone that this marriage isn't a farce," she wailed, tears threatening at the prospect of dragging her father's name through the proverbial mud when she failed. "The schedule is a prime example. I would have come on duty the next day and not thought a thing about it."

"Do you honestly believe I wouldn't have noticed if you'd gotten up at 5:00 a.m.? That I wouldn't have stopped you?"

He sounded incredulous, and hearing him state it like that she felt a twinge of embarrassment before she squared her shoulders and looked him straight in the eye.

"The point is, you would have had to stop me. What happens when you aren't around to correct my blunders? I'll do or say something that will raise questions and then—"

"You're being too hard on yourself," he told her. "In a few days you'll settle into a new routine and you'll be fine."

"And if I'm not?"

"Then everyone will believe my wife is a dizzy blonde and will feel sorry for me," he said soberly.

She narrowed her eyes as his comment sank in. "Did you call

me a dizzy blonde?" Then, as soon as she saw his smile, she knew he'd only been trying to end her pity party, and he'd succeeded. She punched him playfully in his biceps.

"Those are fighting words," she said without heat.

"Noted. As for making mistakes, I hear it's a common phenomenon among newlyweds. After my brother's wedding, he introduced his wife to the German ambassador as his girlfriend, which caused more than a few chuckles, although my sister-in-law didn't find it as humorous as we did."

"I'm sure she didn't."

"The point is, don't worry."

Easier said than done, but his confidence was infectious. "Is that a royal decree?" she asked lightly.

"Absolutely." He tipped her chin up so their gazes met. "Better?"

She nodded. "Yeah. Thanks."

With a feather-light touch, he tucked a lock of her hair behind one ear before he lowered his head and kissed her.

It began softly, tentatively, then became more demanding and certain. He pulled her against him and the heat from his body penetrated her scrub suit and heavy lab coat.

He nibbled on her lower lip and she opened her mouth to tease him in kind before the soft, erotic touch of their tongues meeting made her burst into flames.

Instinctively, she threaded her arms around his neck and stood on tiptoe to press herself against him. His lips moved from her mouth to her cheek, then to her ear, before trailing down her neck. She leaned her head back, eager to offer more of herself to him, until she heard voices outside.

He must have, too, because he instantly stilled, then loosened his hold on her and grinned.

"Do not say a word," she ordered as she ran her hands through her hair and checked her clothing. Nothing seemed amiss, so she flung open the door.

"Gina?" he called.

"What?" She paused on the threshold, irritated by her enthusiastic response as much as she was awed by his kiss.

"You look…" He paused, then smiled.

Once again, she checked herself. "You were saying?"

"Now you look 'engaged'."

Gina clutched the bouquet of flowers Ruark had given her prior to their wedding ceremony in a near death-grip, conscious of Ruark—her *husband!*—following her into his home around ten o'clock the next evening. He looked exceedingly handsome in his black tuxedo and she could imagine how breathtaking he would be if he'd worn his official state dress, complete with ribbons, sashes and sword. Clothes may not make the man, but they certainly dazzled feminine eyes.

And while their wedding had been an impromptu affair, she was glad she'd chosen this calf-length lacy white dress that swirled so invitingly around her legs instead of the business suit she'd initially planned to buy. She hadn't felt this feminine since the last formal ball she'd attended as a med student.

"The ceremony and reception afterward turned out well, didn't it?" she asked as she stood in the hallway and wondered where to go next.

He raised one eyebrow. "Did you expect otherwise?"

"To be honest, I didn't know *what* I was expecting," she admitted. "You truly thought of everything."

He had. The hospital chaplain had performed the ceremony as the thirty guests filled the chapel to capacity. Afterwards, they'd gone to a conference room for a small reception with the required cake and punch. A chamber ensemble had provided the music and a short, homely fellow had bustled around, taking photographs until she'd hardly been able to see anything except spots. Someone had decorated the chapel and the reception room using the same mixed flower theme as in her bouquet.

Somehow Ruark had even managed to book an appointment with her hairdresser and a manicurist for earlier in the day.

She couldn't think of a thing that had been missed. No one could accuse them of shortchanging their wedding—other than the bride and groom not being in love, of course.

Don't think about that, she scolded herself. *You knew what you were agreeing to, as well as Ruark's feelings on the subject. You can't look back. Only forward.*

"I tried," he said as an embarrassed grin appeared. "We're only doing this once so I wanted you to have all the trappings."

Touched by his effort to make this day as special as possible under the circumstances, a lump formed unexpectedly in her throat. "Thank you," she whispered.

"Before you credit me with all the details, I should probably admit my staff reminded me of a few things and handled most of the legwork. The guest book, bows on the pews." He shrugged. "Things like that."

"Regardless, you did a remarkable job on such short notice. Frankly, you delivered more than I expected. Maybe you should go into the wedding planning business," she said lightly, holding her slightly wilted bouquet like a talisman. "You're wasted as a physician."

He visibly shuddered. "Sorry. Give me a trauma, not color schemes and cake flavors."

"Speaking of cake, it was delicious." To be honest, she hadn't actually tasted it until her last two bites, but those two bites had been exquisite.

"Thank Henri. He's been creating since you left the other night," he admitted on a wry note. "He insisted on white but knows I prefer chocolate, so he baked one of each."

"I'll speak to him," she promised.

Ruark loosened his bow-tie and shrugged off his jacket. "I shouldn't be hungry, but I am. Want to raid the refrigerator?"

Her stomach still hadn't settled from her nervous excitement, but sitting in the kitchen appealed far more than unpacking her suitcase or going straight to bed. "Sure, why not?"

But once they'd entered Henri's domain and found him packaging the remnants of their reception for the freezer, he waved his arms and dismissed them.

"What man thinks of food on his wedding night?" the Frenchman chided.

Ruark winked at Gina. "A hungry one."

Henri tutted before promising to bring a tray upstairs, his florid face beaming at the couple. "Now, shoo. Go and enjoy each other."

Literally pushed out of the room, the chef's comment seemed to echo in the empty dining hall. *Enjoy each other.*

For some reason, she found the Frenchman's instructions sweet, although from Ruark's disconcerted expression he did not.

"Does he know about—?" she began.

"Yes, but he's a romantic at heart. So, shall we adjourn upstairs, as we've been commanded?" he said dryly. "Or head for the study to watch television?"

She wasn't ready to enter his bedroom so she chose the alternative. "The study," she answered promptly.

But once there she was too keyed up to focus on world events, the weather forecast, or the current baseball standings. She strolled around the room and noticed the eight-by-ten framed portrait of his family on his desk. It was an official photo because the men wore ribbons, sashes and swords, and the women wore ballgowns, diamonds and rubies. What struck her most was how closely the men resembled each other.

"Tell me about your family," she said, hoping to hear they were like everyone else underneath their royal trappings.

He joined her at his desk. "This is my father, Frederick." He pointed to the distinguished-looking gentleman wearing a gold crown. "He's been the King of Marestonia for the last fifteen years since my grandfather died. My mother, Christina, is from Sweden and stays busy with her charity work. When she's not traveling or fund-raising, she's busy with our family and state events. Don't worry, though, she'll welcome you with open arms."

"I see." She hadn't met the woman and Gina was already intimidated by her activities and accomplishments.

"This is my oldest brother, George. He's married and has two children, both girls, with another baby on the way."

"Boy or girl?"

"The last I knew, they refused to reveal the baby's sex. I suspect it's a boy because George seems to smirk more than usual these days." He grinned. "He's always been the doting papa, though, so I could be wrong.

"Pieter is next. He's quite serious about a young lawyer friend, but they haven't issued any formal announcements as yet."

Which explained why the duty of marrying her had fallen on Ruark.

"I'm third in line and I'm sure you recognize me."

She did, although he looked far more imposing in the photo than in real life.

"The twins are my sisters Beatrix and Mary. Bea is working on her Master's degree in international finance and Mary is finishing her training as a physical therapist." He grinned. "Much to my mother's dismay, both of them are, as you say, footloose and fancy-free."

"High-spirited, are they?"

"No, just not married. My mother wants more grandchildren."

"But she has two already and another on the way."

"My mother won't be satisfied until we've all given her at least two. Have you ever considered how many you'd like to have?"

She grinned. "Grandchildren? I really haven't thought about it."

"Children," he corrected.

"I always dreamed of having four."

"Four?"

"Sure. Two boys, two girls, so each would have a playmate. But it really doesn't matter how many or their sex, as long as they're healthy. What about you?"

"I haven't given the numbers much thought," he admitted before his eyes took on a decided gleam. "I'm more interested in the activities that lead up to having kids."

"Naturally," she said dryly. Then, because the conversation seemed to be traveling in a direction she wasn't prepared to go, she replaced the frame on his desk and returned to the sofa.

There, she kicked off her shoes, dug her toes into the plush carpeting, toyed with her charm bracelet and wondered how she'd manage to sleep with her husband lying beside her—a husband who wasn't interested in a celibate relationship.

After yesterday's stolen kiss in the exam room, she'd been torn between anticipation and dread about this moment. She'd asked for time, but she was only prolonging the inevitable. It wasn't as if she had to manufacture sparks—she could feel them now and he wasn't even within touching distance. And yet, because love wasn't part of the formula of their marriage, wouldn't getting to know each other before becoming intimate make the experience that much better?

Out of the corner of her eye she noticed how carefully he watched the announcers, as if engrossed in every word they said. Irrationally, his attitude irritated her. How could he be so calm and so focused on sports at a time like this?

"Do you play chess?" he asked abruptly.

"It's been a long time," she admitted, releasing her bracelet with a snap.

"Can I interest you in a game?"

She would have agreed to anything. "If you don't mind a rusty opponent, I'd love one."

He pulled a well-used set out of a cupboard and placed it on a small table in the far left corner. "Black or white?" he asked.

"White," she answered.

"Black is my lucky color," he said as he arranged his side of the board.

"White is mine, so look out."

By the time Henri arrived with a tray of champagne, grapes, various cheeses and chocolate-dipped strawberries, Ruark had captured most of her pieces.

"Chess?" The chef frowned as he placed the snacks on the nearby coffee table. "On your wedding night?"

Ruark glared at the fellow and signaled for him to leave. He could think of other, far more pleasurable activities they could be doing without the chef's well-meant interference, but he wasn't about to explain there was method in his madness. After watching Gina fidget for the last twenty minutes, he had to do something to help her relax. While he would prefer a more personal technique, a game of chess would work nicely to divert attention away from her fears.

As Henri silently exited, Ruark captured her queen.

"Darn!" Gina muttered, a cute little wrinkle appearing on her forehead.

He grinned. "Don't lose heart. You still have your king."

While she contemplated her next move, Ruark watched her. The way she worried her lower lip with her teeth, drummed her fingers on the tabletop while touching the heads of her pieces with the other, amused him. She seemed determined not to let him win, or at least not win easily. True, she was a little rusty, as she'd claimed, but if they played on a regular basis, it wouldn't be long before she became a formidable opponent.

A few moves later, he pronounced, "Checkmate," and the game was over.

Gina leaned back in her chair. "I demand a rematch."

"OK, but first Henri's refreshments are waiting." He eyed the platter. "Good thing, because I'm starved."

He probably wouldn't have been if he'd taken time for the light meal Henri had prepared before the ceremony, but after reading the latest news from Marestonia on the Internet, food had been the least of his worries. Making their marriage official had been all he'd cared about. He'd been ninety-nine percent sure Gina wouldn't cry off, but that final one percentage point had nagged at him until he'd seen her at the back of the chapel.

He'd never known relief like at that moment.

He retrieved the champagne and handed a glass to Gina. "How about a strawberry?"

"I'd love one." She bit into the fruit he offered.

"You really don't play all that badly," he said, taking a strawberry for himself. "Did your father teach you?"

"Yes, although I'm not doing justice to his instructions." She chuckled. "When I said I was rusty, I didn't know I was *this* awful. I'm rather embarrassed."

"Would you rather try your luck at something else? Cards, backgammon, poker?" Oh, the possibilities of poker…

"I prefer chess, unless you're tired of my novice skills."

He grinned. "As long as I win, I don't mind."

Two games later, with the food nearly gone and the wins all Ruark's, Gina yawned. "One more match," she begged.

He shook his head, quite aware of his wife's reluctance to go upstairs. "You're half-asleep. You can see if you can best me tomorrow." He tugged her to her feet. "Run along. I'll be there shortly."

She nodded, then padded from the room as her dress swooshed gently with each step. After seeing her only in shapeless scrub suits, the moment she'd walked into the chapel wearing a dress that clung to her slight curves and revealed a pair of shapely legs, he'd been stunned. His imagination definitely hadn't done her justice. And knowing that, he'd been hard pressed not to stare at her like a besotted fool.

He downed the last of the champagne, wishing he'd imbibed enough to fall asleep the moment his head hit the pillow. How would he manage to keep his hands to himself as promised, when her light, floral scent tantalized him and her softness called his name?

Fifteen minutes later, after stalling as long as he could, he flicked off the light switches and trudged upstairs in a state of combined anticipation and frustrated dread.

In his room, he found Gina already in his four-poster bed, the sheet pulled to her waist. She'd left the bedside lamp on for him—such a wifely act—and he caught a glimpse of her negligee's lacy bodice and the bare skin above it.

Determined to act naturally in spite of his body's immediate response, he stripped down to his shorts, flicked off the light, then slid into bed.

For several moments, he lay there, as stiff as a board, aware of Gina doing the same, before he reached a decision.

He rolled toward her, raised himself on one elbow and said, "Gina?"

"Yes." Her voice sounded tentative.

"You were beautiful tonight."

He heard the smile in her voice. "Thank you. You were quite handsome and dashing yourself."

He scooted closer and felt tension radiating off her. "If you don't relax, you'll wake up stiff and sore in the morning."

Her soft sigh made him smile. "Probably."

"So, in the interests of our health…" In a lightning-fast move, he slid one arm under her neck and positioned her against him as he settled onto his back.

She gasped, one hand splayed across his chest. "What…what are you doing?"

He bussed her cheek. "Holding my wife so we can both sleep. Goodnight, Gina."

"Goodnight, Ruark."

For the next few minutes, he waited for a sign to indicate she'd fallen asleep, but none came. Her breathing hadn't changed and she wiggled every so often as if to find a comfortable position.

Her hand stroked his abdominal muscles and he gritted his teeth in a vain attempt to maintain control. What in the world had he been thinking? This whole exercise was to allow her to adjust to being in his bed, not drive him over the edge with desire.

As Ruark lay beside her, his promise warred with his hormones, but he forced himself to freeze. Although he wanted to bury himself inside her, he wouldn't because he couldn't bear to see the wounded look in her eyes if he did. He'd made a vow to her and pride demanded he honor it.

"Ruark?" she asked softly.

"Yeah." His voice was hoarse.

"Did we do the right thing?"

Concentrating on holding his body in check, he didn't follow her question. "With what?"

"Getting married. Especially under our circumstances. Was it the right thing to do?"

Aware of her body plastered against his and the frustration he was suffering, he wondered that himself. No, he decided. Getting married wasn't the problem. Giving her time to adjust to the concept of having a husband and everything it entailed was.

He couldn't complain, though, because he'd brought this on himself with his momentary lapse into chivalry!

"It was." He was certain.

"Convince me," she said.

CHAPTER SEVEN

RUARK stilled. "Convince you?" he echoed.

She shifted her position until she was half-draped across his body and one smooth leg had found its way between his. "Yes."

He didn't want to misunderstand and start something he wouldn't be allowed to finish, so he restated her request. "You want me to convince you that we did the right thing by getting married."

"The circumstances *were* rather unusual," she pointed out. "I know we married out of duty, for the good of the people in two countries, but I just want some reassurance the result wasn't a mistake."

His confused fog lifted. "You mean, a mistake for *us*. Personally."

"Yeah."

She obviously wasn't able to put her fears into words or was too afraid of his answer if she did. Oh, he knew what she wanted to hear—it was the same thing *every* woman wanted. They expected flowery speeches and the I-can't-live-without-you-because-I-love-you remarks, but he owed her complete honesty. At this point, he certainly couldn't profess to love her and probably never would. Love, as far as he was concerned, was simply a euphemism for lust, and he had plenty of that where she was concerned.

"We did what we had to do," he stated firmly. "A lot of people will benefit from this marriage, true. We knew that going into it. But we're benefitting, too."

She didn't comment, but he sensed she was listening carefully. "We each have someone to share our lives with," he said simply. "Someone who'll listen and be supportive, someone to come home to at night."

Realizing how his description could also apply to a pet, which hadn't been his intention, he grinned and tried to lighten the mood. "Someone who prefers white cake and leaves all the chocolate for me."

She chuckled. "If you say so."

"Someone I can beat at chess."

"Give me a few weeks to practice and then we'll see who beats who," she said without heat.

"Regardless of who wins, chess is something enjoyable we can do together. Best of all, we won't have to find a date ever again, much less suffer through the rejections and heartbreaks."

She laughed. "You? Rejected? Heartbroken? Oh, please. I'm sure it was the other way around."

"Au contraire."

"Do you want to talk about it?"

He didn't, but felt he should. Perhaps once he explained, Gina would understand why he held the opinions he did. "This is ancient history, mind you."

"How ancient?"

He shrugged. "Seven, eight years, but it started long before then. Having a title gets in the way of a relationship. It's tough to find a woman who doesn't have an agenda or who can look past my heritage to the man underneath. I learned to be cautious."

"Royalty 101?"

"Something like that."

"But someone slipped past your defenses."

"Yeah." He rubbed his chin. "I met this woman during my residency. To me, Grace was perfect. I loved her and she loved me. Or so she claimed."

"Claimed?"

"We dated for several months. One day she said she loved me, but two weeks later someone better came along, and she left."

"Someone better? How is that possible? You're a prince, for heaven's sake."

He grinned. "Spoken like a loyal wife. Anyway, her 'someone better' was a movie producer who could advance her career more than a prince who practically lived at the hospital. It was my own fault because I should have seen it coming."

"I didn't realize you can predict events."

"The signs were in plain sight, but I ignored them. You see, we didn't have anything in common. Other than attending charity events or her movie opening nights, we led separate lives."

"Have you seen her lately?"

"No. Last I heard, she was on her third marriage and still waiting for her big break."

Gina fell silent as she searched for something appropriate to say. Discussing his former love life while he was in bed with her could be considered tacky, but sometimes it was easier to reveal things in the dead of night rather than in the light of day. In any case, hearing of his experiences explained so much. Now Gina understood why he had such a cynical view about love, why he continued to stress the importance of having mutual interests, of being companions, of sharing a life.

She snuggled against him. "I wish I could feel sorry for this Grace person, but I can't. Anyway, enough about her. I want to hear more about *our* personal benefits."

"More personal benefits. OK, let me think. Here's one. I don't have to worry about choosing the wrong tie because you'll tell me what matches and what doesn't. And I'll reciprocate when you choose the wrong earrings for your dress."

"Fair enough. What else?"

"You have a French chef preparing the most delectable meals on this side of the Mississippi while I won't have to argue with Henri over the menus any longer."

"Something's not quite right with that one, but I'll let it slide," she said dryly, smiling. "Is that all you have?"

"Well…we can share transportation to and from work to save on energy costs," he finished brightly.

"Now you're reaching."

"Yes, but I'm saving the best for last." He moved his head to whisper in her ear. "I find you extremely, *extremely* beautiful, Gina." His voice became rougher, almost raspy, as if he was using all of his energy to keep from acting on that attraction. "And you're my wife," he finished on a distinct note of possessiveness.

She, on the other hand, was grateful the room was too dark for him to see her grinning like an idiot. "I'm flattered."

She felt his shrug. "It's the truth."

"In that case…for the record…the feeling is mutual." There, she'd said it! At the same time, though, she sensed his appeal went beyond his handsome face and his ability to turn her inside out with a mere kiss. She may not have known him for long, but she'd caught glimpses of his character that were as much if not more alluring.

She may not appreciate being married out of duty, but once she'd gotten past the shock and analyzed his motives, his willingness to place other people's needs above his own—his *unselfishness*—she'd been impressed. And when he'd stood behind her with her incident with Frank Horton, when he'd done all he could to give her a wedding ceremony she'd never forget, how could she *not* be attracted to him on more than a physical level?

The question was, what should she do about it? Postpone the inevitable, or allow her wedding day—and night—to be everything it should be? What had he said? People wouldn't care how their romance started, only how it ended?

Why couldn't she heed Henri's advice to enjoy each other? Considering their shared physical attraction, their joining was as inevitable as the sun rising and setting.

"We'll only have one wedding night," she said, hoping he'd hear the invitation in her voice.

Obviously he had, because he froze. "True," he admitted. "But you wanted to wait."

"I changed my mind."

"Once we start, there's no going back," he warned.

"I know. I won't regret this in the morning," she stated firmly, but he still didn't move. "If you're afraid I've drunk too much champagne and don't know what I'm saying, rest easy. I only had one glass."

Determined to convince him of her sincerity, she reached up to cup the side of his face. "You said we'd play this part of our marriage by ear. Well, I heard the music and now I'm ready to dance."

In an instant he'd reversed positions until she was half-undereath him. She sensed rather than saw him lower his head until his lips touched her cheek. Slowly, deliberately, provocatively, he nibbled his way to her ear and trailed his lips down her neck until he reached her collarbone. "Shall we tango…or waltz?" he mumbled against her skin.

"Both."

Time froze under his tender assault. The nightgown she'd purchased that morning disappeared, unneeded and unwanted. Each long stroke, every caress pulled her deeper under his magical spell. Oh, yes, she managed to think…their marriage may have been born out of duty and would be scrutinized by many, but nights like this were not a mistake.

"Your Highness, you must allow me to prepare your breakfast."

Caught in the act of pouring a packet of instant oatmeal into a bowl, Gina smiled at Henri, who'd burst into the kitchen with a look of horror on his face. "Don't be ridiculous. I'm perfectly able to fix my own."

"Of course you are, but it is my pleasure to serve you," the chef said smoothly as he waved her aside. "Would you like toast, fresh fruit, bacon and eggs to accompany this?"

"Just the oatmeal," she told him. "And a refill of this." She raised her mug. "It's the best I've ever tasted."

When she'd awoken that morning, she'd only seen Ruark's indented pillow and a cup of coffee on her nightstand. She normally didn't take time to brew any at home before she reported for her shift and, in fact, didn't need the shot of caffeine to start her day, but having a cup ready and waiting when her eyes popped open would definitely spoil her.

Henri beamed as he grabbed the pot and topped up her cup. "Thank you, Your Highness. I'll bring your breakfast to the dining room shortly."

Clearly dismissed, Gina meandered into the dining room and sat at the huge banquet-sized table. Within minutes Henri delivered a bowl of oatmeal sprinkled with fresh blueberries. He'd also brought a plate of assorted fruit and two slices of whole wheat toast cut in perfect triangles, as well as the morning newspaper.

"Let me know if I can prepare anything else, Your Highness."

"This will be all. Tell me, has Ruark already eaten?"

"Hours ago, ma'am. He's an early riser," Henri explained. "I heard him mention he had correspondence to attend to, so I'm certain he's in his den if you're wondering where to find him."

She was, but didn't want to interrupt him. "Thank you, Henri."

Accustomed to eating alone, she perused the headlines, ate half of what Henri had supplied, then headed for her bedroom. She hadn't made the bed or tidied the room yet, and she still had two suitcases' worth of clothes to unpack.

To her surprise, she found a woman her own age performing all the chores Gina had planned to do after breakfast. The bed was made, the room tidied, and her suitcases were open and half-empty.

"You didn't need to do this for me!" Gina exclaimed, disconcerted to have someone else doing such personal tasks.

"It is my job, Your Highness. I'm happy to do it. I am Inga, by the way. I usually come three days a week to help Mrs Armstrong, but now I'll be here every day."

Mrs Armstrong was the kindly housekeeper responsible for the house's pristine condition, which couldn't have been easy considering the number of people who lived and worked on the property. While Gina was glad the woman had help and Inga had a full-time job, she hoped no one thought she was too lazy to lend a hand or, worse, had extremely high housekeeping standards. As far as she was concerned, a house wasn't complete without several dust bunnies in residence.

Gina watched Inga hang up a pink blouse in the closet. "Thank you, Inga," she said politely. "I'll try not to make too much of a mess for you. Meanwhile, I'll get out of your way."

"The garden flowers are lovely right now," Inga commented. "Perhaps you'd like to see them before the day gets too hot?"

She couldn't hang around the kitchen or her bedroom, and she didn't want to interrupt Ruark, so strolling around the yard seemed a good idea. If she was lucky, she might even find a few weeds to pull. "I will."

But outside the rose bushes were perfectly pruned, the zinnias, petunias, and vinca were well watered, and the small herb garden beautifully tended. Not a weed was in sight, thanks to the two employees who sported *Gary's Gardens* on the back of their uniform shirts.

She sank onto a wicker chair under the covered patio and studied the professionally landscaped yard, wondering what she would do for the next three days. Monday wouldn't come soon enough to suit her. At least at the hospital, she had a place.

In Ruark's home, she was beginning to feel like a useless ornament.

A few minutes later, her new husband strolled outside. "Here you are."

"Yup, here I am," she replied.

He sat in the chair opposite hers. "Have you found your way around? Met all the staff?"

"Oh, yes. They're delightful. Very helpful and eager to serve." That was the problem. She wasn't used to having her every whim catered to. It would take some time to adjust, especially being referred to as "Your Highness".

"Good." He placed her well-used electronic PDA in front of her—the same one she carried in her pocket as a reference guide for all sorts of treatment protocols and drug information. "I apologize for taking this off your dresser without your permission this morning, but you were asleep and I didn't want to wake you."

She hadn't noticed but, then, she hadn't looked for it either. "No problem."

"My secretary updated the calendar with our social engagements. I thought we could review them together."

She navigated the screen to reach the current month. "An interview with *Modern Marestonians*." She glanced at him. "In two *days*?"

"The magazine is a sort of cross between your *Country Living* and *People*. It has a large readership and their reporters tend to be quite congenial. Perfect for your first interview."

"Thanks," she said wryly, then glanced down at the screen again. "A charity event on Friday night?"

"For family crisis centers in the state," he explained. "The numbers of safe havens for victims of domestic violence and their children isn't meeting the demand, unfortunately."

After seeing many of those victims in the ER, the subject was dear to Gina's heart, and she approved of his decision to support the cause. She glanced at the next entry.

"A ribbon-cutting ceremony?"

"For a regional burns center in Chicago."

"Chicago? That's hours away."

"Not by private plane," he informed her. "It won't take any longer than if we drove across town."

Ribbon-cuttings, jetting around the Midwest, an official royal event every week. Obviously his princely duties rolled around more than the few times a year as he'd originally claimed, and she said so.

"We'll be busy for a while because we're news at the moment," he admitted. "Before long, we'll be usurped by an actress arrested for driving under the influence or a politician divorcing his wife because he's gay."

His light-hearted reassurance coaxed a grin out of her. "Do you think we'll be that lucky?"

"Count on it." His tone grew serious. "Just remember, I'll be right beside you."

"You'd better be," she warned, "because I don't have a clue what to say."

"I'll handle it," he promised. "All you have to do is look beautiful and smile like a blushing bride."

A blushing bride. She chose not to point out that brides blushed as a result of their husband's love and as that emotion didn't apply... But considering how far out of her depth she was, she hoped a reporter would attribute her uncertainty at being in the spotlight to her newlywed status.

"Any questions?" he asked.

"About this interview on Sunday," she began. "What sort of questions will she ask?"

"As no one in our country really knows you, she'll be interested in your childhood, your parents, your education. And, of course, in light of events back home, she'll want to see how we're reconciling the past with the present. Just follow my lead and you'll be fine."

"So you say," she muttered.

"It will get easier," he assured her. "I'm fortunate in that my life is really quite boring in comparison to the rest of the royal family's, so the press normally leaves me alone. As soon as talk of our wedding dies down, we'll be practically invisible."

Being invisible couldn't come soon enough, Gina thought as she studied her reflection in the full-length mirror on Sunday afternoon. Ever since the announcement of their marriage, gifts had flooded into their home and Ruark's secretary had been inundated with requests for photos and interviews. To her relief, he freely supplied pictures and rarely granted an audience. She hoped to survive today's session without incident.

It was important for everything to go well because so much rested on the way she presented herself as Ruark's wife. The news from Avelogne and Marestonia over the past couple of days had shown two countries in a state of uncertainty. The mood ranged from hopeful to skeptical about the alliance between their two royal houses, but the violence had stopped, which the political gurus took as a positive sign. However, Gina hadn't needed Ruark or the Marestonian ambassador to tell her how fragile the peace actually was. It was her job during today's interview to convince everyone of their modern-day fairy-tale romance.

A tall order considering how Ruark scoffed at the concept of love and they'd simply married to fulfill a duty.

Duty, not love.

Suddenly, guilt crashed down on her. The past nights in his bed had been wonderful, spectacular even, but they weren't in love. What did it say about her character, her morals, if she could find such enjoyment in the arms of a man who didn't feel anything for her?

Worse yet, what did it say about *her* character if *she* could do the same?

Her guilt turned to horrified shame as she considered how easily she'd succumbed to his charm.

"My, but you look beautiful." Ruark came from the bathroom and adjusted his tie.

Staggering under the weighty question that plagued her, she managed to answer. "Thanks."

He stopped beside her, tall and handsome in his dark gray suit, his frown plain in the mirror's reflection. "What's wrong? Do you feel all right?"

"I'm fine," she insisted. *As fine as any woman who saw a distasteful quality inside herself.*

His frown didn't disappear as he felt her forehead. "You don't look fine."

"Thank you very much for your observation," she said dryly.

"I'm serious. If you're getting sick, you should rest. We can reschedule."

The warmth of his fingers calmed her as much as his obvious concern did, and her momentary guilt and shame vanished. Regardless of the practical reasons behind their marriage, they *were* married. Being married, for better or worse, made it pointless not to find joy in their relationship wherever they could.

She may not feel the grand passion she'd always imagined, but she trusted him, respected him, and enjoyed his company. She had nothing to feel ashamed about. And, if she was honest with herself, he was a man she could easily grow to love.

Oh, who was she kidding? Her intuition said she was halfway there.

As for Ruark, he may not love her, but he clearly cared about her. She'd seen him express concern under a veneer of polite interest—his royal persona—but this was different. His worry was genuine and obviously heartfelt if the look on his face was anything to go by. It might not be the stuff of hearts and roses, but for now it was enough. And with time and patience it might eventually grow into something close to what her parents had.

"No, don't reschedule. I'm just…nervous, I guess. When I think of how our every expression and tone will be scrutinized…"

"Act naturally and the reporter will simply see a happily married couple who've given up a few hours of their precious honeymoon to share their story."

She laughed. "Precious?"

"When you only have three days, every moment counts. Seriously, though, just be yourself."

"Be myself. Got it," she said, pretending confidence when she had none. "But she'll be sorely disappointed once she realizes I think and act like a physician, not a princess."

"But now you are both. I think this will help." He strode across the room to his dresser, opened the top drawer, and pulled out a large, square jeweler's box. "For you."

Her heart pounded with excitement. "What is it?"

"A gift from my parents."

"Your parents? It isn't a tiara or some other princessy thing, is it?" she asked suspiciously, wondering if she'd commit a horrible breach of royal etiquette if she refused to wear it for their interview.

He laughed. "Tiaras are reserved for state events so, no, it isn't. This, however, is something I hope you'll like. It arrived last night." As she hesitated, he urged, "Go ahead. Open it."

She raised the hinged lid to reveal a sparkling teardrop diamond pendant resting on a bed of velvet. She may have had a novice eye when it came to gems, but the size suggested it was horribly expensive. "It's beautiful."

He removed the pendant from the box, then fastened the silver chain around her neck. "This was my mother's. She asks you to wear it with her blessing. My father gave it to her on the day I was born."

Touched by the generosity of his mother, tears threatened to fall as she fingered the diamond's facets. "It's gorgeous. Thank you, and thank your mother for sharing it with me."

"I'm glad you like it." His smile seemed rooted in relief, as if he'd been afraid she would reject a gift that held special significance to him and his family. "But I'll let you thank her yourself."

"I will." She'd spoken to Ruark's parents the morning after their wedding when they'd welcomed her into the family. Their voices had been warm and sincere, and Gina was looking forward to meeting the couple in person, as well as the rest of Ruark's family.

"She's quite anxious for a lengthy chat," he added. "Probably so she can warn you about all my bad habits."

So far, she hadn't noted a single one but, then, they'd only been living together for three days. "Gracious." She pretended horror. "How many do you have?"

"Hundreds, I'm sure. Probably more, depending on who you ask." He grinned.

"Regardless of what she tells me, I'll always treasure this," she said before she stood on tiptoe and pressed her lips lightly against his for just long enough to taste the coffee on his breath.

A lazy half-smile appeared on his face and his eyes gleamed with masculine appreciation. "Remind me to give gifts more often," he said in a lazy drawl. "Even if they aren't my own."

She chuckled at his hopeful expression. "Don't push your luck."

"At the risk of spoiling the moment, after we talk to my parents tonight, your grandmother would appreciate a phone call."

She stiffened instinctively. "I'm sure she would, but I'm not ready."

"You don't have to agree to meet her. Just talk."

"I wouldn't know what to say."

"You could start by thanking her for the gift she sent."

A white linen tablecloth had arrived, exquisitely hand-stitched with the royal crests from both families. It was beautiful, a true work of textile art, and a host of poor souls had probably worked round the clock to create it once she'd agreed to marry Ruark. Either that, or her grandmother had been so certain of the outcome to the royal plan that she'd commissioned it some months ago.

"I'll send a card."

"She wants to visit—at our convenience, of course."

"Sometimes life doesn't give us what we want."

"You can't hold a grudge forever."

"I don't have a grudge. I don't feel…anything." As far as Gina was concerned, she might share a gene pool with the woman, but she was simply a name. Another famous person she would never meet. A complete stranger.

A few short days ago, so was Ruark.

Yes, and look where that had gotten her. She was now his wife.

She slowly exhaled, feeling Ruark's scrutiny. "I appreciate you acting as a mediator, but I'm not ready," she repeated. "She'll have to be content that I agreed to their plan when I could have ignored Avelogne's problems."

He started to speak, then stopped as if he knew she wouldn't budge no matter how hard he pushed. "It's your decision, but keep in mind she isn't getting any younger."

She would have replied, but the doorbell chimed in the distance. Adrenaline surged and panic instantly set in. "Oh, my gosh. She's here, and she's *early*."

Ruark threaded her arm through his and pulled her close. "Look at it this way. You'll have less time to brood."

"Brood? I don't brood. It makes me sound like a chicken," she mumbled as he led her into the hallway toward the staircase.

"You aren't a chicken," he agreed. "You're braver than that."

"Do you think so?"

"Absolutely."

She stopped at the top of the stairs. "Maybe I should change into something more sophisticated, less—"

He tugged on her arm and she followed. "You look fantastic."

Three steps later, she stopped again. "What if she asks a question I can't answer?"

"Squeeze my hand and I'll take over."

"Any other final bits of advice?"

"Remember to smile and look like you adore me."

He winked playfully, and she burst out laughing. "If you insist. One case of adoration coming up."

By the time Ruark had gotten Gina to the bottom of the staircase, he'd accomplished what he'd set out to do—he'd wiped the startled doe-in-the-headlights look off her face. Louise Amandine's first impression of his wife would show her as a relaxed and happy bride.

As the interview progressed, the experienced reporter was far more interested in Gina than in him, which suited Ruark just fine. People in his part of the world clamored to learn everything possible about the new princess, especially because no one had gleaned more than her basic historical facts. He rather enjoyed sitting next to Gina in the formal parlor, holding her hand like an enamored husband as he listened to her share stories and anecdotes about her childhood and her parents.

He was an extremely lucky man, he decided. For a man who'd married only to appease his family's honor, who thought love was an overrated emotion, he was very fortunate to have married a woman he actually liked and enjoyed being with. Gina was beautiful, spirited, intelligent, and after three days of marriage, he couldn't imagine anyone else as his wife.

When he contemplated how easily he might have ended up with a bride he could barely tolerate, he inwardly shuddered, then thanked the fates for the spouse who complemented him in so many ways and on so many levels. He couldn't have chosen better, even if he'd tried.

"Prince Ruark," Louise interrupted his thoughts. "Because your marriage is crucial to the alliance between Avelogne and Marestonia, do you have any plans to hold a more formal ceremony in either country, with both royal families in attendance?"

Although Gina smiled as she glanced at him, he felt her squeeze his hand and saw a flash of uncertainty in her eyes.

"Not at the moment," Ruark answered smoothly.

"Would you *consider* a formal ceremony in Marestonia as a more visible show of unity?" Louise pressed. "As you know, we take pride in our royal family and it's been several years since we've enjoyed the excitement of a royal wedding."

Ruark knew he had to tread carefully. He exchanged a glance with Gina and knew she realized it, too. But while Gina didn't know where Louise's questions were headed, he did.

"Our work schedules are rather tight and we considered ourselves fortunate to marry in the manner we did." He spoke with finality, hoping Louise would accept his answer and move on.

She didn't.

"While the people of Avelogne and Marestonia understand your desire to marry here in the country where you both live and work, some might argue that sharing such a momentous occasion with your people is your duty," Louise said slyly.

"Perhaps," he conceded, "although, as a third son, I doubt if the people would expect the same pomp and ceremony required of my oldest brother."

"Perhaps not the same," she admitted, "but no matter what your place in the line of succession, you *are* a member of the royal family. More importantly, *you* are the one instrumental in resolving the current crisis. What better way to cement good relations with Avelogne than with a celebration to mark the occasion?"

What better way, indeed. Ruark exchanged another glance with Gina and saw both fear and dread in her eyes. He stroked her hand in reassurance.

"We'll take your suggestion under advisement," he said.

"Thank you, Your Highness." She turned to Gina. "It's been a pleasure meeting you, Your Highness. And best wishes for your marriage."

"Thank you," Gina murmured.

Hugh arrived at that moment to escort the two to the door. As soon as they were alone, Gina sank onto the sofa. "I do *not* want to do that again."

"You were great. She was eating out of your hand."

"Perhaps, but she was almost salivating at the prospect of a formal wedding. Frankly, if I hear the word 'duty' one more time, I think I'll scream."

Ruark smiled as he sat beside her and drew her close. "It hasn't been bad so far, has it?"

"No," she admitted. "But you're not seriously considering her suggestion, are you?"

"The possibility always existed," he admitted, "and I'd hoped we could avoid it, but we've come too far to not see this to the end."

Her shoulders slumped. "I know. But…" Her voice faded.

"But what?"

"I just want to be a doctor," she said simply. "I want to go to work every morning and treat patients, not stand in the limelight and pretend to be something I'm not."

He understood better than she knew. He'd found it was far easier to set aside his royal trappings and focus on his profession in a country where he wasn't a household name.

"People should accept we're married without us having to go through a dog and pony show!" she continued.

"They should," he agreed. Unfortunately, as much as he wanted to tell her what she wanted to hear, he couldn't. Comforting her didn't mean giving her false hope and he respected her too much to do that. "However, Louise raised valid points. The royal family is part of the nation's identity. Treating it as something common goes against the very grain of our existence."

She fell silent. "We're going to have to do this, too, aren't we?"

"Perhaps," he prevaricated, although he wrapped his other arm around her to comfort her as best he could. "It's too soon to tell. Besides, Louise Amandine's opinions may not reflect everyone else's. Let's wait and see what happens."

Maybe there *was* a chance the highly visible ceremony wouldn't be necessary, but if Louise had broached the subject, the odds had shrunk to almost nothing. In his heart, he knew a more formal ceremony was inevitable. He wouldn't be surprised if his parents and a few trustworthy staff members had already planned the occasion from the guest list to the dinner menu.

Gina wouldn't be thrilled about this development, and the prospect bothered him. They'd married strictly for practical reasons, but he didn't want her to ever regret her decision. If making her happy served that purpose, then he would move mountains to do so.

Yet he wondered why Gina wasn't eager to go through with a royal wedding. Weren't the horse-drawn carriages, people lining the streets to wave and throw flowers, the sacredness of the cathedral, and the uniform marking his station all part of the fairy-tale ceremony that women dreamed about?

CHAPTER EIGHT

"HERE comes the happy couple!"

"Welcome back!"

Gina smiled at the staff members who greeted them as soon as she and Ruark strolled into the ER on Monday morning. Everything from the phones ringing to the familiar scent of disinfectant made her feel as if she'd finally returned to the familiar. The rest of her life had changed dramatically, but Belmont General remained her anchor.

"It's nice to know we were missed," she said.

"Of course you were," Lucy chided. "It wasn't the same without you."

"Why, thank you." Gina beamed. "It's great to be here." After being pampered like a prize poodle, she was ready for normalcy where she could fill her own coffee mug, zap her own bag of microwave popcorn, and look up a phone number without someone hovering over her.

"How was the honeymoon?" someone asked.

She glanced at Ruark, who appeared as interested in her response as everyone else, and smiled at him. "Wonderful." And it had been. Ruark had provided the one bright spot in her days.

The only bad moment had been when she'd realized their life was still not their own. After surviving an interview, the prospect of facing the fanfare associated with a royal wedding was daunting. It had been sweet of Ruark to hint that it might not be necessary, in order to spare her the worry, but her instincts told her an ostentatious ceremony couldn't be avoided. Especially after Ms Amandine had said the "D" word.

Duty.

Her father truly had bucked tradition by marrying Lizbet in a private ceremony. No doubt the people had felt robbed, and those feelings had resurfaced with a vengeance once Margret's diary had been made public.

Still, nothing was set in stone. And worrying over a possibility was a waste of energy.

"But as wonderful as it was," she continued, "I'm obviously not cut out for a life of leisure."

"Then you're in the right place," Lucy declared, "because we're expecting a trauma any minute. Car accident on the freeway." The distant sound of a siren was cut short, signaling the ambulance's approach.

"I'd say it's here," Gina remarked, already heading for the cart stacked with protective gowns and gloves as she mentally prepared for the patients who would roll through those doors.

It was definitely great to be back where she was needed.

But her sense of purpose was shaken several days later when Ruark called her into his office.

"I wanted you to be the first to know," he said as he perched on the edge of his desk. "Administration has approved my request to hire additional physicians."

"However did you manage that?" she asked, amazed. "Bill had asked for extra staff to expand our clinic services for a long time. Now we can." Seeing his sober expression, her excitement dimmed. "Can't we?"

"The extra positions aren't for the clinic. They're for the ER itself."

She studied him in puzzlement. "But we don't need more staff in the ER. I've handled—"

"Once I saw how many hours you're on duty every week— usually no less than seventy-five—the CEO agreed we had to make a few changes. So I have."

Intuition warned her she wouldn't like the rest of this conversation. "Do I still have a job?" she asked evenly, bracing herself for his answer.

He seemed astonished by her question. "Of course. I'm simply scheduling you for a more acceptable number of hours. You can choose to work three twelve-hour or four ten-hour shifts."

She should have been relieved, even happy, by the news but she wasn't. She'd willingly worked the number of hours she had because it gave her a sense of purpose. Now he was taking it from her without warning. He may be the department's head, but he should have informed her of his plans beforehand. After all, physician coverage wasn't a topic requiring secrecy and they *were* married. That alone had to count for something, didn't it?

Frustration and pain simmered together. "When will this take effect?" she asked evenly, unable to meet his gaze because he'd surely see the hurt there.

"Next week. Until we recruit two more permanent people, we'll be using locums and they'll start on Monday. So which hours would you prefer?"

He certainly wasn't giving her any time to mentally adjust. He'd simply snapped his fingers and it was done, but if he thought she'd thank him for his highhandedness, he could think again.

"Do I really have a choice?" This time she met his gaze, certain she'd masked her inner turmoil well enough. "Or are you going to decide for me?"

His expression was inscrutable. "I certainly could, but I'd rather not."

Gina rubbed her temple, feeling as if she was losing control of the one part of her life that she *could* control.

"This was for the good of the department, Gina," he said, as if he sensed how difficult this was for her. "On my first day here, I mentioned there would be some changes and improvements. Requiring you to cover the number of hours you did isn't in the hospital's or the patients' best interests."

Logically, she knew that, but at the moment, even though he was giving her the courtesy of a choice, she only saw the loss of the most important thing in her life.

The problem was that if she chose the three-day schedule, she'd rattle around his house, bored to tears, for four days instead of three. On the other hand, if she did choose the three day schedule, she could work elsewhere. The free clinic down the street always needed physicians.

"I might mention that your contract doesn't allow you to moonlight," he said offhandedly, as if he'd read her thoughts.

"I can donate my time," she defended.

"True, and if you choose to do that, I won't stop you."

He'd surprised her. "You won't?"

"No, but if you'd rather work round the clock instead of spend time with me, then I must be doing something wrong," he said lightly.

Now he pulled out the husband card, she thought, feeling uncharitable.

Her gut warned she was overreacting to what some might say was a thoughtful gesture on his part. Most people, especially new-lyweds, would be glad to stop working sixty or more hours a week, but she wasn't "most people" or a traditional newlywed. Her career meant everything to her and had governed her life for too many years for her to lose part of it cold turkey without anything to take its place.

You have something to take its place.

Only in a technical sense, she argued. Once she left the

hospital, she had staff to handle every other detail of her life. Her career had been the one thing she'd still felt she could call her own. Now, apparently, she didn't even have that.

While she perversely wanted to take the three twelve-hour days schedule and donate her services to a clinic for the rest of the week, she enjoyed working at Belmont where the staff were like family. She refused to let Ruark take that from her, too.

"I'll take the four ten-hour shifts," she said stiffly.

The tiniest wrinkle of puzzlement appeared on his brow. "Gina, this isn't—"

"Is that all you needed?" She was proud of the cool tone in her voice. "I have patients waiting."

He clearly heard her retreat behind the defined lines of superior-subordinate. He hesitated for a fraction of second before he nodded. "There is one other thing. I heard an interesting tidbit about your former boss today."

"Bill Nevins? What's he done now?"

"He's landed a job as administrator of a fifty-bed hospital in Iowa."

"Administrator?" She was incredulous. "He's certainly moved up in the world."

"Just goes to show how some people are like cats—no matter how they fall, they always land on their feet."

"Who would have guessed?" she mused aloud. "There truly isn't any justice in the world, is there?" Without waiting for his reply, she left.

Ruark watched her close the door before he leaned back in his chair, perplexed. Their conversation hadn't gone quite as he'd expected. She was supposed to be thrilled for the extra free time and the additional staff to lighten the workload, but instead she'd reacted as if he'd cold-bloodedly taken away her most prized possession.

Her comment, *I just want to be a doctor*, whispered in his head. Before its echo disappeared, he understood…

Although she still was and always would work in her profession if she wanted to, losing a third of her working hours clearly had made her feel as if he'd chipped away part of her career along with the rest of her life.

Yet while he regretted not preparing her for the eventuality, he had to make decisions for the good of the department. True, this particular decision would be to his personal benefit as well, but he was confident Gina would see the change as a departmental improvement rather than a personal attack. Given time, she'd see she'd gained more than she'd lost.

Gina forced herself not to fume during odd moments, but by the end of an hour she'd slowly grown to accept what she couldn't change. However, accepting the situation didn't mean she liked it.

Lucy thrust a chart into her hands. "You need to see this woman right away."

"What's wrong?"

"Severe vaginal bleeding. I've seen corpses with more color," Lucy warned.

"Did you call Stella?" Stella Fairchild was the resident house OB-GYN.

"Not yet."

"Go ahead. Meanwhile, I'll see her."

"Before you do, you should also know she's a single mom with three kids in the waiting room."

Gina went inside and found Doreen Roy lying on the bed, her color as pale as the white sheet covering her. "Hi," she said. "I'm Dr Sutton. I understand you're having a few problems."

Doreen nodded. Her light brown hair hung limply around her thin face. Lines bracketed her eyes and mouth and stretched across her forehead. The woman had clearly suffered hard times during her forty-three years.

"My periods have been getting heavier and heavier. The last

few months it hasn't stopped at all. I was going to go to the doctor, but…" she picked at the hem of the sheet "…I just didn't find the time."

Money, rather than time, was probably the issue. Gina had seen cases like Doreen's more often than she cared to count. For whatever reason, the woman had chosen not to use her money on herself. After glancing at her clean but shabby clothes, and knowing three children depended on her, Gina could easily imagine where her money went.

Doreen drew a bracing breath. "I noticed my heart seems to be pounding hard and at times I can't catch my breath, but I've been managing. Then I passed out this morning while I was making breakfast for my kids. Tim, my oldest, insisted I come here. He only knows I fainted—he doesn't know about the bleeding. Some things you just don't talk about to your teenage son."

"I understand. How old is he?" Gina asked as she listened to her heart.

"Thirteen. Molly is seven and Cara is five."

"Any other symptoms you think we need to know about?" Gina asked as she studied Doreen's chart.

"Not really. I'm always cold and I sometimes have a hard time concentrating. Is that important?"

"Possibly," Gina answered. "While we're waiting for our gynecologist to perform a vaginal exam, I'm going to order a few lab tests. Then we'll decide what to do."

"Will the tests take long?"

"About an hour. Two at the most." Sensing the woman's agitation, she said kindly, "It seems like a long time, but it truly isn't."

"No, it's just that, well…I hate to leave my kids alone. I know they're worried."

"After Dr Fairchild examines you, they can wait here instead of in the waiting room. But if we need to admit you, they'll need a place to go."

"My parents are out of town until tomorrow. My neighbor would probably look after them if I asked her." Doreen closed her eyes.

Gina found Lucy in the hallway. "I want a stat CBC and tell them to call the hemoglobin ASAP, basic chemistries, coag studies, with a blood type and antibody screen. Dr Fairchild will want those results so the sooner we draw the blood samples, the better. Oh, and notify Radiology that we'll need an ultrasound."

"Will do."

"Meanwhile, I'm going to check on Mrs Roy's children."

Gina strode into the waiting area where three dark-haired children huddled together in a corner. The smallest sat on her brother's lap with her thumb in her mouth, idly twirling a lock of her shoulder-length hair as he read aloud from a dog-eared copy of *Bert and Ernie Go to the Hospital*.

"Tim?" Gina asked. "Tim Roy?"

He rose, setting his little sister on her feet. "Yes, ma'am?"

"I'm Dr Sutton and I just saw your mother."

"How is she? Is she gonna be alright?" Fear pinched his face and made him seem far older than thirteen.

"We're taking care of her," she assured him. "I've ordered several tests and as soon as we get those results, we'll have an idea of what we need to do." She eyed the trio. All were dressed in faded but clean clothes. The two girls wore matching shorts and vest tops in pink and green while Tim wore a pair of ragged denim shorts and a short-sleeved plaid cotton shirt that was not only faded but also missing two buttons. "As soon as another doctor has seen your mom, you can sit with her. Would you like that?"

The two little girls nodded, their eyes wide. The youngest had popped her thumb back into her mouth.

"It may take a while," Gina warned, "but would you like something to drink while you're waiting? Or a snack?" It was almost eleven and kids were always hungry.

"We're fine," Tim answered, almost defiantly.

"OK, but if you change your mind, soda and snack machines are around the corner."

As Gina had predicted, before the hour was up, Stella had examined Doreen Roy. The preliminary lab results had narrowed her treatment options to one.

"With her critical hemoglobin, I have to take her to surgery," the petite, dark-haired gynecologist announced as she shared the results of the ultrasound. "She's bleeding out before our eyes and until she has a hysterectomy, it won't stop."

This was exactly what Gina had suspected. "I ordered a cross-match for four units as soon as I heard her hemoglobin level. When do you want to operate?"

Stella glanced at the clock. "I can't get a suite until three, which is for the best because Mrs Roy ate this morning and I can't safely anesthetize her before then. Meanwhile, I can infuse a unit or two of blood."

Gina thought of the three children in the waiting room. "Have you broken the news yet?"

"I'd mentioned there was a good chance she would need surgery, either a D and C or a hysterectomy, depending on what the tests showed, but that's all."

"Unfortunately, she has three kids at home." Gina gave their names and ages. "Her parents are out of town until tomorrow."

"She can't wait until then."

"Mrs Roy mentioned a neighbor," Gina said. "I'll ask our social workers to make appropriate arrangements."

"You'd better hurry," Stella said grimly. "I can't, in good conscience, wheel her into surgery until her kids have appropriate guardianship."

"I'll tell the social workers to make this case top priority," Gina promised.

"Meanwhile, I'll talk to Mrs Roy and transfer her upstairs to the surgical floor. Let me know if you run into a problem."

"I will," Gina promised.

After leaving a message for a social worker to visit Doreen, Gina headed for the waiting room. Before she'd gotten too far, the man she'd been trying to avoid fell into step beside her. "Can you sneak away for lunch?"

Instinctively, she stiffened, before she decided that treating him like the enemy wasn't the answer. He did what he thought he had to do, and so would she.

"Not yet," she replied. "I have three kids to see first."

"Then you'll be a while."

"Oh, they aren't sick. Their mother is having an emergency hysterectomy in a few hours and I thought they could wait with her until then." She sighed. "The problem is, she's a single mom and we're trying to sort out what to do with them until her parents return tomorrow."

"I sympathize, but what'll happen to them in the meantime?" He raised an eyebrow.

"I'm working on it."

The corner of the waiting room where she'd previously left the children was empty. "I wonder where they went," she remarked, before she heard a plaintive voice drifting around the corner where the snack machines stood.

She followed the sound and saw little Cara pressing a finger to the soda machine's clear glass window. "Can we have that, Timmy? I'm really thirsty."

"I'll take you to the water fountain," her brother answered.

"I'm hungry, too. That looks good." Cara pointed to something in the snack machine.

"I only have a dollar," he told her. "You have to pick something you can share with Molly."

Immediately, Gina tugged Ruark out of sight. "I'm taking them to lunch."

He nodded. "I had a feeling you would."

"Do you still want to join me?"

He looked surprised. "Why wouldn't I?"

"They're children. They can be messy, not to mention difficult."

His mouth twitched. "I think I can handle the stress."

Gina marched toward the trio who were debating the merits of potato chips against candies. "Hi, guys."

Tim hoisted his little sister to one hip. "How's Mom?"

"She's going to be fine," Gina told him. "But there are a few things we need to talk about. Why don't you come with me where we won't be interrupted? This is Dr Ruark Thomas, by the way."

Ruark said his hellos and shook Tim's hand and smiled at the two girls before Gina led them to a small room used for private discussions with patients' family members.

"Your mom is very sick," she said, noting how Cara sat on Tim's lap with her thumb in her mouth while Molly sat nearby, hugging an oversized bag to her chest. A scruffy brown teddy bear and a doll peeked out of the top.

"How sick?"

"She's going to need surgery. Right away."

"Is that why she fainted?"

"Yes. You see, we all have hemoglobin in our blood which carries the oxygen around our body. If our hemoglobin levels are low, we don't get enough oxygen circulating and we can pass out. Your mom's hemoglobin level is at four and it should be over twelve." She didn't mention that their mother's hemoglobin was well past the critical stage, or that if she'd waited any longer before seeking treatment, she could easily have died.

"Why is her hemoglobin so low?" he asked.

"Because she's been bleeding. Now she needs surgery to fix the problem."

"And then she'll be fine?"

"She should be."

Tim met her gaze, then Ruark's. His green eyes reflected an age far beyond his tender years. "Does she have cancer?"

"We won't know for certain until the lab runs all their tests," Gina said gently. "But let's not worry about that yet, OK?"

"Is she gonna die?" Molly asked.

"Some people who come to the hospital die," Gina explained carefully, "but a lot of people don't. They come here so we can help them get better, which is what we're going to do for your mother." She stroked the girl's hair. "OK?"

Molly nodded.

Gina rose. "The important thing right now is for you three to have lunch."

Molly's and Cara's eyes brightened. Tim frowned. "We're not hungry."

Gina suspected he was too proud to admit to the single dollar in his pocket. "Then you can keep us company while we eat. And if you should change your mind, it'll be my treat." He hesitated and she sweetened the pot. "By the time we're finished, your mom should be ready for visitors and I'll take you to her. But if you'd rather sit in the waiting room until we get back…"

Molly made a noise as she pulled on Tim's pocket to gain his attention. The silent plea she sent her brother was obvious.

He chewed on his bottom lip before he mumbled, "OK. We'll go."

Ruark hadn't seen Gina interact with children before, but from the way she treated adults, he'd expected her to be a natural with little people, too. And he was right. She handled these three like a nanny he'd once had: kind but firm enough to keep him out of mischief.

"If I hang on to the girls," she said in a voice meant for his ears only, "can you carry the food?"

After hearing her sound like his old Gina when she could still be treating him like the enemy, he would have agreed to anything. "No problem."

The girls' eyes widened at the variety spread out before them. Ruark wondered how they'd ever decide what they wanted before their lunch-hour ended, but Gina steered them toward the more kid-friendly choices.

Cara asked for a hot dog, green beans, chocolate pudding, and a side dish of olives. Molly chose macaroni and cheese, red and green gelatin squares, and fish sticks, while Tim gravitated toward the roast beef special.

Gina tossed a tuna salad sandwich on the tray for herself, along with several apples, cartons of both white and chocolate milk, and cookies. "What'll you have?" she asked. "I'm buying."

He grinned. "In that case, toss one of those chicken salad sandwiches on the tray, will you?"

After handing her lunch ticket to the cashier, she herded their group to a table. In less time than Ruark thought possible, the Roy children were wolfing down their meals as if they hadn't eaten in days. They'd certainly not enjoyed a spread like this before.

"How's the food?" he asked.

"'Licious," Cara replied as she poked a green olive on each finger and ate them one at a time.

"It's really good," Tim said as he all but licked his plate clean.

As they ate, Ruark listened as Gina chatted with their guests. In the space of thirty minutes he'd learned which schools the kids attended, what grade and which teachers they would have in the fall, their favorite subjects, how they'd spent their summer so far, and that Tim had been hired as a paper carrier three weeks ago.

Gina asked about Cara's teddy bear—his name was Buster—and Molly's doll—named Pollyanna after a book she'd read. She'd managed to draw Tim out of his shell long enough to learn his bicycle had a flat tire, and had also coaxed out important family information.

"Your mother told me your grandparents went out of town," she began.

"Grandpa took Grandma to visit her sister in Arizona," Tim answered. "They go every year."

"Grandma says this will probably be the last time, though," Molly added, "on account of Aunt Tilly has a bad heart."

"That's too bad," Gina commiserated, "but it's always nice to see people you haven't seen for a long time. Did they drive or fly?"

Tim grinned. "They drove. Grandpa said if man was supposed to fly, God would have given him wings."

The woman was wasted as a physician, Ruark decided. She should be part of a terrorist interrogation team. She could extract information without the other person knowing it.

By the end of the meal the little girls were aglow with happiness and Tim...well, the best thing Ruark could say was that Tim watched her with the same awe a normal teenage boy experienced when an attractive older woman paid him attention. His gaze followed Gina's every move and whenever she asked him a question, he would blush profusely, then stammer an answer.

Gina had three new members in her fan club, and Ruark didn't blame them a bit. Whenever he saw her, he felt as pleased, awed, and amazed as Tim did, because she was *his*.

It became far too easy to imagine her sitting at his dining room table surrounded by *their* children as she cut meat, rescued drinks from tipping over, and wheedled the day's stories out of them while making each feel important.

She was quite a woman, he thought proudly as he eyed the

wide gold band he'd placed on her finger. As ridiculous as it sounded—he would never admit this to anyone—he'd be forever grateful for the furor Aunt Margret's journal had caused. All the commotion had brought Gina into his life. Doing his duty had never been this satisfying.

"What's next on the schedule?" he asked as he and Tim loaded the dirty dishes onto the cafeteria trays.

"We'll pick up a few snacks for the afternoon and then head upstairs to visit their mother. How does that sound?" she asked as she tucked the apples into Molly's bag, next to Buster and Polyanna.

"Thanks," Tim said, "but we won't need snacks, will we, kids? We'll be fine until dinnertime."

Cara frowned and Molly's smile disappeared, but they both dutifully nodded.

"If you aren't hungry, say, around three o'clock, then you can save the treats for tomorrow," Gina said, undaunted by his refusal.

"But you've already spent a lot…" Tim began.

"Friends like to do things for their friends," Gina answered firmly. "A few bags of pretzels or licorice aren't going to break my bank account. Someday, when you're grown up and have a successful career, you can do the same for someone else."

"But—"

"It's settled," Gina said, looking as determined as she sounded. "I want to do it, and that's that."

Ruark clapped his hand on Tim's shoulder. "It's easier to give in than to argue with a woman, especially this one," he told him. "She doesn't give up."

"I do not argue," she said loftily. "I merely point out the obvious."

Ruark exchanged a wink with Tim. "See what I mean?"

The boy's mouth relaxed into a soft smile. "OK, but only for the girls."

As Gina led her group to the vending machines outside the cafeteria, like a female Pied Piper, Ruark watched her purchase plenty for all three. Before long, Molly's bag was stuffed full of goodies and they trooped to the elevator that would carry them to the surgical floor.

"I'll be back in the ER as soon as I deliver them upstairs," Gina said to him. "I won't be long."

"OK." After saying his goodbyes to the children, he took the stairs and headed for his office. It hadn't been the lunch he'd planned, but it hadn't been a waste of time either. He'd seen how unselfishly she gave of herself, just like the other women in his family did. The only difference was that they'd been raised to consider the needs of others as part of their royal responsibilities while Gina did so instinctively and from her heart.

Suddenly something indefinable stirred in his chest. If he were fifteen years younger and less familiar with the games women played, he might be tempted to call it love, but he wasn't as gullible as he'd once been. He'd given up believing he'd ever experience love for himself, so that couldn't be what he was feeling.

As he considered all the things he knew and liked about her, he finally had his answer.

It was pure and utter contentment.

CHAPTER NINE

"I'M NOT going home with you tonight, Ruark," Gina announced after the shift change.

He glanced up from sliding folders into his briefcase. "Excuse me? You're not coming home?"

"I didn't say I wasn't *coming* home. I said I wasn't *going* home. At least not yet," she explained. "The social worker who'd planned to deliver the Roy children to their neighbor's house had to leave for a family emergency, so I volunteered. I'm taking my car so Hugh and Joachim will need to go with you."

After bowing to Ruark's insistence on security, their daily travel arrangements had involved Hugh accompanying Gina to work in her car with Ruark following several hours later with Joachim. At the end of the day she rode with Ruark and the two bodyguards followed.

Today, however, she'd changed the plans.

"OK," he said. "We'll follow you."

"No!" She was horrified. "I'm not taking an entire entourage to their home. I'm quite capable of finding my way. I managed to drive from point A to point B without a bodyguard all these years."

"Life is different now. There are risks."

"Yes, but—"

"I'll drive you, as always," he said firmly. "We'll *both* take the children home. And you won't know Hugh and Joachim are there."

"I didn't realize that being a princess was synonymous with being a prisoner," she accused.

"It isn't," he insisted. "But did it ever occur to you there may be factions in Avelogne and Marestonia who aren't happy about our marriage and the peace it brings? There might actually be people who *want* the two nations at each other's throats, and are looking for ways to undermine what we've done. Harming you comes to mind."

Her anger and irritation deflated. "I never imagined such a thing," she admitted.

"I'm not trying to scare you," he said, "but everyone doesn't think as we do. Some thrive on creating unrest, which is why I have to insist on appropriate security measures even though we're relatively safe living so far away. There will come a time when we won't need to be as vigilant, but it isn't today."

"You should have explained this before now," she retorted, disappointed he hadn't but finally understanding why he'd insisted on Hugh accompanying her to work each morning. She'd thought it had all been part of the pamper-the-princess routine, but she'd obviously been wrong.

"I should have," he agreed, "but you had enough adjustments to make and I didn't want to take away your peace of mind and frighten you to the point where you're looking over your shoulder all the time."

"I appreciate what you were trying to do, but it would have been easier if I'd known this from the beginning," she chided.

"I'm afraid I'm not in the habit of explaining myself," he said ruefully.

"Then you'll have to get in the habit where I'm concerned," she warned.

He smiled. "I see that. In the meantime, as far as matters of security are concerned, I'm asking you to be cautious. Don't place yourself at undue risk by venturing alone into unfamiliar territory or places where there are a lot of strangers."

Once again, she found herself accepting a situation she didn't particularly like. After freely roaming around on her own for years, being curtailed, even if for a good reason, was a difficult pill to swallow. "I won't," she promised reluctantly.

"Good." He closed his briefcase. "While you get the children, I'll tell Hugh and Joachim of our detour. Do you have the address?"

She gave it to him, hoping he wasn't familiar enough with the city to realize the Roy family lived in a rough part of town. If he did, he probably wouldn't allow her within five miles of the place.

"I won't be long," she promised, before she hurried upstairs. After allowing the children a final glimpse of their sleeping mother, who'd sailed through her surgery, she ushered them out to the parking lot where Ruark was waiting.

"Is everyone ready?" he asked as he opened the back door of his car and lifted Cara inside.

"Yes," the little girl chirped. "I been awful quiet so Mama could sleep. Dr Rock, is she supposed to sleep for a long time?"

Gina thought her mispronunciation cute and from Ruark's smile, he was amused as well. "She is," he assured her. "But when you see her tomorrow, she'll be awake."

"Good."

Gina watched Ruark buckle the two girls into the safety seats they'd borrowed from the Pediatrics Department, and as soon as Tim squeezed in beside them, they were off.

"Should we stop for dinner?" Ruark asked her in a low voice.

"The neighbor, Mrs Klimus, said she'd have dinner ready." She pointed to the next intersection. "Turn right."

While Cara and Molly chattered away in the backseat, Gina noticed Ruark's expression harden as they drove farther into the poor neighborhood. She also didn't miss how often he glanced into the rear-view mirror, as if checking on Hugh and Joachim's whereabouts.

At long last Molly cried out, "There's our street!"

Ruark made a final turn into a road that sported more potholes than flat places, then stopped in front of a weathered pink duplex bearing the number Gina had memorized. "We're here," he said cheerfully, although he cast a glance at Gina that promised retribution.

In the blink of an eye the children scampered out of the car and rushed up the cracked and uneven sidewalk.

Ruark grabbed Gina's elbow. "Do not, I repeat, do *not*, wander off," he ground out in a voice meant for her ears only.

"I won't." Although she wanted to explain that she hadn't realized this part of town had deteriorated to this extent, he plainly wasn't in the mood to listen.

Mrs Klimus, who lived on the other side of the duplex, opened the door and welcomed them in with a wide smile on her wrinkled face. She was a portly woman in her sixties and her home, although shabby, was spotless, with the aroma of something tasty drifting out of the kitchen.

"Oh, you poor, poor dears," she said as she hugged Molly and Cara. "Well, not to worry. Your mother's going to be fine." She glanced at Gina for confirmation.

"Yes, she will be," Gina answered, pleased the woman was apparently a good friend of the family. She didn't know what she would have done if they'd delivered them to a house where they weren't welcomed.

"Perfect." The woman beamed. "And don't you worry about these three either. They're practically my own grandchildren."

"I'm glad to hear it," Gina said.

"We hate to run," Ruark said smoothly, "but we have another engagement this evening."

"Of course, of course. It was delightful meeting you," Mrs Klimus said as she ushered them to the door. "Come back and visit anytime. My door is always open."

Outside, Ruark took her arm again. "Ruark, please," she protested. "I'm quite capable of walking without your help."

"I know you are, but stay behind me," he said.

She glanced at him and noticed his expression had turned grim. "What's wrong?"

"Just do as I say."

She followed his gaze and saw a young man and woman, probably in their late teens or early twenties, standing near Ruark's vehicle. Actually, the man was eyeing the vehicle and the girl was leaning against the passenger front tire as if her legs were seconds away from giving out.

As Ruark approached, the young fellow faced them. "Nice wheels," he said nonchalantly, crossing his tattooed arms over a T-shirt-clad scrawny chest before he swiped at his runny nose.

"Nice," the girl repeated in a dreamy fashion. She, too, wore low-rise jeans, but while his revealed his boxer shorts, hers revealed a pierced navel. Her eyes and lips matched the pitch-black hue of her short, spiked hair.

"Thank you," Ruark said politely as he positioned himself between the boy and Gina. "If you don't mind, we're just leaving."

"You can't go yet, man," the boy protested. "Wheels like that cost a pretty penny. You can spare a few bucks, can't you, dude?"

"Sorry, I don't carry cash," Ruark said.

"Hey, man, I'll be happy with a credit card. In fact, that sounds better."

The girl suddenly groaned, clutched her belly and slumped over. "Tony, I don't feel so good."

"A few more minutes," he promised. "Then you'll be fine."

Gina had seen enough cases in the ER to know this woman needed medical attention and soon. She was clearly coming down from her drug-induced high and if her boyfriend gave her another fix, it might well be her last.

"Your friend needs to be in the hospital," she said. "Let us call an ambulance." She reached in her pocket for her cellphone just as he whipped a long, lethal-looking knife out of his pocket.

"No. No ambulance. No cops. No doctors," he said. "Just give me your wallet and you can go."

Ruark held up his hands. "OK. Just relax and it's yours." But before he could move, Gina's own car turned the corner.

The cavalry had arrived.

Apparently realizing he'd lost his advantage because they now had witnesses, the boy flicked the knife closed, then hoisted his girlfriend onto his shoulder before he disappeared between two equally disreputable houses.

Hugh and Joachim jumped out and rushed toward them. "Are you all right, Your Highness?"

"We're fine." Ruark grabbed her arm. "Let's go."

She dug in her heels. "We can't," she protested. "That girl needs help."

Hugh walked toward the area where the two would-be thieves had disappeared. "They're long gone. We won't find them."

"Maybe we can't," she said, "but the police can. We can't just drive away and leave her. We have to do *something*."

"You heard him, Gina," Ruark reminded her. "He said no ambulance, no doctors and no cops. We can't help people who don't want it."

She shook off his grip. "Maybe, but I have to try."

He fell silent, then motioned to Hugh. While the bodyguard punched in numbers on his cellphone, Ruark told her, "This is pointless."

"Maybe, maybe not."

"Regardless, while we're waiting for the police, you will wait in the car."

Sensing she'd pushed him as far as she could, she obeyed. In less than ten minutes a patrol car arrived and the policemen took their statements.

"I understand your concern, Dr Sutton," the middle-aged officer, who'd clearly seen his share of sad situations, said, "but we know Tony and his girlfriend. We won't find them until they want to be found."

"And if she dies in the meantime?" she asked.

He shrugged. "There's nothing we can do short of going on a house-to-house search. I suspect Tony is already miles away. We can't search the entire city for a punk and his drugged-out girlfriend. I'm sorry, but it's a fact of life."

"Then what *can* you do?" she asked.

"We'll put out the word we're looking for her and keep our eyes open. Who knows, we may stumble across her."

Stumble across her body, she wanted to say, but she didn't. It wasn't fair to take her frustration out on the police.

"Thanks," she said. Yet as she gazed at the houses she had an overwhelming urge to knock on doors herself.

Ruark echoed her thanks before grabbing her elbow and propelling her to his car, where he all but lifted her into the backseat.

Deep in her thoughts and disappointed by her perceived failure, she hardly noticed Hugh had taken over the driver's seat. Neither did she pay much attention when Ruark turned around and began scolding her.

"This wasn't my fault," she protested mildly.

"It doesn't matter," he continued. "You went into an area that wasn't safe. You promised you would be cautious."

"I didn't know we'd be accosted," she said, staring out the window. "As for being cautious, I didn't know the neighborhood had deteriorated to the point it had, but I wasn't alone. You were with me. Hugh and Joachim were nearby."

"It wasn't safe," he insisted, as if he hadn't heard a word she'd said. "I need to be able to trust you, Gina. Trust that you'll use good judgment when I'm not with you. What if I hadn't been there? What if Hugh and Joachim hadn't arrived when they had?"

"I'd have given him my purse, as he'd asked," she said practically and evenly, because she was conscious of their audience. "And if he'd wanted the vehicle, I'd have handed him the keys, too." But it was obvious from the way Ruark ran his hands through his hair that he wasn't listening.

"And if it wasn't enough the man pulled a knife on us..." His voice rose. "You probably would have started looking for that girl on your own. Who knows what mess you would have landed in then."

His attack stung and she watched the passing scenery out of her window through tear-filled eyes. She'd said all she could in her defense; she'd show that his tirade rolled off her back instead of lodging in her heart.

Hugh pulled into their driveway and shut off the engine before he silently slipped out of the vehicle. Gina, however, didn't move.

"Well?" Ruark demanded.

"I've said all I'm going to say. I only have one question." She paused. "Are you finished?"

"For the moment," he ground out before he slid out of his seat and jerked open her door.

She strode past him without a word. Ruark followed and when she headed for the dining room, he veered toward his office. A few seconds later the door slammed.

Startled by the sound, she bumped into Hugh. "Excuse me, Your Highness," he said politely.

"It was my fault. I wasn't watching..." She stopped, hating to hear her voice tremble.

He paused and looked down at her kindly. Too kindly for her brittle nerves. It wouldn't do if she threw herself at him and sobbed on his shoulder.

"Prince Ruark doesn't usually show his temper in such a manner."

"I apparently bring out the worst in him."

"He was very worried for you. Otherwise he wouldn't have reacted so strongly to the danger."

"Your loyalty is commendable, Hugh," she said, still smarting from Ruark's wrath. "But what happened was a fluke and I won't be blamed and don't deserve to be chastised for it."

"When he calms down in a few hours, he'll understand this to be true, Your Highness."

She gave him her "yeah, right" look before she shoved aside the swinging door and entered the kitchen. Right now she needed comfort after a day full of unwelcome surprises, and a bowl of her favorite chocolate ice cream seemed perfect.

"Ice cream?" Henri was aghast as he caught her rummaging in the freezer. "You must eat something more substantial first. How about a nice garden salad with plenty of ham and cheese?"

"Don't go to the trouble. I just want ice cream."

"It is no trouble, Your Highness," Henri fussed as he tugged the carton from her hands. "No trouble at all. Just go and sit down and I will bring it to you in a few minutes."

Foiled again! She plopped onto a dining chair and stared sullenly through the window into the back gardens. Her day couldn't have been worse. Her hours had been cut by nearly one-third, her good deed to deliver the Roy children had ended on a sour note, the young woman she'd wanted to help had disappeared, Ruark had yelled at her for something completely out of her control, and now she couldn't even eat what she wanted to!

Feeling completely adrift, she had no idea where or what her place was. Nothing was going as it should. Her husband had turned into a complete dictator after she'd actually thought she might be falling in love with him. Fat chance of that happening, because right now she didn't even *like* the man!

Give him a couple of hours to calm down, Hugh had advised. Fine. She'd give him those hours and gladly. In the meantime, she needed time alone, time to think, but she didn't want it here, in this house, where she felt like a hotel guest and couldn't do anything physical to work off her frustration.

She wanted to go home. Home, where she could eat an entire carton of ice cream without anyone gainsaying her. Home, where she could run the vacuum cleaner, dust, and mow the lawn until she was too tired to think. Home, where she'd have the breathing space to regroup before she faced the dragon again.

An overwhelming desire to escape chased away what little appetite she had. If she could only claim a short time to herself, she wouldn't waste a minute of it by eating.

"Thank you for this, Henri," she said as she carried her bowl into the kitchen, "but I'm not hungry after all. Would you please wrap it for later?"

"Of course, Your Highness."

"Oh, and I'm going out to run an errand," she lied smoothly. "I'll be back shortly."

"Would you like me to call Hugh or Joachim to accompany you?"

"No, that won't be necessary." She smiled at the Frenchman. "I'll find one of them myself."

"Very good, Your Highness."

Gina didn't waste time retrieving her purse or her spare set of car keys. Bracing herself for discovery, she was pleased to find her car still in the driveway, making it easier to slip away.

Carefully, she eased away from the house and rolled down the street, grateful her engine motor purred rather than roared. In a few short minutes she was on her way without anyone the wiser. Less than half an hour later she drove into her single-car garage and lowered the door behind her with a simple press of a button.

She was home.

As crazy as it seemed, as comforting as it was to be in familiar surroundings, she felt Ruark's absence keenly.

No, she didn't, she berated herself. She was infuriated by his utter lack of faith, his harsh words and imperious attitude. She refused to set aside her anger to remember how he'd been so kind and helpful with the Roy children at lunch, how he'd worried about her safety, how he'd positioned himself between her and danger in order to protect her.

She wouldn't dwell on the reasons for his anger because as far as she was concerned, he had none. She'd done nothing wrong to warrant his fury. Instead, she'd concentrate on his disregard for her feelings and how he'd carelessly hurt her. Perhaps his unjustified tirade wouldn't have cut her to the quick if she didn't love him.

Oh, sweet heaven! She loved him.

Now she understood why Ruark wanted a marriage built on friendship instead of love. Love made one vulnerable, especially if it was one-sided. The only question now was, what did she do next?

Every emotion she felt tumbled and swirled together until her chest ached. Before could slide out from behind the steering-wheel and enter her safe haven, she burst into tears.

Ruark left his office some hours later, determined to find Gina and apologize for losing control. He should have trusted his instincts once they'd gotten within a few blocks of the Roy family duplex, called Hugh to stick right on their tail, and waited until his two men arrived before they'd gotten out of the vehicle. But he hadn't, and he'd taken his anger with himself out on her.

He strolled through the house, poking his nose in nearly room looking for her. When he didn't find her he headed for the backyard, certain she'd decided to watch the sunset.

Returning inside, he ran into Hugh. "Have you seen Gina?"

"Not since we arrived, sir," the bodyguard answered.

"I wonder where she is," Ruark mused aloud as a frisson of fear began to wiggle a path down his spine.

"Ah, you're back, Hugh," Henri said as he bustled past. "Did the princess say if she'd like a snack? She wasn't hungry earlier."

"Back?" Hugh frowned. "I never left."

The smile on Henri's cherubic face disappeared. "But…the princess said she had an errand to run. I offered to summon you, but she said she would find you herself." His expression cleared. "She must have taken Joachim."

"He's been here all evening," Hugh said, exchanging a glance with Ruark before hurrying away.

"I don't understand." Concern etched the chef's face as he looked at Ruark.

"Gina is missing," he said grimly.

Hugh returned, breathless. "Her car is gone."

Ruark said two words. "Find her."

Moments later, in Hugh and Joachim's office, which was the base of their security operations, Ruark studied the monitors, which were fed by the surveillance cameras. With other security measures in place, he hadn't insisted on anyone constantly watching the footage, but maybe it was time he did. She would have been stopped within moments, although it would have only reinforced her opinion that she was a prisoner.

"I can't believe she left," he muttered, but in his heart he wasn't surprised.

"Pardon me for saying so, Your Highness," Hugh said carefully as he typed commands on his keyboard, "but you were rather hard on her."

"Thanks for stating the obvious," he snapped. "The question is, where did she go?" He turned to the man who'd seen her last. "Henri?"

He shrugged. "She mentioned an errand. I did not presume to ask what it was."

Joachim accessed the latest surveillance tape of the property and located the footage taken several hours earlier. Sure enough, Gina had climbed into her car and driven away. Ruark took comfort that she only carried her purse and not a suitcase. But where could she have gone?

"Call Belmont," he ordered. "She may be visiting a Mrs Roy on the second-floor surgical unit."

"I don't think so, sir." Hugh accessed another screen on his computer. "The GPS co-ordinates aren't near the hospital. If you'll permit me a few minutes, I can tell you exactly where she is. Or rather where her car is. We are fortunate we took the liberty of installing a GPS receiver in her vehicle when we installed a security system at her home."

Deciding to reward the man later for his foresight, Ruark leaned over Hugh's shoulder for a closer view. "And?" he demanded, impatient for the answer.

The screen zoomed in to reveal the electronic map markings. "The princess is at her old residence."

Ruark bowed his head in relief.

An unfamiliar noise startled Gina out of her deep sleep. So much for her plan to return to Ruark's house before he noticed she'd slipped away from her watchdogs, she thought tiredly. By the time she drove back, he'd be ready to deliver another scathing lecture.

"You're awake." His voice drifted across the room.

She bolted upright. "Ruark! What are…? How did…? I locked the door," she said, brushing at the trails of dried tears on her face. "I know I did so you can't accuse me of being careless."

"You did," he agreed. "Thanks to modern technology, once I realized you were missing, we were able to locate you. As for the door, the lock wasn't a problem." He held up a keyring and jingled it. "Why did you leave?"

She stared at him, incredulous. "Do you have to ask?"

"No, but I'd like to hear your reasons anyway."

"I had to get away," she said stiffly. Then, after deciding to move the inevitable confrontation out of the bedroom, she headed for the living room. "If you're going to yell, get it over with."

"I won't yell."

He'd surprised her, but as she glanced at his face, the coldness she'd seen earlier had disappeared. He almost seemed...contrite, but that wasn't possible. "Then what are you doing here?"

"I wanted to be sure you were all right. I was worried," he said simply. "For the second time today, I might add."

"As you can see, I'm fine." She glanced at the clock. "I hadn't planned to stay this long, but I fell asleep. We can go now."

He shook his head and sat on the sofa. "Not until you explain why you left. If you wanted privacy, there were any number of rooms you could have used. You didn't have to drive across town."

The dam inside her broke and she let loose all the things preying on her mind. "*You* wanted privacy, Ruark, but I wanted something more. I left because I needed a place where I could think and be myself. Where life was *normal*. It isn't *normal* at your house. It might be for you, but it isn't for me. The staff treats me like a guest. And you..." She swallowed hard to clear the sudden lump in her throat. "Today you treated me like a useless, brainless ornament, a stupid, naïve child.

"Here, in my house, I'm me. Gina Sutton. The adult who cleans up her own messes, cooks her own meals, eats ice cream whenever she wants, decides and is accountable for her own actions. And here no one yells at me.

"At your mansion, I don't know who I am, other than a person who's created more work and more worry for everyone. Including you."

He fell silent. "What can I do to make it better?"

"Oh, no," she protested, shaking her head. "Don't you dare be gallant or kind or understanding when a few hours ago…" The words caught in her throat and she blinked rapidly. She'd cried all the tears she intended to cry.

"A few hours ago I acted like a horse's ass," he said bluntly. "I was angry with myself and I took it out on you."

His admission took her by surprise. "Angry with yourself? Why? You weren't responsible for what happened any more than I was."

"I didn't listen to my instincts and as a result you were this close…" he pinched his forefinger and thumb together "…to getting hurt. It was unforgivable to put a woman I'd sworn to honor and protect at risk. I felt as if I'd failed you."

As her proud husband humbled himself, her anger melted into forgiveness. She sank beside him and rested one hand over his.

"You can't plan for every eventuality or protect me from every possible danger," she said softly. "It's sweet of you to try, but you can't predict what will happen and you can't feel guilty if something does. It isn't healthy for either of us."

"I'd rather be too cautious than not cautious enough."

"There has to be a happy medium and it'll take time to find it. Meanwhile, you can't surround me in bubble wrap."

"Maybe not, but you can't disappear like you did either."

"You said to avoid places with strangers and unfamiliar territory," she pointed out. "My house didn't apply."

He raised an imperious eyebrow.

"Next time, I'll tell someone my exact destination," she promised on a long-suffering note, certain there would be instances when she'd chafe at the restriction. "But once you knew where I was, did you really need to check on me? Or did you think I wouldn't go home on my own?"

"You're my wife," he said simply, as if that was all the excuse he needed. "I felt certain you were safe and knew you'd return eventually when tempers cooled, but being here meant I could talk you into coming home sooner rather than later."

"Hmmm." She pretended to consider her options as she ran her finger down the placket of his shirt. "If you take time to persuade me, we won't get home until later. But if you'd rather leave sooner…" She nudged a button out of its hole.

He stilled her hand, then shot to his feet as he pulled her with him. "We'll go later," he said as he led her to the bedroom. "Much later."

CHAPTER TEN

GINA twisted her charm bracelet as she stood at the ballroom entrance on Friday night and surveyed the crowd already assembled. Other than Ruark, she didn't know a soul, although she recognized several guests because she watched television and read newspapers. Her father may have been a prince, but she wasn't accustomed to rubbing elbows with the rich and famous. In spite of her ancestry, she was merely a staff physician at a struggling hospital in a mid- to low-income neighborhood.

As she glanced at the man beside her—the man who was too handsome for words in his black tuxedo—she realized she was wrong. She wasn't only a physician. She was the Prince of Marestonia's wife, a princess, a countess in her own right. This may be her first fancy charity ball, but she belonged there as much as anyone else did.

Yet she couldn't deny she felt more at home in her ER, wearing scrub suits and tennis shoes instead of gorgeous gowns and jewelry.

Ruark took her hand and threaded it through his. "You're fidgeting." He'd leaned over to speak in her ear, appearing as if he'd uttered an endearment rather than a gentle rebuke.

"Sorry," she whispered back. "Can't help it."

"Try."

"But everyone's staring."

"They always do when a beautiful, poised woman makes an entrance."

Having checked herself in the mirror before they'd left, she couldn't deny she looked fantastic. The hairdresser had worked wonders, an expert had applied her makeup, and her simple white evening gown glittered under the crystal chandeliers. As Ruark had mentioned he would, he'd helped her settle on her mother's single strand of pearls and matching earrings.

As for being poised, if she hadn't had Ruark's supporting arm, she'd probably have fallen off her high heels.

"This is quite awesome," she said, noting everything from uniformed waiters and fresh flowers in abundance to elaborate ice sculptures and champagne fountains. "Very glitzy and glamorous."

He glanced across the way, studying the scene as if he were seeing it for the first time. "It is," he agreed.

"I hope the women's shelter project receives a ton of money tonight. Every time a battered woman comes into the ER, I have this overwhelming urge to hunt down the man responsible and give him a dose of his own medicine!"

"I had no idea I'd married such a Valkyrie," he said with a smile. "You'll be pleased to know that women and children's causes are dear to my mother's heart as well."

He motioned ahead. "I see a few people we have to greet. Shall we?"

This was it. "Lead on."

Ruark guided her into the throng where he introduced her to the host of the ball and his wife, then the Marestonian ambassador.

The distinguished white-haired man kissed her hand as he bowed. "Your Highness. What a supreme pleasure to meet you."

She blushed. "Thank you, Ambassador Janssen."

He turned to Ruark with a twinkle in his eye. "Now I understand the rumors of a whirlwind romance. But they were not just rumors, were they, for you to land such a lovely bride?"

Ruark laughed. "One must do whatever is necessary to eliminate any and all competition when such a prize is at stake."

"You have done the royal house and your country proud."

"Thank you."

"The two of you must come to Marestonia soon for a wedding trip. The people are eager to welcome the two of you and will feel slighted should you delay."

Ruark bowed ever so slightly. "As soon as we're able to rearrange our schedules."

Apparently satisfied by Ruark's response, the ambassador moved away.

"I had no idea there was a Marestonian embassy in the vicinity," she said, "much less that an ambassador of your country would attend a ball for a national cause."

"There isn't," he admitted. "However, several of the organizers of this event have ties to Marestonia and Avelogne. As word got out that we were attending, the guest list grew to include more of our countrymen from across the US. You, my dear, were the draw card. I suspect the charity will do quite well as a result."

"Oh, my." The news only increased the pressure she was under to present Ruark and herself in a good light.

"For the record, you dazzled the ambassador."

"Really? How could you tell?"

"A man knows these things," he replied.

"Dazzled or not, was he politely telling us the natives are restless and you need to hurry home?"

"*We*," he corrected her. "*We* need to hurry home, but that's a worry for another day. Would you like to dance?"

She grinned. "I thought you'd never ask. Just don't try anything fancier than a waltz."

"One waltz, coming up."

The next few hours were like living out a fairy tale. The musicians were exceptional, the food mouthwateringly delicious, and the company beyond compare. Having the man she loved at her side made everything else fade into the background.

Gina danced with Ruark as well as several of his compatriots. She met senators and cabinet members, CEOs of several Fortune 500 companies, and several other ambassadors, including Ambassador Antoine Lauwers of Avelogne.

"Prince Ruark," he said as he took Gina's hand and beamed at her, "I congratulate you on finding Prince Arthur's gem."

Ruark smiled. "Thank you."

"May I once again extend the Queen Mother's and King Henrik's invitation to visit Avelogne. Both the royal family and the people of Avelogne would be thrilled to honor the Princess Gina and her husband."

Gina paraphrased Ruark's earlier response. "Should we find ourselves able to rearrange our schedules, we'll consider the invitation."

The ambassador meandered away as an old friend of Ruark's joined their group. After Ruark had introduced her to Jason Dumont, a man he'd known since primary school, Gina excused herself for a trip to the punch bowl. There, she simply watched the guests, wishing she could bottle this moment and share it with Cara and Molly. She easily imagined those two little girls staring at this scene in wide-eyed wonderment.

Thank goodness things had turned out so well for their family. She shuddered to think of how different the situation could have been if friends like Mrs Klimus and relatives hadn't been on the scene.

As she glanced over at her husband and saw him laugh and joke with Jason, she wondered if he missed *his* family, friends, and the culture he'd grown up with. Probably no more than his family missed him. Even with the telephone and Internet, his mother probably hated having an ocean separate them.

Had her grandmother missed her father after he'd moved here and started his new life? No doubt she'd taken his decision to relinquish his claim to the throne as a personal rejection. For the first time she felt the heartache that her grandmother must have suffered because of one poor, misguided woman.

Perhaps it *was* time to accept the olive branch her father's family had extended. It would have been so nice after he'd died to have had the support system the Roy children now enjoyed. Maybe it wasn't too late after all...

But before she would rectify that situation, she had to do something that was far more personal. She had to find a way to tell Ruark she loved him. She could only hope that the care and concern he'd shown for her these past few weeks meant that his cynical views had softened and that love had grown in his heart, as it had in hers.

Jason clapped Ruark on the shoulder. "You always did have remarkable taste in women but you've outdone yourself, my friend. She is a treasure beyond compare and all I can say is you're a lucky dog."

Ruark grinned, delighted by his old school chum's approval. "I am, aren't I?"

"Are you certain she doesn't have a sister hidden away?"

Ruark chuckled at his hopeful tone. "I'm positive."

"She's definitely one of a kind. No wonder you snapped her up without giving us a clue you were in a relationship. When did you two meet and how in the world did you keep your romance a secret?"

"We both attended a medical seminar in California some months ago." Ruark glossed over the details, purposely avoiding any reference to how he'd conducted his supposed romance. "And the rest, as they say, is history."

"Yeah, you've definitely made history," Jason remarked. "I'd heard rumblings of how the problems between Avelogne and Marestonia prompted your marriage, but after seeing you two tonight, anyone with one eye and half a brain would know the gossip isn't true."

Ruark wasn't surprised by the rumors—they'd been bound to surface. However, Jason's observations had piqued his interest and he hoped his friend would elaborate. "Oh?"

"Yeah." Jason grinned. "I noticed as soon as I saw you across the room. You look at your wife as if you can't bear to let her out of your sight. You obviously love her."

Love her? Impossible. He cared about her and appreciated her, but that was all. Unfortunately, he couldn't disagree. Some confidences couldn't be shared even with old friends. If people thought him in love with his wife, then he'd accomplished his mission.

"I have to say," Jason continued, "after your experience with that actress, I never expected you to tie the knot."

"Neither did I," Ruark agreed, because it was true. Had duty not come into play, he'd still be a bachelor. Regardless of how Jason interpreted what he'd seen, he might not love his wife, but he was happy with his marriage.

Contented with the thought, he caught a glimpse of Gina as the crowd parted. She'd been remarkable this evening and had charmed everyone she'd met, as he'd known she would. With her tawny-colored hair and brilliant green eyes, she was a vision in her iridescent white gown, and she was his. He met her gaze and smiled.

Jason reached out and grabbed a bottle of imported beer from a passing waiter. "I'd stay and chat, but I have my eye on a gorgeous redhead and she looks like she's lonely. Give my regards to your wife and if you ever need a godfather, I'm available." He winked as he saluted Ruark, then disappeared into the throng seconds before Gina rejoined him.

"Where did Jason go?" she asked.

"Hunting," he replied. At her puzzled frown, he explained. "For a redhead."

"Ah."

"Is Cinderella ready to leave her first ball, or would she like to stay longer?"

"It's well past midnight," she pointed out. "If we won't commit some horrible breach of etiquette, I'd like to go. As much as I've enjoyed myself, I wouldn't mind slipping out of the spotlight."

"Then we'll go." He was more than eager to cut the evening short. Sharing Gina with so many people had begun to fray his patience. Not only that, but he had a special day planned for tomorrow—today, actually—and he didn't want anything to mar his surprise.

"Wake up, sleepyhead."

Gina groaned at the sound of Ruark's voice. He sounded entirely too chipper for…she glanced at the clock with one eye… 9:00 a.m. He was obviously used to functioning on less sleep than she was because they hadn't gotten home until after two.

Closing both eyes, she stretched. "What's the rush? It's Saturday."

"Exactly. We have places to go, things to do."

Suddenly a T-shirt and a pair of shorts landed on her face, and startled her completely awake. "What?"

Ruark stood above her and grinned, wearing a disreputable pair of jeans and faded cotton shirt. "Come on. We're wasting time. Everyone's waiting. We can't get started until you get up."

A quiet knock at the door summoned him. He returned with a steaming mug of coffee and placed it on the nightstand.

"Henri sent this. You have five minutes or you're coming with me in your pj's."

She jumped out of bed at his threat. "What's going on?"

"You'll see," he said cryptically.

Gina dashed into the bathroom to rush through her morning routine and exchange her nightgown for the clothes Ruark had so graciously chosen for her. She was halfway down the stairs when he met her in the foyer.

"What's going on?" she asked.

"It's moving day," he said.

She stopped short. "Moving? We're moving?"

"Not in the sense you're thinking." He escorted her to the game room, which was a few doors down from his office. Inside, she saw Hugh, Joachim, and Henri dismantling the slate pool table.

"You're moving the pool table?" she asked, wondering why he'd insisted on her presence.

He nodded. "Remember how you said you didn't have a place to call your own? Now you have one. This will be *your* room to organize and use as you see fit."

Gina took in the cathedral ceiling, the window overlooking the flowerbeds in the backyard, the beautiful oak hardwood floor. "It's mine?" she asked, hardly able to believe he was giving up one of his masculine domains for her.

"All yours. As soon as we clear out what you don't want, we can either bring in furniture from your other house or purchase new."

"But your game room," she protested.

"We aren't doing away with it entirely," he said. "We're only relocating it to the empty area over the garage."

Touched by his gesture, she was momentarily speechless. "Oh, Ruark. I don't know what to say. I'm completely overwhelmed. This is so sweet of you."

He grinned, looking remarkably boyish. "Overwhelmed or not, we're operating on a time schedule here. We have to turn the moving van back to the rental company by 8:00 p.m. so before we can cart anything in, this room has to be emptied out."

"Wouldn't it be easier if I took the space over the garage?"

"Not only would you be too far away from the rest of the house but it's an inappropriate location for my wife to receive guests. This," he emphasized, "is your room."

Thinking of some of the women she'd met last night, she realized he was right. "OK. I'll keep the cabinet and the small table. The rest can go. Including the mounted antlers and the bearskin rug."

"Are you sure? Antlers and a bearskin rug are great conversation starters," Ruark teased.

"Then you might want them in *your* office."

"You heard her, guys. We're hauling them upstairs."

With much groaning and moaning, the four men heaved the furniture to its new home. The pieces of slate were the most difficult to maneuver. When Ruark's corner slipped and slammed into his shoulder, nearly knocking him off his feet and down the steps, Gina's heart leaped into her throat.

"This isn't a good idea," she warned. "We should have waited for a crew of experienced movers."

"Don't be ridiculous," Ruark huffed as soon as they reached the top and unceremoniously dropped their load. "This isn't any worse than lifting weights at the gym."

Hugh and Joachim wiped sweaty foreheads with their arms, looking as alarmed as she felt at Ruark's close call with disaster. "Your Highness," Hugh began, "perhaps we should consider recruiting a few more hands for the job?"

"The heaviest piece—the pool table—is done. We can handle the rest."

Gina didn't know if Ruark was determined to show off or simply too stubborn to admit defeat, but she added her muscles to the mix. Before long, the room's contents had been transferred and they were on their way to her old house.

There, she selected several of her favorite pieces, including a roll-top desk, sofa and chairs, an heirloom cedar chest and an elaborately hand-carved wardrobe that had belonged to her parents. She also boxed her frog collection, determined to place the ceramic frog wearing a jaunty expression and a crown on his head in a prominent place because it reminded her of Ruark.

By five o'clock that evening, other than a fresh coat of paint and new window treatments, the Princess's Room, as Henri had dubbed it, was ready.

"I can't thank you all enough," Gina said as she hugged each tired helper to their sheepish embarrassment. "You are all the best."

"We were pleased to do this for you," Hugh said before the three of them disappeared, leaving Gina alone with Ruark.

"They didn't have to rush off," she said, surprised by how quickly they'd left.

"They probably thought they should go before you asked them to rearrange the furniture again," he said dryly.

"I did work them rather hard," she admitted.

"And what about your poor husband?" he asked.

She slipped her arms around his neck. "He was sorely used, too. I'll have to make it up to him."

He groaned as she squeezed. "I believe every muscle in my body aches."

"Why don't you soak in the Jacuzzi for a while? I'll bring a snack to tide us over until Henri calls us to dinner."

"An excellent suggestion," he said, planting a swift kiss on her mouth before they parted company.

Fifteen minutes later, she found him in the master bathroom's whirlpool tub, eyes closed. "How's the water?" she asked as she placed her tray of cheese and fresh fruit on the ledge.

"Great. Care to join me?"

"Maybe later. You need to recharge your batteries first."

As he opened his mouth to protest, she popped in a cube of Cheddar cheese and noticed the purpling bruise on his shoulder.

"You *did* hurt yourself," she accused, hating to think he'd injured himself because of her. If she hadn't loved him before, his actions today would have tipped the balance.

"It's nothing. What else did you bring?" he asked, peering at the tray.

She speared a chunk of pineapple and fed it to him. "Fruit. I chose all of your favorites, so lie back and enjoy."

He leaned back in the whirlpool. "I could get used to this," he said as she offered a grape this time. "We could make this a nightly event."

She chuckled. "Annually."

"Weekly," he countered.

"Monthly."

"Sold."

While they devoured the food she'd brought, they talked of inconsequential things, but Gina knew in her heart that the moment she'd been waiting for, the moment when she opened herself up and revealed her feelings, was fast approaching.

"Last bite," she said as she placed a grape in his mouth.

He grabbed her free arm. "I'm still hungry."

"I'll see if Henri—"

"Not for food," he said as he tugged her shirt upwards. "For you."

She grinned. "But I'm out here and you're in there."

"A problem easily rectified. Join me."

"We can't both fit."

"Trust me. We can and we will."

She didn't hesitate. Her clothes disappeared in short order, discarded in an untidy heap near the tub.

The water was warm and only added to the sensual spell. He positioned her in front of him, between his legs, and she leaned against his chest, enjoying the feel of his muscles against her back. He began soaping her skin as his mouth trailed kisses down the side of her neck. He gently caressed, stroked, and teased every nerve ending of her entire body until she was certain they'd raised the temperature of the water swirling around them.

They might have been there for minutes or hours, she didn't know because she was too caught up in his tender assault of her senses. Finally, he rose with a growl, wrapped a towel around her and himself, then carried her to their bed.

Eager for him, she gratefully accepted his weight as he covered her completely. The ache inside her demanded ease and she dug her fingers into his back as he nuzzled her neck.

"Ruark, please," she murmured.

"Please what?"

"Please…hurry."

With one touch he sent her to the stars. With one smooth thrust he filled her, then began a fierce rhythm that didn't end until he groaned and collapsed against her.

Gina drifted back to earth, her arms and legs intertwined with his as she rested her cheek against his chest and listened to his steady heartbeat. Her scattered thoughts slowly coalesced into one that summed up everything in her heart.

"I love you," she confessed softly as her fingertips traced swirls on his chest.

His grip around her tightened. "I told you we'd be good together."

She heard the pride, the self-satisfaction in his voice. "Pretty sure of yourself, weren't you?"

"You bet."

"And you based this on…?"

"Sixth sense. Intuition. Gut feeling."

Certain she'd taken him by surprise with her declaration of love, she pressed on. "Does your sixth sense tell you anything else besides we're good together?"

He hesitated. "Is it supposed to?"

The excitement of saying she loved him dimmed, but perhaps he simply needed coaxing. "After all this time, I thought maybe our relationship had grown past the we-get-along-great stage."

She sensed his mental withdrawal. "Is that what you want from me?" he asked. "To tell you what you want to hear? To say I love you?"

Hardness had replaced the lazy quality of his voice and she winced at the sudden loss of their closeness. "Only if you mean it," she said.

He rolled off her to sit up on the edge of the bed, his bare back toward her. "We've talked about this concept of love before. You entered into this marriage knowing it was to fulfill a duty, knowing we would build a relationship based on respect and mutual interests, rather than feelings."

"I know what I agreed to," she said. "But my feelings changed."

"Exactly my point. Emotions shift as easily as the tide. Today you say you love me—who knows what you'll feel tomorrow?"

She pulled the sheet around her, suddenly uncomfortable at baring her body as well as her soul. "My feelings didn't just change, Ruark. They *grew*. They'll be the same tomorrow as they are today."

He turned to face her, his expression disbelieving. "What if I suddenly refuse to grant your every whim? To give you the things that you like and enjoy? What then?"

A disquieting thought rushed forward in her mind. "Is that what you've been doing, Ruark?" she asked quietly. "Was today just one more instance of you acting like a benevolent genie? Did you really want a happy marriage, or did you only want the *illusion* of one?"

"I didn't want an illusion," he insisted. "As far as I'm concerned, our marriage is everything we'd expected and tried to make it. Five minutes ago we proved how good it is."

She released the breath she hadn't realized she'd been holding. For a minute there she'd been afraid he'd only been deceiving her, using her as a pleasant perk associated with performing his duty.

"Happiness is a feeling," she pointed out. "But love is stronger because it grows, which is what happened to me. As I got to know you, I fell in love." She paused. "I'd hoped you'd had the same experience."

He turned to face her. "I do care about you," he said soberly. "Why can't that be enough?"

"Because it isn't," she said, saddened that he'd still closed his heart off to her in spite of everything they shared. "Love makes the day seem brighter, problems less insurmountable, life more enjoyable. Without it, you're not really living, only going through the motions."

"Love is simply a word. Nothing more, nothing less."

She rose as regally as possible and twisted the sheet toga-style around herself. "You loved a woman once—"

"I was wrong," he said.

She ignored his interruption. "And she told you what she wanted you to hear. I'm not her, though, so don't transplant her flaws onto me. I have enough of my own.

"I know she left you, but I won't," she stated, knowing that was part of his concern. "Not because I can't give up the princess lifestyle but because I made a promise which I intend to keep. Our marriage can either be heaven or hell. The choice is yours."

She swept from the room and locked herself in the master bathroom. The need to weep swept over her, but she gritted her teeth and held back the sob. Instead, she splashed water on her face and patted her skin dry, wishing she could wash away the pain of his rejection as easily.

He *didn't* love her. Maybe his caring was simply a way to make the performance of his duty more palatable. She couldn't deny they were compatible in many areas, but she didn't want to be his consolation prize, the reward granted to a good obedient little prince for services rendered to the Crown.

For a moment she felt trapped in a loveless marriage, but as she remembered all the things he'd done to ease her into her new life, all the ways he'd made her feel special, she couldn't—*wouldn't*—believe that he didn't feel something beyond companionship. Yesterday he'd worried about failing her, and he wouldn't have done that if she wasn't important to him. He simply couldn't admit that his caring was love in disguise.

Considering all his experiences with women who'd pretended to care because he was a prince, she was fortunate he cared at all. He could so easily have held himself back and turned their relationship into a case of "married singles".

Maybe that was the problem, she thought as hope edged away her sense of entrapment. He was afraid to believe her, afraid to *let* himself love her. Married or not, they'd only known each other for a few weeks and he obviously didn't trust her yet with something as important as his heart. She'd simply have to prove that her declaration hadn't been as a result of her hormones or gratitude for his generosity. That she'd fallen in love with the man, not his title.

It would take patience and effort to smash through his walls of skepticism, she consoled herself. He'd spent years building his defenses, so she couldn't expect to tear them down on her very first try. She'd inherited enough of her father's stubbornness to keep swinging and stay in the game.

She would show him that love, not companionship or mutual interests, made a marriage happy. Teach him that love meant strength, not weakness or vulnerability.

If he didn't learn the lesson? What then?

She didn't know, she thought miserably, but the picture of her life if she failed was too bleak and too miserable to contemplate.

* * *

Ruark jerked on clean clothes, irritated at how easily the afternoon had turned from pure bliss into sheer agony. Gina had known from the beginning that he didn't want or expect love to be a part of their marriage and suddenly, because he'd done a few nice things, she went and changed the rules.

Well, he wouldn't have it. The foundation for their relationship had been set. Trust, companionship, respect, and attraction had been part of the package. He hadn't planned to invest himself emotionally in their arrangement and she shouldn't have either.

Oh, he truly cared about her, more than any other woman he'd spent time with, and that should have satisfied her. Why did she want words that were often uttered carelessly or with deceit? Didn't she know that they only gave false hope and made one vulnerable?

As far as he was concerned, actions spoke louder and more honestly than words ever could. Gina would simply have to accept and be contented by that.

CHAPTER ELEVEN

"HAVE you seen the latest *People* magazine?" Lucy asked Gina a week later.

Gina sighed. Ever since photos of the women's shelter project charity ball had hit the tabloids, her excited staff had gone out of their way to hunt down every bit of publicity about the royal couple they could. At first, it had been sweet, but now she found it irritating, especially as her grand plan seemed to be failing.

She'd done her best to act as she always had, with one exception. Now, every chance she got, she told Ruark both in word and deed that she loved him. Unfortunately, he wasn't replying in kind, and she'd given him ample opportunity.

A relationship expert on the Internet had claimed that men who couldn't say they loved someone had commitment issues. As marriage was a huge commitment which they'd already undertaken, she discarded the theory soon after she'd read it. She was simply expecting too much, too soon, but her continued failure was disheartening.

If only he hadn't been so darned sweet during the past week!

First, he'd ventured into the kitchen and mixed a batch of her favorite double chocolate peanut butter chip cookies with Henri's help. The only way he could have known she enjoyed them so much was if he'd noticed she always added them to her lunch tray.

Then he'd sent her a basket of tiger lilies, admitting he'd known how much she enjoyed them. How he'd learned they were her favorite, she couldn't begin to guess because none of her friends knew just how special those flowers were. Her father would send them on special occasions or whenever she'd had a really tough week at school. She'd deck her parents' graves with them every year on their birthdays and Memorial Day, and whenever she felt especially blue, she bought them for herself.

As for her nights with Ruark, they were as fantastic as always. She would always tell him she loved him, but she'd stay awake long after he did, hoping to hear a whispered endearment before he fell asleep. Unfortunately, she never did.

For the first time in her career she almost wished she'd studied psychology instead of emergency medicine.

"Hello?" Lucy asked. "Anybody home?"

Gina focused on the nurse. "Sorry. Don't mind me. My mind was…elsewhere."

"Can't imagine why," Lucy said cheerfully. "Want to hear what they said about you in *Home and Garden*?"

"No."

"Too bad. It's quite flattering." She closed the magazine and laid it on the stack of other publications that contained some mention of the royal couple.

"I don't know why you guys are collecting all this," Gina said, wishing she could make the pile vanish and knowing she'd cause an outcry if she did. "The entire department sees us almost every day. You don't need photos."

"Hey, these are for posterity," Lucy protested. "You're the closest we'll ever come to knowing a celebrity so we're milking it for all its worth. We get so little enjoyment out of life here in the trenches."

"Yeah, right. Speaking of trenches, do we have the lab work

back on room four?" At Lucy's blank look, Gina pointed to the scheduling board. "Does chest pain ring a bell?"

"Oh, yeah, him. I've been busy with the guy whose nail gun misfired and shot a nail into his hand. Before you ask, Dr Holman is making arrangements to admit him for surgery."

Owen Holman was a top-notch orthopedic surgeon who specialized in hand injuries. "Great. But what about—?"

"The lab work isn't back yet. I checked the printer a few minutes ago. My bet's on indigestion."

"Hold onto your money," Gina advised. "He could fool you. What else do we have?"

"Nothing our PA can't handle. Before I forget, Dr Thomas wants to see you. Preferably before his meeting with Dr Lansing at ten."

Frankly, she'd like some distance from the man until she sorted through her troublesome thoughts, but apparently she wouldn't get any. "OK, but the minute those lab results come through, I want to see them."

"Will do. Oh, and, Gina?"

She turned and faced the nurse. "Yes?"

"You've seemed rather preoccupied today." Lucy's face registered concern. "Is everything OK?"

"Sure. Why wouldn't it be?"

The nurse shrugged. "You seem different. More…restrained, I suppose. Are you feeling well?"

"I'm fine. Truly," she replied, as much to assure Lucy as herself. "And remember, I'm waiting for those results."

As directed, Gina went to Ruark's office. His desk was covered in what she knew were budget proposals and cost analyses, but he was leaning back in his chair, reading a magazine article.

She groaned as she rubbed the back of her neck in abject frustration. "Not you, too."

He grinned sheepishly as he straightened. "Couldn't resist.

According to this, ever since we announced our wedding, the incidents of vandalism and other property crimes have dropped significantly. People are speculating on the details and what long-term effects our marriage will have on the two countries. It's obvious the mood in Avelogne and Marestonia has improved."

Just what she needed—to be reminded of why they'd gotten married. "I'm glad," she said simply. "Is that why you wanted to see me?"

He closed the magazine and tossed it onto his desk. "No." He studied her. "Are you OK?"

Irritated that he was the second person to ask the same question, she ground her teeth together before she evened her tone. "I'm fine. I'm swamped outside, and all this press is getting to me."

"The novelty will wear off soon."

"I hope so."

"As you're busy, I won't keep you, but my father called a few minutes ago. Apparently, in spite of the good news I just told you, the royal family is under pressure for us to have an official state wedding ceremony."

The idea struck fear into her heart. Although part of her had anticipated the possibility, when the subject hadn't resurfaced since the charity ball, she'd hoped it wouldn't.

"Do we have to?" she asked. "I mean, will we start an uprising if we don't?"

"No, but as I've been living in the US for some time, he's afraid the people will believe I'm dismissing my heritage if I don't honor our royal traditions."

"I see." In other words, his duty hadn't ended yet and, if the truth be known, never would. "What would be involved?" she asked, certain she wouldn't like her options.

"Our ceremony won't be as elaborate as my brother's," he

assured her. "A trip down the main thoroughfare in a horse-drawn carriage, I would guess, then on to St Gregory's Cathedral for the formal church blessing. After that, we'll greet the public at the palace and host a small reception for family and friends."

Her breath caught at his mention of the church. "What did you tell him?" she asked.

"Only that I'd discuss it with you."

It had been difficult enough to marry a man who didn't love her the first time, but to repeat the experience? And in such a holy setting? Hardly. She had her limits as to what she was willing to do to right past mistakes.

"Did he indicate when this happy event is supposed to occur?"

If he noticed her sarcastic use of "happy", he didn't indicate it. "Within the month, I expect."

"A month isn't very long to organize an event that elaborate," she remarked.

"My mother has enough staff to pull it together in a week," he said dryly. "So should I tell him to make arrangements?"

There was always the possibility he might come to love her in the few weeks leading up to the royal event, but if he didn't…could she take the risk?

"I'd be honored to marry you again in your country because I love you," she said calmly.

"Then all we have to do is choose a date."

"But I won't."

He frowned. "You won't what?"

"I won't do it. I won't go through another ceremony."

His frown deepened. "I don't understand."

She smiled wanly. "I'm more than happy to marry a man I love in any place he chooses and as many times as he would like, but I refuse to marry one for a second time who doesn't love me.

"I'll visit Marestonia, shake hands and kiss babies like any good royal wife. I'll even add Avelogne to the itinerary in order to see my grandmother, but…" she planted both hands on his desk and leaned toward him "…I will *not* listen to your pledge of love and devotion when you don't mean it and are only reciting trite and meaningless words out of duty. How *dare* you even ask me to consider such a thing?"

She straightened. "So tell your father whatever you like to get yourself off the proverbial hook. Say I'm claustrophobic in churches, allergic to flowers, or that lace makes me break out in hives. I don't care what excuse you give, but I will not repeat holy vows with someone who doesn't love me. I have *some* pride and self-respect."

Shaking with indignation and pleased she'd stated her convictions in no uncertain terms, she swept from the room and returned to work.

Dumbfounded, Ruark watched her leave as if she couldn't escape his presence fast enough. Obligations aside, he'd been so sure she would agree because she loved him. He'd only thought of the ceremony as another event to attend, another duty to perform, but clearly Gina had seen the rite as a symbolic, religious act of two people becoming one.

Sheepishly, he admitted he hadn't considered the vows they would make. He'd only focused on how proud he would be to stand beside the woman who made his life complete by the love and laughter she brought.

He'd greedily taken those gifts, never quite expecting or believing his good fortune. Yet, somewhere along the way, she'd become such an integral part of his existence that he couldn't imagine facing a day without her.

In his thoughtlessness and self-centeredness he'd clearly hurt her, and he berated himself for it. He'd rather cut off his right arm than cause Gina pain. He loved her too much to be responsible for giving her a single moment of grief.

Instantly, something broke in his chest, as if he'd finally been released from his chains of denial. He loved her.

Stunned by the revelation, he tried the words on for size again—he loved her!—and realized he meant every word.

He'd always believed he didn't know what love was or how to recognize it, and now he knew he'd been right. He *hadn't* known what true love was because what he'd felt for Grace had been a mere shadow of what he felt for Gina. Love *was* more than affection, companionship, and compatibility. Love implied a passion that went beyond the physical and into the spiritual. It was a desire to spend every moment of the day with an individual, seeing her at her best as well as her worst, and being delighted with each experience.

If this was what Gina felt, then he understood why she had to tell him every chance she could. Others had uttered "I love you" as a throw-away phrase that was useful on occasion, but Gina had spoken it from her heart. How dense he'd been not to recognize the difference and how foolish to let his cynicism rule him. He'd done her a disservice and if she never forgave him for it, she would be justified.

His path suddenly became clear—he had to make amends. He'd call Henri and ask for a special, romantic dinner with candlelight and flowers. No, tonight was too many hours away. He wanted to tell her *now*.

He jumped up, then stopped short. Unfortunately, his meeting with the budget review committee was scheduled to begin in five minutes. He couldn't postpone it without a valid excuse. Needing a private moment with his wife wouldn't carry enough weight to exempt him from the meeting where upper management decided on his department's funding.

Once again duty demanded his attention and he chafed under

the obligation, wishing his personal wishes could supersede it once in his life.

It would only be an hour, he consoled himself. Then he would set things straight with the love of his life.

"My gut hurts real bad." The forty-five-year-old truck driver hunched his shoulders forward and rubbed his abdomen. "You gotta do something, Doc."

Gina had already examined the man who answered to Glen "Gibb" Gibson, and hadn't found anything suspicious. Normal-sized liver, no signs of fever or jaundice, normal bowel signs, no spasms, no masses, only tenderness in his right upper quadrant. Palpating his abdomen didn't provide any clues as to why he was experiencing such excruciating pain. Of course, that didn't mean anything, only that whatever was wrong wasn't immediately obvious.

"I'm going to order some bloodwork," she informed him. "I want to check your kidney function as well as your pancreas. Those results should narrow down the possibilities."

Because she still hadn't gotten the lab results from her possible MI patient, she decided to save time and collect the blood samples herself. Within minutes she took Gibb's tubes to the nurses' station and handed them to Lucy.

"I want electrolytes, amylase, CBC, glucose, BUN and creatinine, liver profile, and an acute hepatitis profile," she stated, choosing tests that would give her information about Gibb's kidneys, pancreas, and liver. "Get a urine specimen, too, and find out what happened to my cardiac results."

"Will do." The nurse got on the phone and Gina returned to Gibb's cubicle.

"The tests will take about an hour or so," she informed him. "Meanwhile, we'll collect a urine sample, then send you to X-Ray for abdominal films. After that, we'll let you rest."

She'd scarcely finished when everything happened at once. A loud crash barely registered before the walls and ceiling came crashing down. Instinctively, she tried to cover her head with her arms, but she was too late. Something struck her temple and everything faded to black.

Impatient to finish business so he could leave, Ruark tapped his pen against his copy of the budget proposal. Their discussion was dragging on far too long and at this rate he'd be lucky if they finished their inquisition by noon.

Lansing's secretary bustled in and Ruark bit back a groan. The woman had interrupted twice already and obviously intended to do so again. She passed a note to Dr Lansing who scanned it, then frowned.

"When did this happen?" he asked.

"About ten minutes ago," she answered. "The phone lines in the ED are down. We just received the news."

Ruark heard "ED" and his whole body went on alert. "What's wrong?"

"You'd better get downstairs," Lansing said grimly. "Someone's just smashed their vehicle into the ER."

Gina.

Ruark didn't hesitate. He bounded for the exit. "Injuries?" he stopped to ask.

"We don't know. Apparently they're still trying to account for everyone. Don't worry, we'll send all available staff to sort out—"

Ruark didn't stay long enough for the chief of medical staff to finish his comment or implement the hospital's internal disaster plan. He bypassed the elevator and ran for the stairs, arriving at his department in record time.

Once he'd pushed his way through the double doors marked "ED Staff Only", the scene reminded him of other disaster sites. Plaster dust hung heavily in the air and at the far end of the hall where patient cubicles had once been, rubble and a half-demolished Humvee now replaced the outer wall and allowed him to see daylight and the visitors' parking lot.

Staff scurried to and fro in organized chaos. Although the damage to the building was extensive and various pieces of wood, steel and brick had been tossed along the entire length of the department from the force of impact, the worst damage was confined to the two treatment rooms where the Humvee had crashed through. Most of the people appeared shaken, but other than a few who were covered in white dust and held towels to their bleeding faces or extremities the number of casualties seemed minimal, their injuries superficial.

"Where's Dr Sutton?" he demanded of a passing male nurse.

"Haven't seen her."

Undamaged rooms held patients and staff, but Gina wasn't to be found. No one remembered where or when they'd seen her last. With dogged determination he continued his search, hoping she'd gone to Radiology or the cafeteria, but his instinct warned him she hadn't.

He found Lucy near the largest pile of rubble, along with another nurse, Hugh and Joachim. Each worked to move the chunks of ceiling and wall.

"Where's Gina?" he demanded, not caring who answered.

Lucy's face was white, her eyes wide with worry as she pointed. "Underneath that. She and her patient are the only ones we can't account for."

Fear beyond anything he'd ever experienced, including the incident with the man pulling a knife, pierced him, but he reined it in as best he could. He had to be calm and objective or he wouldn't do her any good when they finally reached her.

"Find several backboards and a C-spine collar," he commanded the nurse. While she obeyed, he took her place to work alongside his men.

"Your Highness," Hugh said respectfully, "you should step aside and let us handle this."

"Forget it," he snarled. "I'm staying."

He'd made his intentions plain and Hugh simply nodded and returned to work as if he'd known Ruark wouldn't listen.

"It's so amazing," Lucy said, her voice quivering in apparent shock. "We didn't know what had hit us until we saw the Humvee."

"Anyone check the driver?" he asked.

Joachim didn't waste his breath as he heaved another large piece of plaster to the side. "Dead."

"We're thinking he had a heart attack and plowed right in," Lucy huffed as she lifted several smaller pieces of debris out of the way.

"I see an arm," Hugh called out.

Ruark's gut churned, afraid of what he'd find and afraid of what he wouldn't. He wanted to tear through the splintered wood and bricks to reach Gina, but they were playing a game of pick-up-sticks. Unless they worked slowly and methodically to remove each piece, more could come crashing down.

The ceiling tiles had fallen but the braces were still intact, which Ruark considered a good sign. They wouldn't have to shore up the ceiling or worry about the upper floor crashing on top of them.

A few minutes later they'd uncovered Gina and her patient, both buried underneath the wall cabinets that had toppled over them. "Gina?" Ruark called out as they dealt with the unconscious man who lay in front of her.

She didn't answer.

As soon as they'd placed Gina's patient on a stretcher and carted him to a safer location, Ruark knelt beside her.

Gina's groan was like music to his ears. He called her name as he ran his hands over her head and upper body while others worked to free her trapped legs. A lump on her head, a purplish gash along her hairline, cuts and more bruises on her arms, but no broken bones. So far.

"Hurt...everywhere," she murmured.

"I know," he soothed. "We'll have you out in a minute."

It took ten to immobilize her spine, place her on a backboard and carry her into a treatment room as far away from the destruction as possible. "I want X-ray and lab here, as well as a surgeon," Ruark commanded to no one in particular as Lucy began cutting off Gina's shirt.

Seeing she was going into shock, Ruark barked his orders while the nurse started the IV. He leaned over Gina. "Hang in there," he told her.

"I...will. Have...to."

"You're going to be fine," he promised, willing it to be so because he couldn't accept the alternative.

Her mouth twitched as if she was trying to smile. "Won't be...like the...others. Won't...leave you."

"Darned right you won't," he said fiercely. "I love you."

Her eyelids fluttered closed. As he worked frantically to determine how serious the large, darkening bruising across her hips and abdomen was, he was afraid of one thing.

She hadn't heard him.

For the first time in a number of days, when Gina woke up, she actually felt awake. Tired and worn out, but awake.

Noticing her surroundings—a familiar hospital room—she noticed Ruark sprawled in a nearby chair. She scratched her itchy nose and he sprang out of his seat to stand beside her.

A smile spread across his face until his eyes crinkled. "Good morning, sleepyhead."

She managed a smile. "It doesn't feel like such a good morning."

"You're awake and you're stable. I'd say that's better than good. You've been sedated for several days, you know."

"I didn't realize. No wonder I'm so stiff. I need to sit up." She struggled to find the remote control to raise the head of her bed, but he did the honors.

After she'd settled into a new position, she reached toward his face and stroked his bristly cheek. "You didn't shave," she said inanely.

He clasped her hand and lowered it to his chest. "I spent the night here and haven't gone to the doctors' lounge to change yet. I didn't want to leave you alone."

"Was I that bad?"

He chuckled. "No. I just couldn't go home."

"Why ever not?" she asked. "It isn't like we don't pay our nurses to look after patients."

"True, but I didn't like the idea of you being by yourself. If you had problems, I would have been halfway across town."

"But I didn't have problems," she pointed out.

"Didn't matter. The possibility was there. My parents wanted to fly over as soon as I told them about the accident, including your grandmother, but I told them not to. You see, *I* wanted to be here for you. No one else."

Touched by his statement, she didn't know what to say, so she flexed her aching shoulders and changed the subject. "Are you going to share your diagnosis or do I have to guess?"

"Your liver and kidneys were bruised, but they're healing nicely. We thought we might have to remove your spleen, but Ahmadi decided to wait and see if your blood counts stabilized. So far so good." He grinned. "You also have the usual assortment of scrapes and other bruises, as well as a minor concussion, but it could have been a lot worse."

"My patient? Glen Gibson?"

"Strangely enough, he's in better shape than you. Probably because you'd managed to push him forward enough so the heaviest pieces fell on you instead. You'll also be interested to know his pancreatitis is coming under control."

"I'm glad. Was anyone else hurt?"

"A few had minor injuries, lacerations and the sort. Other than the driver, you and Gibson were the worst."

"How is he?" she asked.

Ruark shook his head. "Massive coronary. According to his wife, he hadn't felt well but insisted on driving himself to the hospital. It's a shame he didn't listen."

"His family must feel terrible," she said, "but it could have been worse. We could have had a full-blown disaster on our hands."

"It's bad enough," he said. "The ER has been shut down until the engineers can check the structural integrity of our end of the building. Then, once they give the OK, they'll start repairs and we'll be back in business."

"What about the patients?"

"We'll handle what we can through the minor emergency center across the street and route the serious cases to St Bridgit's. In the meantime, staff are temporarily reassigned to different units or they're using their earned time." He grinned. "I'm taking a few days off, too."

"Whatever for?"

"I figure I'll need every one of those days to convince my wife how much I love her."

She froze, wondering if the combination of pain medication and wishful thinking had affected her hearing. "You what?"

He carefully perched on the edge of her bed as he held her hand. "I love you, Gina."

"You… How…? What…? I thought you didn't believe in love."

"I didn't, until you came along. Once I realized how I couldn't imagine a day without you, I knew I was wrong."

Tears welled in her eyes. "I thought…I thought…" Unable to deal with her sudden relief, she began to cry quietly because her muscles were too sore for her to let loose real sobs.

He waited until her emotional storm lightened. "You thought what?"

"I imagined all sorts of possibilities," she confessed, wiping her cheeks with the backs of both hands. "I couldn't decide if you truly didn't love me or were just afraid to say so. Then I thought you'd heard it so many times before from so many other women that you didn't believe me."

"I did believe you, Gina. I just had trouble accepting it. Fool that I was, I thought if I showed you how important you were by my actions, everything would be fine. You'd see how much you meant to me, even if I never said so."

"I tried to tell myself that, but a girl needs to hear the words," she finished simply.

He tipped her chin up. "I didn't do this right the first time, so I'm trying again." He paused. "Will you marry me, Gina? Not because of duty or responsibility, not because of our family history or political expedience, but because I love you?"

Tears threatened again, but they were happy tears. "Oh, yes, I will."

He leaned over and kissed her ever so gently as if afraid she would break.

"Come, now," she teased. "Is that the best you can do?"

"For now," he promised. "I'm saving my best for when you're out of this hospital bed."

She giggled. "Promises, promises."

He grinned down at her. "May I call my father and tell him to organize a wedding?"

"Please, do."

"He'll ask for a date," he warned.

"Tomorrow."

He laughed. "Even my mother can't work that huge a miracle. Besides, you need time to recover. How about a month?"

"Perfect." With her spirits restored, she suddenly wanted to share her mood with everyone. "Do you have your phone with you?"

He pulled it out of the case on his hip. "Yes, why?"

"I'll explain in a minute." Grateful for his international calling plan, she scrolled through his contact list to find the name she wanted.

"I can call for you," he began.

"I know, but this is something I have to do myself." After pressing a button, she waited... The number she'd dialed began ringing and a woman answered.

Her crisp accent reminded her so much of her parents' that Gina could hardly speak past the lump in her throat, but somehow she managed.

"Grandmother?" she croaked. "It's me. Gina..."

EPILOGUE

"MY BROTHER would have been so proud to see this day," King Henrik stated as he threaded Gina's arm through his in the vestibule of St Gregory's Cathedral in the heart of Marestonia's capital city.

"I think so, too." She smiled at her uncle, who resembled her father so closely it was uncanny. "Thank you for giving me away."

"It's my honor and privilege." The twinkle in his eyes belied his solemn expression. "I'll be glad when it's over, though," he said. "Planning a royal wedding in less than a month, even a small one like yours, has turned both palaces upside down. Your aunt and grandmother discussed nothing but fabrics and dress designs for days. I can't imagine what Ruark's parents went through to organize their end."

While tradition required the bride marry in her family seat, she and Ruark chose to spread the celebration between both countries in order to avoid slighting anyone. They'd opted to hold the actual ceremony and reception in Marestonia, with her uncle giving her away in lieu of her father. The formal wedding ball would follow in Avelogne.

"I know, and I'm sorry for all the problems I caused."

He patted her hand. "Nonsense, my dear. This event was what everyone needed. It's a shame you'll be returning to America so soon. We haven't had nearly enough time to talk."

"We'll come back to visit," she promised.

Gina could hardly hear the music over the pounding of her heart. She knew the flower girls were slowly scattering the rose petals along the white-carpeted center aisle as they'd practiced during last night's rehearsal. In a few minutes the wedding co-ordinators would cue her uncle and it would be her turn.

While she waited, she fingered the ivory-colored handkerchief that had been in her family for generations and had once been framed and hung in a place of honor in her parents' bedroom. Ten names had been embroidered on it so far, and as part of their tradition Gina's name had been added underneath her mother's. Someday her daughter's name would appear there as well.

Buoyed by the thought of Ruark waiting for her, her jitters faded as the orchestra began playing the *Lohengren*'s Bridal Chorus. "This is your last opportunity to run out the back door," Henrik joked.

"We're already married, so it's not an option," she reminded him with a smile.

The aisle seemed to stretch for miles, but she focused on Ruark as he waited for her in the sanctuary, looking distinguished in his official state regalia with all the accoutrements of his royal family. He might already be her legal husband, but today he would become the husband of her heart.

Her uncle placed her hand in Ruark's, then stepped back while Ruark took his place at her side.

He whispered over the chamber ensemble's performance. "You look beautiful."

"So do you."

"I thought you'd never get here."

"I walked as fast as I could. We didn't have to do this, you know."

"And deny everyone all this excitement? They would never have forgiven us."

For all the fuss and uproar, Gina knew both families had been thrilled by their decision and members of both royal houses had pitched in to help. She'd been more than grateful because she didn't care about flowers, colors, music, or the food. She was only interested in repeating her vows because this time they would both mean them.

As the music began to fade, she teased, "Does His Royal Highness have any final comments before he marries his wife again?"

He squeezed her hand tightly. "How does 'I love you' sound?"

"Perfect. Absolutely perfect."

BABY SURPRISE
FOR THE
DOCTOR PRINCE

ROBIN GIANNA

I'd like to thank my duet partner, Amy Ruttan, for being so great to work with. Let's do it again, sometime, Amy!

Also, another huge shout-out to my wonderful friend Meta Carroll for helping me with the medical scenes in the story—thanks and smooches!

CHAPTER ONE

AUBREY HENDERSON LIFTED her face to the lagoon breeze and smiled, soaking in the incredible history, vivid colors, and sheer amazement that was Venice, Italy. How lucky was she to have snagged a temporary job here? She might have spent only two days in Venice before leaving for her two-month nursing job in Rome, but every detail of those hours felt etched in her brain.

Which included every detail of her illicit, probably ill-advised, and beyond wonderful fling with Enzo Affini. That one night felt burned into her mind—and body, as well—and just the thought of him made her silly heart both skip a beat and burn with annoyance.

Maybe they'd left it a little vague, but hadn't he implied he'd be in touch? What exactly they'd said to one another when they'd parted in the wee hours of the morning didn't seem too clear anymore, but still. She'd expected he'd at least call her while she was in Rome, since he knew she was coming back to Venice around now.

Knowing she might run into him in the flesh had her feeling nervous and excited and ticked off all over again for making her wonder if she'd ever hear from him. Then ticked off at herself for wondering at all.

Then annoyed even more when she realized that when the phrase *in the flesh* had come to mind, an instant all-too-sexy vision of the man's glorious body made her feel a little breathless.

Ridiculous. Time to concentrate on why she'd come to Venice, which had nothing to do with a handsome Italian prince who was obviously the love-'em-and-leave-'em type. Which was okay. She didn't care if she saw him or not. In fact, she had no desire at all to see the guy, since he clearly didn't want to see her.

No, she'd come here before to support her friend Shay, who'd recently married Enzo's brother, Dante. Now she was here to work in the clinic, enjoy that adventure, and meet with the art and architecture preservation society she'd donated more money to in her mother's memory.

Her mom had always been fascinated with Venice and its incredible history, and it had only been her fear of travel and crowds that had kept her from coming to explore it. Seeing the fresco she and her mom had "adopted," paying for its restoration before her mother had died, would be sad but wonderful, too. Her mother's legacy as a preservationist in New England had now been expanded across the ocean, and that thought brought her smile back and her thoughts completely away from Enzo Affini.

Really. She wasn't going to think about him again. Period.

A renewed pep in her step took her down narrow stone passageways in front of colorful homes, over numerous charming footbridges, then across the *piazza* toward the well-marked clinic she'd be working in for the next four months. When she opened the wide glass door, a bell chimed. Inside, a friendly-looking, middle-aged woman sat at a rather spartan desk. Aubrey had been told most of the people here could speak English, but wouldn't they appreciate it if she tried a few of the Italian phrases she'd learned?

"Buongiorno. Mio nome e Aubrey Henderson. Um… sono qui…per lavorare."

She struggled to remember more, then abandoned the effort when she saw the quizzical and amused expression on the poor woman's face. Doubtless she was completely butchering the pronunciation.

"I'm a nurse with the UWWHA, assigned to the clinic here starting today."

"Welcome. We've been expecting you. And let's speak English, shall we?" said the woman, her smile widening.

"That sounds good." Aubrey smiled back. "I'm working on the language, but I'm not too good at it yet, obviously! I'm hoping by the end of the time I'm here, I'll practically fluent."

"Learning a language takes time, but working with patients will teach you much. I am Nora, and you can ask me for anything as you need it, *si*? Come with me." She stood and gestured to the door behind her. "I'll show you where you can put your things. We have a small staff here—you may already know we have just one doctor and nurse working each day, which sometimes gets very hectic. The doctor who is director of the clinic is here today, and he will be the one to show you around. A patient is here right now, though, so the doctor may not be available for me to introduce you at the moment. When you see him, can you introduce yourself? I must greet patients as they arrive, you see."

"Of course. And I confess I don't really know much about how the clinic runs," Aubrey said as she followed Nora down a brightly lit hallway. "I saw the opening in Venice and jumped at the chance to work and explore here." Had jumped at the chance to explore a certain unbelievably sexy prince, too. Except she wasn't thinking about him ever again.

The place was very modern and scrupulously clean. Aubrey glanced into a few rooms to see each had a blue and white examination table, along with the usual medical necessities that you'd see in the United States. Not exactly plush and comfy-looking, but they'd do the job.

Nora opened a tall cupboard door made of the same white material as the rest of the built-in furniture in the space. "Here is a locker for your things, with your uniform inside. I don't see the doctor, so make yourself comfortable and he will be with you soon. Okay?"

"Okay." Nora left her alone and Aubrey was about to put her purse inside the locker until she wondered if maybe she was supposed to change into her uniform right then. Probably yes, since she assumed she would be working with patients right away? Why hadn't she asked Nora those things while she was still here?

Aubrey nearly went back out to the reception area but decided that was silly. If she got into uniform and it turned out to be just an introductory day, it was no big deal. At least she'd be ready, right?

Finding a bathroom, she changed into the crisp white dress, smiling at how it was oddly old-fashioned compared with what nurses wore in the US today, and yet the whole place felt ultramodern. She dropped her clothes and purse into the locker, then hovered around, not sure what to do next. The various drawers and cupboards tempted her to open them up and poke around on her own, but she figured it would be more polite to wait until she was invited to do that.

She stood there for a good ten minutes, and each minute that dragged on felt more awkward. And didn't it make sense to acquaint herself with where things were, in case she needed to take care of a patient sooner rather than later? But luck being the way it was, just as she opened one of the cupboards above the long countertop a deep voice spoke from behind her.

"*Buongiorno.* You must be the new nurse from the US."

Jumping guiltily, she nearly slammed the cupboard shut and turned with a bright smile. Then her heart completely stopped when she saw who stood there.

Enzo Affini. The man who'd unfortunately kept coming to mind since she'd returned to Venice. The man whose hands and mouth had been all over her two months ago. The man who hadn't bothered to call her again after that very intimate night together.

Aubrey felt a little as if she might just fall over, as though she'd been physically struck at the surprise of seeing him right there in front of her. She barely noticed the elderly man standing next to him as Enzo's dark eyes met hers for several breathless heartbeats. He recovered from the shock more quickly than she did, moving next to her to get something from the cupboard she'd just been snooping in, then turning to the elderly man with instructions. Aubrey didn't hear a word he said, feeling utterly frozen as she watched Enzo and the patient move down the hallway, with Enzo opening the door to the reception area for him, then following behind.

Aubrey sagged against the countertop, her hand to her chest, trying to breathe. Did she have any chance of slipping out the back door before he came back? Though if she did, what would that accomplish? She'd come to Venice to work. Was it her fault that he, incredibly, worked at this clinic, too? Gulping down the jittery nerves making her feel numb from head to toe, she forced herself to stand as tall as possible and stared at the door, willing herself to look calm and confident.

Proud that she managed to be standing there in a normal way when the door opened again...assuming he couldn't see her knees shaking...she met his gaze. The look on his face was completely different than the last time she'd seen him, which was the night they'd parted in the wee hours of the morning. Then, his eyes had been filled with warmth, his sensuous lips smiling and soft.

These lips could have belonged to someone else. Hard and firmly pressed together. His silky eyebrows formed a deep V over his nose as he stared at her.

"Aubrey. To say this is a surprise is an understatement. How did you know I work here?" His voice was a little hard, too. Ultra-chilly. She'd have to be dense as one of the posts sunk into the silt of the lagoon if she couldn't read loud and clear that he was not pleased to see her *at all*.

Something painful stabbed in the region of her heart, but the nervousness and, yes, hurt filling her gut slowly made way for a growing anger at the strange suspicion in his eyes. As if she'd come here on purpose to stalk him or something. "I didn't. I didn't even know you were a doctor. Something you conveniently forgot to mention."

"You knew Dante is a doctor."

"So that meant you had to be one, too? From the way you talked about the restoration of the old homes here, I thought you were an architect or in the construction business or something. You at least knew I was a nurse traveling with Shay." She wasn't about to add that her attraction to him and excitement about deciding to let herself enjoy a little carnal pleasure on the trip had been foremost in her mind, not the thought of what he did for a living, since right now *he* clearly had other things on his mind. Like being ticked off that she was there.

Well, he wasn't the only one feeling beyond annoyed right then. It was painfully obvious that he'd never planned to contact her when she was back in Venice, and she wasn't sure if she was angrier at him for that, or at herself for wishing he'd wanted to.

"I assumed you were working at the hospital with Shay."

"Well, you assumed wrong, the same way I did." She tipped her chin and stared him down, her chest pinching tightly at the way he was looking at her. As if she were some black rat that had scurried out of the sewer into his clinic.

A long slow breath left his lips as he stuck his hands in the dress pants that fitted him as impeccably as the ones he'd taken off as fast as possible the last time she'd seen him. His white lab coat was swept back against his hips, and even through his dress shirt his strong physique was obvious. The body she'd gotten to see in all its glorious detail.

The jerk.

"Our time together before was…nice, Aubrey. But this is a problem."

Nice? The most incredible sexual experience of her life had been *nice* for him? "Why?" she challenged, beyond embarrassed and steaming now. "You're obviously a man who enjoys women. I enjoyed our night together, too. But that's long behind us. Now we move into a professional relationship, which won't be a problem for me at all."

Liar, liar, pants on fire, her inner self mocked. Though maybe it was true. Right now, if he tried to kiss her, she just might punch him in the nose.

"Listen." He shoved his hand through his hair. "I think it's better if we look at other options."

Other options? The rise of panic in her chest shoved aside her anger with him. Nora had said he was director of the clinic. Did that mean he could toss her out if he wanted? She knew there weren't any positions available at the hospital. What if there wasn't a single other place to work in all of Venice?

"Enzo, there's no reason we can't work through this. I—"

"Dr. Affini." Nora rushed into the hallway with a boy who looked to be about seven trailing behind. Blood stained his torn pants and dripped onto the floor with every step he took. "Benedetto Rossi is here. He fell off his bike. I tried to call his father and his *nonna* but haven't reached either of them. I'll keep trying."

"All right." Instantly, the frown on Enzo's face disappeared, replaced by a calm, warm smile directed at the boy. "Were you taking the corners too fast again?" he asked in English.

The boy responded in quick Italian, gesturing wildly

and looking panicked. Enzo placed his hand on the boy's shoulder and led him to an examination room as the boy talked, his head tipped toward the child as he listened. Aubrey hurried to follow. Enzo might not want her here, but maybe she could prove he needed her anyway.

The boy stopped talking to take a breath, and Enzo took advantage of the brief break in his recitation. "Sit up here." He swung the child up onto the exam table. "And speak English, please. I know your *papà* likes you to practice, and the nice nurse here is American. I'm going to take a look, okay?"

Benedetto nodded and sucked in a breath as Enzo leaned over to carefully roll back the boy's ripped pants. The skin beneath sported a wide, bleeding abrasion. It was a nasty one, to be sure, but at first glance it didn't look to be deep enough to require stitches. Not that his leg couldn't still be fractured in some way.

Time to show how competent and vital to this clinic she could be, right? Before Enzo booted her out the door for having *nice* sex with him?

Aubrey shoved down the anger and worry and stab of hurt still burning in her chest and opened a few drawers. Pulled out the supplies she'd need to stop the bleeding, washed her hands, and snapped on gloves. "That's an impressive scrape you've got there," she said to the child, smiling to relax him. And herself, if she was honest. She was glad Enzo had asked the boy to speak English, because she hadn't been able to understand a single word he'd said. "You're obviously a very tough guy. Is your bike okay?"

"No." The panicked look came back. "The wheel is bent, and the tire is flat. *Papà* is going to be angry."

"Oh, surely he won't be angry when he sees you were hurt," Aubrey said.

"Yes, he will." He licked his lips and turned his wide-eyed attention back to Enzo. "Nonna will be, too. I was supposed to be getting bread and *seppioline*, but I went to play with Lucio first. And then I fell off my bike near his house."

"Let's worry about that later." Enzo straightened to send the boy another wide smile he should patent to relax a patient. Or kindle some other reaction, depending on the circumstances and who he was sending it to. "First, we're going to stop the bleeding. Then we'll take an X-ray to look inside your leg. Luckily your *papà* signed papers allowing me to treat you the last time you were here."

"X-ray?" Tears sprang into the boy's eyes. "You think my leg might be broken?"

"I don't think so, no. But we'll check just to be sure." Enzo patted the child's shoulder and glanced at Aubrey as she cleaned the wound. "Looks like you have that under control. I'm going to get the portable X-ray."

"Yes, Doctor," she said, oh, so coolly and professionally, staring at the boy's leg because she didn't want to look at Enzo's wickedly handsome face. Be distracted by all his undeniable beauty, and get mad at him all over again.

He returned just minutes later, rolling the cart to the table. "Between the blood and rips, I'm afraid these pants are ruined, Benedetto. I'm going to cut them off so we don't have to slide them down over your leg."

"What? How will I get home without pants?"

"We keep spare clothes here for things just like this. No worries, okay? Nurse Aubrey here will find you something. Now, this won't hurt at all, and you'll get to see a picture of your bones afterward, which I think you'll like."

Enzo was so incredibly gentle as he lifted the child's leg to place the X-ray plate under his calf, her vexation with the man softened slightly. The steady stream of calm, amusing conversation he kept up with the boy actually had the child laughing, which was a dramatic difference from the scared tears of earlier. She had to grudgingly admit that the man had a wonderful bedside manner. In more ways than one, darn it.

Enzo straightened, and his dark eyes lifted to hers. "This will take just a short time to develop."

"I'll wait to dress the wound until you've taken a look. Then find those pants you talked about. Unless you want to wear the ones I brought, Benedetto? They have little flowers on them—quite pretty."

"Eww, no!" He obviously knew she was kidding, because he laughed, and the impish smile she'd so enjoyed on Enzo's face the first moment she'd met him returned as he winked at her.

"Benedetto wearing flowered pants to the fish market just might make the fishermen's day, don't you think, Aubrey?"

"I don't want to wear them, but I want to see you in them, Nurse Aubrey! I like flowers on girls' clothes."

A laugh left Enzo's annoyingly sexy lips, and the eyes that met hers held a hint of the amused look she remembered too well. "You're smart for being so young. Very, very smart. I'll be right back."

Hopefully this proved they could take care of patients and interact just fine, and the weight in Aubrey's chest lifted a little. She absolutely did not want to have to leave Venice before she'd learned more about how her mother's foundation could help restoration projects there. Before she'd barely had a chance to explore this unique city. Enzo Affini might be superficially charming and very irksome, but she was confident she could look past all that and think about him in a strictly professional way while she worked here.

She could and she would.

Aubrey chatted with the child until Enzo returned, and she quickly looked away from him, because every time she let her gaze run over his dress shirt and doctor coat she remembered the strong body, smooth, tanned skin, and soft dark hair on the muscular chest beneath it all. Which made her feel a little warm, and while she wanted to think it was her anger bubbling up again, she knew the ridiculous truth.

Mad at him and hurt by him and needing to keep her distance from him didn't seem to affect being *attracted* to him one bit. What in the world was wrong with her?

"Good news, Benedetto. No fracture." Enzo's voice warmed the whole sparse room. "So Nurse Aubrey is going to get you bandaged up while I go take a look at your bike. See if I can fix it so it's good as new. Is it outside?"

"Sì." The boy's eyes lit in surprised excitement. "Can you do that?"

"I'm going to give it a try. Aubrey, when you're done, please get a tube of topical antibiotic from the drawer for his *papà* to pick up later when he comes back for us to change the dressing. And will you look in the cupboard next to yours to see if there are any pants that would work for him?"

"Of course." She watched his tall frame leave the

room, completely failing in her determination to not admire that beautiful dark hair and his broad shoulders and the elegant way he moved.

Ugh. She quickly turned back to Benedetto. Being sweet to this child and fixing his bike didn't erase the reality that the man had virtually accused her of hunting him down just moments ago. A Jekyll and Hyde type, to be sure.

When she had the boy's leg securely bandaged, she stood and smiled. "I'm going to look for those pants. Be right back."

The first cupboard had a neatly stacked pile of all kinds of clothes, but after fishing through them she couldn't find a single pair of pants. The one next to it had what looked like running shorts and a few T-shirts, and a lone pair of gray sweatpants. More searching proved there was nothing else around, so she took the sweatpants back to the exam room, dug into her purse for her sewing kit, and showed the child the pants. "This is the best I can do, I'm afraid. They're way too big for you, but I'm going to make them fit as best I can. Okay?"

"Okay." He eyed them doubtfully. "How can you make them fit? They are huge."

"Ah, I have many talents, young man. You just wait. Can you stand up without it hurting too much?"

She helped him from the table and held the pants up to his waist. They draped a good foot and a half onto the floor, and she made a pencil mark. Then she took scissors from the drawer, cut off the bottom half of the legs, then cut into the elastic waistband. Removing a big chunk of fabric, she then stitched it back together as the boy patiently watched.

"Eccoli!" she said, feeling pretty satisfied with her work and her ability to come up with a good Italian word to boot. "Step into them and see if they'll stay on you now."

Once he'd pulled them on, he stared down at the pants, then up at her with a big smile. "They are okay! I didn't think you could. Thank you very much."

"You're welcome. Here's that tube of antibiotic Dr. Affini wants put at the front desk for your dad or your *nonna* to pick up. Now, let's go see how he's doing with your bike."

She tried hard to ratchet back the way her heart squished as they stepped out to the *piazza*, trying to shore up her negative feelings about the man currently crouched on the stone pavement. His head was bent over the bicycle wheel as he used some kind of wrench on it. He'd taken off his lab coat, and his necktie was askew and tucked inside the buttons of his shirt. Mid-morning sunshine gleamed in his hair, and his eyes were narrowed as he concentrated on his task.

"Can you fix it, Dr. Affini?" Benedetto sounded both worried and hopeful.

"Good…as…new. You're going to ride like the wind." One last turn of the wrench, then he stood to pump a little more air into the tire. Obviously pleased, he brushed his hands together, beaming a smile at the boy. "How's your leg feel?"

"Okay. Thank you so much. I'm going to get the things my *nonna* wanted, then go straight home."

"Here are the instructions for your *nonna* and *papà* on when to come back, and later, for changing the bandage again and using the antibiotic ointment." He pulled a folded paper from his pocket, and his eyes met Aubrey's. "You did put the ointment at the desk?"

"I gave it to Nora after we set him up with new pants."

"*Bene.* They—" He stopped short as he looked at the child's pants, then, after a long pause, laughed out loud.

"What?" she asked, bristling that he obviously thought her sewing job was amusing. Or bad. Or something. "There wasn't anything that would fit, so I made a bigger pair fit at least a little."

"I see that. They look very good on you, Benedetto. Very good." He reached to give the child a quick hug. "Now you go run your errands. Come back tomorrow to let us take another look and change the dressing, and ask your *nonna* or *papà* to call me before that if they have questions."

"Okay. I don't think Papà will be as mad now that my bike is fixed. Thank you again!"

Aubrey watched the boy mount the bike and ride it slowly and carefully away, and she smiled. "He's being very cautious now, I see."

"Not for long, I'm sure." Enzo's amused gaze met hers. "Good thing you made the pants fit so the legs wouldn't get caught in the chain and make him fall again."

"Yes, good thing. So why were you laughing at my sewing job?"

"I wasn't laughing at your sewing job. I was laughing because those are—were—my pants."

Her mouth fell open. "What? They were in the cupboard you told me to look in! With some shorts and T-shirts and…and…" The vision of the neatly folded shorts and manly T-shirts in that cupboard made her voice fade away. Why hadn't she realized those items were all the same size, when the ones in the other cupboard had been a total mishmash? Heat washed into her face. So much for showing she was indispensable around here. "I'm so sorry. Really sorry. I thought—"

"Aubrey." He pressed his fingertip to her lips. "It's fine. Sometimes I run when the clinic's slow, and I keep clothes here for that. Obviously, they served Benedetto well. Between you and me, his father is very old-school and can be hard on him when he makes mistakes. Not having to show up in bloody, torn pants with a broken bike is a good thing."

"What about his mother?"

"She died a few years ago."

Her heart squeezed for the little boy who had lost his mother far too soon. Having her own mother for twenty-seven years hadn't been nearly long enough. She looked into Enzo's eyes and could see they'd shadowed with sadness for the boy, too. Probably for the child's whole family, since he obviously knew them fairly well, and seeing how much he cared melted her heart. Just a little, though. "Poor little thing," she said softly. "It's good that you fixed his bike for him, then."

"And I thank you for making the pants work. We Venetians take care of our own."

Not being a Venetian, she knew he wasn't talking about her, but somehow it felt absurdly nice to be included in the thought. Which reminded her how much she wanted to stay here for the next few months, and how Enzo Affini had implied just a bit ago that he didn't want to work with her in the clinic at all.

"So." She squared her shoulders and looked him in the eye. "We were having an important conversation about my job and future here, and you need to know I'm not leaving."

"No?" His lips quirked at the same time that suspicious frown dipped between his eyes again. "And if the director of the clinic, who would be me, says you have to? That he'll find you employment somewhere else in Italy?"

"I've already worked two months in Rome. And I've come to Venice now because this is where I want to be. Didn't taking care of Benedetto prove we can work together just fine?"

"Aubrey, I cannot promise that I wouldn't allow myself to be seduced by you again."

Her mouth fell open. "I didn't seduce you! I believe it was you who seduced me. And I *can* promise that it won't happen again. I don't even find you attractive anymore." Which was kind of true. For good reason. And yes, her nose was growing a little, but she'd stick with that half-truth if it killed her.

A slight smile softened the hard lines on his face. "That I know is a lie. Shall we agree that the seduction was on both sides? And that's the problem, because I can't have an affair with someone who works at the clinic."

"Listen. I know we only got together at first that night because you wanted to ask me questions about Shay." Knowing that hadn't kept her from jumping into bed with him, though, had it? "It was just a one-night thing. I have zero desire to…to co-seduce you again."

"And if I can't say the same thing?"

She wondered if he knew he spoke the words in the same low, sexy rumble he'd used when they'd kissed and made love, and she sucked in a breath as memories of all that shimmered between them. "Then that's your problem, not mine. Though you clearly didn't want to anyway, since you never called me in Rome."

Oh, hell. Did those words really fall out of her mouth? Implying she'd wanted him to, and wondered if he would, and hadn't liked that he hadn't? Lord, that was the last thing she'd wanted to admit.

"Aubrey. It wasn't—"

"Skip it." She held up her hand, desperate to stop him from giving her some lame excuse he didn't really mean. "We'll just have to figure out how to work together. I have no doubt we can act like mere acquaintances and pretend that night never happened."

"That would be extremely difficult. For me, at least."

"Uh-huh. And since we're going to have a professional relationship, please stop with that tone of voice and…and those kinds of comments."

"I thought you no longer find me attractive, so why is that a problem?"

The way her heart fluttered and her breath caught at his physical beauty and sexiness and utter male appeal, she knew it would be tough going to learn to be immune to it.

"It's not. Now, I'd appreciate it if you'd give me a tour of the facility, so I'll know where everything is when a patient arrives, Dr. Affini." She moved past him to the clinic door and paused there. "Shall we?"

CHAPTER TWO

ENZO STUDIED THE woman standing there by the door, looking expectantly at him. Coolly, her pretty chin tipped up as her eyes challenged him. Those eyes had seduced him the second he'd met her two months ago, at the same time he'd wondered what her story was, and her friend Shay's, too, who'd shown up in his brother's life pregnant.

He still had no idea if the two women had an agenda that included snagging two doctors who also happened to be princes, and whose problems with their inheritance had been well-documented in the press. He'd planned to just talk with Aubrey the night they'd spent together, but talking and laughing had led to kissing, then touching, which had led to other, more than pleasurable and memorable things he hadn't been able to stop thinking about ever since.

But getting involved with a woman—a woman he wasn't sure he could trust—at the same time he was trying to save his heritage had seemed like a bad idea.

And now here she was, in his clinic, in all her beautiful glory. *Stunned* would be the only word that could describe how he'd felt when he'd seen her standing there, looking sexier than anyone should be able to look in a nurse's uniform. How coincidental was it that she'd just happened to be signed up for employment there?

Too coincidental, as far as he was concerned.

"You working somewhere else makes more sense. I'll make a few phone calls to the hospital and the other clinic. I can't promise to find you a position there but can also look at Verona or Padua for temporary nursing opportunities."

"This is ridiculous." She folded her arms across her chest and stared him down with such laser intensity, a lesser man might have caved right then and there. "You need a nurse here, obviously, or I wouldn't have been hired. I want the job, I'm qualified for the job, and I'm here now ready to work. Did I do well helping with Benedetto?"

"Yes. But that's irrelevant to the problem."

"Are you saying that you're so chauvinistic and weak around women that you wouldn't be able to behave professionally around me?"

"What? Of course not." He couldn't decide whether to laugh, or be irritated, or both. And admit that their night together had happened because he'd been unable to resist being with her then, so yeah, maybe he was weak. "You're pretty sassy for a woman who wants her boss to keep her around."

"And you're pretty insulting, implying I hunted you down in coming to work here." She stepped closer and poked her finger into his chest, her eyes flashing blue-gray fire. "I can show you the letter from the UWWHA confirming my employment here, which is dated long before we met. And I'm not going to let a mistake from two months ago keep me from having this job now. So you're stuck with me, and I'm stuck with you."

He grasped her hand in his, planning to move her finger from his sternum, but found himself curling it against his chest instead. "A mistake, was it? You didn't seem to think so that night."

"That night, I didn't know what I know now." She yanked her hand from his. "And neither did you. So we act like adults and work together like adults. Professional relationship, pure and simple. Now, let's get on with you showing me around here, before more patients show up."

He felt his lips curve, despite knowing that if he agreed to keep her here, it might well be a disaster waiting to happen. He'd been attracted to her smarts and beauty and sense of humor before. Add to that her spunk and tough attitude?

Irresistible.

Dio. He sighed and stepped around her to open the door. "I have a bad feeling the next few months are going to challenge me at a time I have too many challenges already," he said. "Lead on, Aubrey Henderson. I'll show you the ropes if you promise not to hang me with them."

"I never make promises I'm not sure I can keep," she said in the sweetest of tones, smiling up at him, her eyes filled with victory, flashes of exasperation, and a touch of the teasing look he'd fallen for before. "But I'll do my best, Dr. Affini. That I can promise."

Several days working at the clinic hadn't dimmed Aubrey's enthusiasm for the job, it had made her even more excited about it. Seeing the clinic sign up ahead had her stepping up her pace the same way it had the first day she was there. She was so glad she'd embarked on this adventure, in spite of Enzo Affini's insulting attitude and the uncomfortable tension between them.

Why in the world had she decided to sleep with him that first night she'd met him? What a mistake that had turned out to be! It was so obvious now that she never should have gotten involved with him, especially since she'd known all along that the main reason he'd offered to show her around Venice was because he'd wanted to pick her brain about Shay.

Except she just hadn't been able to resist, fool that she was.

Now, though, she was going to concentrate on work and only work. Thank goodness Enzo hadn't made her go somewhere else, since taking care of mostly tourists was so interesting. In some ways completely different than what she'd done back at home, and in other ways it was exactly the same. And the locals she'd seen so far in the clinic had been a fascinating mix of characters, from charming and sweet to gruff to downright cranky. Though she supposed that would describe all the people in the world—when it came down to it, everyone was much more alike than they were different, weren't they?

She changed into her crisp white dress and glanced in the locker-room mirror. Caught herself thinking about how surprisingly well it fit and how flattering it was and how Enzo just might think so, too, and why did even her simple uniform make her think about the man? Pathetic. What was wrong with her that she still caught herself feeling doe-eyed over a guy who'd wondered if she was trying to trap him or something?

Cool, professional relationship only. No fighting or kissing allowed. They'd done pretty well with that the past couple days. Surely after a few more it would feel as if their time together before had never happened?

Yeah, right. Whenever they were alone in a room, the low sizzle humming between them was very hard to ignore.

Nora poked her head into the locker room. "I have a British couple here to see the doctor. A Mr. and Mrs. Conway. You want to get started with them first?"

"Of course." She ushered the middle-aged couple to one of the exam rooms. "Hello, I'm Aubrey Henderson, the nurse on staff today. Can you tell me what you're here for?"

"I've been pecked by a bird," the woman exclaimed. "By an awful dirty bird, and it hurts!"

"All right. Let's have a look." Aubrey was about to shut the door for privacy when Enzo appeared, filling the doorway with his big, irritating, masculine presence.

"Mind if I stay?" he asked. His face was impassive, but she could see a glint of amusement in the depths of his dark eyes at the woman's dramatic statement. "I need to evaluate how our American nurse is doing."

"Of course," Aubrey said before the patient could answer. And was that what he really wanted, or was he there to just rattle her again, knowing this was probably not a serious situation? "This is Dr. Affini."

"I'd like to see what the doctor thinks about this!" the woman exclaimed. "I've probably got some disgusting disease."

"Mrs. Conway, why don't you sit on the table here and show me where it hurts? Sir, you can sit in one of these chairs."

"Right on the top of my head, that's where it hurts!

Bleeding, too." She held up a tissue with some specks of blood on it, waving it first at Aubrey, then Enzo. "What if I've been exposed to some terrible bird infection?"

Aubrey donned gloves and gently pushed the woman's hair aside to find a small, reddened indentation. "I can see this probably hurts. But I don't think it's too serious. Let me get some antiseptic to clean it with."

"Not too serious? You'll change your mind when I tell you the story." The woman sat straighter and waved her hands. "I'm minding my own business on a park bench in that big main square where the basilica is. Pigeons were walking around, and I pulled a little treat from my purse to give to one. Then this great, giant black bird dive-bombs me from the sky and grabs the treat from the pigeon!"

Aubrey pulled the cotton and antiseptic from the cupboard, and, when she turned, saw Enzo's eyes dancing and his lips obviously working to not smile at the dramatic recitation. Feeling her own mouth dangerously quiver, she quickly turned back to her patient to keep from looking at him. "And then? How did your head get pecked?"

"So I pull another treat from my purse, and the nasty black bird takes it, drops it, then scares me to death when he suddenly flies up, flapping his great wings in my face as he does. Lands there, right on my head! I shrieked, of course, and jumped up, and it pecked me. Hard! Why, I'm lucky it wasn't my eye he put out."

Aubrey glanced at Enzo. Fatal mistake, as his expression clearly showed he wanted to laugh, and a chuckle bubbled in her own chest when she saw how he was struggling.

Turn away. Do. Not. Look. At. Him.

She quickly turned to the woman's husband, who appeared more weary than worried. "Did you see what kind of bird it was?"

"Some black bird. Don't know what kind, I'm not a birdman. Especially Italian birds. Medium sized. Yellow beak, I think." He turned to his wife. "You brought it on yourself, you know. Who gives a pigeon mints to eat? The bird that pecked you was probably so shocked and ticked off, it felt it had a right to attack."

"Well, I never!" The woman looked beyond insulted as she flung her hand toward her husband. "And this is the kind of support I get after giving him thirty years of my life!"

Oh, Lord. Aubrey held her breath. Dang it, she would have been fine if not for Enzo's unholy grin. She would.

"I...I think I've cleaned it well, Mrs. Conway," she said.

"What do you think, Doctor? Don't you think I may get some nasty infection or disease? A filthy bird in a filthy square full of filthy people is bound to have given me something awful. Don't I need an antibiotic or something?"

Aubrey was impressed at how carefully he looked at the tiny wound, since he knew as well as she did that it was nothing. "Nurse Henderson has done a good job of cleaning it, Mrs. Conway. I'm sure you'll be fine, but if you have any problems with it, be sure to stop back and we'll take another look."

"We're leaving tomorrow anyway. Thank heavens for that. And what a waste of time to come here for help." Looking miffed and completely unsatisfied, she slid off the table, and Aubrey led her back out to the lobby, making sure to not look at Enzo as they passed. The woman's parting words before she walked out the door had Aubrey holding her breath hard again when she went back to the room to be sure it was clean for the next patient.

Enzo appeared again in the doorway. "Ah, she's the kind of patient that makes this job worthwhile. A pick-me-up from the more serious stuff we deal with, don't you think?"

Aubrey couldn't hold it in another second, and she pressed her hands against her mouth to subdue the laugh that spilled out. "That's for sure. You know what she said when she left?"

He folded his arms across his chest. "What?"

"She said, 'What does that doctor know about birds? He's obviously a quack.'"

His sexy laughter joined hers, and she quickly pulled him into the room and shut the door behind them. "Shh! They might have come back for something! What if they hear us?"

"Hear us what?"

She looked up into his eyes, still filled with mirth, but something else, too. That dangerous glint that made her heart flutter and her skin tingle.

She drew in a deep breath. "What is it with you? One minute you're unpleasant, and the next you're throwing out sexual innuendos. Didn't we agree we had to be professional with one another? I think I'm holding up my end here."

"I also said I didn't think we should work together because I knew I'd have problems with that."

Oh, my gosh. Why did he keep saying things he

shouldn't in that deep, rumbly voice that sent a warm flush across her skin, reminding her of their first day and night together?

"Enzo." After his name, words seemed to dry up on her tongue and she just stared at him.

"Yes?" He took a step closer. He smelled wonderful, and his body heat seemed to envelop her. He obviously knew what unwelcome thoughts had suddenly crowded her brain, because his gaze settled on her lips.

Which parted involuntarily, and her own small movement toward him that brought her nearly against his chest was completely involuntary, too, and when his arms wrapped around her and his head lowered toward hers all protest and common sense left her mind as her eyes drifted closed in breathless anticipation.

"Dr. Affini? Aubrey?"

Her eyes snapped open to see his, dark and dangerous and full of heat, staring right back at her. Time seemed to halt for several heartbeats until they both managed to gather their wits at the same time. She stepped back as he let her go, his chest lifting in a deep breath.

"Saved by Nora." He stared at her for one more second before turning to open the door.

She watched him disappear into the hallway, and the air she'd been holding in her lungs whooshed out. She was in so much trouble here. No matter how many times she remembered his suspicions, no matter how often she reminded herself they had to keep a professional distance, she just kept forgetting.

And it clearly wasn't her imagination that he kept forgetting, too.

CHAPTER THREE

ENZO WAS MORE than glad the Restore Venice Association meeting was about to start. That people were finally wandering off to find seats instead of asking him endless questions about the house that was no longer his, talking about how it was going to be ruined if he didn't get it back, and grilling him on what he was going to do to save it.

He sat toward the back of the room, resisting the urge to slouch in his seat to become semi-invisible. And yes, that probably made him a coward. But since he had no real answers yet, having endless conversations about the house that represented the past seven hundred years of his mother's family history, and his own, and how he had to keep it from going under the wrecking ball, made his gut churn.

He pulled the program from the pocket of his jacket and just as he was about to look at the meeting schedule, a flash of something bright blue or green in the aisle near him caught his eye. He looked up to see that the flash of color was a dress on what looked to be a very attractive body, at least from the back. The fabric skimmed the curves of a sexy feminine derriere that swayed slightly as she walked.

Who was she? He knew most of the people who attended these meetings and definitely would have remembered that body. The woman turned her head to smile at the person standing to let her sit next to him, and Enzo's lungs froze in his chest.

Aubrey.

What the hell was she doing here?

Her silky golden-brown hair skimmed her cheek as she sat, and a slender hand shoved it behind one ear as she dug into her purse for something, coming up with the same program he held in his hand.

He and Aubrey had managed to work together without fighting, or, worse, kissing, if he didn't count that one near miss yesterday. But now the suspicions about her that had stayed on a low simmer—along with the sexual attraction between them—came bubbling into full boil. First she showed up at his clinic to work, and now she'd decided to come to an art and architecture meeting attended only by Venetians and academics from universities in other countries?

Tourists never came. Neither did many Italians from other areas, because they had their own preservation concerns. And yet here she was, and how was he to believe it was about anything other than her ingratiating herself into his life even more? Doubtless knowing all about his family's problems and the house he loved that she happened to be currently living in.

Did she know he'd owned it before and had rented it out to the UWWHA as he'd planned its renovation? Know that his father had sold it out from under him, and it was about to be resold at a profit? Was renting it from the UWWHA part of her plan somehow?

Enzo's blood ran cold. If Aubrey was trying to

charmingly, spunkily wiggle her way into his life, did that mean Shay had done the same thing with his brother? Was there any way this could be another big coincidence?

Seemed incredibly unlikely, but suspicion without proof just festered, and Enzo had enough to worry about right then. So the only solution was to be brutally frank with Aubrey. To ask her some hard questions, and hopefully be able to figure out if she was being honest with him or not. Which might be very difficult, considering he'd had to consciously fight being attracted to her seeming sweetness and smarts and beauty every hour they'd worked together the past few days, but he had to give it a try.

Barely paying attention to the speakers and conversation, Enzo sat through the first half of the meeting trying to decide if he should tackle Aubrey during the break, or wait until it was over. Feeling on edge, he was still pondering that question during the break when the decision was made for him.

A flash of color had him turning from the coffee stand in the front hallway to see her marching right up to him, a militant expression on her beautiful face.

"Just so you know, I had no idea you'd be here today."

"No?" The woman must be a mind reader. "Then why are you here?"

"Because I'm interested in Venice's future. In the restoration of its buildings and artwork."

"So you know nothing about my current situation." He said it mockingly, and she frowned at his tone.

"What situation? Unless you're referring to having

to work with me, which you've made more than clear is something you'd rather not do."

"I've seen you're a woman who says what she thinks. So I'm just going to come right out and tell you what I'm thinking. Which is that it's really bizarre that Shay shows up announcing she's pregnant with Dante's baby, and within days she's married to my brother. Then you and I get together, and two months later you magically show up at my clinic to work." He set his coffee down and folded his arms across his chest. "And now you claim to have an interest in the restoration of Venice's buildings, which…shockingly…is my passion, too."

She stared at him, an even deeper frown creasing her brow. "I'm not following."

"Then let me be clearer." He stepped closer, hoping to intimidate her and make her come clean. "What I'm saying is that I can't help but wonder if you and Shay researched Dante and me, and decided two doctor princes would be a nice catch, then figured out how to weasel your way into our lives."

"What?" Her mouth fell open in a gasp. "You have an ego the size of Mount Vesuvius, you know that? I'm not even going to dignify that accusation with an answer. You can believe what you want to believe. But if you think insulting me is going to get me to leave the clinic, you've got another think coming. I'm staying until my contract is over, so just deal with it. And you're going to feel pretty ridiculous when you realize your fantasies of me wanting to trap you into something were all in your own small mind."

She spun away and stalked off, and he stood there long seconds just watching that sexy behind of hers until she went through the doorway to the meeting room again.

He let out a long breath. Maybe his strategy had backfired this time. But if she and Shay weren't what they seemed, he had to believe that, sooner or later, one of them would tip their hand and the truth would come out.

The president of the association spoke in English as he opened the second half of the meeting. The back of Enzo's brain absently noted that there must be university guests from other countries for this portion of the presentation and discussion. Then his focus snapped big-time to the speaker when the next words out of the man's mouth were a name.

Aubrey Henderson.

What the…? He sat up straighter to watch her stand and make her way to the lectern, noticing that plenty of the men in the room seemed to be admiring her swaying walk as much as he had been earlier. Until he'd been shocked to see whose enticing body was wearing that dress.

"Two years ago, Ms. Henderson graciously adopted the renovation of the large fresco depicting angels and warriors in one of the churches at San Sebastiano. The twenty-five thousand dollars she donated have brought this art treasure back to life, and we encourage all of you to visit and admire it. In recognition of this gift, we present this plaque to show our appreciation."

Applause greeted Aubrey as she accepted the plaque, then stood with the president as photos were snapped. If he'd been surprised before, this time Enzo could barely wrap his brain around what he was witnessing.

Aubrey had donated money to a restoration project in Venice? Two years ago? And not just a little money, but a very nice chunk—enough to completely pay for that project, which was one of so many beautiful old masterpieces in Venice that needed repairs.

Her smile seemed to light the whole room as she leaned toward the microphone, holding the plaque to her breasts. "Thank you. I appreciate this recognition, but it was our privilege to be able to adopt the fresco project. My late mother, Lydia Henderson, lived her life working to save old buildings from being demolished instead of renovated. She led numerous architectural review boards in Massachusetts and elsewhere in New England. During her illness, we decided to donate to this project because she was fascinated with the history of Venice and had always been drawn to images of angels and warriors. She often said that all of us had a chance to be both in our lives. I'm proud to say that she truly was an angel and a warrior, and I hope to live my life at least a little bit like she did."

Even from the back of the room, Enzo could see her blinking back tears as she said one more thank you, then headed back to her seat. It seemed she'd taken only a few steps before her gaze lifted to his. Her eyes narrowed and her graceful gait seemed to falter for a moment before she turned her attention to finding her seat again.

Dio. What was he supposed to think now?

He stared at the back of her silky head and had no idea of the answer to that question. But one thing he did know?

He owed her an apology.

Obviously, she had good reason to be at the meeting that had nothing to do with him, and, yeah, she'd been right. He did feel ridiculous that he'd assumed otherwise.

He huffed out a breath, not wanting to have to give her that *mea culpa*, but knew he had no choice. The meeting seemed to drag on forever, his eyes on the back of her head instead of the speaker for most of it. Finally, the crowd stood and he jostled his way through the throng until he was able to catch her just as she was walking out the door.

"Aubrey. Wait. I need to talk to you."

She stared straight ahead across the *piazza*, walking faster. "You've already said plenty, Dr. Affini."

"I want to apologize."

"For what?" She finally turned to look at him, and if the daggers she was sending from her furious gaze had been real, he'd be lying dead on the pavement. "Accusing me of showing up at your clinic to trap you? Of stalking you at the architecture meeting? Of faking an interest in restoration? You overestimate yourself."

"I know. And I'm sorry. I am. Truly."

"Hmmph." The sound she made wasn't exactly an acceptance of his apology, but at least she slowed down a little, instead of surging through the crowd as if she were in a sprint race.

He reached for her arm to slow her even more and was glad but a little surprised that she didn't yank it loose. "Aubrey. Things are…difficult right now. Which maybe is making me think and act in a way I shouldn't."

"Now, isn't that an understatement."

"So can we put this behind us?" He tugged on her arm to force her to look at him. He wanted to see her soften and forgive him, and why that felt so important, he had no idea, since he still wasn't sure what to think about her.

"I'll do my best." She finally turned to him, and the blaze in her eyes had thankfully cooled. "But only because I love being here and enjoy working at the clinic. And I'm not going to let you ruin either one of those things for me."

This time, she did pull her arm loose, and without another word she took off at a fast pace again. He slowed and decided to let her go. Time to think up a new strategy on how to handle beautiful and mysterious Aubrey Henderson.

"Stop being negative. We still have time," Enzo said to his accountant and fellow preservationist, Leonardo. Not sure if he was trying to convince Leonardo or himself, he paced the upper floor of the one home he had left in his possession in Venice, staring unseeingly at the finely woven antique carpet covering the *terrazzo* floor. "I'm working on raising more money for the purchase and have also liquidated some assets, which you'll see transferred to the account in a few days. Almost all our vineyards had a good harvest, with more grapes sold this year to other wineries than last, and our own vintages are selling well. Dante gave me the numbers a few days ago. It's coming together."

At least, he hoped it was. His gut tightened at how much money he still needed to buy back the childhood home he loved, but he was determined to make it happen.

"But the new owner told me he expected the sale

to the hotel chain to go through within the next three weeks," Leonardo said.

"Which gives us two and a half to beat them to it."

"I was looking through all the photos of the house you gave me. Whether the sale goes through or not, I'll need more of the exterior, the internal courtyard, and the bedrooms to provide to the commission proactively, so they'll agree to a six-month delay of the interior demolition the hotel is planning. Buy us some time to convince the commission to refuse to allow it. If the sale ends up going through to the hotel, maybe they'd end up selling it back to you if they can't remodel it the way they want to. So can you get those for me?"

"Yes." Or at least, he hoped he could. He might not be the one who owned and rented the property to the UWWHA anymore, but he did know a certain beautiful, questionable tenant living there. If she wasn't so angry she refused to talk to him anymore, let alone allow him in the house. "I'll get them to you as soon as possible. *Arrivederci.*"

Familiar burning anger swelled in Enzo's chest as he hung up, but he fought it down. Holding close the bitterness and fury he felt was a distraction he couldn't afford. Despising his father and his selfish actions didn't change a damn thing.

No, Enzo just had to work harder and outbid the hotel chain. That was all there was to it.

Thinking of the house had his thoughts turning to Aubrey again. He could picture her sleeping in one of the run-down but still beautiful bedrooms, her shining hair spread across the pillow. Curled up reading a book in a chair in front of one of the massive stone fireplaces. Wandering the halls admiring the amazing rooms and artwork and antiquities.

He dropped into a chair to stare out over the Grand Canal. *Confused* was probably the best word to describe how he felt about her. Along with suspicious and extremely attracted.

Were she and Dante's lover—no, wife, now—two women with an agenda? So many things pointed to *yes, maybe*. Then again, there was something so appealing, so seemingly genuine about Aubrey, something that drew him to her in a way that he couldn't quite remember happening with another woman. He'd seen it when she'd cared for Benedetto, then fixed up Enzo's pants for the child, which made him chuckle all over again. And a number of other times as they'd taken care of patients together.

Yet there were all those coincidences that made it hard to believe she was for real.

So where did that leave him?

The same place he'd always been. Still planning to save his inheritance here and in Arezzo a different way. Through hard work. Still planning to never marry, regardless of what that meant to the future of the properties that should be his.

Except Aubrey didn't know that.

Feeling oddly unsettled, he decided to give Dante a call. Between his brother's new wife and his always busy job as a trauma surgeon, Enzo hadn't seen the man in weeks. He hoped that meant everything was reasonably fine, but he wanted to hear that for himself. With any luck he'd be available to talk, and not in the middle of surgery, and Enzo was glad Dante picked up after only two rings.

"To what do I owe the honor of hearing from my brother, since you haven't called me for weeks?" Dante said in his ear.

"The phone works both ways, you know. I figured you were busy with Shay and didn't want to bother you."

"You've been bothering me your whole life, so why change things now?"

"Point taken." The smile in his brother's voice made Enzo smile, too. "How's work?"

"Busy. So busy that we haven't been able to get back to Arezzo for a while, but we plan to soon. How about you?"

Hearing his brother say "we" when it came to his life and travels sounded so strange, but, with a baby on the way, he'd be saying that for the rest of his life, wouldn't he? Something everyone would have to get used to. "Busy, too. Always is during the heavy tourist season, as you know. How's Shay? Feeling all right?"

"She's well. Getting more round, but feeling good."

Why the conversation felt so awkward to him, Enzo wasn't sure, but he sensed that his brother wasn't feeling awkward at all. He sounded happy, maybe? Excited? Enzo hoped so, and also hoped his brother's heart wasn't going to get mashed up over all of it. "Glad to hear it. Well, I just wanted—"

"What's the situation with the house?" his brother interrupted. "Last time we talked you were having trouble raising enough funds."

"Still working on it." No point in adding to his brother's concerns, since they'd already collaborated to borrow as much as possible against their wineries.

"I heard that Aubrey Henderson is back in Venice with the UWWHA and living at your house now."

"It's not my house anymore, remember?"

"It will always be your house." Dante's voice was fierce. "I'm still exploring a few other possibilities for raising money, and I know you're going to find some way to buy it back. No one is as determined as you when you set a goal for yourself."

"Thanks. And I am determined." Somehow, his brother's vote of confidence eased the tightness in his chest a little, even if they were just words and not money in the bank.

"So how's it going with Aubrey working at the clinic, or shouldn't I ask?"

"How did you hear about that?"

"You know how women like to talk," his brother said drily. "I heard it from Shay. But she didn't have to tell me you went out with Aubrey. I had a gut feeling you'd end up in bed with her when you told me you were going to introduce yourself to ask questions about Shay. Despite my telling you I knew the child was mine."

His brother's voice was chiding, but he didn't sound annoyed with him anymore. But who wouldn't have wanted to find out more about the woman his brother wanted to marry? "Maybe your gut feeling was just indigestion."

"Or not. Aubrey's a beautiful, smart woman and I knew you wouldn't be able to resist. And neither would she. If there's one thing the Affini men are good at, it's charming women, right?"

"I hope we have more going for us than that, since

it's one of the many things about our father that we both despise."

"Yeah." Dante's joking tone disappeared. "Listen, I just got a surgery consult. Thanks for calling, and I'll talk to you soon."

Enzo stood to shove his phone in his pocket, sling his camera around his neck, and grab the keys to his boat. He jogged down the curved stone staircase of one of the several homes that had been in the Affini royal family for centuries.

It struck him that the way to find answers to his questions about Aubrey seemed obvious. What was that old saying? Keep your friends close and your enemies closer? He had no idea if Aubrey was friend or foe, but keeping his distance from her wasn't the answer, since he couldn't feel good about making her leave the clinic and find a job somewhere else, especially now that her wanting to be in Venice might be partly because of her late mother. He understood that kind of loss, and if staying here helped Aubrey heal a little, she should have that chance.

And hopefully, spending time with her both at work and socially would eventually tell him the truth.

If he could keep his damned libido out of the picture, that was. Keeping the enemy close was one thing. Sleeping with the enemy? That was something he was sure never ended well.

It was handy that he was the one who drew up the clinic work calendar. That allowed him to be sure to have her time off scheduled for when he wanted it to be, and the thought made him smile for reasons he shouldn't be smiling. Before he started the motor to his boat, he pulled out his phone again. The sound of her answering with a cheerful hello on the other end of the line made him smile even more, and he shook his head at himself. Hadn't he just reminded himself moments ago that he had to keep an emotional distance from her?

If just the sound of her voice made him smile, that wasn't going to be easy. Though he had a feeling that smile would go away quickly when she learned it was him calling.

"Aubrey, it's Enzo. I was wondering if by chance you were at the house you're renting. I need to get inside to take a few photos."

CHAPTER FOUR

"TAKE A FEW PHOTOS?" Aubrey's voice in his ear sounded beyond surprised. "What do you mean?"

"I'll explain when I see you. If you're available?"

"Why should I be? Oh, wait, it's because I'm trying to snag a prince doctor for another notch on my bedpost."

"That's not exactly what I said."

"That's right. It actually was that I'm trying to *weasel* my way into your life. Because I'm cunning and deceitful and…and squirmy."

"But you're a beautiful squirmy weasel." He couldn't help it, something about her outrage made him want to tease her even more, though he could hardly blame her for being angry about all he'd said. "If I apologize again, will you let me take the photos?"

"I'll consider it, if it's a good apology and you tell me why you need the photos."

"I apologize for being suspicious of you and your motives." He wouldn't share that he still was. "And I'll tell you when I get there."

"Well, I'm not there right now. I just finished lunch and am outside the restaurant."

"Where?"

"I don't know, exactly. I'm a little lost, to be honest."

He could picture her face scrunched up in thought the way it did at the clinic sometimes. "What's the name of the restaurant?"

"It's called…um…Trattoria da Agnolo. It's off some *piazza*, a little way from a small canal."

He had to chuckle at her description. "Everything is just a little way from a small canal in Venice, or off some *piazza*, but I know where you are. Walk back to the canal. I'll pick you up and drive you back to the house."

"Drive? What do you mean?"

"Drive in Venice means by boat. I thought you said you'd done your homework?"

"If you want me to let you in the house, you'd better be extra, super nice, Dr. Affini, to make up for being so nasty to me."

"I'm not going to be nasty anymore. But I don't have to be super nice, either, because your employment at the clinic is in my hands, remember?"

"And you might remember that the UWWHA has very strict rules about the conduct of the health centers that employ their nurses. They don't like doctors who insult us and try to lord it over us."

Her words pulled a chuckle from his chest that he couldn't hold back. The woman was such an attractive mix of smart and spunky, and he wondered if she knew it. If all that was designed to sucker unsuspecting men into falling for her before she snagged them in her net, or if she really was as wonderful as she seemed. "I'll be there in five minutes to pick you up."

"No, that's all right. I can find my way back to the

house. I'm pretty sure it's not too far. I'll just meet you there."

"I'm happy to—"

"No," she interrupted, and her voice sounded nearly panicky. Surely she didn't think he'd fire her if they spent time together that wasn't strictly professional? Then again, he'd said some pretty unpleasant things, so he couldn't exactly blame her for wanting to keep her distance.

He maneuvered his boat through the canal, and as he approached the house he looked for her. Even with a number of people walking on both sides of the canal in front of his house—correction, *formerly* his house—he spotted Aubrey instantly. The golden highlights in her shiny brown hair caught the early-afternoon sunshine, and her gorgeous body wore a sundress that stopped a few inches above her knees, showing off her shapely legs. The sound of his motor must have caught her attention, because she turned, then instantly sent him a half scowl. The boat skimmed to a stop in front of her, and he stood to grab a wooden post to steady the boat and tie it.

"Ciao. Thanks for letting me come by," he said as he climbed onto the walkway to stand next to her.

"I'm still mad at you. But I confess I'm curious why you want to take photos here. Do you have some connection to this house?"

He looked down at her, wondering how much he should share. How much she might already know. Since the sad and infuriating truth was public knowledge at this point, he didn't see a reason to try to keep it a secret.

"I do. I'll tell you about it as I take the photos."

Aubrey concentrated on carefully putting the old, intricately forged key into the lock and turning it this way and that, her tongue cutely poking out of the side of her mouth as she did. It had been tricky to manage for as long as Enzo could remember, and he couldn't help but tease her about it.

"For a woman so good at creating a small pair of pants from a large one, you seem to be having some mechanical difficulties."

"It's hard to open. I swear I've stood out here five minutes every time—why doesn't whoever rents this house to the UWWHA put on a new knob and lock?"

"It's important to keep the original hardware and historic charm when possible. I thought you said you were a preservationist."

"I am. And you're right." She huffed out a frustrated breath. "I need to have the kind of relaxed attitude the ancient Venetians had, instead of my twentieth-century hurry-up impatience, don't I?"

"Yes." He reached around her, his arm skimming against her warm skin, to take the key from her hand. He inserted it again, and, with a quick turn to the left, the lock clicked and the door swung open.

She stared up at him. "How did you do that?"

"Magic fingers." He wiggled them at her, and she frowned.

"Huh. I don't want to think about the various times you use that line. And what you might be referring to."

"What do you think I might be referring to?" They stepped inside the large entryway, wide sunbeams striping the *terrazzo* floor from every west-facing window. He knew exactly what her words made him think of, and he found himself leaning close to her.

A little test to see if she'd take it as an opportunity to start flirting with him again. "Are you remembering our night together?"

"No." Pink tinged her skin. "I just figured a guy like you enjoys making sexual innuendoes to either make women feel uncomfortable, or to think bad thoughts."

"And which are you experiencing at the moment?"

With her hands on her hips, she took a quick step left and frowned up at him. "Listen. You can't be all nasty and accuse me of stalking you, then the next day come on to me. We agreed that if we're going to work together, we need to keep our distance. Treat one another professionally. So tell me why you want to take photos of this place, and how you're connected to it."

He didn't want to talk about the dire situation he faced, but he might be able to tell if she already knew. "Do you know that this place is close to being sold to a large hotel chain? Afterward to be gutted of everything historic except its exterior and turned into a modern hotel?"

"What? That's terrible!" The surprised dismay on her face seemed real. "How can that be allowed?"

"We live in a democracy, and, while we have architectural rules in place, the economics of Venice are a worrying reality. More and more tourists, fewer residents. Many of us are trying to reverse that to some degree, but it's a complicated and difficult task. A lot of houses are now empty, some even slated for demolition. The cost is great to restore them, and when you do you must have someone who can afford to live there."

"I saw in the meeting that there's an architectural review board that a hotel chain or whoever has to go through for permission to tear up a house like this one. It's so incredibly beautiful, I can't imagine it."

His heart warmed at her words, even as he wondered again if she already knew all the truth about it. "It's in great disrepair, as I'm sure you've seen. At times, even some of the tenants working with the UWWHA have complained about the bathrooms, the broken flooring, the peeling frescoes."

"Then they're just stupid," Aubrey said hotly. "If they can't see beyond superficial things like that to love and adore the amazing handwork of the tiling and *terrazzo* and artwork, the incredible design, the awe-inspiring history of a place like this, they should go work somewhere like the US, where a house just eighty years old is considered historic. Every time I walk in this house, I love it more."

"A woman after my own heart," he heard himself murmur. Then mentally stepped back. Distance, remember? *She may not be who she seems.*

The eyes looking up at him were wide and worried. "So, you said you have a connection to this house? Do you think you'll be able to stop the hotel from gutting it?"

"I'm doing everything I can to prevent them from buying it. Getting it into the hands of someone who will renovate and preserve it the way it deserves to be. Who will live in it and love it for the rest of their life."

"Do you have someone in mind? Someone who wants to buy it?"

"Yes. I do." He looked down at her seemingly earnest face. "That someone is me."

Aubrey blinked up at Enzo in shock. "You're trying to buy this house? But what about the house you live in now? Are you hoping to renovate it, then resell it?"

"No." She watched him move around the spectacular room, absently picking up a vase here and a decorative plate there, which Aubrey had been surprised to see lying around. Surely a few of the tenants might have had sticky fingers, unable to resist taking home an antique "souvenir."

"Then what?"

He turned to look at her, his expression deeply serious. Even pained. "This home has been in my late mother's family since the portal was built in the fourteenth century. The second and third floors were added in the fifteenth century, and the top floor, always my favorite as a child, was built in 1756."

Surprise left her staring for a long moment. "So you visited family here as a child?"

"I lived here as a child. Grew up in this house from nearly the day I was born. Of all the properties my family has owned, this one means the most to me. My father kept mistresses in a few of the homes belonging to his side of the family. Always claimed it was his right to do with his own properties as he pleased. And he continues to prove he believes that today, selling away what rightfully should belong to Dante and to me, having been held in trust for us. Except my father has control of that trust."

The bitterness in his tone was unmistakable. "This was one of the houses he sold out from under you and your brother." She didn't say it as a question, because the truth of that was obvious, and her chest filled with a mix of emotions. She wasn't sure what they all were, but she knew for certain the main one was anger. A different anger than she'd felt toward Enzo when he'd been so accusatory at the architectural meeting.

This anger was on behalf of a man who had lost the

home he obviously loved. Fury that the buyers didn't care at all about it, ready to pass it on to a hotel chain that couldn't care less about destroying its history, wanting only to transform it into a modern, money-making hotel. Disgust and pain swept through her. Sympathy for both men that their father was as self-ish, coldhearted, and uncaring about his sons as her own had proven to feel toward her.

"Yes." Intense dark eyes met hers again.

"But if it was your mother's, how did your father have control of it?"

"When they married, she signed over her property to him. I never asked her why, if it was just expected, or if he insisted. I didn't realize what could happen until she was gone, and it was too late. Now I'm doing all I can to get it back."

"I'm glad, then, that I decided to look past your meanness yesterday." She said it to lighten the weight in her chest, at the same time reminding him she hadn't forgotten about it. And that she expected him to be nicer from now on. "What do you need pictures of?"

"I need better ones of the outside, but will do that last, because any changes to the exterior are regulated much more than the interiors are. And, Aubrey?" His serious dark eyes met hers. "I am sorry about yester-day. I should have kept my mouth shut and not let my worries push me to say things I shouldn't. But I need to look after my brother, you know? We've both had our share of women pretending to be attracted to us just because of our titles and profession. Forgive me?"

She found it hard to believe any woman would have to pretend to be attracted to either of them, but she wasn't about to say so. "Yes. So long as it doesn't happen again."

"Thank you." A real smile touched his eyes. "Okay with you if I go to the bedrooms and baths? Then I want to take pictures of the top floor."

"This way." She started to walk, then stopped to shake her head at herself. "Wait. You know this house a lot better than I do. Lead on, Dr. Affini."

She followed him up the stairs and watched as he snapped photos of some of the incredible things that had amazed her from the second she'd first walked in the place. "I couldn't believe it when I saw the first fresco in the entry. Then about fell over at the sight of all the gilded stucco on the next level. And the art on the ceiling!" She knew she sounded like a little kid in a candy shop, but that was exactly how she felt. "Just like something out of one of the museums I went to in Rome. I never dreamed I'd ever get to live in a place like this. When I heard the UWWHA had a house to rent, I figured it would be some plain, utilitarian thing."

"I'm glad you're enjoying it." His smile was back in all its attractive glory, and the power of that alone made her feel stupidly weak in the knees. "Wanting to share it for a while was part of the reason I first offered it out to rent as I made plans for its renovation, until my father sold it. The house I'm living in now was already in the process of being restored, and being there as much as possible to supervise it all had seemed like the best plan."

"Well, getting to live here for a while is like a dream come true." She realized that was insensitive, since it had been yanked out from under him. "I'm sorry. Here I am going on about getting to live here, and you can't anymore. Which really makes me mad, just so you know."

"Thank you. Makes me really mad, too." His impish smile widened to show his straight white teeth. "And I have to tell you that your American accent and the way you say things is very cute."

"I don't have an accent. Except maybe when I'm trying to badly speak in Italian."

"Oh, you definitely do."

His warm expression made her lungs feel a little squishy and she frowned to hide it. She refused to think about his words and the low, sexy tone he'd spoken them in as they moved up the intricately carved stone staircase. A complete reversal from the hard words he'd flung at her yesterday.

"One of my favorite rooms here is the library," she said, both to distract herself and because it was true. "So huge! And the ceiling is stunning. The bookcases are in remarkably good shape, too. But the windows are quite leaky and let in an awful lot of light that is doubtless damaging the paintings in the ceiling, not to mention being hard on the books. What are your options for replacing those while still making them look original?"

He stopped dead as they reached the next level, staring at her. "I guess you really do have an interest in historic renovation."

"So you truly thought I went to yesterday's meeting just to stalk you?" She folded her arms across her chest. "Like I said, you're unbelievably egotistical. For your information, my mother's passion for restoration is a part of me. And while doctor princes aren't one of my interests, I have lots of other ones. To me, people who don't are boring as heck."

"Which you most definitely are not, Ms. Henderson." Their gazes seemed fused together for long seconds before he moved toward the bedroom she was currently using. Which made her suddenly, horrifyingly, remember that she'd left clothes strewn around, including some personal items she'd rather not have this hunk of a man see, and never mind that he'd seen a whole lot more of her than just her underwear.

She pushed past him and rushed into the room, grabbing clothes up off the floor and from her bed. And why did it have to be this day of all days that she hadn't taken time to make it?

"Um…let me get this stuff out of your photos."

"It looks like you have more clothes out of the drawers and armoire than I have inside mine. But I think you should leave them." The amused eyes meeting hers danced as he reached out with the curve of his finger to hook the pink underwear lying on the bedspread. "I'll be presenting these photos to the Preserve Venice Committee. I suspect they'll be even more interested if I show how people actually live here, don't you?"

"No, I don't." Heat rushed into her face as she snatched her underwear from his grasp. "I don't normally leave my stuff lying around, so I'm really sorry about that."

"Are you kidding? You're apologizing for leaving your underwear and nightwear out?" He picked up her flimsy black gown by the spaghetti straps and held it up to her. His smile faded a little, his eyes darkened, and his voice went even lower than before. "This bedroom was mine as a child. As a teen, I had many sexual fantasies in this room, and, believe me, seeing what you sleep in has made my day almost as much as it would have back then. Problem is, I'll probably be imagining you in it when we're working together tomorrow."

Oh, Lord. There it was, shimmering between them like a hot, bright light. The connection that had drawn her to him from the moment she'd met him. The chemistry that had sent her headlong into his arms and his bed before she'd thought too hard about it.

No doubt he could see exactly what she was thinking and feeling, despite desperately trying to shore up her past anger with him. Because he leaned closer to brush his mouth against her cheek. Slipped it across her mouth, his breath mingling with hers before he pulled away. The sizzling thoughts swirling in her brain were clear on his face, too. Just as she took a step back and started inwardly scolding herself for letting herself think about the annoying man that way, she could see him mentally and physically retreat, too.

"Got to get these pictures taken. Thanks for letting me in to get this done." He slipped the camera off his neck and seemed to concentrate awfully hard on adjusting the lens. "The hotel's supposed to close on the house in three weeks, so you'll be around for the news."

"Good luck. Let me know if there's anything I can do to help." Probably shouldn't be offering, considering everything, but wouldn't anyone feel bad about his situation?

His gaze moved from the camera back to her. If he was trying to put cool and collected between them instead of hot and alive, he failed miserably. Because it looked for all the world as if he was mentally undressing her, and she just couldn't help the quiver her body responded with.

"I think you know that's an offer I can barely resist, Aubrey Henderson." His chest lifted in a long breath, then, as he turned to walk to the next room, she heard him murmur, "Just barely."

CHAPTER FIVE

How was Aubrey supposed to actually get any sleep in the bedroom she'd unfortunately learned had been Enzo's as a child?

A bedroom he'd apparently slept in from childhood until recently. *Recently* being when he'd decided to rent it for a short time while he renovated his other house, a move his father had apparently taken as a green light to sell the home Enzo loved. Not that it sounded as if the man who was both Enzo's and Dante's father needed any real excuse to steal from his sons.

That awful reality still burned in her gut for both of them. She couldn't even imagine how that must have felt—how upsetting it would have been for Enzo in particular, selling off this house that held centuries of his mother's history, and his own.

Thinking she couldn't imagine how that felt wasn't exactly true, though, was it? She sure knew from painful personal experience how deceitful and self-centered some fathers could be.

Aubrey glanced at her watch, trying to process all the emotions swirling around inside her. Sympathy for Enzo and what he was going through. Annoyance with his weird suspicions and insults. Confusion about why he seemed to run hot and cold with her, which made her determination to keep things professional and stay angry with him none too easy.

Since she had twenty minutes before she needed to be at the clinic, the burning need to talk to Shay about it all conflicted with her worries that she shouldn't bother her friend at this strange time in Shay's life. And was "strange" an understatement, or what? Aubrey could only hope she was doing okay, and wanting to know that, too, prompted her to give in. To stop walking and sit on a warm wooden bench in the *piazza* near the clinic and pull out her cell phone. All kinds of tourists walked by, from young and old couples, to big tour groups, to families, as she soaked in the amazing beauty and sense of community that was Venice. Children laughed and played, pampered dogs on leashes nosed their way around, and pigeons pecked at invisible delicacies from the old stone at her feet as she dialed Shay's number.

"Hello?" Shay's voice came through, strong and vibrant. "Aubrey?"

"Hey, you! I was wondering how you're feeling. How it's going. You okay?"

"Life has certainly taken a new twist for me, but I'm doing all right. You probably remember the past couple months I was feeling really tired, but now I feel great."

"I hope you're taking good care of yourself. Making sure you get plenty of rest and keeping a little easier pace than usual."

"That's what Dante said."

Was Aubrey imagining a smile in her friend's voice? She hoped and prayed that, however things turned out

long-term, it would prove to be good for everyone involved, including the little baby Shay carried.

"I'm glad he's taking care of you, and I hope you
listen to that resting thing." Now that she felt good
about her friend's health and state of mind, she licked
her lips to move on to the other subject on her mind.
"What's Enzo been like to you? Has he been a jerk?"

"A jerk?" Shay sounded surprised. "No. I've only
seen him a couple times, and he was a little cool but
not a jerk. Why, has he been nasty to you?"

The way he spoke to her at the meeting had definitely qualified as *nasty*, but his apology for that had
seemed sincere. Hopefully. She had to work with the
man, after all, and he'd been pleasant yesterday—and
the brief brush of his lips on hers had been more than
pleasant.

She shook her head in annoyance that she'd let herself enjoy it. "Never mind. We're managing to work together. And by the way, I wanted to ask, did you know
that Enzo used to own the house we rented from the
UWWHA? That he and Dante grew up there?"

"I did know. Enzo took me there to get my clothes
when I moved in with Dante, and told me then. Though
he acted kind of stiff and odd about it. I'm not sure
how much of that was because of me and the baby and
Dante, and how much was about their dad selling off
the property."

"I can't believe their father is so selfish and awful."
Though she shouldn't have any trouble believing it,
considering she'd experienced the same thing for a
short time, too.

"I can't, either. And it's such a beautiful house,
standing so tall with those small canals on both sides

of it. Almost like an island itself, isn't it? I can't imagine how Enzo feels about losing it. And this house that's Dante's? It's amazing, too. Incredible, really."

"Who would have thought you'd meet a prince and marry him?"

"Not me, that's for sure," Shay said. "I don't need anyone to take care of me. At least, I didn't think so until I got involved with someone famous. Who I didn't even know was a prince or famous, and that has sure complicated things. But it's just temporary, you know. We're only staying married for a year. Until the crazy stalker camera people out there forget about me, and when the excitement of an Affini heir is old news. So the baby and I can stay safe."

"It's been that bad?"

"Unbelievable. They practically knocked me over a few times getting pictures." Shay sounded angry, and who could blame her? "I have to admit it was scary, which is the only reason I went along with his marriage suggestion."

Aubrey still found all of it hard to believe, especially their sudden marriage. But since she'd never been in such an odd and difficult situation, she definitely couldn't and wouldn't judge her friend. She moved on to more basic conversation, asking Shay how her work at the hospital had been, and sharing a few of her experiences at the clinic. Yakking with her the way they had in the past had her smiling so much, she nearly forgot to check the time. "Oh, my gosh, it's late! I've got to get to work now. Don't be a stranger! Call me with any news, promise?"

"I promise. You keep me posted, too, okay?"

"I will. Talk to you soon." Aubrey hung up and

stood, feeling so much better now that she'd talked to Shay. Thankfully, she'd sounded pretty good, so Dante must be treating her well. Not that she was surprised, since, despite Enzo's weirdness with her, she'd seen that, for the most part, he was basically a good guy.

Which was such a bland, understated way to describe the dynamic, sometimes-charming, caring doctor Prince, it didn't even come close.

"Aubrey." Enzo moved into the doorway of the clinic room she was tidying, and she looked up. Her eyes locked on his broad chest, then moved up to that absurdly handsome face, and she quickly busied herself with finishing her cleaning before he could catch her absurdly and inappropriately eyeing him.

"Yes?"

"I'm going on a house call. Hotel call, actually, not too far from here. I may need you. If we get a patient here that needs immediate attention, one of us can come back."

"Okay." Being around a patient and having work to do would be the distraction she needed to get her head on straight. Or at least she sure hoped it would.

"We're going to see an elderly tourist, female, who's been walking a lot the past couple of days, apparently more than she's supposed to. My friend who manages the hotel told me she isn't feeling very well, but doesn't seem in enough distress to warrant a hospital visit. She has a history of congestive heart failure, but of course we'd need to confirm that's what the problem is. The granddaughter doesn't want her walking here, though, so we're going to go to her."

"What do I need to bring? Nitropaste? Lasix?"

"And a little morphine, in case it is congestive heart failure. Blood-pressure unit and cuff, phlebotomy items and an IV line."

She nodded. "I'll have it all ready shortly."

"Thanks. I'll be in my office."

Proud that she'd resisted the urge to watch him leave, Aubrey gathered up the items, put them in a plastic Ziploc bag she found in the cupboard, then found herself glancing in the mirror. Her ponytail was looking a little loose and she pulled the band out, brushing it to tidy it again. She tried to convince herself it was so she'd look professional for the patient, but she shook her head at the stupid reality that it was partly so she'd look good, period.

Even walking briskly along the wide promenade to the hotel, Enzo proved to be a good tour guide, pointing out historic buildings, homes, and hotels and giving a brief history of each. The hotel manager greeted Enzo warmly, was cordial to Aubrey, then ushered them up elegant floral-carpeted stairs to a small but beautifully appointed room.

"Thank you so much for coming," said an obviously American woman about Aubrey's age as she opened the door wide. "I feel bad that my grandma and I may have overdone it walking and seeing the sights. Should have kept a closer eye on her and not pushed it, but Venice is so tremendous that we got carried away." She frowned and glanced at the older woman sitting across the room in a plush, wingback chair. "I didn't want to put her through the ordeal of going to a hospital if we don't have to, but I felt we needed to know if we should be worried or not."

"That's why we're here," Enzo said, introducing

himself and Aubrey, and the woman in turn introduced her grandmother. Aubrey could see by the way the younger woman stared at Enzo that she was as dazzled by his easy smile and good looks as Aubrey had been from the second she met him. As every woman on the planet would be, no doubt, if they didn't know what a split personality he had.

He crouched in front of the white-haired woman, who leaned against the back of the chair holding both hands pressed to her chest. "Tell me how you're feeling."

"Short of breath. But it's barely anything. Really. My granddaughter just likes to worry about me."

Aubrey could immediately see that the woman's breathing was a little labored, but Enzo just smiled as though they were having a regular conversation. "Because that's what granddaughters are supposed to do when it comes to their beloved *nonnas*."

"We've had such a wonderful time." The woman's eyes shone, and her wrinkled face smiled broadly. "The basilica—why, it was more incredible than I ever would have dreamed. And going up the tower to see the islands, and the terra-cotta rooftops of the city! And taking that boat thing down the canal to see the houses along the water—the history! Unbelievable. Seeing Venice in pictures isn't anything close to actually being here, is it?"

"No, it most definitely is not." His smile widened and the way he glanced up at Aubrey made her heart do that annoying, squishy thing again. "You are a woman after my own heart, Mrs. Knorr."

"You're so handsome I'm sure there are lots of women after your heart, young man. I'd heard Italian men were beautiful, and have seen for myself it's true. And here you're proving it again."

"Thank you. Sometimes it is true that women show up in my life, but they are not necessarily after my heart." Another glance up at Aubrey, this one odd and questioning, and her throat tightened that he obviously wasn't completely over wondering about her. "Does your chest hurt?"

Yes, Aubrey wanted to say, *because of you and your attitude*. But of course she knew he was asking the patient and not her.

"Just a few twinges," Mrs. Knorr said. "Really, I don't want to be a bother. I'm sure I'm fine, and I'm having a wonderful time. Just a little tired."

"Let me take a listen anyway." Enzo pressed his stethoscope against various parts of her chest, his face inscrutable. "May I look at your ankles?"

She stuck out her foot, and he gently tugged her socks down to press his fingers against the obviously swollen flesh. He drew the socks back up before reaching for her hands and the nail beds were clearly purple. Aubrey hadn't listened to their patient's lungs, but it was pretty apparent that heart failure was likely the problem.

Enzo pulled up a chair and sat in front of the woman, looking at her. "Your heart is a little out of rhythm. Does that happen sometimes?"

She nodded as the granddaughter answered. "She's had fibrillation on and off for some time. Takes a heart medicine to control it. And a little water pill in the mornings."

"They work. They do, Doctor." The eyes that had looked so excited before now reflected the worry on her granddaughter's face. "I don't want to ruin our trip and don't want anyone fussing over me. I'll be fine."

"Only the right amount of fussing, I promise." He patted the woman's hand, and the sweetness of the gesture and the warm expression on his face made her own darn heart about go out of rhythm, too. How could the man be beautiful and smart, so incredibly caring, and the best kisser in the Northern Hemisphere at the same time he was so skeptical and wary with her?

"You are having a little congestive heart failure. But I don't think you need to go to the hospital. So here's what we're going to do," he said. "We're going to have you take the water pill three times a day for three days, and see if that helps with the fluid in your lungs. Increase your beta-blocker, too. Don't worry—" more patting and sweet smiling "—I'll write all this down for you. Aubrey is going to take your blood pressure, and we'll see if we need to tweak the medicine for that, as well. Then draw your blood, just to check a few things, like your potassium and sodium, and to make sure you're not anemic. Okay?"

"Okay. That all sounds good." She gave him an obviously relieved smile.

He stood, and Aubrey worked to do as he'd asked while he spoke to the granddaughter. "When are you leaving Venice?"

"We were supposed to leave tomorrow, to go on to Florence, then the Tuscan countryside. But maybe we shouldn't. Maybe we should arrange to go home."

"Can you stay in Venice three more days, so we can look at her again? If she's feeling better, I don't see any reason why you can't continue your vacation with maybe a couple fewer stops."

"That's what I want to do," Mrs. Knorr chimed in. Aubrey smiled at the stubbornness that suddenly was loud and clear in her voice. She reminded her a lot of Aubrey's nanny, the retired nurse who'd been obstinate and awesome and was the reason she'd decided on that profession. "I love it here. Three more days sounds perfect, and we can just cut a few days off the rest of our trip somewhere else."

"I love it here, too," Aubrey said, hoping to distract her as she drew the woman's blood. "I get to be here for four months, and I know even that isn't going to feel like long enough."

As she capped off the vials Enzo's gaze caught hers. Held. The man was becoming more and more of a mystery, because she had no idea if he was thinking good things or bad things about her, and decided she couldn't worry about it.

As if that were possible. She focused on being efficient as she worked to gather everything up while Enzo wrote down his instructions, going over them with both women again before they left to go back to the clinic.

"You were so good with her, Dr. Affini," she said as they walked. That was matter of fact, right? Just honestly expressing her admiration with his bedside manner. *Oops. No thinking about his bedside manner.* "Are all elderly patients smitten with you?"

"Definitely not." He grinned at her. "I had one lady throw every pillow on her settee at me the second I walked in her house. And older Italian men tend to be the worst patients in the world, believe me. I'm sure you'll experience one or two while you're here."

"Older men in general are the worst patients, if you'll pardon me saying so. Sexist though that might be. You think you'll be cranky in your old age? I mean, crankier than you already are?"

He laughed. "Most definitely. In fact, it's in my genes. Along with other unfortunate traits."

He didn't look as if he was kidding, but she didn't ask what other traits he could be talking about. Keeping it professional. She could do it.

The rest of the day went by in a blur. Aubrey felt downright exhausted after the influx of patients they'd taken care of all day. Everything from tourists who got overheated to cuts that needed to be stitched to a broken arm and gashed head after a poor guy intently admiring the city fell down a long set of stone steps. They ended up keeping the doors open until seven o'clock when finally the last patients had been treated and were on their way.

With a last swipe of antibacterial wipes along the countertops, she stepped back, satisfied that the exam rooms were ready for the following day. Time to maybe do some evening walking around the city she still had barely toured, then have another wonderful dinner somewhere. Her breath suddenly hitched in her chest as she stood at the sink washing her hands, and she didn't have to turn to know the figure that came to stand close behind her was Enzo. And how did her heart and lungs know work was over and she could think about *him* again, darn it? Being able to concentrate on their patient load all day had convinced her she was over it.

Trying hard to pretend she wasn't ridiculously aware of him, she nonchalantly dried her hands on a towel. Which was tugged from her fingers before a large warm hand grasped hers, the other sliding a cool glass of sparkling water into her palm.

"You've had a long day, and you're probably thirsty. Thanks for hanging in there so long."

"You did, too." She let her eyes meet his over the glass as she took a drink, thinking how very thoughtful he was to have brought it to her. She hadn't even realized she was thirsty—how had he? "And no thanks are needed. That's why I'm here."

"Still, you did a great job. Even not speaking Italian, it amazes me how well you're able to communicate with the locals anyway."

"Hey, I'm learning to speak Italian! A little, anyway. A few words and phrases."

"Yes, you are. Even Venetian Italian." He smiled. "Pretty soon you'll be talking like a native."

"Wouldn't that be wonderful? Sadly, that's probably not a reality, in just a few months." And she'd probably forget all of it after she went back home. Still, the idea of being able to pretend for at least a little while that she was part of this amazing city filled her heart with some emotion she couldn't quite place.

"You never know. I'm impressed with your progress."

"Um…thanks." The admiration in his gaze made her feel warm, or maybe it was his closeness, and she took another big swig of water to cool it before setting the glass on the sink. "I better get going."

"To where?"

She moved to her cupboard to grab her things, hyperaware that he followed. Since she didn't yet have any idea where, and didn't want to think too hard about what *he* might be up to that night, she tried for a joke.

A joke she couldn't deny she hoped would needle him a little. "Maybe I have a date."

Even from the corner of her eye, she could see him stop dead. "A date?"

"You know, where you eat somewhere with someone, and explore a bit? A date."

"With who?"

She turned to him and folded her arms across her chest, absurdly pleased that she'd gotten the surprised and disconcerted expression from him she'd wanted. "What's with the questions? You got out of me all I know about Shay, and, since you accomplished that on *our* date, what I do outside the clinic isn't really your business, is it? Maybe me going on a date would finally prove to you that I'm not here because I was pursuing you or something."

"First, you knew when we met that I wanted to learn more about the woman my brother was to marry. Second, I've apologized for the things I said. I realize how stupid it was of me, now that I've gotten to know you better and see the kind of person you are. I'm truly sorry it even crossed my mind to accuse you of that. But there probably is one thing you don't know that you should." The small hallway felt even smaller as he moved close. "Which is that being with you that night was the best thing that's happened to me in a long time."

For once, the eyes meeting hers weren't laughing, or suspicious. His brows weren't dipped into a frown. His lips weren't curved into a teasing smile. Instead, his expression was serious and sincere and her heart started beating in double time. She tried to shore up her defenses because the last thing she needed was the complication of a man who hadn't tried to get in touch with her after their oh-so-memorable night together, who'd been suspicious of her when she'd first come back to Venice, and who was her boss to boot.

And never mind that it was a beyond tempting complication that seemed more tempting with every second that passed.

"I've got to go." She turned and hurriedly grabbed her stuff, shut the cupboard door, and started to move past him, but his hand reached for her arm to stop her. Slid slowly down her skin to twine his warm fingers with hers.

"A long day deserves a nice night," he said quietly. "For both of us. Would you join me for dinner? Then a little more touring of Venice to see things we didn't see last time? Unless you must honor your date, of course."

"I…I think it can be rescheduled." She couldn't help that her response sounded a little breathy, because the way he was looking at her and touching her seemed to steal every molecule of oxygen from her lungs. Making her feel the same way she'd felt two months ago that first night they'd met.

"*Bene*. You have a change of clothes here? I think you'll like what I have in mind."

CHAPTER SIX

"I'M PRETTY SURE that was the best dinner I've ever had. Though I fear I may gain ten pounds by the time I leave here." Aubrey sat back in her chair and watched Enzo pay the bill, his head tipped downward as he did. The night lights by the canal touched the silky black hair that he wore slightly long, and she couldn't help but admire the adorable little waves curling against his neck that were usually a bit hidden by his lab coat. When he looked back up at her with the smile that had dazzled her two months ago and again tonight, her silly heart skipped a beat.

The evening with him had been wonderful, as she'd known it would be. Magical, just like the first night she'd met him. Getting to roam romantic and incredible Venice, not just once, but twice with a man as amusing, intelligent, and physically beautiful as Enzo Affini was something she'd never forget.

Hadn't forgotten even a little in her two months away from Venice.

No wonder she'd fallen into bed with him last time. Not that she had any intention of repeating that all too memorable experience, especially knowing now that he wasn't really perfect in every way.

"Between seeing patients and touring the city, we've walked a lot today. You needed the sustenance." Enzo stood, and why did just his smile keep making her feel a little weak in the knees? His hand wrapped around hers as it had on and off all evening, and it felt perfect and electric and she wasn't sure how much of that was the magic of Venice, and how much was the magic of Enzo Affini. A very lethal combination. "Let's take the *vaporetto* to my boat, hmm? Then I will take you to your house."

Boat? Her tummy tightened at the suggestion—as much as she adored Venice, being on the water made her nervous—and she drew a deep breath to calm it. "You mean your house."

"It's not my house again yet. Unless you mean you want to go back to the house I'm living in, instead?"

His eyebrows were raised, and his dark eyes shone with both amusement and the banked-down heat she'd seen in them on and off all day.

"No way. I could be a stalker, remember? Not smart of you to take a chance. And we work together now. But I appreciate your asking for clarification," she said in a prim voice that got a chuckle out of him.

They headed toward the water taxi, and the closer they got, the more her breath quickened until she felt she might hyperventilate.

Stop being stupid. Being around water all the time while you're here is going to help you get over this, right?

Still, staring at the dark sky surrounded by even darker water as they stepped onto the taxi, she found herself gritting her teeth and hanging tightly on to his arm. She was glad it was far less crowded than earlier that night, which had just added to her anxiety somehow. Despite having plenty of room, he slid his arms around her waist and pulled her back against him just as he had when there had been a few dozen people pressing shoulder to shoulder. The way he held her made her feel safer, ridiculously, and even as she reminded herself again how silly her fears were she found herself clutching the forearms looped across her stomach.

"You don't have to hold me this close anymore, you know." She'd said it to force herself to be brave, but she was more than glad when the arms around her didn't loosen. Her words had come out a little breathy, but she couldn't help that. Between his closeness and her worry, she was surprised she could breathe at all. "I can stand up on a moving boat quite well when people aren't jostling me."

"I know. Which should tell you that's not why I'm holding you close." His voice was soft, his lips right next to her ear in a feather touch against the shell before moving slowly down to rest below the lobe.

For a split second she was surprised. Until the feel of his mouth on her skin had her relaxing, melting back against him at the deliciousness of it and making her forget that they were on dark water that might swallow her up. That he was her boss and all the other reasons she shouldn't let him kiss her again.

Her head tipped back against his collarbone as her hands caressed the large, warm ones pressing against her belly. It wasn't a conscious invitation for him to explore further, but he obviously read it that way, since she could feel his lips smile against her skin before his mouth moved down her throat, the tip of his tongue touching the base.

"It's a good thing the stop near my boat is close by," he said. "Otherwise I might have to kiss you right here in front of everyone. Not that Venetians would mind, but tourists, maybe yes."

"I thought kissing wasn't allowed between clinic employees."

"It's not. But for just this moment, I want to pretend we don't work together."

"But we do work together." And why had she said that, when only negative things could come of it? Those things being that he'd make her stop working at the clinic after all, or he'd decide not to kiss her. And she definitely wanted both of those things a whole lot whether she should or not.

"Sorry, I can't hear you. The wind's in my ears." With his warm, slightly rough cheek touching her temple, they rode across the water without another word passing between them as the breeze caressed her. It felt wonderful, but not nearly as wonderful as the feel of his skin against hers and the exquisite sensory overload that completely overpowered the fear that had squeezed her chest just moments ago.

The *vaporetto* finally docked, and Enzo released her for just a second before grasping her hand to help her off. That familiar fear skittered down her spine again, and she was beyond glad to be off the darn boat. Also glad Enzo had found a very nice way to distract her, and sure hoped she didn't freak out riding on his small boat.

"My skiff is just over there." The pace he kept was so fast, she might have tripped if she hadn't been in the comfy, crepe-soled sandals that were her favorite for long tourist walks.

"Do you have a curfew or something?" she asked breathlessly, feeling nearly dragged behind him as he held her hand tight. "Do you turn into a pumpkin at midnight? Oh, wait, that was Cinderella's coach, not the Prince."

He turned his head to flash a grin at her that somehow managed to look impish and sexily seductive at the same time. "Guess you'll have to stay with me until midnight to find out, hmm?"

Then just as he'd practically started sprinting the second they got off the boat, he came to such an abrupt stop in the shadows beyond a streetlamp, she collided into him as he turned toward her.

"Gee, give a girl a warning, would you?" She pressed her free hand to his chest to separate them and found hard muscle there, and heat, and...and... what had she been about to say?

"Sorry. Here's your warning. I'm going to kiss you now."

And with that promise rumbling deeply from his throat, he pulled her flush against that warm, firm chest, lowered his head to hers, and did exactly that.

The kiss started out gentle, sweet, his mouth moving on hers in an unhurried exploration that stole her breath and sent her heart into slow, rhythmic thuds against her ribs. He tasted a little of the Chianti they'd shared, and of fantasies come to life again, and of him.

Especially him.

The hands she had pressed flat against his pectorals slipped upward of their own will to wrap around the back of his neck, and she could feel his palms splay wide on her back as his arms tightened around her. The kiss deepened, their tongues danced, and Aubrey hung on for dear life as her knees weakened under the sweet assault that felt so beyond a mere kiss there wasn't a name for it.

His lips separated from hers, just enough to let her drag in a much-needed breath at the same time his chest heaved against hers. "You taste amazing, *mia bellezza*. Just like you did the last time we were together."

"You...you do, too." And wow, was that ever true. She stared up into his eyes, and even through the darkness she could see the blaze in their deep brown depths. That taste filled her with a hunger she'd felt only one time before, which had been the last time they'd kissed. A hunger for the life adventures she'd promised herself, for moving on from betrayal, for...for Enzo Affini, smart or not.

"I have to tell you something," he said.

The blaze in his eyes was suddenly joined by an odd seriousness. Maybe even troubled, and her chest felt as if it caved in a little. "Oh. You're...you're involved with someone else?"

"No."

"Okay, that's good." More than good, but then that left lots of other possibilities of something even worse. "You still think I'm a stalker? You murder unsuspecting tourist employees and throw them to the sharks?"

"No. Didn't I already tell you I knew I'd been stupid?" His lips curved slightly. "And I don't believe I've ever seen a shark in the lagoon, or one of the canals. But the truth is almost as bad. The Affini men are a bad bet. I hope Shay knows that. And I want you to know it, too."

"Why?" She searched his face, wondering why he'd gone from kissing her breathless to pulling back like this. And should she really be worried about her friend? "In what way are you a bad bet?"

"Just take my word for it." His expression was downright grim now, even as his eyes still looked at her as if kissing her again was as high on his list of desires as it was on hers, and his hands held her waist so tightly she expected to be pulled back against that hard chest at any moment.

"Shay's a big girl. She's planning on her relationship with your brother to be temporary, and what's best for the baby," she said. "As for me, I'm a big girl, too. I'm not betting on you. I'm just enjoying kissing you. A lot. And I don't think kissing and…and stuff has anything to do with betting. Does it? You're completely confusing me here."

"Aubrey." He said her name in a low voice that held a smile and something else that made every inch of her insides vibrate, and she found herself moving against him instead of waiting for him to draw her closer. "I know you can't be confused about how much I enjoy kissing you. Even though I shouldn't. And if you are, I'll have to make it clearer."

And with that, he lowered his mouth to hers. Kissed her until all thoughts and questions disappeared, replaced by heat and want and a desire so intense, she felt woozy from it. After long, breathless minutes, he raised his head, lifting one warm hand to cup her cheek, running his thumb across her moist lower lip.

"Are you sure you don't want to quit working at the clinic and just have a hot affair with me instead?"

"Not fair to ask me that question right after you've

kissed me like that." And was that ever true. The way her insides were quivering told her to hand in her notice that very second. Who needed work when she could have Enzo Affini for a few months? "But, no, much as I'm tempted, working at the clinic is important to me."

"I know." He smiled and slowly pressed his lips to first one cheek, then the other before lightly kissing her mouth. "I was kidding. Sort of."

He released her and stepped back, and she instantly missed his warmth. "I should get home now. To your home. I mean, your home that's temporarily my home." Lord, kissing the man had clearly shaken her brain as much as the rest of her.

"Thanks for making that clear." Enzo's impish smile was back in full force, and he reached for her hand. "Tomorrow when we see one another at work, we'll pretend tonight didn't happen. If we can."

"Yes. I'm sure I can manage that." Which was a total lie. Her still-tingling lips and wobbly knees told her that, for her at least, pretending that would be impossible.

For the first time all day, there was a lull in the action at the clinic, and Aubrey took the opportunity to get a cold drink and catch her breath, glad the office was about to close. Crazy busy days there had left her with little time to think about the evening she'd spent exploring the city with Enzo. To think about how it had felt when he'd held her and kissed her, which was a very good thing.

During clinic hours, there hadn't been more than a few quick moments to reflect on their odd and confusing relationship. Learning they worked well together, and were able to set aside their attraction to one another while taking care of patients, was a relief. But the other times? When there were gaps between patients? The heat they kept on a back burner would suddenly flare into a warm simmer in an instant.

A teasing grin, or a gentle finger flick to her cheek, or a long look from his dark eyes, would tell her he was remembering their kisses, or maybe even thinking about that first night they'd met over two months ago. Then she'd recall exactly how all that had felt, which would leave her a little short of breath.

So, what were they going to do about it? Was Enzo going to stick to the "keep their distance" thing? Did she want to? And really, hadn't they already violated that rule at least a little?

She had no idea what the answers were, but maybe trying to make a few friends in Venice would keep her from thinking about him so much when they weren't working together. Meet some of the UWWHA nurses who worked at the hospital, or get involved with the various restoration and preservation groups and learn more about the city and its history and challenges.

Yes. That would be a good plan. Learn something, maybe contribute as well, and have more things on her mind than Enzo Affini.

Aubrey was just about to pull out her tablet to see about any meetings the organizations might have scheduled, and look at the UWWHA social loop to see if any of the nurses might be planning a get-together that night, when Nora came into the back hallway.

"We have a Russian couple here. Wife is twenty-five weeks pregnant and is feeling uncomfortable. I'm going to bring her to exam room two."

"All right." Aubrey washed her hands, then greeted the couple with a smile. "Hello. Tell me why you're here."

"My wife is pregnant. Not feeling okay." The man's expression was strained, and his English was hard to understand. Aubrey knew difficulty communicating usually made patients feel even more anxious, and she smiled wider to try to reassure him.

"Tell me how you're not feeling okay," she said to the dark-haired woman, who looked to be in her thirties and reminded Aubrey a little of their Russian housekeeper, Yana, who'd ruled the roost for years when she'd been growing up. "Are you in pain?" Aubrey repeated the word in Russian, hoping to gain her confidence. She didn't speak much of the language, but could manage the basics.

"No." The woman looked at her with surprise, then a smile as she cupped her hands around her round belly, speaking rapidly in Russian until Aubrey had to stop her.

"I'm sorry, I don't understand. I only know a few words, from an old friend."

The woman stopped speaking, but still smiled. "Okay. Just, um, balling. Here."

"Cramping?"

"Yes." She nodded and seemed a little relieved that Aubrey understood what she was trying to say. "Cramping."

"All right. Let's put a gown on you, then get your feet up, and I'll take a listen to baby." She helped the woman undress, then had her lie down on the exam table. After putting a few pillows beneath her legs, she pressed a stethoscope to the woman's belly, relieved to hear a steady heartbeat there. "Baby's heartbeat is normal, so that's good. I'm going to talk to the doctor, okay? Be right back." She patted the woman's shoulder, adjusted the pillows, then went to look for Enzo.

His office door was open, and she was glad to find him there filling out paperwork. "We have a patient who's twenty-five weeks pregnant and experiencing cramping. Baby's heartbeat is steady. Do you want me to do an ultrasound? Or do you want to do an internal exam first?"

He looked up and her heart gave an unfortunate little kick when his dark eyes met hers. Hadn't she just been feeling proud that the simmer between them was mostly absent when they were working? "I'll come do the exam, then we'll decide."

Enzo gave the couple his usual, calm smile, asked questions about how she was feeling, explained what he was going to do, then snapped on gloves as Aubrey helped adjust the patient's position. "You'll feel me touching you, and some pressure, okay? This will just take a moment."

Aubrey watched Enzo's face as he examined the woman's cervix, and though his expression didn't change she could tell instantly that he didn't like what he'd found.

He took off his gloves as Aubrey moved their patient into a more modest position, keeping her legs elevated on the pillows. "I'm afraid there is some dilation of the cervix. Not much, but more than should be there at twenty-five weeks. I want you to go to the hospital for treatment that we can't give you here."

"Hospital? No." The woman suddenly looked a little mulish. "We are on vacation. No hospital."

Enzo glanced at Aubrey, and his look told her loud and clear that he might need backup about this. "If you go into preterm labor, your baby could be born way too soon. It's important that you have the baby monitored for a bit. If they determine that baby is trying to come too early, there are medications that can be given to you through an IV that will stop the process and let baby grow inside you longer. Depending on what they find, they may even want to give you steroid injections to be sure baby's lungs will develop before it's born."

"We go home soon. I will see the doctor there."

The husband hadn't said a word, and it seemed clear that he'd go along with whatever his wife wanted.

"Please let me call the hospital. An extra day or two here is worth your baby being born healthy, isn't it?"

"No. Thank you."

The woman swung her legs over the table and picked up her clothes, clearly intent on leaving. Enzo opened his mouth to say something more, but Aubrey put her hand on his arm to stop him. Her Russian might not be very good, but she understood this woman a little and wanted to give it a try.

A halting conversation with the patient finally had her yielding, and her expression went from stubborn to resigned. Enzo's eyebrows were raised, but he didn't say another word except to tell Aubrey he'd call for the ambulance boat to take the woman to the hospital, probably worried that he'd jinx the process and she'd change her mind.

By the time the ambulance came the office was closed for the day, and it was all Aubrey could do not to drop into a chair and stay there awhile. Enzo returned through the back door after talking with the EMTs, raising his eyebrows at her.

"When were you going to tell me you had special skills with difficult patients? That was amazing."

"I just got lucky." She had to admit she felt good the situation had gone well. Glad the woman and her baby were going to get the help they needed. "Our Russian housekeeper, Yana, was the most stubborn woman I've ever known. She was very suspicious of doctors and hospitals, and refused to see anyone but a Russian doctor whose practice was almost a hundred miles from our town. I channeled my memories of why she felt the way she did when I was talking to our patient. I guess it worked."

"I guess it did." He reached for her hand and brought it to his lips, his eyes smiling at her above it. Heating, too, as that *thing* that was always simmering there between them started to boil a little higher. "You are a constant surprise, Aubrey Henderson."

"I try to keep you guessing and on your toes, Dr. Affini," she said lightly, hoping he couldn't tell that just the touch of his lips on her hand and the way he was looking at her had her heart doing a little tap dance.

"You successfully do that every day. In more ways than one."

The dark eyes meeting hers were full of admiration, maybe a little confusion, and a whole lot of desire. She recognized it, because she could feel it melting her bones.

"Aubrey."

His deep voice vibrated through her, and her answer back was breathless. "Yes?"

"Would you join me for a cruise on the water to see

some of the islands in the northern lagoon? They're very different from the glamorous Venice you've seen, and one has interesting buildings and church ruins I believe you'd enjoy. I'll pick up some things for a picnic dinner. What do you say?"

He was watching her with the small smile touching his lips that was always so appealing, but the question in his eyes seemed to say that what he was asking was important to him. And how could she say no to an excursion to a part of the lagoon she might not get to see her entire time here, if not for him? The thought of cruising on that dark water made her stomach squeeze, but she knew if there was one person who could make her face her fear of that, it was this caring and empathetic man.

"I'd love to. But I'm happy to get the food together."

"Let me. I have favorite delis I know that will pack us a picnic you won't forget. I'll pick you up at the house at six, *si*?"

"*Si.*" Her chest bubbled with pleasure just at the thought of spending another evening with Enzo Affini, even as she promised herself it absolutely would not end anything like the first delicious one they'd shared.

CHAPTER SEVEN

With bags of food and a few bottles of wine from one of the family wineries at his feet, Enzo sent his boat through the canal toward his old home. He hadn't looked forward to an evening with a woman this much in a long time. Not since the recent night they'd spent touring and eating and kissing. Not since the incredible night he'd spent with Aubrey two months ago, and he didn't have to think too hard about what all that meant.

Maybe this was a bad idea. Maybe it wasn't. Maybe it didn't matter either way, because he'd given up on keeping their relationship strictly business, not just because he'd failed miserably at it. Because he'd come to believe that, unbelievably coincidental as it had seemed that Aubrey had shown up in his life, there'd been a reason for it. And not the reason he'd originally wondered.

It was meant to be that he and Aubrey would have four amazing months to spend time together. For her to have a native Venetian show her the most amazing city in the world. For him to have something in his life to enjoy while he dealt with the very stressful and un-enjoyable battle to get his mother's house back from the brink of destruction, and into the family fold again.

The more he was around Aubrey, the more he

wanted her. Warm and smart and a little sassy, and how was he to resist that lethal combination?

Clearly, the answer was that he couldn't. And he'd given up trying.

His heart gave a strange little kick in his chest when he saw Aubrey waiting for him next to the dock. She smiled and waved, and he nearly ran the boat into one of the wooden posts, he was so intent on looking at her beautiful face and body, her silky hair lifting a little in the breeze.

He managed to safely secure the boat right next to her. A gust of wind blew her dress up a little, and was it his fault that he was below her and had to look?

"Hey!" Both her hands pressed down her skirt and she frowned at him. "No peeking up my dress."

"Need I point out that I've already had the pleasure of seeing way more of you than that?"

She gasped, but it almost sounded like a shocked laugh, so he was pretty sure her offense was mock. Though why he'd let such a thing fall out of his mouth, he wasn't sure. Or maybe he was, because he couldn't help that the vision of her beautiful, naked body often filled his mind.

"That kind of remark definitely doesn't qualify for us having that professional, friendly relationship we're trying to have."

"That was friendly, wasn't it?"

"Maybe in Italy. At home it's called sexual harassment."

"Is it? To me, sexual harassment is more like—"

"Stop now, before I call the UWWHA on you. And refuse to come on this excursion after all."

He'd already told himself to shut up already and

laughed at how outraged she somehow managed to look, even when her beautiful eyes were twinkling. "Sorry. I'll behave. Come on. Your chariot awaits."

"Does Prince Affini say that to all the girls he picks up?"

"Only the ones he wants to picnic with." He reached for her hand. "Watch your step."

She hesitated for a moment before finally extending her hand. He folded her soft palm in his, surprised at the strength of her grip as she stepped carefully into the boat. So carefully, in fact, he looked up at her instead of at her sexily sandaled feet, suddenly realizing she looked surprisingly scared. "Does getting into the boat worry you?"

"Of course not. Um…okay, yes. I'd hoped I'd be so brave you wouldn't notice."

Her teeth sank into that delectably full lower lip of hers, and he let go of the post to grasp her elbow, keeping her steady on the gently bobbing boat as he lowered her onto the seat. "What should I have noticed?" But he had a feeling he already knew.

Wide blue-gray eyes met his, filled with embarrassment and worry. "I'm…I'm afraid of water. Like, dark lake water or ocean water. It's silly, I know. Ridiculous. I can even swim fine and have no problem in a clear swimming pool. But when I was really little, I fell off the dock of the big pond on our property and thought I was going to drown for sure until one of our groundskeepers jumped in and fished me out. I've been weirded out by it ever since."

He hadn't asked about her background, but if they had housekeepers and groundskeepers, that usually meant wealth. But, of course, he'd figured she must be well-to-do when he'd first learned about her donation to restore that fresco.

He remembered the way she'd clung to him on the *vaporetto*, realizing now that perhaps it had been as much about her fear as about wanting to be close to him. Had he not noticed because all he'd been able to think about that night was how much he wanted to kiss and touch her? The alarm in her eyes was more than real, and he thrashed himself for not seeing it before.

"I'm sorry I didn't realize you were scared. I wish you'd told me before now." He sat close enough to wrap his arm around her, this time to comfort instead of maneuvering into a good position to kiss her, though he couldn't help but think about that, too. "Perhaps driving around on the canals and riding more often in the *vaporetto* will help you manage it better, hmm? Though I have to say I'm surprised at your insistence on staying in Venice instead of going to the mainland. A woman with a fear of water clearly likes to torture herself if she wants to live in a city built on water."

He smiled at her, relieved to see her smile back, even if it was a weak effort. "Actually, I did it on purpose. Not to torture myself, but to deal with it. Get past it. My mother had a terrible fear of being in public places around a lot of people, and it was paralyzing for her. I promised myself I wouldn't live my life like that, that I'd figure out a way to get over it. Four months here should do the trick, don't you think?"

"When did your mother pass?" he asked quietly, understanding well that pain and loss.

"Just over a year ago." She looked away across the water, and the pain on her face was so intense, he squeezed her shoulder in support. When she turned back to him, her smile was wider, but still forced. A clear message that they were closing the subject. "I'm starving and very excited about this picnic idea. Where are we going again?"

"To an island in the northern lagoon that's mostly deserted, but beautiful in its own way. The marshes and mud flats around it are totally different from here, and much of the island itself is marshy with rough fields. It's quiet, unlike the busyness of Venice. I think you'll like it. And, Aubrey?"

"What?"

"I promise I won't let you fall overboard."

She smiled, but it didn't banish the worry in her eyes, and his mouth lowered to hers for a soft kiss to reassure her before he'd even realized he'd done it. And that simple touch of his lips to hers made him want so much more.

When his lips parted from hers, he was glad he'd kissed her, because the eyes wide on his were filled with something very different from worry now, and it was all he could do not to go back for another, deeper kiss.

He drew in a breath and forced himself to stand again, his arm around her waist as he moved them to the rear seat.

"Sit in the back with me. It'll make the bow sit a little high in the water, but you'll be close to me." Normally he would have had her stay in the center of the boat for better weight distribution, but he wanted to keep his arm around her. Make her feel secure. And it had nothing to do with wanting to touch her soft skin and hold her close. And he was getting really good at kidding himself when it came to Aubrey Henderson.

They passed boats like his, larger tour boats, and the ferry that stopped at a few of the islands. Her excited exclamations at the various sights made him smile, glad he'd had the idea to bring her here. He watched her point at old buildings and churches as they went by, and each time she did she'd turn to look at him with a bright smile. He stared into her eyes as she talked, wondering how she described their color. Sometimes they were the gray of the water, tinted with a blue reflection of the sky. Other times they seemed more blue than gray, with interesting flecks of green and gold. Holding a smile inside that she was able to enjoy the ride in spite of her fear, he felt as buoyant as the boat skimming across the water.

"So, where exactly does Dante live? And, I guess Shay now, too."

Her odd tone of voice had him stealing another look at her. She wore a slight frown, and her lips were cutely twisted as though she was wondering about that marriage as he was, which lightened Enzo's heart even more. If she wasn't too sure about the two of them marrying, that would mean there was no agenda on Shay's part, just a situation where a night of lovemaking had led to unexpected consequences.

"Dante's home is on the Lido di Venezia. The very long island you can see past Guidecca, which is across from San Marco's."

"Is it as old as yours? I mean, the house I'm living in now?"

"No. His is practically new. Built in the fifteen-hundreds. Needs a bit of work, though."

She laughed. "Only in Italy is something built in the fifteen-hundreds practically new."

"Much of the rest of Europe would object to that statement. Though I believe our history is the most interesting, which isn't bias, of course."

"It is. It's incredible. Imagine knowing who your ancestors were so long ago, and that they lived and loved in the very house you grew up in. You have to get that house back, no matter what."

The fierceness on her face reflected just how his heart and gut felt on the matter, and it amazed him that she seemed to understand that. "I agree, *bellezza*. Believe me. And I will, no matter what it takes."

He didn't want to think about all that now, and the tough odds against him. He wanted to enjoy a special evening with this very special woman.

They sat in silence as they approached the island, and he didn't try to analyze the sense of peace he felt being with her at the same time he felt utterly wired. "I'm going to dock here. We'll walk along the canal, but, unlike the ones you've seen before, this one will be practically deserted. Then I'll show you the old churches, and then we'll have our picnic on a favorite green space Dante and I used to bring girls."

"I can imagine what you both had planned when you did that."

"And sometimes those plans would backfire if the mosquitoes came out. Smelly repellent isn't quite as appealing as cologne."

"Except rubbing it on the girls would have been a good excuse to touch them."

"There was that, yes."

Her soft laughter slid inside him, and he reached to tuck the silky strands of hair that had escaped her ponytail behind her ear. Let his fingers travel down her jaw before sliding his hand down her arm to hold hers as they exited the boat.

Her exclamations and excitement as they walked along the deserted canal made him feel as if he were seeing everything with new eyes himself, despite having been there dozens of times. They trudged over the grasslands and saw the ancient churches and abandoned homes, and she seemed so pleased, he was glad he'd brought her out here, despite her fear of the water.

"You're right—this place is very different from Venice." Aubrey spread the blanket over the flat, overgrown grass next to the lagoon. "Feels almost wild, you know?"

"Yeah." He wanted to tell her that watching her tempting rear move around as she bent over to straighten the blanket was making him feel a little wild, too. Because hauling her into his arms, lying down on that blanket, and kissing her until neither of them could breathe seemed like a much better idea than a picnic. He inhaled a deep breath of the salty air and concentrated on pulling out the food. "After we eat, we'll take the boat to meander through the channels a little more, where we'll probably see wildlife, then we'll head back."

The picnic food seemed to taste even better than usual, and he was glad he'd brought one of their wineries' best vintages to share with her. "Did Shay tell you about the Affini estates in Tuscany? We have extensive vineyards, and several wineries. Dante and I are pretty happy with this batch of Chianti. I hope you like it."

"It's really good." Her eyes closed briefly as she took a sip, apparently letting it linger in her mouth. The expression on her face reminded him of the night they'd made love, and he turned his attention to the horizon to subdue the way his body reacted to the memories. "And believe it or not, Shay and I really haven't had a chance to talk about more than the, um, situation. I don't really know much about the Affini family other than what you've shared with me."

"And that's probably just as well." Talking about his family situation was one sure way to kill his libido, and he managed to get them settled onto the blanket without laying her down on it and kissing her breathless.

As they ate they shared stories of patients that had both of them laughing, along with a few that brought tears to Aubrey's eyes, turning them into another fascinating shade of gray-blue tinted with green.

"What color are your eyes?"

She paused from eating a chunk of bread and looked up in surprise. "My eyes?"

"Yes. I'm slightly color blind, and every time I look at them, I wonder."

"That must be so strange! Do you have to spend your life figuring out what color things are, or are you just used to not being sure?"

"Neither. Most of the time I don't particularly care." He leaned closer, lifted his hands to cup the softness of her cheeks as he turned her face, watching her pretty eyes catch the lowering sunlight. "But knowing the color of your eyes feels important."

"They're…they're just a mix of colors. Change with what I'm wearing, and the light, and how I'm feeling, I guess. I always wished I could say they were blue or green or gray, but never knew how to answer that on my driver's license questionnaire."

She smiled, but he could feel her pulse fluttering against his fingers, her breath skittering across his face, and knew she felt the electricity strumming the air between them, too.

He lowered his mouth to hers, sipping the Chianti from her lush lower lip before delving deeper, feeling the hot connection zing between them that happened every time their mouths met. Kept kissing her as she slid her arms around his neck and pulled him close. Felt her melting into him, and he lowered her slowly to the blanket before both of them ended up just toppling over.

His hand found its way to the soft skin of her thigh, tracking up inside her skirt, and her gasp into his mouth inflamed him. The only thought in his head was getting her naked and kissing and touching her everywhere and he was making progress on that mission until the sound of voices and laughter somehow made it through the sexual fog in his brain.

He barely managed to break the kiss, lifting his head toward the sounds. Sure enough, not too far down the grassy area, a group of people, likely tourists who'd decided to go off the beaten path, had unloaded off a hired boat.

"Well, damn." He dropped another quick kiss to her mouth before he made himself sit up, taking her hand to help her do the same.

"I thought you said this island is practically deserted." Somehow her eyes were laughing a little at the same time they looked as dazed as he felt. Her tongue slipped out to lick her lips, and he nearly groaned, thinking about what they'd been doing just seconds ago and how good it had felt and where it might have been headed next.

"It is. Usually. Just our luck, hmm?"

"Maybe the gods of professional relationships are looking out for us."

That got a laugh out of him. "I hope not. Roman gods can be pretty ruthless. And I don't know about you, but I'm seriously thinking about crossing them."

Golden fingers of light spilled across her shining hair as she let out a low laugh, which had him pulling her close for another soft kiss. Behind her, the sun sank to just above the grasses and murky water, and Enzo let go of her to pick up his wineglass and tip the last of it into his mouth. But the taste of Aubrey still lingered.

"We better get going before it's so dark you can't see a bit of the lagoon life."

"Okay." Her last sip of her own wine was followed by what sounded like a very happy sigh, and she sent him a smile almost as brilliant as the setting sun. "I bet I'll more than like it. This has been wonderful. Thank you for bringing me."

"Thank you for joining me." He helped her back into the boat and couldn't remember a time he'd felt quite this deeply connected with a woman. "I love it out here. Haven't found a good reason to come lately. You're my reason."

"I like being your reason."

Their gazes met and held. Something about the words made them seem more important than they should have. He didn't know exactly why, but the feeling hung between them, sweet and intimate and suspended in the thick lagoon air. Enzo found himself just looking at her as they sat close on the small seat, her hip and arm warm against his, and it felt about as right as anything he'd ever felt before.

"I have to ask you something," she said, her gaze

steady on his. "Why didn't you ever call me when I was in Rome?"

An easy question with a hard answer. "I thought about it more times than I could count. Had the phone in my hand ready to dial, but stopped myself. I wasn't sure about Shay and my brother, and if she had planned what happened. And you were her friend, which seemed like it could be a problem. Plus I had the issues with the house going on, and I just... I guess I felt like being with you was a complication I didn't need."

"And then it just got more complicated."

"Yeah. But somehow that complication seems more than worth it now." He drew her close for another long, sweet kiss, until he managed to pull back to get the boat on its way. The movement put an inch or two between them, and he instantly missed the feel of her body touching his.

"Soon I'll be turning off the motor and using the oars so we can slip quietly through the channel. Parts of it are only two feet deep." Maybe talking about the place would get his mind back on track. Away from her soft skin and lush mouth. "Depending on the flow of the rivers and wash of tides from the Adriatic, if you lean over you'll see fish, crab, squid—all of the many things you can find on restaurant menus in the city."

"It almost reminds me of the fish farming on the coast near my house."

"Venetians like to scoff at talk about the 'new' art of fish farming, since we've been doing it for hundreds of years."

"You Venetians seem to like to scoff a lot at anyone who doesn't have the history you do."

"Which is most everyone, Ms. New World."

They exchanged grins as he cut the motor and let the boat slide into the marshy channel. Aubrey leaned over just a couple inches to peer over the side of the boat, then, as the boat slightly rocked, grabbed his arm so tightly it hurt.

"Ouch," he said, extricating her fingernails from his skin, holding her arm up against his body instead. "I'm wishing this boat had a mast for you to hold on to instead of my flesh." He dropped a kiss onto her cheek and smiled at her, hoping she'd relax.

"I'm sorry."

"No need to be sorry. But remember what I said? Only two or three feet deep here. If you did fall out, you'd get a mud bath as much as you'd get wet. But you won't fall—the boat is steady, promise. I'm here to steady you, too. Making you feel safe is, right now, my priority in life."

"That's a...a very sweet thing to say. And being scared is so silly, I know." She sat up straighter and looked embarrassed, which made him wish he hadn't teased her. "I'm trying."

"I know. And that impresses me more than you know." He stroked her soft inner arm as he tucked her closer. "Do you have any idea how many people just accept their fears and don't try to do a thing about it? You're already way ahead of every one of them."

"Thank you." Her eyes were wide and troubled as they clung to his. "I'll get there. I— Oh!" She pointed behind him. "Look at that huge bird! What is it? Is it stuck in the lagoon?"

CHAPTER EIGHT

ENZO TURNED TO see the bird, which had doubtless just dived into the water. "It's a cormorant. They're everywhere out here. The lagoon's bounty of fish and shellfish are a daily buffet."

"It looks trapped or something."

He looked again, then even closer. Was the bird really floundering? "Let's go take a look." With the oar shoved into the mud, he pushed the boat through the marshland.

"You look like a gondolier when you do that. Is that another of your many skills?"

"Is that a real question of a man who grew up here? I look exceptionally good in the striped shirt and be-ribboned hat."

Her laughter faded as they drifted up close to the bird and it became clear that it truly was in distress. "Is that…? What is that on it? Oil?"

"Don't know. Something like that." He tried to maneuver the boat close enough to see if there was something they could do without making the bird panic, jamming the oar deep into the mud to bring the boat to a stop. "With the industrial plants at Marghera and near the causeway, chemicals from agriculture, and all the tankers and cruise ships that come by, our pollution problems have gotten worse. We've put in buffer strips of trees and shrubs along the edges of the lagoon to try to catch it, but it's not a perfect solution."

"Poor bird!" Aubrey leaned over the edge of the boat toward the bird, obviously forgetting about being afraid of the water. "What can we do?"

"It's not completely covered in the oil, so that's good. Probably just dived into a single gob that had fallen off a ship. It still looks fairly healthy, I think." He glanced at her. Normally, when things like this happened, he'd get the bird on the boat and take it to one of his veterinary friends, but he knew from experience that sometimes the birds didn't like that too well. He didn't want to see Aubrey get splattered with the oil or, worse, pecked and injured, especially when they were on the water, which worried her.

"It won't be healthy for long. You know as well as I do that it won't be able to clean itself enough, or if it does the oil it eats off its feathers will make it sick."

"And how do you know this?"

"Just because you're a doctor and a prince and a native Venetian doesn't mean nobody else knows as much as you, Dr. Affini," she said with great dignity. "I volunteered off the coast of California when there was an oil slick once."

"A woman of many talents." He had to laugh as he said it, even as one or two of those talents that came to mind weren't funny, they were amazing, and he shouldn't be thinking about them. "So you won't freak out if I bring it on board and it flaps around? We'll have to try to secure it with something."

"The blanket will work." While she rummaged

through the picnic bag, he got the medical bag he always kept with him in case there was an emergency, and snapped on the gloves.

"If we do this, I can't promise that you won't get covered with oil, or even bitten."

"I can handle both of those things. And I know a certain quack doctor who is very knowledgeable about bird bites and pecks." Her eyes laughed into his. "But we just need to hold him tight, right?"

"Hopefully right. But sometimes things don't always go as planned, you know?" He grinned back. "All right, then. After I put him in it, I'll keep his beak closed while you wrap him and hold him as tight as you can. Tell me when you're ready."

"Ready."

He draped the blanket over her shoulders, then smoothed it down over her legs as much as possible, and was it his fault he had to linger on each of those spots as he did?

"What kind of man uses rescuing a bird as an excuse to fondle a woman?"

"A man who keeps trying not to touch you, but can't help himself."

The seductive look she sent back to him jabbed him right in the solar plexus, along with a few other notable places, and that thing that kept shimmering between them lit the air. This time it was Aubrey who leaned in for the kiss, and he was only too happy to meet her halfway. Her mouth was sweet and soft and pliant, and if he hadn't had the damn gloves on he would have held her face in his hands, tipped it back, and kissed her until neither of them could think anymore, but that would have to wait.

He pulled back, loving the way her lips stayed parted as she stared at him. "Hold that thought, okay? We have a good deed to do."

Maybe she was having as much trouble talking as he was, because she just nodded. He turned to slowly, carefully reach for the bird, bracing himself in case it tried to fly up into him. When he grasped its body, holding its wings down as firmly as he could, he was glad the bird only wrestled weakly to get away.

"Coming to you on the count of three. One, two, three." He pulled the bird from the water, pressed it into the cloth over Aubrey's waiting arms, then lifted one hand to slide his fingers around the bird's beak as she wrapped it and held it close to her breasts.

Lucky bird.

"I...I think I'm good," she said. Enzo used his free hand to help wrap it, while holding the beak tightly as the bird jerked its head up and down, trying to get loose. He took from his wrist the rubber band that he'd grabbed from his bag earlier and wrapped it around the beak. For having fairly small arms, it looked as if Aubrey had the huge bird held good and tight.

"I'm going to let go now, okay?" He watched carefully, ready to contain it if he had to, but the bird seemed to have given up the argument, and Aubrey's elated eyes met his.

"We did it!"

"Haven't gotten him back yet. So don't count your cormorants before they're hatched. Or something like that." She laughed as he snapped off the oily gloves to get the motor going. "I'm not going to go too fast, so it doesn't get scared."

"And so *I* don't get scared, wimp that I am." She said

it without one bit of fear on her excited face, and Enzo's chest filled with something absurd, like maybe pride in her toughness, as he reached to stroke her soft cheek.

"You? A wimp? Wonderful nurse, fear-facer, and bird-rescuer? You, Aubrey Henderson, are a warrior."

All the way back, she talked to the bird in a soothing voice, and Enzo had to smile at how cute she was. His vet friend, Bartolomeo, met them at the dock, and the handoff proved to be a little awkward. Getting Aubrey out of the boat at the same time she held the bird tight wasn't easy, but finally she was standing on the walkway, able to carefully pass the bird to Bart.

"Is it going to be all right, do you think?" Aubrey asked, her happy expression dimmed with concern now.

"Do not worry, *signorina*," Bart said. "You have brought him in good shape. I have all I need to get it cleaned up and hydrated, and an assistant who enjoys helping with birds in trouble. Come to our office to see it in a few days—with a little luck, I think you'll be pleased."

"I'd like that. Seeing how you do things there would be interesting, too."

"Aubrey has told me about some of her many interests, Bart." Enzo smiled at the excitement on her face, despite the splotches of oil on various parts of her skin and dress. "She's participated in bird rescue in the past."

"Maybe you could come work at my veterinary clinic. We can always use extra hands."

"No way," Enzo said, stepping in fast before she had a chance to think about that. "I need her nursing skills at the clinic more than you need her giving shots to dogs and cats."

"No promises that I won't try to woo her over to my clinic instead, Enzo."

His friend's face might be grinning, but it showed loud and clear that he was attracted to Aubrey, too, and what man in his right mind wouldn't be? The feeling of possessiveness that suddenly filled Enzo's chest was unfamiliar, but there was no denying that emotion was what drove him to reach for her hand. To place a kiss to her forehead in a clear message to Bart as to whom she belonged to.

For the moment, at least.

"I appreciate the offer, but I think nursing humans is my calling at this point. Thank you, though," Aubrey said, and Enzo felt relieved that she didn't scowl at him for answering before she could say a word, but squeezed his hand instead.

"Let me know if you change your mind. And now I'd best get this bird taken care of before he decides to dive back into the lagoon. *Arrivederci.*"

Glad the man and the bird were gone, Enzo was able to focus on just Aubrey again. He ran his fingers across the black smudges on her forehead and jaw, only managing to smear them even more. "You're a bit of a mess. And I am, too. The clinic is close by, so I suggest we go there to shower. Unless you gave away my change of clothes again?"

"Funny." She playfully swatted his arm. "I don't have extra clothes there, though. Maybe you should just take me home so I can clean up there."

"No. Because that would be the end of our evening together, and I'm not ready for that." The truth of his statement had him tugging her against him, not caring that the bits of oil on her skin would find their way to his shirt and pants. "Are you?"

"No," she said softly, and the way she smiled into his eyes and snaked her hands around his neck stole his breath. "I'm not."

He touched his lips to her nose and the places on her face that weren't smeared with oil before kissing her for real, and the heat of her mouth felt so arousing, so right, he had to break the kiss and suck in a deep breath before he stripped her naked right there in public.

"Come on. Let's get that oil off you." He grasped her hand and nearly ran the few blocks it took to get to the clinic. He quickly pushed the code into the keypad outside the back door and practically hauled her inside, not able to stop until they were in the locker room next to the shower.

"I'll go in first," she said in a prim voice totally at odds with the twinkle and heat in her eyes. "I'll let you know when it's your turn, Dr. Affini."

"Uh-uh. This job requires two people." He grabbed towels from the stack on the shelf, then washcloths, too, before reaching for her hem. He had the dress off and over her head in one quick movement, then reached around her to get the bra off, too.

"What kind of job are you referring to?" Her fingers were already working his belt, then the button and zipper, too, shoving his pants down his legs. One second later, she had her hands around the waistband of his boxer shorts, inflaming his obvious desire even further until he nearly groaned. "I think I'm handling this okay solo, don't you?"

"You're doing a fine job, yes," he said, his voice a

little hoarse. "But once we've taken care of this part, the next jobs will take both of us."

"Jobs, plural? I might need more instruction on this job you're referring to. You might do it differently in this clinic than we do at home." Those beautiful, mysteriously colored eyes met his, and the heat and humor in them weakened his knees almost as much as the way she was touching him.

He opened the shower door, turned the water on, and finished getting both of them naked as fast as he could. "Pretty universal techniques around the world, I'd think. Except there's not one single thing that's just 'usual' when it comes to you, Aubrey Henderson."

The water spraying his back was still a little cold, so he pulled her in front of him to shield her from it until it warmed. Once he'd gotten a washcloth wet, he slathered it with soap. "Here's the two-person job. You can't see the black stuff smeared on your face, and this oil is tough stuff, so I'll have to wash it for you."

The frustration on her face made him chuckle as he gently washed the spot on her forehead. "If this is strictly medical, with you cleaning me like your friend is cleaning the bird, I might have to kill you."

"You had something else in mind, *bellezza*?" He scrubbed off the spot on her jaw, then slowly moved the washcloth down her throat, across her collarbone, and down to her nipple, following with his lips and tongue.

"Um…no. I can see this is…an excellent way to address the problem." She tipped her head back, and as he licked the water from the hollow of her throat and slid the cloth slowly back and forth across her breasts and down between her thighs, her little gasping breaths and the way she touched and stroked him back nearly sent him to his knees.

Which might not be a bad place to be.

So go there, he did. Kneeling before her, he held her sexy, round bottom in his hands and drew her to his mouth. Kissed and touched the slick sweetness of her center as she tangled her hands in his wet hair and made little sounds and it was so good he didn't notice how much her legs were shaking until she dropped to her knees, too, pushing him back onto his rear as she did.

"That was… I couldn't…" She stopped talking. With her lips parted, she stopped talking. Just stared at him with eyes that were filled with the same intense want that rushed uncontrollably through his veins and his mind and his heart.

"I know."

It was good that words weren't necessary any longer, since neither of them seemed able to say more than two of them in a row. She reached to touch him, her hands caressing his cheeks down to his shoulders as he lifted her to him, pressing her warm, wet breasts against his chest. He was barely aware of the water pouring over their heads and bodies. All he could think about was how she felt against him as she positioned herself and eased onto him. All he could see was how incredible she looked as she moved on him, needing to touch every part of her he could reach as she did. Her breasts, her hips. Her thighs and waist and where they were intimately joined. Her soft cheeks as he brought her mouth to his for a deep kiss that seemed to shake his very soul even as their orgasms shook their bodies. And when she pressed her torso to his, resting her face against his throat as their chests rose and fell in unison, he knew with certainty that he'd never before experienced anything like the physical pleasure and emotional closeness and mental connection all layered together that he felt at that moment with Aubrey in his arms.

Which was incredible and confusing and scary as hell.

CHAPTER NINE

AUBREY BLINKED AT the orange-yellow early-morning sunlight that spilled through the huge windows of Enzo's childhood home and across the thick cotton comforter. She turned her head and focused her bleary eyes on the oh-so-close chiseled features of Enzo, his head propped up on one hand and his sculpted lips curved in a smile.

"Buongiorno, mia bellezza," he murmured.

He pressed a soft kiss to her forehead, then lazily began twining a strand of her hair through his fingers. His slumberous dark brown eyes were looking at her in a way that told her he was ready to take up where they'd left off last night, and how that could be she had no clue, since three times in one night had been more incredible sex than she'd ever enjoyed in her life.

Than she ever expected to enjoy as much again.

"How can you be so wide-awake? We were up half the night." She rolled slightly toward him because she wanted to feel the warmth of his skin again. Wanted to feel the thud of his heart against her hands as she pressed them to that wide, well-defined chest. Wanted to slip her arms around his strong body and stay held close in his arms for the rest of the day.

For the rest of the time she'd be in Venice, and suddenly a few months didn't feel nearly long enough.

"Sleeping seems like a waste of time when I'm with you."

Oh. Well. When he put it that way, she'd have to agree. "Except sleep is kind of a necessity when we have to be at work in an hour. Or at least I do. Are you working today, too?" It suddenly struck her that Enzo might have scheduled her to work with the other clinic doctor—the one she hadn't even met yet—since their plans to keep that professional distance had gone up in smoke, then seriously hot flames, last night.

"You think I'd have you work with Antonio instead of me? No way. Women fall all over him, and he takes advantage of that. You're stuck working with me instead, Nurse Aubrey, for better or for worse."

She sat up. Did he mean that the way it had sounded? "So what you're saying is you think I'd sleep with any handsome man? Just because I slept with you that first night we met, I want you to know—"

"No, feisty one." He effectively stopped her by pressing his mouth to hers before propping his head on his hand again. He tugged at the strand of hair in his fingers, and the way he grinned in response seemed to show he was enjoying her annoyance. "I'm saying that I don't trust him to not come on to you, then I'd have to beat him up, and the clinic would be down to one doctor. Not the best thing for our many patients, do you think?"

She sank back into the mattress and snuggled up against him, liking his words more than she should. Since when had she ever been attracted to a possessive man?

Apparently, when that man was fun, smart, delectable Enzo Affini. And since they'd now moved way beyond a simple hookup, she wanted to learn more about him.

"That first night we met," she started to say, "you—"

"Couldn't resist kissing you."

"And prying for information about Shay. Which I told you I know is why you went out with me at all."

"Ah, you're wrong about that. I did want to find out more about the woman my brother was going to marry, but that was most definitely not the only reason I went out with you." Heat emanated from his body as he tugged her closer, and as he nuzzled her neck it was very apparent that he was ready for round four. "The second I spied you from across the room, I was extremely attracted, which alarmed me greatly."

"Alarmed you?"

"Because I thought you were Shay. Remember I told you I'm slightly color blind? Dante had told me she was wearing a green dress, and I thought yours was green." She could tell that the lips traveling across her throat and down to her collarbone were smiling. "Very bad form to lust after your future sister-in-law."

She started to laugh, then squeaked when his mouth found her breast. "I'm trying to have a conversation with you here." He didn't seem to listen, as he moved his attention lower to start nipping at her ribs, but maybe that had something to do with the fact that she was clutching the back of his head and holding him close.

"Converse away." His tongue slipped back up across her nipple and she gasped with the goodness of it before she managed to speak again.

"Tell me why you say you and your brother are bad bets."

She hadn't necessarily wanted to stop his very exciting ministrations, but her question had him lifting his head to look at her, all playfulness gone from his face.

"Because we are."

"People aren't just born bad bets, Enzo."

"And you would be wrong about that." His heavy sigh slid across her skin as he rolled to his back, bringing her with him. He just looked at her, seeming to think awhile before he finally spoke. "The Affini men are afflicted with a bad personality trait. My father's father was notorious for the number of women he kept, with my grandmother pretending to look the other way. My father was even worse, but my mother didn't pretend it wasn't happening. She spent their whole married life trying to change him."

"Did they fight?"

"I'm not sure you could call it that." He turned his head to look at her, and his dark eyes were filled with a peculiar mix of pain and anger and disgust. "My mother would cry and beg for him to stop and love only her, and he would respond that he knew she loved him enough for both of them. I never understood why, but that appeared to be the truth."

"That's…that's terrible! Why did she stay with him? Because of you and Dante?" Aubrey just couldn't imagine having the man she loved constantly cheating. She looked at Enzo as he held her naked body close to his, and realized that if she found out he'd been with another woman while they were sleeping together, it would tear her up inside. That they'd been together only once over two months ago, and a matter of days since then, wouldn't change that. Being together for years? Having children together? Impossible to imagine.

"No." He stroked his finger down her cheek. "We wanted her to leave him. My mother was a happy, loving, joy-filled woman except for this one, terribly painful thing in her life. We knew our home would be a more cheerful place, a better place, if he was out of the house. But even on the day she died, as he stood by her bedside, she told him how much she loved him."

"He must have felt terrible then. Must have told her how much he loved her, too."

A bitter laugh left Enzo's throat. "No. The only person my father loves is himself."

Her throat clogged for the poor woman who had loved a man who hadn't loved her back the same way. For the sons who'd grown up with a cold, selfish man for a father, doubtless feeling confused and hurt about all of it. Thought about her own mother. She'd never spoken of Aubrey's father, which had left Aubrey's imagination to create a larger-than-life dad.

Had her mother loved him? Had he left her? Was that why she'd done what she'd done?"

"And so you see why we are bad bets." He brought her mouth to his for a kiss so sweet, it was hard to imagine that he truly believed that about himself.

"Just because your dad isn't a good person doesn't mean you're not. You know that."

His answer was to kiss her again. "Your turn," he said, tucking her close and playing with her hair some more. "Tell me about your family."

She didn't really want to talk about it. But he'd answered her questions, hadn't he? Fair was fair.

"My mother was a very special person. So smart,

and a wonderful, loving mom. We did everything together, until she got sick with cancer." She closed her eyes against the tears that threatened, but he turned her face to make her look into his warm and sympathetic eyes.

"Aubrey. It's okay to cry. I cried when I lost my mother, too. Sometimes I still do, when I think about losing the house she loved. So tell me about the wonderful woman who created such a special daughter."

She swallowed and forced herself to go on. "I told you she was afraid of crowds, of being around more than a few people. But in small groups, she was such an amazing leader. Her passion for the history of our city in Massachusetts, for our home and the other historic homes there, led her to start a number of architectural boards, and to get laws passed that would keep that history, that heritage, from being torn down or irreparably changed."

"We would have gotten along well, your mother and I."

"Yes." That thought managed to make her smile. "You would have."

"And your father?"

That, she definitely didn't want to talk about. "Let's just say he and your father have a lot in common."

"He cheated on her?" His voice had gone low and hard.

"No. Or at least, I have no idea about that. I never knew him until after she died. Other than telling me she got pregnant accidentally when she was only nineteen, she never talked about him. So, growing up, I created who he might be in my mind. Strong and handsome and fun. Someone everybody adored. My imaginary dad loved to fish with me, to travel places my mom didn't like to go. He loved to ride our horses, and he loved me."

Hearing herself say her childhood fantasies out loud made her feel ridiculous and embarrassed, and she turned her head away from the serious dark eyes listening so intently. "What time is it? I need to get showered. Get ready to go to the clinic."

"In a moment." A large, gentle hand nudged her gaze back to his. "So you met him after your mother died. And he wasn't anything like your imaginary dad."

"At first, I thought he was. I was so thrilled to meet him, and he seemed like everything I'd ever dreamed he'd be. So handsome for a man in his fifties, well-groomed, with an easy, charming smile. He told me he hadn't known about me until my mother died, when her lawyer contacted him about some money in her will. Said he felt terrible he hadn't been part of my life growing up, but that he couldn't wait to make up for all the time we'd lost together." She shut her eyes, hating to think about how gullible she'd been. In some ways, still the little girl who'd long dreamed of her superhero dad. When she opened them, she could see Enzo's were still warm and sympathetic, but getting a little hard again, too. Smart man knew this story wasn't going anywhere good.

She was silent a long moment, but Enzo didn't speak. Just ran his hand slowly up and down her side, over her hip and back, not in a sensual way, but in a caring, soothing way. Giving her time. And that comforting touch made her want to talk about it after all.

She sucked in a breath and forged on. "He started coming around all the time, four or five times a week.

We rode the horses together. Went on quite a few excursions. He seemed so interested in my nursing career, even sometimes came to a few of the architectural review meetings that I'd taken over for my mom, saying he wanted to support her passion, too. He was fun and exciting and I just felt so blessed to have finally met him. I'd lost my mom, but, after all these years, God had helped me find my dad."

"And then what happened?"

"He told me about a project he needed money for. Just a loan, to help him refurbish a few old homes he'd bought in another state. It was a lot of money, but I knew my mom would have wanted that, too. So I gave it to him."

"Oh, *tesoro*." The hand cupping her face was full of tenderness. "I'm guessing that was the last you saw of the money."

"The money, and my father." It angered her that it still hurt. She didn't even know the man, really. They shared only genes. So how could she let his dishonesty, his manipulation, his lack of moral character, hurt her at all? "Once he had the money, he disappeared. No more visits, no more telling me how happy he was to have me in his life. I soon found out through my mom's lawyer that she'd been paying him money for years to stay away, and when it stopped coming, that's when he found out she'd died. I have no idea if she paid him because she didn't want to see him, or if she knew her teen crush had turned out to be a gambler and a con man, or what. All I know is that she didn't want him to be part of my life. And I feel so stupid that I fell for the charade and for his lies."

"What a terrible thing for you to have to go

through." The way he tucked her face against his neck and hugged her close felt so good, she found herself clinging to him. Hungrily soaking in the warmth and comfort he offered. "But you must tell yourself what Dante and I eventually learned. Our father's cold, selfish heart isn't the way it is because of anything we did, and no amount of love from our mother could've changed him. That's true for you, too. You wanted and deserved a good father who loved you, and it's his loss that he will never have the kind of relationship with you that you could have offered him. I'd feel sorry for him if I didn't want to beat the hell out of him."

"Thank you." Trust him to make her smile, even as she thought about how much she hated being used by the man. "If he shows up again wanting more money, can I give him your address as the place to pick it up, so you can punch his lights out?"

"It would be my pleasure. As is this, *mia belleza*." He ran his hand down her hip again, before pulling her thigh over his. It was very apparent that their serious conversation hadn't affected his libido, and even as she was thinking they were going to be late for work, she wrapped her leg farther around him, tangled her fingers in his hair, and kissed him.

Bing-bong. The jarring sound was so loud, she jumped and nearly knocked her skull into the huge, carved wood headboard as she clutched her hand to her chest. "What was that?"

He frowned and sat up. "The doorbell. Is there another UWWHA nurse coming to stay here?"

"Not until next month, as far as I know." She hated to leave the sizzling warmth that had been zinging between them, but maybe it was for the best. "Saved by the bell, maybe? Otherwise we might have had an annoyed line of patients at the clinic before we even got there."

He responded with a heated grin as the bell gonged again, and she slid out of the bed to shove on her robe and see who the heck could be ringing.

"I'll get it." Enzo was putting his pants on with some difficulty, since his body apparently hadn't figured out they weren't doing *that* after all.

"I have my robe on already. Besides, I don't want to get a bad reputation around here with a sexy, half-naked man answering my door. Be right back."

She ran her hands through the current mess on her head as she trotted down the stone stairs, not wanting to look as if she'd just gotten lucky, even though she sure had last night. Very, very lucky. The giant door was heavy, and she slowly pulled it open to see a man standing there, formally dressed in a suit and tie and carrying a briefcase.

"May I help you?"

"Are you Aubrey Henderson?"

"Yes."

"The owner of this house has informed the UWWHA about this but wants to let you, as the current tenant, know personally, as well."

"Know what?"

"This property is almost in contract with a new buyer. The funding will be finalized within the next few days. When the purchase is complete, I'm afraid this home will no longer be available to rent, as it will go under construction immediately. The UWWHA tells me they will be contacting you about new housing.

My client is giving you a three-day notice to be moved out. You will be refunded your rent accordingly."

He pulled several papers from his briefcase to hand to her, but Aubrey could barely see them as she reached for them with icy hands. All she was seeing was Enzo's determined face when he said he'd do anything he could to save the house he'd grown up in. All she was hearing was his voice telling her how much he loved this home.

Her voice shook with the big question she needed answered. "May I ask who the new buyer is?"

"Proviso Hotels. They will do a magnificent job remodeling this run-down place. You will have to come stay here again when it's finished. I am sure you will marvel at its transformation to the kind of new and modern hotel tourists will love."

CHAPTER TEN

"I TOLD YOU to sell those a week ago! Why aren't I seeing the funds as available in the account yet?"

Enzo paced his small office in the clinic, worry and frustration gnawing at his gut. Was Leonardo inept? Hadn't he made it clear to the man that he needed to immediately liquidate the assets that he'd outlined in detail?

"I did sell them. I don't know why it's not showing up as cash yet, but I'll find out right now."

"Find out sooner than right now. I need to know exactly how much more I need to outbid Proviso so I can figure out a way to get the rest by tomorrow."

He flicked through the reams of papers he'd pulled from his briefcase and laid on his desk at the clinic. He leaned his palms on his desk as he did, fighting a sickening feeling of impending defeat. Never before had he brought this kind of work to the clinic. Had always tried to keep his medical work separate from the vineyards and wineries he and Dante helped operate, and from his other business investments.

But today wasn't the day to care about that kind of separation. Desperate times called for desperate measures, as the saying went, and if he had to stare at the numbers and what else could be quickly sold to get fast cash in between seeing patients, that was what he'd have to do. Maybe there was some solution he wasn't seeing yet. Or maybe there was no solution, and his fight would end in failure, which he'd refused, until this moment, to believe could really happen.

In the midst of his intense concentration, he heard a soft knock on his office door. *"Entra."*

"Enzo."

He looked up to see Aubrey staring at him, her fingers twining anxiously together as if she had some bad news.

"What is it? Someone I need to see?"

"No. The last couple of patients have all had simple problems I could take care of without bothering you."

"Then…?"

"I want to talk to you about your house."

"Aubrey." For some inexplicable reason, just looking at her sweetly earnest face helped his lungs breathe a little easier. Which made no sense. Her caring and warmth and beauty weren't going to save his mother's house. The house she'd loved so much, that he had, too, and that he'd so wanted to keep forever. The house he'd never dreamed would be lost to him in yet another selfish sweep by his father.

Her worried eyes stayed glued to his for a long moment before she spoke again. "Your house. We need to talk."

"I appreciate that you care. I do, more than you know." And the truth of that loosened the tense knots bunching in every muscle. "But talking isn't going to fix this problem, *bellezza*. Money is going to fix this problem, and I'm doing all I can to get it together in time to save it."

"Well, that's what I want to talk about." She licked her lips, and just as he was going to tell her not to worry, that it wasn't her problem to stress about, Nora swept into the room.

"Franca Onofrio just called. She said Carlo looks very ill, but he is refusing to go to the hospital to see what the problem is. Are you able to go see him today?"

"You want me to go by myself while you work on this?" Aubrey asked. "It might be something I can handle on my own, and if not I can call you."

"A very nice offer that I appreciate. But my first responsibility is to my job and the patients in this city, and Carlo's English is hard to follow. He's diabetic and had to have one leg removed below the knee a couple years ago. I should come to see what's going on."

"All right. I'll get both our bags together and meet you out back in, what, five minutes?"

"Yes. *Grazie.*"

He watched her rush out, wondering how he could ever have been suspicious of her motives for coming to Venice, and for working in his clinic. The woman was not only beautiful and exuberant, she was all about what she could do for others, not for what others could do for her. Something not at all true about many of the women he'd dated over the years.

After gathering the items he always took on house calls, they walked through narrow passageways and over cobbled bridges on their way to Carlo's house. "Are you glad he lives close enough that we didn't need to ride on the *vaporetto*?" he asked.

"I'm slowly getting used to the water. The risk of

hyperventilating the next time I'm on a boat is getting less and less, I think."

"Bene." He liked the cute way she poked fun at herself, and, since he seemed to always be looking for a reason to touch her, he put his arm around her and tugged her against him, dropping a kiss on her forehead. "You may end up buying a boat of your own when you go back home."

He'd said the words without thinking, but when they came out of his mouth it struck him how much he would miss her. The months would go by too quickly, of that he was sure. But he also knew, deep in his soul, how lucky he was to have met her for this brief time. And since he'd been given that unexpected gift, maybe that meant he'd find a way to save his mother's house, too.

"Maybe." She looked away from him and after a pause began exclaiming brightly about the various doorways she liked to admire. Too brightly, really, and he looked closer at her, wondering if she was bothered by walking so close to the canal, or if her chatter was hiding something else.

Then she abruptly stopped talking, turning to him with an odd look of determination on her face. "About your house."

"So that's what's bothering you." He pressed a lingering kiss to her soft cheek, wanting to show her how much it meant to him that she cared. "Please stop worrying about it. I hope to have some numbers in hand later today, and I need to talk to Dante about a few of our joint liquid assets, as well."

She opened her mouth to say something else, but he

dropped a quick kiss to her lips before she could speak. "Here we are at the Onofrios'. It's time to get to work."

They rang the bell and within seconds Franca had opened the door for them, ushering them inside. Enzo nudged Aubrey in ahead of him, following her through the arched stone doorway that was so low, he had to duck his head beneath it.

They followed Franca to another room, listening to her talk the whole time about how stubborn Carlo was, and how he wouldn't do a thing she asked him to. Enzo smiled to himself, thinking Aubrey would have appreciated the diatribe if she understood fast Italian, but when her amused eyes met his he could tell she got the gist of it anyway. Because it was in the center of a row of houses, the interior was fairly dark, and it took a moment for his eyes to adjust before he spotted Carlo sitting in a chair in the corner.

"I hear you're not feeling too well. What's the problem?" He felt a little rude speaking in Italian when he knew Aubrey couldn't follow, but their patient's comfort was the most important thing and he'd fill her in as he could.

"I'm okay. Franca just likes to worry and nag me."

"Which makes you a lucky man."

Carlo huffed an annoyed breath, and Enzo noted how dry his lips looked. Eyes looked a little sunken, too, so he'd guess the man was very dehydrated. He switched to English. "Aubrey, please take his vital signs. Also check his blood sugars."

She nodded and went about getting his blood pressure and sugar levels while Enzo listened to his chest. "Have you been taking your insulin the way you're supposed to?"

"Yes. Well, not this week, because I ran out."

"You ran out?" Enzo looked at him in surprise. "You know how important it is to keep your insulin levels on target. Did you—"

Franca interrupted him to loudly scold her husband, even smacking him on the shoulder as he shook his head and apparently tuned her out. Enzo glanced over to see Aubrey's eyebrows raised at the argument, and he gave her a quick grin. He'd been taking care of both of them for quite a while and couldn't remember a single time when they hadn't gotten into it over something.

"Aubrey, what's his sugar reading?"

She peered at the monitor, then her mouth dropped open as she stared up at him. "Top reading is five hundred, and it's over that."

Enzo cursed under his breath and turned to the fighting couple, needing to get this thing moving before Carlo got any worse. "You two do know I'm charging you by the minute, don't you?" He said it with a grin and this time it was his arm that Franca whacked. "In all seriousness, Carlo, your sugars are way high. Your potassium is high, and your sodium is low. Since you don't have any insulin in the house, and since you're obviously dehydrated, too, I want you to go to the hospital to get insulin right away, and some fluids."

"I don't want to go to the hospital. Franca will go get my insulin, and I'll be fine."

"I'm not arguing with you about this. I'm calling the ambulance boat, and you're going."

The man looked mulish, as if he was going to argue some more, but apparently could tell Enzo meant business and just scowled. Enzo quickly called the ambulance with the information, then turned to Franca, telling her about how soon they'd arrive. "I'll come back in a couple days to check on him. And please get his insulin prescription filled right away."

Thanking him, and nicely including Aubrey in her nods, she told them to wait a moment, returning with a bag of cookies she insisted they take. "You'll love Franca's biscotti," he said to Aubrey as they headed out the door. "Maybe we should take a coffee break to enjoy them with." Taking a short break with Aubrey, away from the clinic and the financial statements hanging over his head in his office, sounded better than good.

"I thought you had more paperwork you had to deal with."

"An hour isn't going to make a difference." He looked at her and realized how badly he needed and wanted a break that included spending real time with her. "There's no doubt in my mind that an hour with you would boost my spirits."

"Sounds like a lot of responsibility, Dr. Affini, but you know what? I just might have an idea on what would cheer you up."

Bright sunshine poured down on them as they walked down the canal toward one of Enzo's favorite coffee shops. He wrapped his arm around Aubrey's waist, and just tugging her close was enough to boost his spirits already.

"Isn't it a beautiful day? Not a cloud in the sky." The smile she turned to him was wide and full of the joy he'd seen in her so often, but at the same time he could tell it was shadowed with concern. "Though I know it's hard to enjoy when you have such a tough situation going on right now. I can't tell you how sorry I am about that."

"I'll figure it out." He had no idea if that was true, but what was the point of her worrying, too?

They moved from the narrow passage to a walkway by one of the small canals. Children were kicking a ball back and forth across it, laughing and good-naturedly arguing when the ball plopped into the water.

"Is this a game you played as a kid?" she asked, holding her hand above her eyes to shield them from the high, midday sun.

"Dante and our friends were always cooking up new games to play when older games got boring, but I'm not sure about this one. Looks like they're trying to either catch the ball, or kick it into one of the boats."

"I can just see you as a boy playing here."

"Because I seem childlike to you?"

"Um…that would be a definite no." There was a teasing smile on her lips as she looked up at him, but her gaze didn't seem smiling at all. It seemed hot and filled with sexy thoughts, and he was so mesmerized by it, he didn't see the ball heading straight toward his head until it smacked right into him, practically knocking him sideways.

"Oh, my gosh!" Aubrey rested her soft palm against his temple. It throbbed and hurt like crazy, but he wasn't going to let her know that. "Are you all right?"

"Good thing it hit my head. Dante would say it's the hardest part of me."

"That's because he doesn't know what's *really* the hardest part of you."

That made a laugh burst out of his chest, which made his head ache even worse. He leaned toward her, loving the coy look on her face that was making that sometimes hard part of him start to do exactly what she was talking about. "Ah, *bellezza*. I'm more than happy to—"

The boys interrupted him with a spate of shouts, and he turned to see the ball floating down the canal, out of their reach.

"They want you to fetch the ball, I'm guessing?"

"Your Italian is getting good, Ms. Henderson."

"Don't have to speak Italian to figure that out." She grinned. "Need help?"

"No. I'll use a fishing net from one of these boats. Be right back."

It took just a few minutes, and as he was shaking water from the ball before he carried it back he heard the children screaming, then Aubrey shrieking.

What the...? He looked up just in time to see Aubrey's white skirt flying into the air in front of her fluttering legs and shoed feet before she did a belly flop straight into the canal.

CHAPTER ELEVEN

MIO DIO. WITH HIS heart pounding straight up into his throat, Enzo sprinted to the spot she'd gone in, about to jump in himself when Aubrey's head came back up. Her soaking hair was streaming into her eyes and he could tell she was catching her breath, but was obviously treading water as she held a crying, very small little girl in her arms. She was talking in a breathless but soothing voice to the child, pushing the girl's black hair out of her eyes as she did. Since Aubrey wasn't using her hands to swim, she must have been doing some kind of scissor kick, as she was making her way over to the wall of the canal. Several children were standing there ready to grab the little one, but Enzo stepped in front of them, pulled her from Aubrey's arms, handed her to one of the older kids, then reached for Aubrey.

Hardly able to breathe, as if he'd been the one underwater, he shoved his hands deep down to grasp her waist. Lifting her out of the canal and high into his arms, he smashed her tightly against his chest as he pressed his cheek to hers. After barely starting up again from the scare of seeing her go into that water, his heart now slammed hard against hers, and he wasn't sure if it was her shaking from the chill of the water, or him shaking, or both of them.

"What were you thinking? Why in the world did you do that? Can you even swim?"

"I told you, I can swim. I swim in pools all the time. It's dark lake and river water that scares me."

"Which the canal is. *Dio!*" He lifted his head just enough to look in her eyes, and that they were shining and happy made him want to shake her. "Seeing you go in that water took ten years off my life."

"I'm sorry." From the gleam in her eyes, it didn't seem like she was sorry at all. "But we need to check on the little one. Hold on."

She pulled herself from his arms, smoothed the rest of her wet hair from her face, and crouched down to the child, who Enzo could now see was probably only three years old, or so. She was still crying, but just a little, sniffling and nodding and looking a little shy as Aubrey spoke to her. Enzo had a feeling the child had no idea what Aubrey was saying, but the way she smiled at her was a universal language, wasn't it?

Aubrey gave her a quick hug as the older children thanked her, picked up the ball Enzo had dropped when he'd fished them both out of the canal, and went off to play again.

"Are you done playing hero for today?" He folded his arms across his chest, wanting her to know that, even though it had turned out well, he still couldn't believe she'd put herself at risk like that, scaring him to death in the process, when it should have been him going in after the child.

"For today, yes." She grinned at him. "Oh, come

on. If you'd been standing there, you would have gone in, too."

"In case you hadn't noticed, I was plenty close enough to have done the jumping in. Not to mention that I'm not afraid of water, which might have sent you into a panic, which you know as well as I do is often the reason people drown."

"You're being dramatic. I knew you were close by." She waved her hand before she used it to pull his wet, clinging shirt away from his skin. "But I am sorry I got you all wet. And that you were worried."

Exactly how worried still shocked him. He couldn't deny that the instant terror he'd felt had been a little unnecessary. Extreme, even. And what exactly that said, he didn't want to analyze too much.

"We should get back to the clinic." His voice was gruff, and he knew the arm he wrapped around her waist was a little too tight, but that was too bad. He needed to feel it there. Needed to hold her close.

That closeness had him finally thinking less about how upset he'd been and what had just happened and more about her and her discomfort when he felt her shivering against him. He stopped to rub his hands briskly over the goose bumps on her arms. "You're cold. How about I get you a water taxi back to the house? You can take a hot shower, change into dry clothes, and relax without worrying about coming back to work."

"I'm fine." She ran her hands up his damp shirt to wrap them around his neck as she pressed her smiling mouth against his as he folded her close, feeling the tension of the past five minutes slip away as he held her.

"I'll take a shower at the clinic. Get into a dry uniform there. But you're sweet to want to take care of me."

Surprising was the word he'd use, since wanting to take care of her seemed extremely important. Remembering all they'd done in that shower got his heart rate cranking all over again, and he kissed her again, a little deeper this time. When he came up for air, he heard some giggling and realized a few of the kids were watching.

"The Italian version of the peanut gallery," he said drily as he took her hand. "Let's get you into that shower, and, Aubrey?"

"Yes?"

"Warning you that I just might use having my clothes wet, too, as a great excuse to join you there."

With the last patient of the day gone and the clinic closed, Aubrey paced in front of Enzo's office door. After they'd returned yesterday to dry off after her canal plunge, he'd spent most of the afternoon in there. Today, he'd been closeted inside the entire time he wasn't seeing patients, studying spreadsheets, making long private phone calls, and disappearing periodically. Clearly, he hadn't found a solution yet.

She wasn't sure she should disturb him, and even less sure what exactly she should say, even though she'd been pondering it for two solid days. Thinking about her forced move date from his house—former house—tomorrow. He'd been so busy with it, the other doctor had come to the clinic for a few hours to take over some of the patient load. And while Dr. Lambre was nice enough, and a good doctor, work hadn't been the same without Enzo patiently working along with her. Exuding his potent charm and sending that impish grin to some patients, while getting gently tough—a seeming oxymoron he amazingly managed—with the most difficult patients.

Despite their rocky start when she'd first returned to Venice, she'd come to see that he was a good man. A very special man. And because he was, and because she wanted to help him and *could* help him, she stiffened her spine and forced herself to knock on the door.

"*Entra.*"

Holding her breath, she pushed open the door, expecting him to be looking up at her. Instead, his head was lowered to the papers in front of him, a deep frown creased his brow, and, even worse, his fingertips were pressed against his closed eyes.

That utter picture of stress and despair made her heart squeeze hard in her chest. Made her wish she were a huge, burly man who could go find his father and beat the heck out of him for doing this to his son, the way Enzo had said he would do to her own father if he could. But it also made what she had to say easier.

"I'm sorry to bother you. But can we talk for a minute?"

His hands dropped to the desk as he looked up and gave her a smile. If you could call it a smile, because it was a forced, gray shadow of his usual, adorable grin. "Of course. I'm sorry that I've been busy and... absent. I hope working with Antonio has been okay?"

"It's been fine." She sucked in another fortifying breath and forged on. "I know you have a lot going on, but can we maybe get a drink somewhere in the fresh air? It's a beautiful evening, and I know you probably need a break."

The eyes that looked back at her were dark and scarily lacking all their usual warmth and vivacity, but she could see him trying hard to push past the darkness obviously consuming him right now.

"A break and a drink sounds good. Better than good, if it's with you."

Relief weakened her knees, and she walked to his desk to reach out her hand. "You promised to be my Venetian tour guide, His Excellency Dr. Prince Affini. Where's the best place close to here for a perfect Italian Bellini?"

"Bellinis are a bit fruity for my taste, but, if that's what you want, I know of a good place a bit past all the tourist spots, but not too far."

That it had taken a long moment for him to grasp her hand worried her, and the half smile he gave her worried her, too, but she'd get him out of the clinic any way she could. Because they had important things to talk about, and maybe those things would bring the smile she'd come to love back to his handsome face.

The sun was hiding behind thick clouds on the horizon as they walked along the Riva Degli Schiavoni toward the restaurant and bar Enzo had suggested with obvious reluctance. Aubrey pondered when and how to broach the subject they needed to talk about. The evening was alive with tourists walking the promenade, and vendors of all kinds were working to sell their wares, but one in particular caught her eye.

"Those watercolors are beautiful, don't you think? Do you mind if we look? I'm going to need a few souvenirs to take home."

She didn't really want to think about souvenirs, and about going home, but hoped maybe a benign distraction and conversation would be a good thing before she tackled what she really wanted to talk about over that Bellini.

"You do realize there are dozens of artists selling paintings of Venice everywhere you go here." The smile Enzo sent her was better, a little more real, than the one they'd started this excursion with, and her heart lifted a little that it was a start.

"I know. But I might find the perfect one when I least expect it, right? Why wait until the day before I'm leaving for the States?"

He seemed to look at her a long time before he answered. "Yes. Why wait?"

Her stomach jittered with nerves, and she made some lighthearted conversation about all the touristy stuff for sale, trying to bring them back to their former relaxed banter. As they walked along there were artists who were painting at the same time they chatted to tourists. Others sat on folding chairs, looking a little bored as people walked by to admire their work.

"I can guess which artists are selling more, can't you?" Just as she said it in a grinning undertone her heart jolted in her chest at one of the watercolors on display.

"Look!" So surprised, she felt a little breathless as she tugged him toward the various canvases propped on easels next to stacks of other artwork. "It's your house. Your beautiful house. Right there, in the painting!"

"Sì." His arm wrapped around her waist and held her close to his hard body as he looked down at her, and not the painting. "It's a very famous house. One often photographed as being quintessential Venetian,

standing tall and proud in the middle of two canals. You've already noticed its unique design. One of the many important buildings that are part of our history. Part of the fortunes and extravagance of nobles and aristocracy from bygone days."

She stared up at him as his dark gaze met hers. For those who might not know him, his expression seemed impassive. Matter of fact. But she knew differently. Knew that beyond the calm facade he tried to portray to others lay a world of emotion. A deep love for this city and his ancestral home and, yes, for his mother. A love that went far beyond the connection Aubrey felt to her house in Massachusetts that her mother had held dear to her heart. The home in this painting, this amazing place built more than seven hundred years ago, the house he'd grown up in, could never be replaced. Because it was irreplaceable.

That certain conviction gave her the strength she needed. "Are we getting close to that Bellini? Because I'm dying of thirst."

"That's surprising, since you decided to drink some canal water yesterday." He dropped a smiling kiss to her forehead. "Don't worry, it's not much farther."

Aubrey was glad that an outside table set slightly apart from the others was available for them. Sitting there looking out over the darkening water, she clutched her cold glass and glanced at Enzo as she breathed in the lagoon air for strength. Nerves jittered in every muscle, and, while it seemed ridiculous, she knew it wasn't because what she was about to say was important to only her. She knew it was important to him, too, and also knew it was going to be very hard to convince him to accept her help. And learning ex-

actly where everything stood and what weighed in the
balance had to come first.

"So, tell me what progress you've made on buying
the house back."

His eyes met hers, dark and brooding and so somber,
she wanted to reach for him before they said another
word. She tightened her fingers on her drink and bit
her tongue to keep from touching him or saying anything else, because, as hard as it was to be patient, she
knew she had to give him a chance to talk.

"If you're wanting me to say that all is fixed and I've
bought the house back and you can keep living there,
I'm afraid I can't."

"The house sale is due to close day after tomorrow."

"This I know. Your point?"

"I want to help."

His chest heaved in a deep sigh as he reached for
her hand. "And I thank you for that. But this is a battle
I must finish on my own."

"Why? Are you too proud to accept help?"

"Aubrey. There is no way for you to help." He said
her name on a long breath, a quiet defeat in his voice
as he brought her hand to his mouth, holding his lips
there until she loosened it to hold his cheek in her
palm instead.

"Maybe that's because you haven't yet listened to
what I have to say."

A sad smile that was so unlike any Enzo smile she'd
seen before touched his lips. "Then of course I'm more
than willing to hear it. You have much wisdom in that
amazing brain of yours."

"Thank you. But this isn't about wisdom." She
licked her lips and stared into the brown eyes she'd

come to care about so much, praying he'd accept her proposal. "This is about practicality and business, pure and simple."

"You have a business proposition for me?" This time, his smile looked a little more real. "Talented nurse, architectural historian, child rescuer, and a businesswoman, too? I'm all ears."

"I'm glad to hear that. How much money do you still need to outbid Proviso?"

"About one hundred thirty-five thousand euro. Which today is approximately one hundred fifty thousand dollars."

"I'm guessing you're having a hard time getting it by tomorrow."

"You already know that most of the land we own is held in trust, and I don't have access to it to sell it. I've liquidated a number of my assets, but many others aren't liquid. And I can't take out more loans, because that would be irresponsible. I have to think about the people who work for me on my various properties. Dipping into the accounts that pay them would be wrong. So I'm coming up short but am still working on it."

"But it's not looking good."

"No." The dark eyes that met hers communicated much more than that simple word. "It's not looking good."

"I have a solution." She drew breath, afraid to say it because she had a bad feeling he'd flatly say no. "I'd like to give one hundred fifty thousand dollars to the fund you have set up to buy it back."

His stunned expression would have been comical if there had been anything funny about the situation he faced. "What? No."

"Yes." She reached for his hand. "I love that house, too, and I've lived there barely two weeks. I can't imagine you losing it when you and your mother grew up there. You know that saving historical homes is important to me and was important to *my* mother. Seeing her money, which is now mine, go to keeping a historic landmark from being gutted would make her happy. And it would make me happy, too."

"Aubrey." He shook his head as he stared at her. "I can't accept that. It might take me a long time to pay you back."

"You wouldn't have to pay it back. It would come out of the same fund I accessed to adopt the fresco. That my mother set up years ago for preserving homes like yours. Well, not exactly, because there's nothing like yours in the US." She smiled, wanting to make him smile, too. To see that it really was all right for him to accept her offer.

He lifted her hand and brought it to his lips as he had before, then leaned across the table to kiss her mouth. Soft and sweet and so full of emotion, it felt as if the kiss sneaked all the way into her heart. She clutched at his shoulders to draw him closer, and when their lips finally parted, their eyes met in the silent connection she'd felt since the first moment they met.

"Say yes," she breathed.

His lips brushed hers as he shook his head. "No, *tesoro*. I can't. I'm moved more than I can say by your generous offer, but this is my battle to fight."

"So you won't let anyone else on the battlefield to fight with you?"

"Not you, not anyone except my brother and my bankers. But there is one thing you can do for me."

"What?"

He held her face in his hands, and the eyes meeting hers held something like awe along with the heat that made her quiver. "Let me spend one more night in the house with you. One more sweet night with a special woman to join the many important memories I already have there. Please?"

As if he had to ask. And maybe, just maybe, after another night of lovemaking she could change his mind. She pressed her lips to his and whispered, "Your wish is my command, Your Excellency."

CHAPTER TWELVE

ENZO WAS GLAD that the clinic had been filled with patients all morning, and that Aubrey hadn't been there with him. Focusing on work was probably the only way to take his mind off the reality of what was happening today. That it was moving day for Aubrey, with the sale of the house going through soon. His stomach had churned about it for days now, but today he felt more resigned to the harsh reality that it would soon no longer be the house it had been for so many centuries, but transformed into some monstrosity instead.

He knew that making love with Aubrey again last night was part of the reason he felt calmer about it. Something about being with her had filled the empty hollow in his chest when he'd finally seen there was almost no chance that he could buy the house in time. Took some of the sadness away, too. Even some of the exhaustion he'd felt when it became painfully clear that defeat was imminent.

That she'd offered him so much money to help him blew his mind. Free and clear and with no strings attached just because she knew it was important to him. Yes, he knew she liked the house, and was fascinated by its history, but that could be said of any number of houses in Venice ready to go on the chopping block, and probably a few of the older homes in the States that her mother had cared about.

No, he knew she'd offered it because she cared about him. Which humbled him. Overwhelmed him. And when he'd made love with her last night, his heart had felt strangely light and heavy at the same time. Had felt a reverence for her when he'd kissed her and touched her that was completely foreign to his existence. Emotions he'd never felt or experienced before, and he knew he was teetering dangerously close to loving her.

And that would be bad. Very bad for her. He knew it but selfishly couldn't bring himself to end things just yet. They both knew there was an end date for their relationship, didn't they? She had a life and home to go back to in the States after she was done with her tenure here. Just thinking about how much he would miss her when she left stabbed his heart before it had even happened. But he knew that a few more months with her would be more than worth the pain and emptiness he'd feel after she was gone.

The ring of his cell phone startled him and he fished it out of his pocket to see it was Leonardo. A few days ago he might have gotten hyped up about a phone call, wondering if there was good news, but today he knew the conversation would be more about closure. About what to do with the funds they'd liquidated into cash now that they couldn't buy the house.

"Have you seen this, Enzo?" Leonardo's voice was loud and excited and Enzo strode into his office, wondering what the man could possibly be so excited about.

"What?"

"There's enough money in the fund!"

"What do you mean?"

"There's been a big cash transfer. We've done it! I've sent it all over to the Realtor and lawyer to get the transaction expedited and completed, hopefully today. If all goes well, that house will be yours again by tomorrow, Enzo. Congratulations."

He dropped down into his chair, and a sudden, sickening feeling joined the cautious optimism that swirled around his gut. "Where did this cash transfer come from?"

"It's from a trust in the States. Henderson LLC. Do you know who that is?"

Dio.

He scrubbed his hand down his face. What should he do? Should he accept Aubrey's incredibly generous gift? Let the sale go through? Getting to keep that house and eventually renovating it would all be due to Aubrey if he did.

A deep sigh left his aching chest. He wanted to. *Dio*, he wanted to more than he could say. But what kind of person would that make him? Taking that kind of money from a woman so incredibly special, so amazing, so loving and giving, while offering her absolutely nothing in return would be all kinds of wrong.

He wasn't a fool. He knew women. He knew Aubrey was coming to care for him the way he was her, even though he didn't deserve it. That she was on the verge of loving him, which last night had proven to both of them.

He couldn't let himself be the kind of rat his father was, using her to his own ends without being able to commit to her. Loving her while she was here, yes, but he couldn't love her forever because that would just end up in pain and sorrow for Aubrey, and she deserved so much more than that.

She deserved the world from a man who wasn't a bad bet, and he knew at that moment with absolute certainty that he had to save her from him. He already wanted to keep her close. The way he felt about her filled his chest and heart in a way he'd never experienced before. Big and overwhelming, and because of that he could see himself making promises he couldn't keep.

He absolutely could not selfishly hurt her that way.

No. He'd send her money back to her and keep his distance. Work opposite shifts, and have Antonio work with her instead of him. Maybe he'd even take some vacation time away from the clinic, go see how the vineyards and wineries were doing. Spend time with his brother and get to know Shay.

Losing both Aubrey and the house at the same time made his heart feel as if it had turned into a heavy stone weight, but it was the only choice he could make.

He refused to be the man his father was. He would not be the man who broke Aubrey Henderson's beautiful heart.

"We can't accept the money, Leonardo. Don't argue with me, please. I'm telling you we can't. Transfer it back to the trust with our thanks and regrets."

"Buongiorno, Aubrey." Antonio Lambre gave her a smile as she walked into the clinic. "No patients here yet, so take your time changing."

"Thanks, Dr. Lambre. I'll be ready shortly." She moved to the locker room, and her stomach lurched the way it had the past seven days. A rising anger had joined her confusion and the sick feeling in her belly every day that she'd come to the clinic and Enzo hadn't been there.

She knew he'd been in Venice the entire past week, because of course she'd had to look at the work schedule. Which he'd carefully written to have them work on days opposite one another. She'd called him a couple times, too, to see how he was feeling now that the house sale had gone through and ask if he was happy and if he was going to move there, since the UWWHA nurses weren't renting it anymore. To ask if he wanted to come see the awful little modern apartment they'd stuck her in and laugh about it.

And how unbearably humiliating was all that? Calling him like a moonstruck teen, even though it was now beyond clear he was avoiding her big-time. Embarrassing beyond belief that she'd secretly hoped he'd ask her if she wanted to move back to his house, now that he owned it free and clear. The paperwork from her financial advisor and lawyers had come through showing he'd happily accepted the money he'd claimed he didn't want. And she'd seen in the newspaper just that morning that the house was officially back in the royal family again.

Was it possible that he was just super busy with finalizing everything? But how could he be so busy that he wouldn't even call her? Wouldn't want to celebrate with her?

She moved toward the new week's schedule, hating to have to see how he'd written it this time, at the same time stupidly hoping she was wrong, that he wasn't avoiding her, that there was some other explanation. That they'd be working together again. Sharing picnics again. Making love again. Then stared when she saw he wasn't on the schedule at all.

"Just step right in here, Madame Durand. The nurse will be with you in a moment."

Aubrey ran her suddenly icy hands down her skirt and stepped to the hallway as Nora closed the exam-room door.

"I have a patient for you, Aubrey. Room two."

She nodded and licked her lips to moisten her dry mouth. Her heart was thumping so hard she could hear it in her ears, and she was having so much trouble breathing she had to suck in air twice before she spoke. "Nora. I see that Dr. Affini isn't on the schedule for this next week. Do you know why?"

"He took some time off to go to his home in Tuscany. Left a couple days ago. He has property there, you know, and needs to check on it now and then, I think. He hasn't been there for quite some time. I'm not sure how long he'll be gone."

"Thank you." She needed to get out of there for a minute before she saw her patient. She stumbled out the back door and breathed in the lagoon air she'd come to love almost as much as she loved Enzo.

Lying, deceiving rat that he was. Because the only explanation for his suddenly steering clear of her, even leaving for another part of the country, which he apparently hadn't done for a long while, was loud and painfully clear.

Funny how he'd been so unpleasant to her until the meeting where he'd learned she'd donated money to restore the fresco. Suddenly he was apologizing, then all nice and charming the following day. He'd accused her of having an agenda? What a joke.

He'd gotten what he wanted, then he'd taken off, just like her father.

Barely able to swallow the bitter taste of that reality, she forced herself to go back to do her job. But as she walked inside the clinic she thought about all he'd said about his mother. How she'd loved his father even though she knew he didn't love her back, and here Aubrey was, doing the exact same thing.

Pining for a man who didn't truly care about her.

She stood there a long moment, facing that horrifying realization. Pictured herself working in this clinic day after day, checking the schedule over and over again. Knowing she'd dread seeing him at the same time she craved it, might even forgive him the way she had after he'd been so nasty just a few weeks ago. Thinking about how easily she'd done that forced her to see what had to happen.

She couldn't stay in Venice any longer.

She had to go home. As soon as possible. And yes, that made her weak and pathetic, but being those things was better than staying in this city she loved without the man she'd pitifully come to love, too. Thinking of him as she walked along the canals and looked at all the fascinating buildings, hearing the sexy rumble of his voice as he talked about it all. Wishing he were beside her as she rode the *vaporetto*, telling her how brave she was. Missing his touch, his kisses, the way he'd looked at her and held her with such an incredible intimacy, she'd fallen headlong in love with a lie.

Except there was one thing he'd said that hadn't been a lie. He'd been absolutely truthful when he'd told her he was a bad bet for any woman. She could only hope her battered, deluded heart would eventually truly believe it.

Enzo tipped his forehead against the airplane window and looked down at the city he loved, waiting for the smile that always came as he did. Instead, a peculiar mix of anxiety and nervous anticipation roiled in his belly. There was a sense of grief, too, over losing his mother's house, but he'd worked hard to put that behind him. To roam the beautiful hillsides of the Affini estates, to walk the vineyards and enjoy time in the villa he still owned that had always been an enjoyable respite for him and Dante and his mother when they'd needed a short break from the close quarters and summer heat of Venice.

He tried to conjure the bit of happiness he felt that his brother, at least, had saved his own properties from their father's selfishness. Dante hadn't planned it, but clearly it had been meant to be for him to have a child with Shay. And Enzo had to admit he was looking forward to playing with his niece or nephew in the same rolling hills he and Dante had played in as kids.

How to handle being back at the clinic and having to see Aubrey was something he hadn't figured out yet. Scheduling Antonio to work the same shifts she did had worked in the short-term, but he knew there would come a time when that wasn't feasible. So then what?

Working with her again would be sweet torture. He wanted to look into her beautiful eyes, see her dazzling smile, listen to her laugh. But he knew not reaching to touch her and hold her, not kissing her or wanting to enjoy more time with her on the lagoon or anywhere else would be nearly impossible. He honestly didn't know if he could do it, so where did that leave him?

In serious trouble, that was where.

He leaned his head back against the seat and closed his eyes. Aubrey. How had she become so deeply nestled inside him in such a short period of time? She was on his mind as he rode the water taxi from the airport, looking out over the island where they'd picnicked and laughed and kissed. He thought of her as he watched the cormorants fly and dive for fish, remembering the oil smudged on her beautiful face, her happy smile as they'd rescued the bird. The way she'd clung to him on both his small boat and the *vaporetto*, forcing herself to face her fear, then actually leaping into the canal to save that little girl.

Whenever he'd been gone from Venice for a while, the lagoon air filling his lungs on the taxi ride from the airport was another thing that usually made him smile. This time, the air felt thick and heavy instead of invigorating.

He slowly walked from the *vaporetto* stop to his house, feeling as if he had lead weights in his feet. Aubrey was still on his mind as he passed the old doors that fascinated her, and he wondered where the UWWHA had put her up after she'd had to move from his old home. Was she happy there? Finding new places in Venice to explore without him? He hoped she was. Hoped she didn't miss him the way he was missing her. Which brought back to mind the huge problem of working with her again.

How was he going to handle it?

Piles of mail that his housekeeper had stacked on the old wooden table in his foyer needed attention and he started sifting through them to see which seemed the most urgent. A larger envelope delivered by certified mail was tucked in between bills and letters and catalogs, and he tore it open. Then stared.

It was the deed to his mother's house.

What the...? His breath backed up in his lungs, and it felt as if his heart stopped for a long moment before lurching back into rhythm. He stared at it again, but there it was in black and white. His name on the deed. He owned the house.

How had this happened?

A letter was enclosed in the envelope, too, and he slowly slipped it out to read it. Then read it again. His lawyer outlined the details of the transaction and the final price, ending the letter with a hearty congratulations on his success getting the funding together in time.

Except he hadn't. Which left only one explanation. Somehow Aubrey's money hadn't been sent back to her, after all.

Head spinning, he hoped he was wrong. That something else had come through in time. He practically staggered to a chair and dropped into it, pulling out his phone to dial Leonardo.

"Can you explain why the deed to the house is now in my name and in my possession? Can you also tell me why all this went through, and nobody bothered to tell me? Would maybe a phone call have been in order?"

"I assumed you knew. I got a copy of the letter the lawyer sent you weeks ago."

"I was out of town and didn't get my mail." Hiding away from Aubrey, and look what had happened because of his cowardice.

"Well, there was a little mix-up." Now Leonardo sounded sheepish and contrite and a little worried. "I did what you asked with the Henderson money, except I'd already transferred the fund over to the Realtor and your lawyer before I'd talked to you. Then neither of them answered my call at first, and by the time they called me back, it was a done deal. Because we—you— bought it with cash at a slightly higher price than Proviso had offered, the seller was happy to take it and run. So, um, a belated congratulations!"

Dio mio. "Leo. This is a huge problem." He rubbed his hand across his forehead as emotions ping-ponged all over the place. The house was his. For real. The house he loved more than anything. Except maybe not. The way he felt at that moment told him that maybe he loved Aubrey even more, and if he did how could he possibly accept her gift? Giving her nothing back but probably a deep disappointment in him that he wasn't the man she'd doubtless believed he was? That he wished he could be?

"Why is this such a big deal?" Leonardo asked. "If it's the money from Henderson LLC, we can always pay it back, you know. Consider that it just bought you more time to raise the money you needed. So we keep working to raise more cash over the next few months, then you can pay it back. With interest, if that's important to you. This isn't the problem you're making it out to be, Enzo. Consider it heaven-sent, instead."

Heaven-sent. That was Aubrey, not the money, and he had to go see her right away. Talk to her about all this.

"Plan to pay the money back, Leo. I'll be working on raising it."

He hung up and called Aubrey, shocked that his hand was actually shaking as he dialed. Then everything inside was shaking, too, when it went to voice mail. He strode out the door again and headed straight to the clinic. It wouldn't close for another hour. He had no idea if she'd be there, since he'd been gone for almost three weeks, and Antonio had been doing the scheduling. But if she wasn't, at least Nora would surely know where Aubrey was living now.

He went in the back door, his stomach in knots. The exam doors were both closed, so presumably patients were inside, and he headed to the front desk to find Nora. More patients waiting to be seen sat in the few chairs, and he came up behind Nora, leaning down close to her ear.

"Can we talk for a minute?"

She looked up and her mouth dropped open in surprise. "Dr. Affini! When did you get back?"

"Just now." He lowered his voice even more. "Is Aubrey working today?"

She looked perplexed, tipping her head sideways to look up at him. "No. She apparently told the UWWHA she wanted to be reassigned somewhere else later in the year. I believe she went back to the States."

Enzo stared at her, wondering if he'd heard right. "She's not in Venice?"

"No. She left about two weeks ago. Do you want to meet the new nurse? She's—"

"I'll meet her another time." Since the world seemed to tilt on its axis, making Enzo feel a little dizzy, he'd barely been able to answer. "Do you by chance know where Aubrey lives in the States?"

"I have no idea. You could probably find out from

the UWWHA." Nora was looking at him with great interest, which made him wonder what his face looked like.

"Good suggestion." He drew in a deep, shaky breath. "Thanks." His legs felt a little numb as he walked out the door, having no idea where he was even going.

Aubrey had left Venice? Gone home, or maybe even somewhere else in the States? How in the world was he going to find her? He had to clear up this mistake. Let her know how much he appreciated her help and that he'd pay her back.

He walked through the city he loved, and every step he took made him think of her. All the things she loved about it, all the things he'd loved showing her. His feet took him past the artists selling paintings of the buildings and his house and that made him think of her, too.

How had every part of this city become filled with memories of her in a matter of weeks? *Dio*, he wanted to have her there with him. Kiss her and hold her and make love with her again, but as he stood there he forced himself to realize that her being gone was for the best, taking all temptation with her. He wouldn't have to go through trying to work with her while keeping his distance, which had been torture before he'd gone to Tuscany.

She was the most special woman he'd ever been privileged to be with, and nothing had changed about that. Which also meant nothing had changed about needing to stay away from her so there was no chance he could hurt her. She deserved a man who could give her his heart and soul and a forever after, and as he stood there picturing her beautiful face and shining eyes, hearing her inquisitive questions and infectious laughter, the thought of her with someone else made him feel as if he were bleeding inside.

None of that mattered. Her feelings were what mattered. And as he stared out over the water, the deep ache in his chest he wasn't sure would ever completely go away told him that calling her would be a bad idea. Hearing her sweet voice might make him do something stupid, like beg her to come back to Venice, or let him visit her in Massachusetts or wherever she was so he could see her one more time. Touch her once more. And how selfish would that be?

No, as soon as he was able to find out from the UWWHA where she was living, he'd have his lawyer send her a letter about the transaction. Tell her that he would be returning the money with interest as soon as he had it. He'd write her a letter, too, thanking her for her generosity and telling her he wished her all the best for her life.

Somehow, he'd keep it cool and professional as he'd tried to do before, until he'd completely caved to the allure of Aubrey Henderson. Then he'd go back to his old life. Except that life now, at the clinic and this city, would hold memories of her everywhere, and he had no idea how he was going to deal with the pain of her being gone.

CHAPTER THIRTEEN

AUBREY STOOD IN the old bedroom she'd grown up in and changed out of her uniform, thinking about how mundane her life felt now. Hoped that feeling would change once some time had passed, bringing back her interest in all the places nearby she'd always loved to go. Assumed that working at the nearby hospital again would start to feel challenging and interesting instead of days she just needed to get through.

As she wandered across the grass to the stable she scolded herself for that thought. She'd had some lovely patients she'd enjoyed taking care of, and had managed to have some fun with friends, too, right? And with her old nanny, Maggie, who lived in one of the guest houses. Anyone would feel a little let down coming back to the life they'd lived for years after the adventure of living and working in a place as incredible as Venice.

Maybe it was because she'd been feeling tired. Kind of sick, really. Queasy and a little dizzy, and she hoped she wasn't coming down with some kind of stomach bug.

That must be it. Her malaise had nothing to do with Enzo Affini. Okay, maybe it did, but that just made her mad because he didn't deserve for her to be moping around about him. Wasn't worth her heart still hurting and her stomach feeling all twisted around at the way he'd used her.

How had she let herself fall in love with a mirage? A prince doctor used to having people fall all over him, and using that to his advantage, deceiving them with his charm and easy smile and a sexiness that would wow anyone?

No, it wasn't her fault. If she kept reminding herself she disliked him now, one of these days her heart would finally catch on and life would get back to normal.

Except right now, normal felt very, very dull compared to being with a handsome, charming, manipulative man in beautiful Italy.

She made her way into the barn, waving when she saw that Maggie was at the far end, feeding one of the horses a treat. "Hey, Maggie! Going riding tonight?"

"Planning to." The nurse and nanny who had been part of the family for years beamed her sweet smile. "Want to join me?"

"Thanks, but not today. I'm not feeling too good." She put her hand to her stomach because the queasiness seemed worse. Maybe after she went back inside, she'd make herself some chicken soup or something to see if that would help.

But first, she'd say hi to one of her favorite horses. She headed to his stall to rub his nose. "Do you think I'm an idiot, Applejax? You know how my dad turned out to be a jerk. But you had no idea he was like that, did you? Should I have known? Am I just a really bad judge of character, being taken in by both of them?"

The horse bobbed his nose up and down in agreement, and she grimaced. Yeah, maybe she was just bad at reading people, and she wondered if there were lessons on how to get better at it.

Her stomach lurched a little more, and the realization that she might actually get sick had her deciding to get back to the house sooner rather than later. But as she turned, her head strangely swam, the light seemed to glitter, then fade, and her legs felt as if they just crumpled beneath her.

Blinking open her eyes, she looked up into Maggie's anxious face just above her. It took her a second to realize she was lying flat on her back, and when she lifted her hand to her head she felt some straw stuck in her hair.

"What…what happened?"

"You fainted dead away, sweetie. About gave me a heart attack."

"Fainted? What?"

She could see Maggie looking at her closely as she helped her sit up. "Feel like you can stand now?"

"Yes. I feel okay. I can't imagine how that happened."

"Well, there could be lots of reasons. Take your time walking, and lean on me, okay?"

They slowly walked back to the house, with Maggie's arm wrapped around her waist as she'd often done when Aubrey was little. "How are you feeling now?"

"I'm fine. Really. I think I have a bug. Been feeling light-headed and queasy on and off the past couple of days."

Maggie didn't speak for a long moment, then asked, "Any chance you could be pregnant?"

"What?" She stared in disbelief that Maggie had

even asked her that. "Of course not! I'm on the Pill. I mean, I did miss a couple of periods, but that happens sometimes with the one I'm taking, and, well…" Her voice faded off as a cold chill came over her that didn't have anything to do with her bug.

Surely there was no way she could be pregnant. Was there?

"You know I have all kinds of nursing supplies at my house, including a pregnancy test." She tucked Aubrey into her favorite chair and briskly plumped pillows behind her head, then got her a cold drink. "You get comfy and I'll be right back."

With her figurative nursing hat firmly in place, Maggie was speaking in a no-nonsense voice, and while Aubrey wanted to say she didn't need the test, the suddenly really scared part of her had to know.

Getting comfy wasn't possible, despite sitting in the plush chair with her feet up while she waited for Maggie. Aubrey sipped her water and thought about Enzo.

What if she really was pregnant? As Shay had gotten pregnant by Dante? What in the world would she do? And would Enzo think she'd done it on purpose, since he'd been suspicious of why she'd shown up to work at the clinic that first day?

The thought sent another cold chill sliding down her spine and made her feel even sicker than she had before.

It seemed like an eternity before Maggie got back with the test. All too soon, the answer was terrifyingly clear in the form of an intense pink dot. She stared at it for long minutes, feeling as if she might faint all over again. She sucked in deep breaths and looked into the mirror to see her shocked eyes staring back at her.

How in the world had this happened?

Somehow getting her wobbly legs to work, she finally made it back to the living room to see Maggie. The result must have been more than obvious on her face, because Maggie stood up and came to hug her.

"Ah, sweetie. Come sit down and let's talk."

"Oh, my God. What am I going to do?"

"Who is the father? Someone you like?" She gently pushed Aubrey back into the chair and patted her knee. "Is he here or in Italy?"

She stared up into Maggie's wrinkled face, and the calm, nonjudgmental way she asked the question helped Aubrey start breathing again. "He lives in Venice. He's a doctor. And a prince." *And a jerk.*

Maggie grinned. "Trust you to do it right, little one."

"Do it right? This is awful!"

"Is he a good man?"

"I thought he was. But then he did something that showed me he isn't." And was that an understatement, or what? Took the money, then ran hard and fast the other way.

"Well, I'm sorry to hear that." She patted Aubrey's knee again. "But you'll have to tell him soon, and, after you talk, you both can figure out how you want to handle this."

The thought of telling Enzo made her feel faint all over again. He'd be horrified to be having a child at all, let alone with her, since he obviously didn't feel any of the things for her that she'd believed he did. Not to mention he'd all but accused her of trying to trap him when she came to work at the clinic. He'd probably think this was proof of that, since she must have gotten pregnant that very first time they were together. "I don't think I'll tell him, Maggie. I'll just raise it myself. He lives halfway across the world, anyway."

"Italy isn't exactly halfway across the world from the east coast of the US, now, is it?" Maggie said with a chiding smile. "And do you really want to raise a child alone? Have it grow up like you did, always wondering who your dad was?"

Everything inside her stilled at Maggie's words. All the memories came tumbling back, all the fantasies, all the melancholy she'd felt her whole life knowing that her father must not love her, because if he did he'd come around sometimes. Memories of drawing pictures, imagining who he might be. A pilot or a football player or a dragon slayer. Memories of asking her mother questions that were never answered. Memories of that sad, empty feeling inside that other kids had a dad, knew who he was, and spent happy times with him.

They never had to imagine who he might be, because they knew.

She lifted her gaze to Maggie's face and reached for her gnarled hand. "Thank you. You're right. No matter how hard it will be to tell him, I have to. I can't let my baby grow up like I did, not knowing. Because that was the only thing about my life that wasn't good."

"That's my girl." Maggie's hand squeezed hers. "And do it soon, or otherwise you'll be stewing about it instead of planning your future, and the future of your baby."

"Thanks so much for your good advice." She leaned forward to hug the woman who'd always been there for her since she was eight years old. "I feel so lucky to have had both you and Mom in my life. Two people who loved me and who I knew always had my back."

It was true. And as she pictured Enzo's impish smile, remembering how wonderful he'd been with little Benedetto, reassuring him and fixing his bike, and with all the other children they'd taken care of, she knew, in her heart, that he'd be there for his own child. Not what he'd planned maybe, but he would be. Yes, he'd used her in a way that hurt even more than her father's betrayal. One thing she knew for sure, though?

Family was important to him.

"You know, I think I'm going to call him right now, before I lose my nerve. Get it over with."

"Way to go," Maggie said, and the high-five hand-slap the older woman gave her, as she'd done since Aubrey was a kid, actually managed to make her smile as she faced the toughest thing she'd ever done.

"I don't understand why you can't give me her address," he said to yet another UWWHA employee. "She worked for me!"

Enzo felt as if all he'd done since he'd gotten back to Venice was pace the floor somewhere. His other house, the clinic, the walkway streaming with people as he'd spoken with his lawyer and the UWWHA and the guy he'd bought his house back from, since he'd been renting it to Aubrey before she'd had to move out.

Pacing this house, too. The one he now owned only because of Aubrey. He'd made so many of the calls from here, now that he'd moved back, because this house somehow felt as if Aubrey were a part of it. But every person he'd reached had claimed they either didn't have her address, or couldn't legally give it to him.

He was close to pointing out he was Italian royalty to see if that loosened their tight lips, which was something he never did. But if he had to, he would, and just as he opened his mouth to see if that would work he heard another call coming in. When he looked at his phone to see who it was, he almost fell over.

"I have to take this call." He abruptly hung up on the person and punched the answer button with a shaking hand. "Aubrey."

"Hi, Enzo." The sound of her voice poured into him like the finest wine, and his fingers tightened on the phone, holding it like a lifeline. "I…I have to talk to you about something. Something important."

"I have to talk to you about something important, too." *Dio*, his heart felt as if it were pounding in his throat, making it hard to breathe. "I've been trying to get your address to send you a letter about it. You need to know that the money transfer from your trust wasn't supposed to go through. It was supposed to go back to you because I couldn't accept it, but there was a mistake and it went through anyway."

The silence from the other end rang in his ears. It struck him that he hadn't thanked her for her incredible generosity, even though he couldn't take the money, and stumbled to get it out coherently. "And I want to thank you for…for caring about the house and I do own it now, so thank you, it's amazing to have it when I thought there was no way it could happen, but I'm in the process of raising the money to pay you back. With interest. So you don't need to worry about that."

He cursed under his breath, knowing he sounded

like a raging idiot. But he might never have the chance to talk to her again, and the stress of that knowledge made it difficult to know, exactly, what to say. Difficult to remember how to talk at all.

More silence. "Hello? Are you there?"

"You were going to send me a letter."

She said it in a flat voice as a statement, not a question, and Enzo hurried to answer. "Yes, I wanted to tell you all that I just said, about the mistake, and that I was going to make it right."

"Make it right." Another flat statement. "Picking up the phone was out of the question because you didn't want to talk to me, apparently."

It was true, he hadn't wanted to talk to her. Hadn't wanted to risk letting her know how much he'd come to care for her, had needed to keep her safe and far away from a man who couldn't be the kind of lover she deserved. "It wasn't that I didn't want to talk to you, it was—"

"Save it. I don't need any explanation. It was all crystal clear. You got the money, then suddenly we were working different shifts, you weren't answering *my* phone calls, then you disappear to Tuscany without a word to me. I may not be very smart, but I figured out pretty fast that our...relationship wasn't as it had seemed to me."

"Aubrey." Horror left him frozen to the floor. Did she really think he was that kind of monster? Hearing her voice so hard and cold showed that the awful truth was that she did. "That's not how it happened. I enjoyed our time together. I—"

"Again, save it, please. That's not what I called

about. I'm calling about the time we enjoyed together, unfortunately."

Surely, after lambasting him for the past few minutes, she wasn't about to tell him she wanted to see him again, was she? And if she did, what should he say? He'd already told her he was a bad bet, which she apparently fully believed.

This time, he was the one who stayed silent, deciding he'd blabbered and upset her too much already and needed to listen instead.

"I hope you're sitting down, because—" he heard her draw a deep breath "—I'm pregnant. And you're the father."

"What?" The floor beneath his feet felt as if it were moving, and he had to try twice before he could say more. "How do you know?"

"How do I know that I'm pregnant, or that you're the father? Thanks for the insult."

That hard voice had gotten even harder, which kept him from saying, *both*. He stumbled to a chair to sit and try to process the grenade that she'd dropped in his lap.

Thoughts of his brother slowly came to mind, about Shay showing up pregnant and his wondering if that had been her plan all along. Wondering about Aubrey, too, and now he couldn't help but wonder again how much Shay had told her about the Affini family trust that said his properties would all come to him if he married and produced an heir by age thirty-five.

"I know this is a shock. It was for me, too."

Her voice had softened into the Aubrey he knew. He absorbed the sound of it, and as he did his blood seemed to finally start pumping again, reducing the numbness he'd felt creep through every muscle at her stunning announcement.

He thought of all the wonderful things he knew about her. The way she stepped up to take care of everyone around her. Her bravery facing her fear of the water. Her adventurous spirit, and her sweetness with patients and with him. Her genuine love for the architecture and history of the city he loved, too.

The truth came as clear as the glass windows in his library that she'd admired.

She hadn't done this on purpose. She hadn't planned to manipulate him or force him into marriage. She hadn't wanted anything from him, other than the very special time they'd spent together. Instead, she'd given him so much, expecting nothing but his friendship and caring in return.

"We need to talk." He wasn't sure about what, other than their baby. Confusion and fear blurred his vision, and he needed time to think. But he had to see her. Look into her eyes and see her beautiful face as they worked through how to handle this. "Come back to Venice. Or I'll come see you. Which would you rather?"

"Neither. There's no reason for us to see one another right now. I knew I had a responsibility to you and to our baby to tell you, and I've done that." He heard the sudden tears in her voice, heard her breathe in a long, shuddery breath, and the sound of her distress made him want to reach through the phone and hold her close. Let her know that he was here for her. Tell her it would somehow be okay.

"I should be available to you if—"

"There's no 'should' in this. I don't want you to

do anything you don't want to do. I'm not like your mother, Enzo, who kept a man in her life who didn't love her. I'm perfectly fine on my own. I'll let you know when it's getting near the time it will be born. We can talk then about when you can come see it, and how we're going to handle things after that."

"Aubrey, no. We need to—"

"*Arrivederci*, Enzo."

The way she said goodbye, low and gentle, pulled hard at his heart. Because goodbye sounded so final, and he realized he'd avoided saying that to her before by leaving Venice altogether. Her soft tone reminded him of the times they'd made love, and that she'd spoken to him that way after being so angry, and then telling him she didn't want to see him, brought a lump to his throat, too.

He sat with the silent phone held limply in his hand for a long time after she'd hung up, finally getting up to move in a slow stride that was far different than the agitated pacing he'd been doing before she called.

Dio mio. A baby. A child created through lovemaking as he'd never experienced in his life, with a woman so beautiful and special in every possible way. Missing her filled him with a hollow ache. Of not getting to see her joyous smile, or feel her silky skin, or tease her inquisitive mind. Of never again sharing coffee with her, or holding her close on a boat ride, or listening to her many knowledgeable ideas.

He moved through his mother's house—his house— and thought of Aubrey as he had nearly every moment since he'd been back. Had slept in a different bedroom than the one she'd used because he couldn't bear to be in it without seeing her beautiful hair spilling across the pillow, her eyes smiling at him as she awakened, feeling her warm, soft body tucked closely against his.

Thought about her as he wandered through each room, picking up the artwork and little things she'd admired. Touched the books in the library she'd loved, and thought about her comments about the windows, and the light in the room. Looked up at the painting on the ceiling, and realized one of the angels depicted there looked a little like her.

Slowly, he made his way into the office he'd just recently brought all his things to, and picked up the deed to the house. Stared at it for a long time, and as he did the confusion he felt lifted, cleared, and he knew with absolute certainty what he wanted to do. Because there was nothing confusing about how he felt about Aubrey.

He loved her.

Loved her in a way he'd never loved anyone before. A woman who deserved a man who would care for her and be loyal and faithful to her forever. He wanted to be that man, so much that for a long moment he tried to convince himself he could be. But he was his father's son, and he couldn't bear to ever hurt her the way his father had hurt his mother.

He couldn't give himself to her, because that wouldn't be the kind of gift she deserved. There was one thing, though, that he could give her. The perfect and right thing. He would give this house to the woman he loved, and to the unborn child they'd made together. She loved Venice, had said she loved this house, and he knew she would bring their child here to learn its history, and discover his or her own deep heritage. An Affini growing up right here where he and Dante had grown up. A new child following a long line of generations of his mother's family, and he actually smiled when he pictured his mother smiling, too, because he knew she would be.

Of course he'd be a part of his baby's life and help it grow up as best he could. Seeing Aubrey and not being able to hold her and love her would unbearably hurt, he knew, but he'd keep away from her as much as possible to protect them both.

CHAPTER FOURTEEN

Aubrey stilled when she saw the certified letter post-marked from Venice, Italy. There were two possibilities what it could be. One: that it was from the UWWHA about the brief time she'd worked there. Or two: it was from Enzo.

With her heart skipping around and her stomach tight, she opened the envelope and slid out a folded letter, along with an official-looking document and a piece of stiff manila paper. Then stared at the document, her heart now in her throat, barely able to process what she was looking at.

The deed to Enzo's house. With her name on it.

What in the world…?

With shaking hands, she slowly unfolded the letter, handwritten in the familiar bold scrawl she'd seen Enzo use on clinic paperwork and prescriptions.

Dear Aubrey,
It is my privilege to be able to give you and our baby this house beloved by my mother's family, by her, and by me. I believe it was beloved by you, too, in the short time you were here.
Thinking of our child spending time there with

his or her very special mother makes me smile more than anything has made me smile in a long time. Except for my time with you, because that brought me many smiles, as well.

I hope you'll decide to live there at least part of the year, which also will give me a chance to spend time with our child while you're in Venice. Also know, of course, that if you choose to stay in the States, I'll visit regularly to be a part of our baby's life.

I look forward to hearing from you when the time comes for our bimba *to be born, because I want so much to be there with you for what will be an incredible moment in both of our lives.*
All my love,
Enzo

Aubrey stared at the letter, then the deed, then read the letter three more times, not quite believing what she was seeing.

He'd given her the house he grew up in? The house he loved so much; that he'd worked so hard to try to buy back? The house that had been so important to him, he'd made her think he liked her so she'd help with the purchase?

Except, that obviously couldn't be true. If it was, she wouldn't be holding this deed in her hand.

She laid the deed and letter on the kitchen counter and picked up the third paper that had been enclosed with them in the envelope, turning it over to see what it was. Then what little breath she had left swooshed from her lungs.

It was the watercolor painting of Enzo's home they'd

seen when they walked along the waterside. The place considered to be a particularly special example of an amazing house in a city full of incredible houses. The rich colors leaped from the page, bringing memories of the short time she'd been able to live there, of making love there with Enzo, of his plans to restore it to its original glory.

It is my privilege to be able to give you and our baby this house beloved by my mother's family, by her, and by me.

She stared at those words on Enzo's letter, then looked back at the beautiful painting he'd obviously made a special effort to get for her.

Did her being wrong about him using her to buy the house for himself mean she could also be wrong about how Enzo felt about her? Was there any way it was possible that he loved her the way she loved him?

All my love,
Enzo

Slowly, she shook her head. Who knew, maybe a deceitfully charming man like him signed letters like that all the time. But as she thought about him, this crazy man she stupidly still loved, the man who'd given her this incredible gift and, unexpectedly, a baby as well, she knew that, no matter how hard it might be, she had to find out.

The thought of baring her soul and telling him how much she loved him felt beyond terrifying. But hadn't he said she was brave? Amazing to face her fears?

Dealing with her fear of water was a good thing, but not essential to happiness and living her life to the fullest. Risking telling Enzo she loved him? Shoving that fear aside to find out if maybe he loved her, too? That was worth everything. She had nothing to lose but her pride, right? And if he didn't, she'd simply be standing in the same place she stood right now.

A place that didn't feel nearly full enough without Enzo by her side.

How the tiny premature infants in the neonatal intensive care unit at the Hospital San Pietro could stand the glare of harsh white light above them was beyond Enzo. Not to mention the annoyance of the steadily beeping screens above the bassinets, and the way they were hooked up to IVs and external monitors of all kinds. He'd never been bothered by it before, when he'd taken care of patients in the hospital, and knowing all that was helping them get well. But thankfully the babies seemed utterly oblivious to it, sleeping peacefully.

Especially his new little niece, Sophia Maria Affini.

Looking at her tiny face, he couldn't help but think about how much his mother, with only two mischievous sons growing up in her house, would have loved having a granddaughter. Hoped that maybe his niece might look a little like her someday. Dante was convinced that the baby looked just like him, except for the heart shape of her face like Shay's.

Enzo personally thought that, at the moment, the skinny baby looked more like a tiny monkey than his mother or brother or sister-in-law, but he'd kept that to himself. Had a feeling Dante wouldn't appreciate that opinion.

What would his own child look like? Would it be a girl with gray-blue eyes and golden-brown hair? A boy with his beautiful mother's coloring, or would it, girl or boy, be darkly Italian?

Never had he imagined his brother or himself having a new little life they were responsible for. And yet staring at Sophia Maria's tiny pink face, he knew both he and Dante had been given an amazing gift. Gifts they hadn't planned on, and maybe didn't deserve, but perhaps that was the best kind of gift. The kind you didn't even know you wanted until you held it in your hands.

His gift wasn't here yet, wouldn't be for too many months, and it took nearly all his strength to not hop on a plane, find Aubrey, and bring her back to Venice until their baby was born. Take care of her, and be there for her in any way she wanted him to be.

Except she'd made it very clear she didn't want that. Respecting her wishes was more important than his need to see her. More important than pandering to his own desires, which was something he'd spent his lifetime doing. But that was about to change. Soon he'd have a new life to think about, and he'd already realized that having a child was going to make him a better man.

"Goodbye, little one." He patted the glass surrounding the sleeping infant. "Sweet dreams, and your uncle Enzo will come see you again very soon."

He pushed to his feet and headed to a local restaurant, leaving with his dinner in a bag to head back to his house. The worry that had been nagging at him for the past few days came back as soon as he was in his boat.

Why hadn't Aubrey ever called him about the deed? What if she hadn't gotten it?

Then told himself—again—that his worry about that was stupid. He'd received notice that it had been delivered to her house and signed for, hadn't he? So the reason he hadn't heard from her was obvious.

Clearly, she still didn't want to talk to him, and he could hardly blame her. Hadn't he avoided calling her from the day he'd left for Tuscany while she was still in Venice? He probably wouldn't have talked to her ever again if she weren't pregnant with his baby, and thinking about that reality squeezed his heart so hard he wondered how it could continue beating.

He pulled the boat up to his dock and secured it, leaning down to grab the dinner he'd be eating alone, and a heavy feeling hung on his shoulders. He couldn't remember ever feeling lonely before, but loving Aubrey and missing her were all new things he would just have to get used to.

He fished his house key from his pocket as he rounded the corner to the front door, stopping abruptly when he saw two sandaled feet with pink toenails... shapely legs stretched across his doorstep. He let his gaze travel up those beautiful legs to the yellow skirt skimming her thighs, and his stomach dived and pitched and smashed right into his heart at the sight.

"Aubrey?"

"*Buonasera*, Enzo."

He stared down into the eyes he'd missed so much, at the curve of her sweet lips, and practically fell to his knees as he crouched down in front of her, dropping the bag to reach for her hands. "Are you all right? Is something wrong?"

"I'm fine. The baby is fine, too."

His heart started up again in slow, lurching thuds as he sucked in a steadying breath. "Then why are you here, sitting on a hard stone step? You need to take better care of yourself! How did you even know I would be here? You might have sat there for hours, getting a chill." He lifted her to her feet and it was all he could do to not pull her into his arms and beg her to stay with him forever.

"I got Shay to ask Dante which house you were living in, and if you were in Venice. Then I talked to Nora, and she told me you'd worked today. Then I came here, though I admit I was a little worried you might not come home, or would have some woman with you."

He could tell the joking tone and half smile on her face were forced, and her gaze was searching his for something, but he had no idea what.

"I haven't wanted to be with another woman since you left Venice that first time." Had wondered if he'd want to be with anyone other than Aubrey ever again. "For heaven's sake, please get up off the hard pavement and tell me why you're here."

He knew why he wanted her to be here, which was to take up where they'd left off, but he couldn't let that happen, could he? His important reason and conviction about staying away from her faded from memory as he absorbed the feel of her hands in his, that she was here in this house again—her house now—where every room he went into she was on his mind and in his heart.

"Why I'm here? Are you accusing me of stalking you again?"

"You're ridiculous," he managed to mutter. "I want you to be here, but I'm confused because you said you didn't want to see me."

"I didn't. But now I'm here because I have something to say that couldn't be said on the phone."

She licked her lips and he could almost see her shoring up the inner strength she had that made her fight her fear of water and go for what she wanted.

"What?"

"I'm here to tell you that I love you. Not because I'm pregnant with your baby, because I loved you before I left Venice. I think I fell a little in love with you that very first night we were together, and every time I was with you, I fell a little harder. When you fixed Benedetto's bike, and when you were so sweet with the lady who had heart failure. When you held me to make me feel safe on the water, and when you rescued that bird. And I decided that I had to tell you. Even if you don't love me back, I wanted you to know."

His heart pounded hard in his chest as he looked into the beautiful eyes he loved, reflecting that love right back at him. To see it there humbled him more than he'd ever been humbled in his life, because he knew he'd never done a thing to deserve the love of a woman like her.

She took a step forward, looking up at him with hope and fear and uncertainty swimming in the blue-gray depths of her eyes. His hands closed around her arms, but he didn't let himself pull her close. Didn't speak. Didn't know what to say or how to say it.

"Enzo, I flew across the ocean to tell you I love you, and to see if you might love me, too. I need for you to give me an honest answer back. Please. That's all I'm asking for."

All she was asking for. So easy to give her the honest answer she wanted, but so incredibly hard to know if he should. "You know I'm a bad bet, Aubrey. Remember?"

"I don't believe that. You might not love me back, but, no matter what, I would bet on you any day." She brought one of her hands to his cheek. "You're a good man. A special man. A man who would give the house he loves to a woman he may not love, and to an unborn child he didn't plan on and hasn't even met yet. That tells me you have the kind of deep moral character that should tell *you* that you're not at all like your father."

Admiration had joined the other emotions in the eyes gazing into his, and his hands tightened to tug her closer. Whether or not she was right, he owed her the truth. "I do love you, Aubrey. I love you more than I knew it was possible to love a woman. And because I love you so much, I'm afraid to ask you to be with me forever. I'm afraid I might hurt you, and I couldn't bear for that to happen."

"You helped me with my fear of the water. What do you say I help you with your fear of hurting me? We spend the next six months making love and fixing up this house and working and adventuring together. After little Prince or Princess Affini shows up, if you feel like being with another woman, feel those bad genes taking over, I won't try to keep you. You can decide then to let me go. What do you say?"

Another emotion in those eyes. Trust. So clear and real, it brought a thick lump to his throat. Listening to her words, looking into her eyes as he held her close, made him finally know.

He'd never be like his father.

Aubrey was the only woman he would always want to be with. To love her and cherish her and do whatever he could for her. He wanted to marry her and spend the rest of his life with her and be the best bet she'd ever made in her life.

"What do I say?" His answer was to kiss her. Softly and slowly the way he'd thought about kissing her every hour of every day for the past six weeks, breathing in her sweet scent, tasting the lips he'd never thought he'd get to taste again.

When she eventually broke the kiss and leaned back, she gave him the smile that had dazzled him from that very first day they'd met. He held both their hands to the slightly rounded belly that, incredibly, held the baby they'd created together, and pressed his forehead to hers, swallowing down the emotion overwhelming him. "I say that I don't need six months. I only need as much time as you want to put a wedding together. Can't have little one born out of wedlock, can we?"

"I guess Prince or Princess Affini won't need that kind of attention from the tabloids." She wrapped her arms around his neck. "What do you think about getting married on a boat out on the lagoon?"

He laughed against her mouth. "A celebration of both of us moving past our fears? I can't think of anything better than that."

EPILOGUE

AUBREY KNEW THAT no one expected peace and quiet at a one-year-old's birthday party, but she had to wonder if the insistent banging on the ancient *terrazzo* floor just might be getting on the nerves of at least one of the thirty or so guests by now.

She crouched down next to her baby son, Gabriel Dante Affini, and waved a new toy in front of him. His instantly fascinated eyes were so like his daddy's, it filled her heart with overwhelming emotion the way it did every time she looked at him. Gabriel's focus switched to the dangling, colorful rings from the plastic hammer he had been pounding.

"How are we ever going to get the renovation on this house finished if you won't let him work on it?" Enzo said in her ear as he leaned over both of them, his warm lips sliding down her cheek while his big hand rested on their son's soft black hair.

"With or without his help, we have a long way to go, and I think he's examined the floor enough for today. But we'll get there, don't you worry." She lifted her lips to meet his, still amazed that this man was hers. That he loved her as much as she loved him. That the touch of his mouth always made her feel breathless. "Even though it's not close to livable yet, I'm so happy we decided to have Sophia Maria's one-year birthday party here. In the house where her *nonna* and daddy and uncle grew up. Do you think the smell of paint and sawdust will make everyone extra hungry for the cake?"

Enzo chuckled and glanced over at his niece, who seemed deeply focused on taking off her pink birthday hat, then trying to put it back on again, much to her parents' amusement. "I find the construction scent very pleasing and appetizing. But not nearly as pleasing and appetizing as you."

His mouth met hers again for a long kiss that had her clutching his shirt as he sat on the floor to pull her close, until something fluttered into their faces to separate them.

Aubrey and Enzo both turned to see the birthday hat lying between them, and Sophia laughing as she lurched in her adorable, learning-to-walk way to retrieve it.

"Hey, you two, enough of that. This is a birthday party, not a date night," Dante jokingly chided as he pulled Shay close against him.

"Every night is date night with my wife," Enzo responded with a grin. "And the sooner your daughter opens her presents, the sooner we can get on with our date."

"Enzo!" Aubrey swatted his arm as Dante and Shay laughed.

"My brother and I have always had an understanding. And today that means he knows I'd just as soon finish celebrating, too, then get home with my wife and daughter to celebrate some more. After Sophia Maria is in bed." Dante kissed Shay's forehead as she rested against his shoulder, turning to Aubrey with a wide smile.

"We had no idea what we were getting ourselves into when we came to Italy, did we?"

"No, we sure didn't." Aubrey watched her handsome husband lift their baby into his arms, who gently bonked him on the head with the plastic hammer as Gabriel laughed. "I thought I was coming here to work. To cure my fear of water and have an adventure. And what did I get?"

She stood to lean over Enzo and Gabriel, wrapping her arms around them. Holding them close to the wonder that filled her heart.

"I don't know, *bellezza*," Enzo murmured against her temple. "What did you get?"

The answer was so enormous, a mere sentence couldn't cover it. "I got our beautiful son. A new life and new dreams. This wonderful and special house. And you." She kissed him again, not caring if Dante complained. "My perfect and amazing husband, who I'm betting will keep making me happy every day for the rest of my life."

* * * * *

MILLS & BOON
True Love
Romance from the Heart

Celebrate true love with tender stories of heartfelt romance, from the rush of falling in love to the joy a new baby can bring, and a focus on the emotional heart of a relationship.

JOIN US ON SOCIAL MEDIA!

Stay up to date with our latest releases, author news and gossip, special offers and discounts, and all the behind-the-scenes action from Mills & Boon...

 millsandboon

 millsandboonuk

millsandboon

t might just be true love...